"Don't be surprised if you find yourself sleeping with the lights on."

—*Parade*

"*A Good and Happy Child* is a rare achievement—a literary horror story that's deeply intelligent, beautifully written, and seriously chilling. If Justin Evans's provocative and creepy first novel doesn't keep you awake at night, you must be taking some pretty strong medication."

—Tom Perrotta, author of *Little Children*

"Evans has written a debut novel that will keep readers thinking, and checking under their bed, long after they've finished the last page."

—*St. Louis Post-Dispatch*

"[Evans has] a good feel for psychological horror. . . . [He] also cleverly poses the story's central dilemma: Is George merely imagining the demon that torments him, or is he truly the victim of an extraordinary possession?"

—*Miami Herald*

"[A] compelling novel."

—*Charlotte Observer*

"Everyone has a little demon inside them. And some darkness. But it's the revelation that makes *A Good and Happy Child* so incredibly scary and unnerving. Man, did this get under my skin in the very best way. Get ready to face your demon."

—Brad Meltzer, author of *The Book of Fate*

"This stunning novel marks the debut of a serious talent. Evans manages to take a familiar concept and infuse it with psychological depth and riveting suspense. . . . Evans subtly evokes terror and anxiety with effective understatement. The intelligence and humanity of this thriller should help launch it onto bestseller lists."

—*Publishers Weekly* (starred review)

"This debut novel grips readers from the first chapter. . . . Evans delivers a creepy and entertaining story full of perfectly written characters."

—*Library Journal* (starred review)

"A psychological thriller that keeps the reader on edge until the last page. . . . A haunting story."   —*Kirkus Reviews* (starred review)

"This is an edgy, compelling read—more unnerving than scary—that will slide its hooks deep inside and throttle you more than a few times before it's all over."   —*Booklist*

"*A Good and Happy Child* unsettles the imagination with its twisting path into a private hell. Evans's story tingles with psychological suspense as it explores the subterranean world where faith meets fear, reminding us how hard it is to rid ourselves of our demons."

—Keith Donohue, author of *The Stolen Child*

Justin Evans

a
good
and
happy
child

a novel

THREE RIVERS PRESS
NEW YORK

Published in the United States by Three Rivers Press, an imprint of the
Crown Publishing Group, a division of Random House, Inc., New York.
www.crownpublishing.com

Three Rivers Press and the Tugboat design are registered trademarks
of Random House, Inc.

Originally published in hardcover in the United States by Shaye Areheart Books,
an imprint of the Crown Publishing Group, a division of Random House, Inc.,
in New York, in 2007.

Library of Congress Cataloging-in-Publication Data
Evans, Justin.
A good and happy child : a novel / Justin Evans.— 1st ed.
p.   cm.
1. Psychotherapist and patient—Fiction.   I. Title.
PS3605.V366G66   2007
813'.6—dc22   2006025824

ISBN 978-0-307-35128-9

Printed in the United States of America

Design by Lynne Amft

10 9 8 7 6 5 4 3 2 1

First Paperback Edition

for Maria and Nicholas

All the conventions conspire
To make this fort assume
The furniture of home;
Lest we should see where we are,
Lost in a haunted wood,
Children afraid of the night
Who have never been happy or good

— W. H. Auden

December, Last Year

It was a tidy brownstone on Ninth Street near my home, one that I had passed many times without noticing. Stone stairs and a comfortable warm light inside. On the sidewalk, a lady walked her dog, a bug-eyed Boston terrier, black. She smiled at me. I wondered if she knew somehow that I was a soul in need.

My recent problem made me think of an instructor I had in college, an Israeli, who was always laughing at American naïveté, who was fond of saying, "With Freud, we are all poets in our dreams." To him, analysis and dream interpretation were ways of converting our little personal miseries into big, robust myths. I had no intention of doing this when I arrived at your office. My problem, while maybe uncommon, seemed more like a hang-up than a crisis; I had no wish to dramatize myself, become the hero who asks the right questions, solves the riddles, and slays the dragon in an epic sung on the streets of Manhattan. In fact, I can honestly say I had no memory of the events I describe in these pages—meaning no conscious memory, no current memory. They are things I experienced in childhood, then tucked away in a file along with the soccer games, the Christmas presents, and the illicit midnight Nutter Butters. With both my parents now dead, and no siblings—and with many old ties severed—the only way to my past led through my own mind. Strange, then, and a tribute to you, that you exposed this the very first day you met me.

The foyer smelled of damp carpet, and the lightbulb was burned out. An inauspicious start, I thought. The brownstone was obviously a private residence. There were mailboxes in the hall and a mountain bike tucked under the stairwell. I reached the apartment with the tag "DR. H. SURMAN." I knocked, and you appeared, shaking my hand, smiling, leading me inside to your office, to a wicker chair in a pleasant room with plenty of daylight (but discreet shutters on the lower halves of the windows), hanging plants, throw pillows, and a cinnamon smell that might be some kind of aromatherapy (why not? I thought, get my money's worth). You folded your hands and your greet smile changed to a nice-business smile. I ran my hands over the chair's arms and noticed dents in the wicker.

"I wonder how many people have picked at that in fits of mental anguish," I said, forcing a laugh.

You smiled like a sphinx. Now we were genuinely in shrink territory: I had made a revealing comment, you had dodged a bullet by refusing to disclose information about your other patients or to join me in mocking their suffering. Good for you.

"So," you said, "what brings you here?"

Funny, how trite we patients must be to you. Like hundreds before me, I walked in convinced that a handful of irritations and sadnesses were "my problems." And then, like hundreds of others, I was to see how the facts, laid out, began showing patterns. I sensed an underlying logic to my distress even in that first hour, but only dimly. It was just a quaver, which would later broaden and deepen and, at times, threaten to engulf me. But I was a greenhorn that first day; a city kid preparing to canoe the Amazon, smelling the damp air and feeling the first bumps of the Jeep ride and thinking, "Oh, this isn't so bad," when we hadn't even taken the boats off the roof of the car.

I told you about my son. "I can't hold him," I said.

I told you how in the early days it had seemed like normal anxiety: near-crazed from sleeplessness, jumping up at 3:00 A.M. to check the baby's breathing, anxiety that I might somehow break him. But, I confessed to you, days passed, and then weeks, and I could still not stand to hold him—hardly to touch him. When, for brief moments, I was alone with him, I would leave him in his crib and sit nearby, smelling his delicious baby smell and feeling terrified, as if I might fall off the earth, unstuck from gravity, and go hurtling into space.

"That sounds a little extreme," you acknowledged.

At the end of the first month, I hoped my negligence might be chalked up to paternal jitters. Would anyone notice if I worked longer hours than usual; left the room when my wife carried him into it; avoided my wife when she breast-fed; would not change him, bathe him, touch him? I passed off my behavior as old-fashioned: I was a man's man. But I changed in other ways. I became edgy, sour, suddenly suspicious of my wife. After two months playing the surrogate dad, my mother-in-law began to make remarks. Behind my back at first, but ultimately to my face. My wife defended me for a time. But the extra work exhausted her—and my seeming indolence wore her down. Cutting remarks and criticisms escalated into arguments, arguments into warfare.

Finally, with tears streaming down her face, she admitted she could no longer give me the benefit of the doubt based on four years of marriage and nine months of tenderness during her pregnancy. Seeing my coldness now made her think she had never known me; she was disillusioned; she fretted about our son's future, and her own. My behavior was inexplicable, unforgivable. How could she stay married to a man who couldn't care for his own child? She wanted me to offer an explanation, or seek help. Either way, my choice was to change or leave. *And Jesus, think about our son,* she had said, so pitifully that I confessed to her that in the presence of the baby, I was paralyzed. Sometimes I would just tremble; other times I would disappear into a trance for a half hour, an hour. Not from the usual parental anxiety; from a profound feeling of nullity, shock, disorientation. It was terrible for me, too. I promised her

I loved her and our son more than anything. But the feeling that came over me seemed out of my control. I had waited for it to pass. But it never did.

My wife was relieved to hear it was not she who was crazy. We promised each other we would try to work it out. And here I was.

"Have you experienced anxiety attacks like this in the past?" you asked me.

Never, I told you.

You asked me about my job, my education, my medical history, my physical health. I answered all your questions.

"Well," you said, and frowned.

You offered a review of what I had described. I agreed that you grasped the issues. Then there was a lull, which, being nervous, I leapt to fill.

"This isn't my first time to a therapist, come to think of it," I said, looking around.

If you had been a dog, I would have seen one ear prick up.

"Really?"

"Yeah," I replied, "I saw one when I was a kid."

"How old?"

"I was eleven."

"Was it a good experience?"

"Yeah, I guess it was. I felt better afterward."

"Good. I like to hear about people having positive experiences with therapy. It makes things easier the next time around. Not that the work gets any easier."

"Of course not."

"Do you mind if I ask why you saw the therapist then?"

"I was . . . depressed."

You cocked your head. You have good intuition.

"You sound as if you're not sure."

"I guess . . ." I hesitated. "I tend to say 'depressed' because it's short-hand for a lot of things." Then I laughed. "Put it this way. If I told you, you wouldn't believe me."

"You're not giving me much credit."

"It's nothing to do with you."

You waited.

"Um," I said. "It had to do with . . . spooky stuff."

"Spooky meaning strange? Now I'm intrigued."

"It's really hard to explain."

"Okay."

Plunk. The word sat there. I wasn't sure whether you were giving me permission to move on to something else, or waiting for me to elaborate. I was getting stressed out by this shrink act.

"Listen," I began. "So few people nowadays are religious. Especially in the city. They don't like to talk about religion, or the supernatural, or even allow that things like that exist—except on cable shows. You get this cold contempt; you're branded a hick, someone from the Bible Belt—I'm from Virginia. And frankly . . . well, you're a scientist of the mind. I would hate to see things I believe in viewed as specimens, or metaphors, or popped like a balloon with professional skepticism. I'm sure you've worked in a mental hospital at least once in your career and treated crazies ranting about God and angels and demons, and I don't want a prescription for Haldol," I puffed. "No offense."

"So every psychiatrist is an Upper West Side Jewish intellectual atheist who scoffs at Christianity?"

"That's not what I meant."

"It's okay," you replied. "You don't have to talk about anything you don't want to talk about. But," you continued with a smile, "I can tell you right now from looking at you, there will be no need for Haldol."

I raised my eyebrows. "Wanna bet?"

For a brief moment, tension crackled between us.

"Can we talk about the present instead?" I offered.

"Absolutely," you said, sounding relieved.

We lapsed back into good manners and wrapped up the session. The fifty minutes had passed quickly. But I was distracted, as if I had an extra channel open, feeling a tide of memory pulling at me. Despite the momentary friction, or maybe because of it, I extended my hand

and agreed to continue the visits. I liked you. You're smart. As I walked out you stopped me.

"You say you enjoy writing in a journal," you said, referring to a comment I'd made in passing.

"Yes."

"Maybe you can write something for me. For us, here."

"Okay."

"Since I agree that our energies are best spent on the present, perhaps working on the past is something you can begin on your own. Start a notebook. Here, I'll even give you one, to take away that opportunity for neurotic delay. . . ." You pulled down a couple of spiral notebooks from a shelf. "Same ones I use. Write me about that last therapy visit— the one when you were eleven. You don't have to show me anything. Okay?"

I took the pads.

"Yes, sure." I found myself hoarse.

"Would you like a pen, too?"

"I think I can manage."

"Good." You held the door and smiled again. "I'm looking forward to working together."

Outside, on the steps, the light had changed. Daylight quits so early in winter. The street was steeped in gloomy blue twilight. I should have known, walking into a therapist's office, that I would emerge back onto the same street as if it were a different planet. I stopped for a moment. A woman in a black overcoat and fancy shoes clopped toward me. She carried a bulky shopping bag, and she brushed me as she passed so I was forced to catch my balance on the cast-iron rail. I opened my mouth to say something, but as she walked by, I realized I could not see her face, just a blur where a face should be, and my mouth hung open with the obnoxious *Watch it* stuck there. The street went quiet, the way it can in New York. I sank onto the stoop, with your notebooks in my hand, remembering rotten things.

Intellectual

There were three of them. Are names important? Toby, Byrd, and Dean. They were lined up against me uphill. I was standing with my back to the steep incline carrying an NFL lunchbox in one hand, and in the other, a French horn.

"Your dad died from VD, everybody knows that," Dean taunted. "Probably fucking a whore over there."

"More like a sheep," added Byrd. "Or a goat."

"Oh, yeah—*goat dick,*" grinned Dean. "Your dick turns blue. Pus oozes out of the tip."

"Then it falls off," Byrd laughed.

"Your dad died with no dick, right?" continued Dean. "That's how you knew."

At this age, I was an awkward-phase test case: pudgy from a cookie addiction and zero exercise habits, little granny-style wire-frame spectacles that fit poorly and sent my blond hair up in tufts over both ears, and altogether disorganized. But the French horn exemplified everything. It was unwieldy, heavy, in a black carrying case shaped like a giant snail. I carried this load to school three times a week for band. The three other boys were also in band, but they played cooler instruments. Byrd, trumpet; Toby, snare drum; Dean, trombone. Playing in the band proved they weren't hicks—the poor, twang-talking county folk who also attended Julius Patchett Middle School and who seldom took an interest in things like band. These guys were supposed to be my compatriots. Their fathers had known my father. But their fathers were members of a local fat-cat class of real-estate brokers, developers, and architects—men who were beginning to transform Preston into a polished nexus of the horse industry. Not eccentric professors with weird ideas about *beautiful melodic instruments*. I was eleven years old, and my father had been dead for three months.

Until that afternoon I would have referred to Toby Van der Valk as my best friend, but it would have been a stretch. Toby was a chub like me. With white-blond hair, apple cheeks, a belly fed by an overattentive mother (he was an only child), and a tendency to trip, Toby was approachable, appealing. The previous summer at an Early College arts and crafts day camp, Toby and I had been inseparable. But when school resumed—and I joined his class after skipping from fifth grade to seventh, the result of test scores and a Gifted and Talented acceleration program—this friendship between fatties was subsumed by Toby's prior obligations: to glamorous, golf-playing Byrd; to cruel Dean; to Toby's own reputation within the clique as the entertaining clown. I, the new kid with the dead dad and the bad breath, did little to enhance his status. He tolerated me amiably but I could not steer his allegiance to me, and I was therefore continually stung by—up to now—small betrayals.

"Look at him, he's about to cry."

"My dad did not die from VD," I said, choking on the words.

"Then why is everybody saying it?" remarked Byrd, grinning. Byrd was tall, broad, a golfer who entered tournaments with his father at the country club, and who was, I thought, pretty dumb. Even in bullying he was dumb. He smiled like this was a lark we would forget in an hour.

"Then what *did* he die of?" asked Dean. "He came home and saw your face."

"Hu*blughh*," Byrd made a barfing noise.

Dean laughed. "Oh-my-god-my-son-is-so-ugly-hu*blughhhh.*"

"You guys are every bit as ugly as I am," I said.

"Every bit."

"Such an intellectual," Dean pronounced, with withering contempt.

"In-tell-ec-tual," sang Byrd.

This was their song for me. Once during gym, I jogged alongside Dean and Byrd. *What we're doing now, jogging slowly, metabolizes fat. When you run more quickly, that's when you metabolize muscle and build strength.* They exchanged mocking glances. I had heard my mother say it. She had probably read it in a magazine. I had no idea that what I was doing or saying was strange—it was the natural speech of my home. I wasn't sure what these kids' conversations with their parents were like, but at my house, when my father was alive, my parents got steamed at dinnertime arguing about the Counter-Reformation. Sometimes they would argue in German. My father taught me Latin and Greek and Old English etymologies over dinner, and during dessert, quizzed me about saints' days.

My parents met in graduate school at Columbia University. Though it was fairly common to meet PhDs in a college town like Preston, with Early College and Fort Virginia at the center of local commerce and culture, I sensed that my parents took learning and scholarship more seriously than most. At my friends' houses—even my friends whose parents were also professors—the television would be on, or the dad would play Nerf football in the backyard, or they would hike, or play tennis, or do yard work. Not my parents. My mother had her office; and my father had his study; and the house would be breathlessly quiet. My father would announce the end of the workday by abruptly cranking Mahler on his hi-fi; then would follow the rattling sounds of pans in the kitchen as my mother prepared dinner. No words passed between them. It was my duty to come home every day from school and read in my room. I also drew, with pencil, on sheets of my father's typing paper. I drew elaborate, Rube Goldberg contraptions, or I copied scenes

from Asterix comics or from the Mannerist prints my father had
hung throughout the house—the beheading of Holofernes, a detail of
Michelangelo's *Last Judgement*. I remember re-creating in pencil the
wrinkles of St. Bartholomew's flayed skin, and my mother admiring
how I used shadow on the folds.

So we may have been eccentric. My mother, absorbed in her writing, was not much at keeping house. Our kitchen was littered with
crumbs. Under every ledge were dust mice; dirty towels licked over the
edge of the wicker laundry basket dumped in our upstairs hallway for
a hamper; grime coated the windows of the front hall. An impolite pal
once told me bluntly, "Your house smells." It was a meandering wood
house built in the 1870s with rooms pointing off in many directions—
alcoves, attics, porches—with layers of white paint on the walls and
doors, columns on the front porch, and inside, dozens of oriental rugs,
shimmering designs in orange, blue, red, and white, all collecting
mildew and dust. The walls were half decorated with my father's print
collection, the other half with photographs my mother preferred—
black and white angles on Bauhaus architecture, or Diane Arbus–type
shots of freaky staring-eyed people in poor towns. It was a house
halfway between this and that, between upper-middle-class luxuries
and absentminded squalor. My father had been too distracted, while he
was alive, to teach me about showering regularly, or that it was necessary to brush my teeth in the morning, elements that became more
important when I was expelled from the garden, as it were, and thrust
before my time into seventh grade, into the ring with the likes of
Dean Pranz.

Dean Pranz was the son of a local real-estate developer, thick-
limbed and strong, a gifted basketball player—the high scorer of the
local junior team, frequently mentioned by name in the local papers—
with bushy black hair, wide-set, almost froggy, eyes, and a perpetual
sulk. But he was not stupid. He could be funny and crafty and playful,
performed a dozen "magic" tricks at a moment's notice—"the dead
man's hand," "the broken arm," "zombie eyes"—and was a gifted

mimic; but he usually presented a face so gloomy and bored he might have been taking cough medicine from a patch. When I encountered Dean in school, and then befriended him, he would give me nick-names and horse around; then, just when I would begin to laugh, let loose, let myself get goofy like a pal does, I would turn around and find myself facing Dean, somber and sulking, nodding slowly and judgmentally at me, as if I had just confirmed his worst suspicions. What those suspicions were, I do not know. I couldn't play basketball. I spoke like my parents. I smelled and had bad breath. I had befriended Toby Van der Valk, one of his gang, but to Dean I was an annoyance, and now he wanted me out. The look in his eyes told me as much.

And now he was inches away from my face.

The other boys had backed away and let Dean come forward. His face was transformed from his usual sulk into something different: alight, alive, and enjoying this spectacle, his place in center stage.

"I hate your guts," he breathed.

We were so close, I could smell him. Musty, unbathed little-boy smell; the odor of corduroys and armpits and dirt. A ball of hate curled up hot and furious in my stomach as I stared back into Dean's eyes. With what I felt was a war cry, but probably sounded like a yelp, I reared back with my right arm, pulled the French horn's bulk behind me—then swung it at Dean. Dean leapt backward. The momentum of the French horn pulled me over. I fell heavily onto the pavement—which was almost as painful as the howls of delighted laughter that followed.

To his credit, Toby asked me whether I was okay before he trailed Dean and Byrd down the hill.

"You have to admit, it was kind of funny," he said, as he crouched over me.

"Let him alone," was the last I heard from Dean. "He just wants attention."

The entertainment was over; his voice had grown bored again.

I opened our front door and heard the radio playing faintly downstairs. I knew without seeing my mother's briefcase and jacket thrown over the chair that she had no classes and was in the basement writing. Suddenly my mother was included in my fury. *They hate me,* I thought to myself, *and she won't even notice.* I raced to my bedroom and slammed the door. I leaned against it. *Will she hear it?* I asked myself. *Will my mother hear the slamming door and know that I'm upset and come upstairs and check on me?* I waited, listening, but no sound came. I sagged. Of course she could not hear me. I went to my dresser. There, tucked under the socks, was the penknife my father had given me. *Every boy should have one.* I flipped open the long blade. I plunged the knife into the wood of my bookshelf. A half-dozen books tumbled to the floor. *My mother won't hear that, either,* I thought. I began to stab them. For one or two I only slashed the covers. But my eye landed on one, a thick hardcover, a library book. The cover was hard to penetrate. I needed to bring the knife over my head in order to force the knife through. The knife sank into the pages, two, three inches deep. I buried it to the red, plastic hilt. I repeated this action many times.

I heard a knock at the front door and looked up. I wondered how long I had been doing this. The book was in shreds.

The knock came again, louder. Since my mother could not hear I would need to answer it. I stuffed the book under my mattress, but the blade of my Swiss Army knife was bent at the hilt and would not close. I stuffed it back into the drawer. Then I ran downstairs.

Someone was already standing in the hall.

"I let myself in," he said. "The door was open."

It was Tom Harris.

Everyone called him that—Tom Harris—as if the names were stuck together. I never heard anybody refer to him in the third person as just Tom, not even my parents. When my father was alive, Tom Harris dined with us weekly. He had been my father's best friend, his roommate at Calhoun College, the tiny but distinguished men's institution atop Wilder's Mountain in South Carolina. My father was a relative sophisticate from Greenville (one of the town's two *aesthetes,* he had told me, drily), but Tom Harris was from a hill town near Calhoun itself, called Hogback—*the kind they don't put on the map,* my father had told me, *with real dirt-eating mountain folk*—and by the time he entered Calhoun, he had never left Wilder's Mountain. The admissions officer handling Tom Harris's file had made the journey personally to the Harris house to determine whether these grades and admissions essays could really have been authored by a high school boy from Hogback; and he found there a dirty, cramped cabin that had nonetheless been populated with nearly every volume from the public library. (*Tom Harris found he was the only one checking them out,* my father said, *so he decided to keep them.*) Tom Harris arrived at Calhoun with a single suitcase, wearing trousers too small for his six-foot-three frame, and an oversized flannel shirt, *which stank,* my father attested. Even now, a Harvard doctorate, a full professorship, and many published monographs later, there were signs of the mountain on him. His face was craggy, his cheeks sunken, his hair was greasy and looked as though it had been cut and combed by three angry barbers at once. He wore droopy and mismatched clothes: mustard-colored slacks that bagged between his legs, and a mud-colored sweater. I thought of Tom Harris as an ironic old tree. He stood at a lopsided angle, leaning so far over on one leg or another you expected to hear a creak. While he seldom laughed, the corners of his mouth would often tug down in a suppressed smile. My mother used to say he needed a wife to clean him up, to which my father replied Tom Harris would need to clean up first, because no woman could stand that smell.

But it had been some months now since Tom Harris came, arguing good-naturedly and praising our dinner fare and pretending to steal my dessert. My mother said he missed my father. But I felt a strange hostility just then, seeing him there in our hall. It was his first visit since the funeral.

I just stared.

"I could hear the music downstairs, so I came in," he offered, seeing my expression. Then, joking: "But now that you're here, maybe I should step outside and knock again?" He took a theatrical step toward the door.

"That's okay."

He gave a mocking little bow. "You're very kind."

"What are you doing here?"

"I was invited for supper," he said. "What are you cooking?"

"I'm not cooking."

"You're not cooking! Well. I guess we'll just have to eat what your mother makes. Blegh," he made a sound of disgust.

Ordinarily, I would have giggled at this.

"What do you care?" I said, glaring. "You're eating for free."

"No, no. I insist on paying." When this garnered no reaction, he gave up. "I'll see myself in," he said. He threw his coat on a chair and went down into the basement, releasing a burst of Vivaldi when he opened the door.

⚜ ⚜ ⚜

"So Tom, tell us this *story*!"

My mother stirred a pan of red spaghetti sauce with a wooden spoon. Steam whirled from a great aluminum pasta pot. I glowered at Tom Harris across the kitchen table; he had been holding forth for a half hour.

"Ah yes," he said. "Last weekend, Gary Bannister—you know him? Asian languages . . ."

"Of course."

"Gary persuaded me to go to a Pentecostal meeting."

"Tom! You're joking!" Mom's voice rang with interest, but her expression—visible only to the stove, and to me—seemed wary.

"Oh, you see signs for these revival meetings up and down Route 11. Gary's from Boston. He thought they might detect a Yankee, so he dragged me along for protection. There was no need—they expect visitors and you sit in special bleachers. The preacher whooped into a microphone, they sang along with electric guitars, then finally came the speaking in tongues."

"Mom, can I stir the spaghetti?" I said, stamping over to the stove with theatrical boredom.

"Members of the congregation came forward, starting swooning, going into trances," continued Tom Harris, kicking out his long legs, folding his arms behind his head. "Average folk in jeans and sneakers. But there they are on their knees, eyes rolling back in their heads, speaking in tongues—which, by the way, sounds just like baby talk. Gary was thrilled. Then, before I know it," Tom Harris paused, "Gary is grabbing my arm. I look at him, and he's white as a sheet. 'Let's go,' he says—and he bolts!"

I plunged a spoon into the roiling water, sour with self-pity. Wasn't anyone going to ask what had happened to me today?

"I followed him to the parking lot," continued our guest. "*Tom, you saw the woman near us?* he asked. I had—a dark-haired woman, quite pretty. *She was speaking a dialect of Cantonese that I happen to know,* Gary tells me. *And she was cursing the name of God up and down.*"

"What?" my mother exclaimed. "How could a county woman from Preston speak Chinese? And even if she could . . . why would she curse God in church?"

"That, my dear, is the point of the story," Tom Harris pronounced. He paused. "It was a demon."

My mother's hand, stirring the sauce, stopped momentarily in its clockwise path. "Really," she said.

These sorts of pronouncements had once been common in our house. With my mother and me as the audience, often at the dinner table by candlelight, my father and Tom Harris competed with tales of religious mysteries. The bishop in Dark Age Britain who chopped down a grove of trees sacred to the druids and built a chapel out of them to harness their power for the church. The 1960s housewife in Tennessee who miraculously appeared in two places at once, washing dinner dishes at home and feeding the poor in a soup kitchen across town. My mother playing foil—*How could they prove that?* or a teasing *Come on!*—Tom Harris's eyes twinkling; my father caught up in the momentum of his own diatribes, the evening ending only when he would at last stop speaking and stare down at the table, spent and glassy-eyed from wine. The subject was always church lore, history, and ritual, and it was fed by a contrarian streak—*the twentieth century has been culturally bleached by Marxism, and TV!* The stories left my mother bemused and maybe a little lonely; but me, wide-eyed.

"Certainly!" said Tom Harris, in response to my mother. "Ecstatics like these actively seek to put themselves in the hands of another power. But there's the problem. If you open the door," he said, "you never know what will come through."

"Spaghetti's ready," I called out, interrupting.

"You have to taste it," said my mother.

"*Taste* it?"

She crossed to the stove and reached for the wooden spoon.

"No, I want to do it," I protested, tugging it back from her.

"Let me—" said my mother, but it was too late. I had pulled her arm against the hot rim of the pot. She cried out.

In an instant, Tom Harris was on his feet with his arms wrapped around my mother, shepherding her to the sink, running cold water, gingerly placing her forearm under the stream.

Soon we were seated around the table; Tom Harris sat off to the side, his bent knees splayed like butterflies' wings.

"Something's bothering young George today," he declared.

"Why, what's the matter?" said my mother quickly.

"We'll have to ask him," he said. "He's very mysterious."

My mother turned to me.

"Is something wrong, George?"

"No," I said, staring at my placemat. But my mother's voice, kind, inquiring, brought all the frustration and pain of the Dean incident back. "The kids at school hate me," I choked.

My mother reached over to embrace me, and coaxed the story out of me, all under the hawk eye of Tom Harris, whom I chose to ignore.

"That Dean," she said angrily. "Why does he have to do that? If he doesn't like you, why can't he just leave you alone?"

"And then I come home and find *him* here," I said.

"Now George," my mother said, her tone changing from sympathy to warning. "Tom Harris is our guest. Bad day or no bad day, if you don't behave you can eat your supper in your room."

"FINE!" I screamed, and ran upstairs.

⚜   ⚜   ⚜

I sat at the top of the stairs, listening. In our house, the tall ceilings and planked floors echoed.

"How is it out there, by yourself?" my mother asked. "It must get lonely."

"The wind howls and the stairs creak," Tom Harris joked. "But for company I have my neighbors, Farmer Mutispaw and his charming sheep." He chuckled. "What about you?"

Mom sighed a deep, sad sigh. "Oh, Tom. It gets very hard." She sighed again. "It would have been so much better if I could have spoken with him one more time. He was so verbal . . ."

"I feel the same way," he said somberly. "It's been, what—?"

"Three months. Thirteen weeks," my mother said. "You know, with sabbaticals or research trips, we've been apart for almost this long before. Sometimes, I putter around the house thinking he'll be home any minute. Then I catch myself."

"Maybe you're the one who shouldn't be alone."

That sounded corny for Tom Harris—could he be courting my mother?

"I'm not sentimentalizing," she said, a hardness in her voice.

"Sometimes I get . . . just furious. Why would he *do* it? He wasn't risking his life. He was risking *ours!*" She sighed. "I should have pushed harder. Asked more questions." She moaned. "That's the worst part. The regrets."

"Paul wanted to do good," said Tom Harris. "He had reasons to prove himself. For one thing, he was no longer able to publish."

"He never got over that book," said my mother.

I had heard about *that book*. In recent days it was referred to only occasionally in our house, but I had dim memories of arguments, my father shouting in the living room at night, after bedtime, and my mother crying; or the reverse: my father catatonic on a sofa, my mother stroking his shoulders in sympathy. *That book* had only been explained to me once; as with so many things at that age, I swallowed the explanation whole and never asked for more: *A book your father worked on a long time was published and some people didn't like it.* Did you like it? I asked my mother. *Your father's brilliant,* answered my mother. Then they're mean, I said. *That's what your father thinks, too,* nodded my mother.

"I miss him every day, Tom," my mother sighed. "But he was hard to live with."

The blood throbbed in my ears. How could she say that?

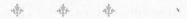

I undressed and stepped into the shower, cranking the hot water into a steamy roar. Pictures of my father flickered in my memory. Spankings, furious outbursts, my mother crying sometimes, me others. But then I would hear the words that made me leap like a puppy: *Let's take a walk.* Around the corner and up Hill Avenue we would go in the springtime, past dogwood blooms, and alongside freshly rained-on lawns, with the odor of mud and grass and crisp wild air blown down from the mountains—*the Blue Ridge Mountains,* my father was the first to tell me (one fact among thousands)—fresh in our nostrils. He told me whole histories as we tromped in Slopers Creek Park in autumn, through patches of green globulous hedge apples fallen from leafless trees. In winter we hiked past Revolution Hall, the old college destroyed by fire in the 1780s, now just a stone chimney and some hollow walls rising against the sky. We trudged up and down long slopes in the snow, and with the rhythm of our walking my father would talk ... about baroque churches; how Byzantium fell to the Turks; the real Thomist meaning of transubstantiation; all the "oversophisticated" things my mother objected to, fought with him over (in discussions overheard from the top step), saying they made me strange for my age group and made me awkward. But it was these dialogues which made me feel, even for a brief time—scrambling beside him as he strode with his long paces; looking up at his somber, dark face—that I, above everyone else, more than his close friends like Tom Harris or his many fawning students, was his chosen apprentice, his favorite.

The bathroom was steaming up. Droplets ran down the transparent shower door, reminding me of rain on a car windshield. The tile glowed white and clean. It was in that sterile, safe cocoon, turning to soap my belly, that I saw it for the first time.

What is the reaction a person should have, seeing a strange face staring at them in the shower?

I might have screamed, like someone in the movies. But a scream, however instinctive it might seem, is in fact an act of logic: when confronted with an intruder a person should scream because screaming will bring help. But what if there is no opening and shutting of the door, no rustling movement of clothing, no indication of physical presence?

I knew what I was seeing was impossible. In retrospect I could say my brain went off the rails; I felt a sickening lurch as my senses heaved out of their tracks, and I trembled despite the fact that I was standing in a hot shower. I felt myself teeter. I turned and balanced myself on the cool tile. I closed my eyes and said to myself, "When you turn around, it will be gone." I opened my eyes. The face continued to stare.

My breath returned to my lungs. I let out a scream, and I fell.

Next I saw Tom Harris standing in the doorway of the bathroom. He was tall and stern, sweeping the room with his eyes. He spotted me and bolted to the bathtub where I lay. He knelt down beside me. My mother appeared, her hand covering her mouth. Then I fainted.

The Boy in the Window

I woke in my bedroom, bright and full of daylight, great white bolts of sun pouring in the window catching motes. I was in white pj's, swimming in white cotton sheets. My mother sat on the bed next to me, stroking my hair, coaxing me out of my dreams. She gazed at me, her mouth tucked into a concerned frown, and I wondered how, in all this suffusion of light and warmth, she could wear such a worried expression. And then I remembered: I fell in the shower; I had lain against the porcelain with the droplets still falling, and I watched my mother through half-lidded eyes as she fetched towel, then aspirin, then water glass, her voice rising and rising with fright in that choking-close bathroom, still filled with steam, as Tom Harris tried to calm her and pressed a cool palm on my forehead.

My mother, at that time, was like two women trussed together, like rosebushes my father tied to a single stake to make them look more full.

On the one hand there was Mother, the Scholar: a CV boasting a PhD, two books, and bylines in academic journals. She kept multiple copies of these on a special shelf in her makeshift office in the basement.

I browsed them periodically and saw their titles—"Sexuality and Poststructuralism" and "The Frankfurt School and the Erotic Self." I was thrilled not so much by her prose, which was incomprehensible to me with all its slashes ("the woman/vessel"), but by the appearance of so much apparently dirty material. Despite—or perhaps because of—my mother's long-shanked, Gloria Steinem beauty, her cutting-edge library, her books and bylines, her degree from Smith and her doctorate at Columbia, she was unable to secure any position at Early College except the German grammar-instructor position reserved for women instructors (instructors, not professors). This I learned from listening to my mother's side of various phone conversations:

Early College is an old southern institution, she would say. *Paul loves it, he has this reverence for southern aristocracy. But it's one of the last all-male institutions in the United States. Feminists are like killer bees to these people; they're hoping we don't really exist, and if we do, they'd rather not be the ones to find out. You should see the chairman of Modern Languages; he looks at me like I might try and castrate him on the spot.*

And so my mother commuted to The Women's College of Central Virginia (shortened to "Central" for convenience, a nickname put to smutty purposes—as in "Pussy Central"—by the Early boys), a small women's college of almost no consequence in nearby Foxcoe, where she was permitted to teach German, but where she again met with trouble, politics, obstacles. To find failure and obstruction in such a place—they had, for instance, no maternity leave policy at the time, hard as this may be to believe—infuriated her. But her opponents sensed her outrage—the *hauteur* of the overqualified—took offense at the snub, and dug in deeper:

Central is not about to change its tenure track for a woman professor to take time off to have a child. It's a women's college, but all the positions of power are held by men: the head of my department, the dean of faculty, the trustees. They're going to make me start again, from the beginning, because of my son. From the very beginning.

Like a bonneted wife in the nineteenth century, carried by wagon away from her "people" (in my mother's case, from Killingworth,

Connecticut), Mother the Scholar had been brought to this town nestled in the Valley of Virginia. Preston had sprouted up around its colleges—Fort Virginia, a military institute, and Early College, one of the country's oldest, renamed in the 1860s after a Civil War general, Jubal Early, renowned not so much for his battle tactics (he once lost his brigade in the woods) but for establishing a revisionist camp of southern historians, who tended the tragic, heroic flame of Robert E. Lee and the Lost Cause. The hues of Preston were the rust of hundred-year-old brick, and the white-wash of Doric columns; its tourist attraction, the ivied mansions along its broad avenues (a few were still private residences, but most had been bought by the college); its backdrop, the Blue Ridge Mountains. These formed around the town a hazy, rolling, protective ring—keeping such notions as Women's Studies out, and enclosing a stifling society, which was split into three camps.

First there was the Old School: families dating back generations to Revolutionary War officers and eighteenth-century Presbyterians, whose scions were so pompous, bow-tied, and erect (streets bore their last names: MacFarlane and Piggott and Bibb) that few actually envied them, and instead happily left them to their dingy country club—the one a few miles past the Hayfield development, with its algae-bottomed pool and the Sunday dinners with greasy gray steak.

The alternative was the Bohemian Cluster, a clique of restaura-teurs, lawyers, real-estate types, and theater folk, all in their thirties and forties, all slim and vain, who smoked reefer, cultivated a taste for local moonshine and bluegrass, and slummed with the town hippies (a mix of local craftsmen and musicians, blacksmiths and banjo players). This group created a mini California culture of wife-swapping divorces and brutal gossip: impotents and drunks; lawyers who cheated clients; wives who cheated on husbands; embezzlers, bankrupts, even toxic waste dumpers (there was a factory in nearby Canaan). The gossip thrown off by this group entertained my parents many a night, but, I honestly think, never inspired a glimmer of real curiosity. My father was too pas-sionately religious; my mother's fantasy of fulfillment, I suspect, was liv-ing in Berlin, androgynous, underdressed, and steeped in literary theory.

The rest of Preston society, such as it was, was a constant flow of professional professors. These were the straight arrows, the folks who took their jobs, if not their intellectual calling, seriously; academics who lived in Preston as strangers to the South and who suffered from the same ironic fate as type A New Yorkers who quit the rat race, move to "quaint" New England towns, and find themselves in a place that, due to its deep roots, has zero use for them. The aristocratic brotherhood of Preston did not care if the new Romance languages professor had studied at the Sorbonne. Preston had its own gods, its own shrines and temples: the mountains, the houses, the families, the horses. Professors had been coming and going for generations. Each one arrived polishing his vanity, ready to lend a little culture to this tiny, pretty, culturally impoverished village. Each one, just as inevitably, grew puzzled when the town did not display the proper gratitude. Then, according to kind, the professor would adjust: buy a house and take up tennis; kick up vicious academic controversies; or duck out of public view, and through isolation, grow odder and odder. Adapt, rebel, or withdraw.

My parents were more or less of this last group. My mother was not tempted by the rewards of becoming a local artist or a lady of the garden club. She was determined to clear herself of the backwater by sheer labor. Her basement office was less a study than a factory. Afternoons, evenings, weekends she spent crouched over sheaves of photocopied manuscripts, her long, sandy brown hair tied back, peering through her glasses like a diamond cutter. In these manuscripts she made notes; the notes flowed into prose on legal pads; the legal pads were typed into articles, books, reviews. All the while she pursued new ideas, new grants. She planned trips to academic conferences and devoured the latest *Lingua Franca*.

The result of this labor, this ideation as industrial toil, was two shelves of journal articles, and three slender books. But it only amounted to, at the time, a tiny flutter; bringing her maybe a foot or two into the national view; drew some attention; earned another contract at a university press. In the meantime—I think she realized with a sigh—she had a family to attend to: her difficult husband, and me.

That was Mother the Scholar. Her other face was the Mommy Mother, the fussy mother, harmless ditzy confidante and pal. This was a role she played with assurance, and, I think, some joy. My mother had a goofy laugh; she plonked big plastic glasses over her elegant features; she packed my lunch every day into the NFL lunchbox (and its predecessor, the Peanuts lunchbox); she shopped for toys and Halloween costumes and kindergarten supplies. She listened carefully; she deflated self-pity and drama with precise observations, followed by practical suggestions. She learned how to soothe, to calm, to pacify. And though I was always grateful for her patience and her care, these attributes sometimes felt studied—like she was carefully executing memorized steps. At some level I fretted that if she came across a problem to which her tools did not apply—one that would require her to reach for something deeper and different than her training had prepared her for—she would be lost. In the meantime, she put on her serious face and addressed each problem with aplomb. And it was this mother, the pacifier, who appeared in my bedroom that morning after I fell in the shower.

"I let you sleep in today," she said, still stroking my hair.

"Don't you have work?"

"I canceled my classes."

I thought about this. This only happened when things were serious, like somebody had to go to the hospital. Then I remembered the face.

I must have held my breath, because my mother's hair-stroking paused.

"Sweetie," Mom said, "do you remember what you told us last night?"

"No."

"You said you saw somebody looking at you while you were in the shower."

"I did?"

"Yes. Do you remember anything about that?"

Had it been real? I wasn't sure. "Maybe."

"You saw someone, then?"

"I guess."

"Well, sweetie," she said, fighting frustration, "tell me what you mean. What did you see?"

"I saw a face."

"Was it a man?" she said, urgently. "Did you hear anybody come in?"

"It was just a face," I said. Then I added, to be clear: "No body."

My mother took this in a moment.

"George," she said carefully. "It's been difficult for you since your father died. But just because things are tough doesn't mean you need to suffer. Maybe Clarissa Bing can recommend someone at the clinic. Someone to talk to."

I had the sensation of having been pitched off the end of a pier: a lurching free-fall feeling. *The clinic* had been a phrase I'd heard around the house for years, usually in the context of grown-up professional, psychological chatter; the words *therapy* and *analysis* and *Freud* and *Lacan* were perpetually in the air. The idea that I would now, at eleven, be a target for all that technique seemed, at minimum, a little unfair.

"Okay," I said. Then, a little mournfully: "I guess I'm prematurely complicated."

My mother smiled. "Let's see."

After dinner, I heard my mother call Clarissa Bing.

Clarissa was a psychologist at the Mental Health Clinic and shared my mother's passionate interest in things psychoanalytic. A strong-minded eccentric, she rehabilitated hillbilly drunks and gave succor to beaten county housewives, and she once threw a patient out of her office for saying "nigger." My mother viewed Clarissa as an odd duck, another outsider, and an ally.

I listened to my mother's voice, beginning high-pitched, sociable, charming, then shifting gears into professional straight talk. Then concluding: "Thaaank you, Clarissa, thank you so much, this is really helpful. Mm. Thank you so much." She hung up and came in to give me the skinny: there was a man Clarissa highly recommended, experienced with children, slot available. I said fine. Mom smiled and patted my leg.

"I think you'll be glad you did this."

Later, as I got ready for bed, the phone rang. I heard Mom talking on the phone in her bedroom. Thinking it was Clarissa Bing again I sidled up to her cracked door and listened. Mom had just gotten out of the shower. She was wrapped in a towel and sat at the edge of the bed. But to my surprise she spoke in murmurs and laughed softly into the receiver, her back turned to me. "Of course I would," she said, and her voice had transformed; it had grown warmer and softer, and it was as if she were pouring it through the phone like melted butter. "I would really enjoy that," she said. Then, "Yes. Yes, I said yes." Then a laugh, not the haw-haw goofy laugh that I knew, but one beginning low in the throat and rising into a glittering giggle. Finally, "See you then." She stood to replace the phone on the receiver, then turned to look at herself in the mirror. She stood, gazing and drying, turning herself absent-mindedly. She let the towel drop. I moved away quickly.

I lay in my pj's in the dark. The savage daydreams about Dean resumed, mingled with anxiety about facing him. I imagined the school hallways filled with hostile students—the hicks, the black kids, the cold-eyed developers' kids—and realized with apprehension that after the incident on the hill yesterday I would probably be ostracized for weeks. Socially radioactive. Dean was not finished. It was nearly midnight when I fell asleep.

I woke from a dream to the sound of my own name.

George.

My room was dark, no hall light visible under the door. Moonlight pooled around the radiator by the window. I rubbed my eyes.

George.

With a jolt I realized the voice was not inside the room—I was alone. Yet there it came again. My fingertips tingled.

George.

I inched down my bed, and on instinct I peered out the window.

There was a figure outside my window looking in at me. It was the same face that watched me in the shower. Only now I saw it more clearly, as if I were more used to it and could focus on its presence: it was a boy, like me, standing on the branches of the tree. He had straw-like hair and scruffy clothes. He reminded me of Huckleberry Finn.

I registered two things very quickly. First, the boy was suspended on the thin branches at the end of the bough. Those twigs could not support his weight. Second, I glanced at the clock. It read 2:14. I was certain I was not dreaming.

The room, though dark, felt still and strangely vivid. Shadows leapt out at me in blue and pale shapes. The window seemed to grow in size. It was a giant luminous square, big as a movie screen that seemed to grow big-bellied and convex, as if it were pulsing toward me.

"Yes?" I answered.

Yes, yes, yes, came the voice inside my head, almost exulting. A rush filled my ears. It was like a crowd roaring at a football game. I smiled. I felt I had answered a question correctly, and the boy on the branch seemed to smile, though his face was a blur. The bough bobbed with him on it.

What's your name? I asked him.

At this question I felt a sudden growl of anger and restlessness from the boy. I regretted asking; even felt a flash of fear. But the boy recovered, and answered sadly, so that my momentary worry turned to pity.

I don't have one, he said.

It was as if the boy did not even need to speak to communicate with me; we seemed to be using images, ideas. I asked him how he appeared there, and whether he was the same frightening figure that had come to the shower the night before. He answered that before, he had only been becoming aware of me. *How?* I asked. *I knew you could be my friend,* he answered simply. He told me he had only showed me part of himself, like an introduction. He told me how this was the better part, his favorite part, the whole. I knew what he meant. I knew then the boy would be my friend, and I resolved privately to call him that, to myself.

Suddenly, into my mind crawled a picture so vivid, I felt as if the floor had dropped out from under me: I was suspended. Not in air, not in water, but in something warm and buoyant, gray and thick, where I had complete movement of my limbs, and I could breathe freely. It was like hanging on a rope upside down with a blindfold on; I was not sure which direction "up" was. After a few seconds it became impossible to remember which direction "up" had ever been; after a minute, I stopped searching for "up" at all and simply realigned myself. *Like walking in a spaceship in flight,* I thought. *That's right,* came the answer with an appreciative laugh, and I laughed, too, happy at last to have a friend who got my jokes, my oddball comparisons. This thinking, so free and liquid and supple, was like something I had been hungering for. All my stilted conversation, my awkwardness with people, just disappeared. I was like an eel slithering in oil, quick as lightning and impossible to catch. *Yes, this is the best,* I agreed.

I followed my Friend through this ether, neither aware nor caring where the "real" space of my bedroom had gone. Eventually, we came to a long, black shape, like a giant battleship seen from underneath. *What is that?* I asked. *That's the earth.* I looked again. Notches appeared in the shape, like windows in a skyscraper, and the battleship grew and grew until it surrounded us. It was like swimming into a sunken vessel, a shipwreck, that was miles deep and miles across, silent, and black. I noticed that, every once in a while, one of the "windows" in the shipwreck would light up a pale yellow-white. Some of the windows were dim and pulsed only briefly; others kept beating like insistent hearts.

What are those? I asked.

Those are Beacons.

I was puzzled. *What's a Beacon?*

A Beacon, he said, *is anybody who is interesting.*

And who is interesting? I asked, desperately hoping that I was one of those interesting people.

My Friend suddenly flooded my mind with that delicious oil slick of ideation that I was coming to crave. *Someone interesting is anyone who takes an Interest.*

An Interest! Interesting! It was like some crazy pun that I could not quite get, circling around in my head. I laughed a delighted, nervous laugh, and my Friend laughed with me, and I felt relief to be understood, and above all, to be wanted.

Exhausted. I woke up curled in a ball on the floor. I was shivering with cold in my pajama bottoms. My mind was full of echoes of my night journey. With the light streaming in my window, my room felt heavy, ugly. I peered out the window: the bough, and its twiggy fingers, bobbed quite normally in the wind. I checked closer to see if there were any telltale marks on the branches: a footprint, a scratch. There was nothing.

"George, you look awful!" my mother exclaimed as I came into the kitchen. "Didn't you sleep well?"

I thought about this.

"I'm not sure," I said truthfully. "It was hard to tell."

I could feel her eyes on me after I gave this answer. But I could not explain what I had seen in my bedroom. My mother was already sending me to a therapist; telling her about the figure, about traveling in the ether, would only frighten her. And her, trying to get to work on time, after making sandwiches, after already taking one day off . . . No, I could not tell her.

But I recognized one other thing: I was so spent, so hollow feeling now, only because the world my Friend showed me was so rich. I wanted more.

Frequent Headaches,
Inability to Sleep

It was October now. Windbreaker season. I left Julius Patchett Middle School with my lunchbox and took out the paper crumpled in my pocket. *11 Slopers Creek Road.* I started my journey.

School was festooned with Halloween decorations: wobbly-limbed scarecrows, Sesame Street vampires, cardboard witches with warts, all Scotch-taped to the walls, above the lockers. My father had told me about Halloween—the real one. It was a Celtic holiday, he said. In ancient times, people celebrated winter as the season of death, and the day that season began, they believed spirits visited the earth. They held a festival; they slaughtered winter livestock. Ghosts and goblins and the shades of dead ancestors walked among living people. *That's how trick-or-treating began,* he said. *Imagine being a farmer back then. No electricity, no street lamps. Walking home from the fields, you're prey to all sorts of spirits. The only way to avoid attack is to go in disguise.* The earth, on that night, was crammed with spiritual energy, he told me. Women who practiced magic—*yes, real witches, in the sense that, without a pharmacist and medical treatments, every village had some old woman who would look at your cancer and give you a piece of parsley and mumble a few words, which was the best they could do for you*—saved their charms for that night, in order to be assisted by the power of the dead. *People put out meals for their dead relatives, the way we do for Santa Claus. If you didn't appease them with hospitality, they might play a trick: drag you down to hell, to the sound of wild animals snarling!* My mother was pissed when he told me that. She told him I was too young to hear such things. (I was four at the time.) He told her it came from the legend of Saint Andrew.

Preston, too, I observed as I walked up Main Street, my lunch-box plunking against my leg, was bedecked with Halloween decor. McCrumb's drugstore had paper monsters taped to the windows. In the Hobby Shop gossamer streamers and plastic bats hung in the display window alongside the airplane models and electric trains. The public library had propped a life-size gorilla outside its doors.

By contrast the Mental Health Clinic bore no reference to the holiday, except for a small jack-o'-lantern full of Tootsie Rolls by the receptionist's desk. The clinic was a low, brown brick building in a generic suburban office-style building, there in a quiet corner on a back street alongside Slopers Creek Park. The lobby smelled vaguely of disinfectant, and the waiting area was in the same milk-chocolate color as the brick, with plastic seats like at an airport gate.

I gave my name to the receptionist.

"Did your mom come with you?"

"She's at work."

A frown. "Take a seat."

I sat near a man with wispy hair and colorless skin, and a head shaped like a spaghetti squash. He stared at his hands. He looked poor. His clothes, too, were colorless, the kind of crappy Kmart clothes my mom always said fell apart five days after you bought them. He gave off a faint odor. There was nobody with him, either.

The receptionist handed me a clipboard with a yellow sheet to fill out. It asked which of these things applied to me:

Problems with coworkers/supervisor
Frequent headaches
Inability to sleep

Frequent/excessive drinking
Use of illegal drugs
Blackouts/memory loss

I checked "Inability to sleep" and "Frequent headaches." I looked at the rest of the list: rotten-sounding things that only applied to grown-ups. Then I looked at the ghostly man with his eyes downcast, sitting by himself. I wondered which of these he had checked off. Eventually the receptionist called my name.

"George Davies? Richard Manning will see you now."

He was never "Mr. Manning" or "Doctor" anything. He was always Richard. Richard. Funny how the name came to mean calm, and kindness, when before, "Richard" was a dashing fellow, a blond, a guy in an ascot with a sportscar, also known as "Alan" or "Ken." My Richard, the child psychologist, had a sad face—two layers of big brown rings under each eye, as if his heart had been broken a decade ago, and he hadn't slept since. He was in his forties, but looked older. He had a bushy mustache and a mane of brown hair, both running gray. He wore slacks and a yellow cardigan. When he greeted me, he had the air of some old craftsman meeting me at the door of a shop. I felt a sense of pride there, maybe tinged with sadness. I told my mother this. She said, "It must be an occupational hazard for therapists. Half the time they're not sure whether they succeed or fail—and when they do, they can't tell anyone. Especially in a town like Preston. They work alone."

"George Davies," he declared.

I sat in the chair he offered me, a slightly too large, nylon-upholstered affair. The office was clean, modern, carpeted. Richard sat not at the desk, but in a chair identical to mine across from me. I noticed that his chair was as much too small for him as mine was too big for me. I liked that. If the world was designed for normal people, neither Richard nor I quite fit.

He asked me my age. "Eleven and a half," I replied. He smiled. What grade was I in? Seventh, I told him. He frowned. "You're young for your grade?" I nodded: "I skipped sixth." Then he asked me if I knew why I was there. I told him, "Not exactly."

"Your mother says you've been sad lately."

I nodded.

"Why do you think you've been sad?"

I shrugged. "I've been having trouble with my friends."

"Friends at school?"

I nodded.

"What about them?"

I explained: about Dean, and how Toby Van der Valk had been my best friend—though even as I said it, I knew it had hardly been true—and that he had betrayed me. Richard let me talk. He asked me how it made me feel. I told him about coming home and shutting myself in my room.

"But how did it make you feel?" he said.

"What do you mean?"

He seemed nonplussed by this. "Um," he said, "describe the emotions you had, when Dean told you he hated you."

"I felt bad."

"Okay."

"I felt . . . I don't know. Sad." Bad, sad. My quavering disappeared. This was turning into an unexpected exercise in vocabulary. I didn't know what he wanted.

"Let's try a little role-playing," Richard suggested, sensing my struggle.

For the next half hour, Richard acted the part of Dean, Toby, and eventually, my mother. I played the part of me. It was a funny feeling. I was Hansel and Gretel, following a trail of my own conflicts and encounters, and picking up the crumbs I had left behind.

"This is really interesting," I said at last.

Richard cocked his head.

"Why interesting?"

"It's like . . . artificial life."

Richard threw back his head and laughed. I laughed, too, but I wasn't sure why.

"I probably shouldn't say this," said Richard, "but you're a very unusual boy. You perceive and express things many adults would not be able to."

I glowed.

"We only have a few more minutes," he said, in a softening voice— I soon learned Richard's voice always went quiet when he approached a serious subject. "But I'd like to discuss your father a little bit. When did he die?"

"Um . . ." I stirred in my seat. "Over the summer."

"How did you find out?"

"My mother."

I had been in my room, playing a game of chess with myself, and cheating, when I heard a howl from my mother's bedroom. I did not even connect the sound with the phone ringing, which I had tuned out in the throes of my game. I froze, on my knees next to the bed, holding a black rook suspended over the board, listening.

Richard nodded sympathetically. "Was your father in an accident?"

"He was sick."

Richard waited.

"He had been in Honduras."

Surprise. "Ah." Then: "Your mother didn't mention that."

"He was a volunteer worker," I informed him, "at a refugee camp."

Hesitation. Richard must have been trying to figure out how the hell a man who lived in Preston, Virginia, with a wife and child would find himself trotting around Honduran refugee camps. "I see. Did he get sick down there?'

I nodded. "He was sick, and . . ." It was strange. I had almost forgotten. The details of his death were so much less important than the all-absorbing *fact* of his death. Then the phrase returned to me: "He didn't recover." *He's not going to recover.* Those were the first words from the doctor's mouth, outside the hospital room, as my mother and I waited.

"That must have been very difficult."

I said nothing.

"Do you think about your father?"

I shrugged again.

Richard held his gaze on me a few moments. "Maybe we should discuss this more," he said, "next time. I think there's more here for us to talk about."

"Okay," I agreed.

"Well, then, until next time." He smiled.

I stared at him.

"Oh," I said, finally understanding. "Do I go home now?"

"Yes, George."

Outside, it was a chilly autumn evening. My mother's car idled at the end of the walk. The headlights were on, exhaust curling from the muffler. The cold grabbed my neck, an icy hand. I shivered. I had the feeling that, just behind me, something had slipped out the clinic door, like the wild stray dogs that followed people down at Slopers Creek sometimes, hoping for scraps. Practically breathing on me now. I ran to the car.

That night I collapsed into bed and wrapped myself in blankets. Richard Manning's probing had exhausted me. It also filled me with an unexpected sense of safety: I felt that, in the care of those sympathetic, sad eyes, there were certain things I could let go of, stop fretting over: if Richard handled the artificial life, I could get on with the real one. I drifted into a deep and grateful sleep.

When I awoke, it was the middle of the night, and I felt groggy. I stirred, and it took me several seconds to open my eyes. When I did, I jerked upright with a horrified gasp.

"Wha's that?"

I sat there, chest damp, exposed and chilled. The room was entombed in darkness: the hour of night when not so much as a squeaky brake disturbed the silence. But I had seen something in an instant, a single flash. A child lying next to me in the bed. Grinning, eyes narrowed in mischievous glee, chewing its fingers, wondering if it would be caught in a naughty, practical joke. I sighed. Of course—it had been my Friend.

"Are you there?" I whispered. "Are you there?"

✦   ✦   ✦

After school. An uneventful Monday. Byrd and Toby, with their adjacent lockers, barked details to each other about an after-school basketball game. I stood watching, balancing with difficulty my French horn, lunchbox, and bookbag, waiting to be invited.

"There's a basketball game?" I said, finally.

"Yeah," said Toby, studiously filling his backpack. "But there are too many people already. I'm not sure I'm gonna go."

"Oh, there are too many people?"

"Yeah."

"Oh, okay."

A voice came into my head.

Maybe I'll go for a walk.

"Maybe I'll go for a walk," I heard myself saying.

Byrd's voice dripped with contempt. "Go for it," he said.

I made my way outside and walked alone down the steep incline of Ruby Hill, past blocks of small, sooty houses.

The Julius Patchett Middle School, the town's formerly "colored-only" school, now integrated, was named for a 1940s black minister and civic leader who had grown up on Ruby Hill—symbol of the town's black section, the north-facing slope that descended to Main Street and the trickling creek that ran alongside it. Next to the columned mansions on Early Avenue, the homes on Ruby Hill were dollhouses. The narrow streets clung to the scrubby hillside; each lot seemed cramped between the curbs; and on a single block, prim yellow wood-framed houses with fresh paint and hanging plants might alternate with shacks, built from crates whose Sunbeam and Coca-Cola insignias remained branded on the wood.

Every day white kids were driven here, in Audis and Mercedes, to attend a school named for an integrationist. They came from the prosperous white sections, lined with long drives and houses with two-car garages and swimming pools and rec rooms, on streets named for Confederates—Hill Avenue or Beauregard Road. Their parents were lawyers, dentists, realtors. The old "white school" now served as the elementary school; and the high school—Preston High, *Go Hornets!*—closed the loop of school system and social class by linking Preston students to the county—to Pumphouse Hill, Home of the Hicks.

In Preston ethnography, the hicks were the black kids' natural enemy, so it was only natural that, from a topographic perspective, Pumphouse Hill actually abutted Ruby Hill, with only a dip in the landscape and three hundred yards between them. It was equally natural that, to drive between them, you would need to circumnavigate a three-mile loop—no street connected the two. Aluminum-sided houses, studded with satellite dishes and pickup trucks, characterized Pumphouse Hill; and if the rich white kids with their white-and-watermelon turtlenecks had pretentious names such as Tobias and Violet and Byrd; and the black kids had names (female) like Tameka, Latrina, Sharnaya, with the boys seemingly all named Boo; then the hick kids, tending to the fat, had perhaps the most unintentionally comical names of all: sets of twins named Goldie and Pearl, or Earl and Erwin; and boys with such doggedly unoriginal handles as J.J., or Tex.

I walked down Ruby Hill, and I felt alongside me the presence from the night in my room—my Friend. He was like a shadow, following right out of the corner of my eye. He made no noise, but as he walked behind I constantly fought the desire to jerk my head to the side and catch a glimpse of that tremor or flicker on the border of my vision.

We'll go for a walk, and I'll show you something.

All right.

That feeling of hyperreality came over me. Two tiny, identical, scruffy houses lay ahead, where a girl I went to school with lived with her nine brothers and sisters (lore had it the family was so large they lived in two houses). The afternoon sun struck the whitewashed walls and they glowed a despairing yellow-gold—*Like the color of surrender,* my Friend suggested. He was filling my mind with pictures, sensations. I tried to focus on walking—the lunchbox under my arm and the French horn in my hand—but I could not keep my eyes from the yellow houses; the intensity of the color was almost overwhelming, hypnotizing; the quarter mile down Ruby Hill dragged like five. I wondered whether I would ever reach the bottom.

It's because it's daytime, came the voice.

What is?

The harshness.

I reached the grounds of Early College. That campus, normally a French garden of a university—all red colonial brick and whitewashed Doric columns rising over trim lawns—became a rage of noise. They surfeited my senses: the students, young men in khakis and baseball caps boisterously crowded at picnic tables eating junk food; the bulletin boards overstapled with flyers announcing a Fiji Night or a concert by The Bar Codes; yards of chained bicycles; the boxwoods planted in banks of pine mulch, their cloying odors rising. It was too much; *Too much,* I told him, though he continued to lead me with his voice, that whisper just slightly beyond my hearing, until I reached the footbridge, and then at last the harshness and the grating colors and the noise began to peel away. I knew from my father that the bridge was the longest footbridge in the United States, a stone-and-concrete structure fifteen feet wide and some three hundred feet long, spanning the gorge dug by Slopers Creek and offering a view of the mountains that sprang up beyond the football and soccer fields of campus. That day the footbridge was empty, or nearly so; there ahead of me at the midpoint, my Friend waited for me. He stood bareheaded, his sandy hair scruffy and wild, his face obscured by a smudge. We crossed the bridge together in silence. We passed all those landmarks of order and community that the university imposed on this fringe of the countryside—its modest football gridiron, the tennis courts with their broken fences and weeds choking the pavement, the chalk-lined green sports fields—toward the wilder places, beyond campus. We climbed the hill on a dusty track, until the ruins of the old Revolution

Hall stood before us, that husk of hearth and stone wall, held together by preservationists' wire. Beyond it was a brush of thistles and bracken and reeds, cooked brown by the autumn sun, giving way to uninterrupted miles of rolling forest.

Ready?

Okay okay okay okay.

We plunged into the brush, following a narrow dirt path. My vulnerability to sensation, here in the woods, was rewarded by heightened perception—every twig snap, fluttering bird, or subtle shift in afternoon light caught my eye and caused me to shiver with pleasure. We were tromping downward, on a path cut by cross-country runners, toward the river.

It's about your father, said my Friend.

What is?

All of this. I understood at once that he meant the walk. My father and I had followed this route many times.

What about him? I was breathless.

We were down by the James River now, at the bottom of the trail where the river opened up fat and sluggish under a thick overhang of pines. My Friend was serious, importunate, showing me yet another side of himself. Suddenly his voice was like a hiss. His blurry face was close to mine—though I could not make out its features, I sensed a grimace—and he spoke with such wild urgency it was almost a shriek.

Somebody knows what happened to your father!

I recoiled from the outburst. But the face kept coming nearer.

Somebody knows!

I put my arm up to shield myself, but felt my Friend come closer and closer, so that I fell over backward into the brush.

What do you mean, knows? Everybody knows how he died, he was sick.

Somebody knows, somebody wanted it!

The voice was loud and thin and unbearable.

Who? Who knows?

And then, in a horrible gesture I will never forget, my Friend turned—slowly, smilingly—toward the path that stretched along the river. His voice simultaneously mocked, insinuated, and exulted into a squeaky high pitch, and he lifted a finger to point.

He's coming this way!

I looked, in horror, but at first saw nothing. Heard nothing. My Friend had disappeared. I was alone, listening to the whisper of drying leaves in a wind and the faint rush of the river heaving along below. Then, bit by bit, I began to hear the rhythmic rustle of footsteps along the path where my Friend had indicated. I sat frozen. The rustling came closer. I squinted ahead. Suddenly a figure appeared. It *was* something from a nightmare: a towering figure in long coat. Then, it stopped. It had spotted me.

I tried getting to my feet but the underbrush made me lose traction. I heard footsteps move rapidly toward me. I scrambled to my feet and tried to run away. An iron grip seized my arm.

"George!"

I whirled around. Then I screamed.

I saw a face, strangely familiar, and yet horrible: it was ashen and flimsy, and the flesh of its cheeks seemed to quiver as if they were not quite attached to the skull underneath. It peered at me fervently, imploringly, its mouth moving but no words coming. The anatomy of the thing was horribly apparent, like a model from a biology classroom made from real human tissue by mistake: it was a study in death. *This is what happens when you die,* a voice said inside me. *This is what your father looked like inside his casket. Just a piece of meat that rots when you leave it out of the fridge.* The face opened its mouth and roared. I closed my eyes. The blackness in that throat would swallow me.

"George!" it said. "George!"

"Get away!" I squeaked.

"George, what are you doing here?" The voice was familiar.

"I don't want to see," I said, still scrambling to get away.

"See what? George, look at me!"

I turned. The white, clouded sunlight glared. I lifted my hand to shade my eyes. Finally I was able to focus.

Crouched over me was Tom Harris, in a bulky black overcoat with the collar turned up around his face like bats' ears. His face was pinched and pale.

"George, it's me, Tom!"

"You!" I said.

"Yes, me. Who did you expect?"

"I didn't know. I didn't know who to expect," I said, a phrase that puzzled Tom Harris. "What are you doing here?"

"I come out here all the time. Clears my head, after a lecture. But what are you doing? Why did you try to get away from me just now? Didn't you recognize me?"

But I was not listening. What did this mean? *Somebody knows, somebody wanted it.* Wanted what? My father to die? Tom Harris, who came to my house, who spoke to my mother about *not being alone anymore?* At that moment, everything my Friend said suddenly made sense. I felt a wave of gratitude.

"I do now," I said, and gave him a knowing glance. Though I had not intended them to, the words escaped with an insinuating tone.

He had been trying to dislodge a stubborn leaf from my pant leg. Now he stopped. "What do you mean?" he said.

I pulled away from him and began backing away to make sure he did not follow.

"Just leave us alone," I said.

He stood watching me, his face grave.

"Who is *us?*" he said.

But I turned and began walking, trotting, running back toward town. He called after me, following with his long stride; but whenever he caught up, I would run, so at last he simply trailed me at about twenty yards. We walked that way all the way into town. I turned several times, but he was always there, watching me, a tall figure in black following with his gangly-legged walk. At the sidewalk to my house I turned one last time. He was gone.

January, This Year

My wife lay in bed, her face in the pillow, her mass of curly black hair splaying across the bed. Street light filtered through the blinds. I smelled cigarette smoke—the night doorman, three floors down, would be pacing under the awning in his coveralls. It was between 2:00 and 3:00 A.M. Generally I knew from the noise level on Second Avenue what time of night it was. Until two, even on weeknights, revelers from the bar around the corner—cabs, trucks, garbagemen, yowling party girls stumbling home late—kept the Manhattan streets near our apartment abuzz. Between two and four, peace reigned. After four, the day slowly churned to a start again, with the buses and the delivery trucks, the commuters pouring through the bridges and tunnels.

Now the apartment lay in unaccustomed quiet. I sat up in bed, listening hard.

There's nothing, I told myself. Go back to sleep.

But I remained rigid. I focused on the sliver of hallway visible from the bed. Is it better to get up and check, or stay here? I asked myself. *What are you afraid of?* came the answer. *You're supposed to be the man of the house. What are you going to do—shake Maggie awake and ask her to check for noises?*

Yaw, it said.

That was it—the noise that woke me up.

Yaw. Um.

I lay there, heart pounding. Without thinking, I began to pray. *Our father, who art in heaven, hollow be thy name.*

Hollow? No, I corrected. Why did that insidious word spring to mind? Hallowed, not hollow . . .

Stop torturing yourself, I said, shaking it off. *Your son is there by himself. Whatever it is that made the noise might be going into his bedroom. Staring at him. Leaning over his crib.*

I made my way to the hall in my bare feet. The house was silent—but never dark. Light filtered in from the stairwells on the air shaft, from the streetlights, from the clock on the microwave.

Mm, came the noise again.

I rounded the corner to the baby's room. I moved forward slowly. I was not sure what I expected to see there. The nightlight in the corner cast an amber glow through the slats in my son's crib. My pulse beat in my ears. *Yaw, um.* The noise was my son's unformed voice, calling an unseen person. He wore footy pajamas and lay in the crib surrounded by lions, lambs, dragons. His little figure thrashed its legs. *Mm.*

He's having a bad dream, I said to myself. You read the book. He goes through sleep cycles, and during REM sleep the limbs move, he reacts to stimuli from his brain, processing what he's seen today, the Baby Einstein video, the songs, the feedings, the fall from the sofa.

Something wild has got him, came a voice in my mind. I stepped away from him until my back touched the wall. I fought the urge to run from the room, fought to catch my breath. I checked to see that the Celtic cross, placed there by my sentimental-Irish but not religious-Irish wife, still hung over the doorframe. It did.

You can't leave him, came the voice again. *Stay, and watch.*

I sank onto my haunches. I listened to the thrashing, balling my hands until my knuckles went white. He's fine, I told myself, at the same time fighting the urge to leap up, turn on the lights, fling open the windows, wake my wife. *We need to help him. Something's inside of him!*

I fought these urges down until his thrashes became murmurs; his murmurs, sighs of sleep.

Dawn came. It spread white light over the poster of Babar, and over me—a figure crouched in the corner, circles under my eyes.

"What are you doing?" came a sharp, accusatory voice.

Maggie stood in the doorway. Her nightgown pictured an orderly garden of patterned lilacs—but her hair was a whirlwind of dark curls. She had a long, delicately hooked nose, with refined nostrils that flared when she grew angry; green eyes; and porcelain skin smattered with freckles. I used to flatter her by comparing her to Snow White; more recently I'd come to notice a resemblance to the Wicked Witch.

"Nothing," I sulked. I had been reduced to a naughty child in six seconds.

"Get out of there, he's sleeping," she hissed.

I tried getting to my feet. My muscles had cramped from squatting so long. I groaned loudly.

"What's the matter with you?" She started tugging on my arm.

"Let go!" I yelped.

The baby moaned.

"Great," said Maggie through gritted teeth. "He's awake. And neither of us have showered. I told you I had an early meeting. What were you doing in here anyway?"

"I was . . . watching him."

"Watching him sleep?" she replied. "Why?"

I stood speechless.

Maggie's eyes flickered with understanding. "Your thing again?" she asked, more gently. "Oh, George," she sighed, and pressed herself to me, smelling sweet and sleepy, a garden of lilacs. "What are we going to do with you?"

That's what would have happened three months ago. What really happened was this:

Maggie rolled her eyes. "*God.* Go start the coffee," she said angrily. "I'll change him." For the next hour we stomped around our tiny apartment without speaking—bumper cars with road rage.

• • •

Con Edison workmen were repairing a gas main up the street. They had wheeled out an industrial-sized saw with a three-foot blade and were cutting into the asphalt in long slices. The result was a preposterous cacophony. You winced, apologized for the noise, and got up to close one of the windows that was open a crack.

"Now," you said, "where were we?"

"Things have been getting worse," I said.

At home my wife and I had descended into a mutual silent treatment. "We haven't skulked around the house like this since we were first married," I said. "Passing each other in the hall. Making curt remarks. But then it was kind of fun: newlywed quarrels."

"And now?" you asked.

"It's just miserable."

I told you how my wife was spending weekends at her parents'. How I rolled the problem over in my head constantly during the day. My work suffered as a result. I surfed parenting websites, reading advice about "Sex for the New Dad" and "Making Time for Making Love," or pieces about postpartum depression, topics that I balefully wished applied to me. "So I would have an excuse," I told you. I would make resolutions in my head . . . convince myself I could walk into my apartment, see my son, and suddenly be able to . . .

I stumbled.

"Be able to what?" you prompted.

"Be able to reach him. Hold him. But something stops me. I can't be a father."

You sprang up like a pointer. I had a feeling I'd made your day. "Why not, George? What does it mean to you, to be a father?"

We discussed the challenges of parenthood. I ticked them off: "Responsibility. Love. The desire to raise a good and happy child."

"You see yourself as having these traits?"

"I think I'm a responsible person. And I love him almost more than I can handle."

"You left out something."

"Sorry?"

"From your list. You mentioned responsibility and love. But you left out 'raising a good and happy child.' Why is that?" you asked. "Do you think you can raise a good and happy child?"

"I guess," I said.

"You don't sound very certain." You prompted me: "In your estimation, what does that require?"

"Not sure. Confidence? Good genes? Moral intelligence?" I laughed at my own pretentious phrase.

"Moral intelligence," you repeated.

"I was kidding."

"Were you?"

"Yeah, I was."

"Do you have that quality?" you probed. "And for the record, 'moral intelligence' sounds like an Ivy Leaguer's way of saying 'good.' George, are you good?"

"What?"

"I said, are you good?"

"I don't know! Of course. I mean, no one would walk around thinking they're not good. By definition . . . I mean, even Hitler probably thought he was good. Inside his mind. Wouldn't he? So even if I were a monster, and you asked me that question, I would say the same thing. I would say I was good. So yeah, by definition, I think I'm good."

You regarded me a moment. "Are you comparing yourself to Hitler?"

"No! I was just trying to make a point."

"It sounded like a defensive response. I asked you if you consider yourself a good person," you said, "and you immediately compare yourself to Hitler. To a monster. I'm just pointing that out."

I brooded.

"You've been thinking a lot about your own father lately," you said, changing tacks. "Your notebooks are full of very strong feelings about him."

I was momentarily stunned.

I had handed over a half dozen small spiral memo notebooks to you the week before, but it never occurred to me you would even open them, much less work your way through them. Each page was filled with line after line of scribble, in ballpoint, felt-tip, roll-tip pen, in black and blue ink, and stained with rings from where they'd been used as bedside coasters. In the margins were geometric doodles and a page of hastily jotted phone numbers of divorce lawyers whom I'd called and consulted, but never called back.

"You read them?"

"Absolutely. In fact I'm patting myself on the back—this is an out-pouring. They've obviously touched a nerve. In addition to the inherent satisfaction of being able to read someone else's journal," you said with a wry smile, "it's a fast track behind the veil. I mean, look at you. You come into my office. You wear an expensive suit, you work at a Fortune 500 company. You *care* what other people think about you. Take your comments today—it kills you that your in-laws are angry with you, right? I bet you write thank-you notes after every Sunday dinner."

"So what?" I said, embarrassed.

You laughed.

"See? You have no problem expressing socially appropriate feelings of affection," you continued. "But when it comes to expressing anger, fear, confusion . . . What was the word you used before? Paralysis. Misery." You paused and fixed me with a look. "Now, I read those journals and I said to myself: Aha. George *used* to have a way of coping."

"When?" I said, confused. "You mean, when I was a kid?"

"Have you ever heard," you said, "of the idea of the shadow self?"

Sure, I told you. It was one of the Jungian archetypes—one of the symbols of the collective unconscious. That was pretty much all I remembered from college.

"Not bad. Do you know what function it plays, in analysis?" you asked. I shook my head. You continued. "The shadow is a frequent fig-ure in dreams. It can appear as a kind of doppelgänger; an evil twin. It embodies our repressed desires. The dark stuff. The shameful stuff. The you-want-to-fuck-your-mother stuff."

"I get the idea."

"Do you?" you said. "Now, look at the memories from your journals. How do you interpret the hallucinations you had? The ones you had of 'your friend'?"

"Hallucinations," I repeated, distastefully. "I really don't know. This is the first time I've really reflected on them."

"Fair enough. Let's examine them now. When you saw your 'friend,' he was a little boy, just like you. Only he was—how did you describe him? Scruffy? Like Huck Finn?"

"Right."

"Tell me about Huck Finn."

Taken aback, I answered the question straight. "He's an orphan in Mississippi. He runs away from home and lives on Jackson's Island with Jim, the runaway slave. They go fishing, um . . . they kill rattlesnakes, and in the end . . ."

"Runs away from home, lives in the wild," you said. "Sound like somebody who writes thank-you notes?"

"No."

"No. But for you, at that age, this Huck Finn–like 'friend' was a way of expressing the terrifying feelings you had. George Davies still had to go to school and get good grades, because *he* was gifted and talented. But Huck Finn doesn't give a crap!"

I shifted uncomfortably.

"Now look at George Davies, all grown up. Frightening feelings choke you. They're so terrible you can't hold your own baby. Your child, your marriage, your career. You would rather destroy them all than face these feelings!"

"No," I said feebly.

"Well, that's what you're doing," you snapped. "And why? Because you have no way of letting these terrifying feelings free. You're socialized, presentable. But your shadow doesn't go away, George. He's standing right beside you now. I can see him, even if you can't. He's speaking to me. And do you know what he's saying?"

I gripped the handles of my chair. I forced myself to look forward. You leaned forward and shouted.

"He's saying *you can't be a father!*"

I felt as if I'd been struck.

"Do you believe it?" you said. Your voice was urgent. "Do you?"

"No," I said, weakly.

"Good," you said. "Me neither. That's why we're here. To discover why you would believe a lie like that." You grinned. "You didn't really believe Huck Finn was standing behind you, did you?"

"No, no," I made myself chuckle. I sounded like a drowning frog.

"Keep up the journal writing," you said cheerfully, ending our session. "But be ready for what comes out. When you lock something in a box for twenty years . . . it begins to stink."

Into the Night

T hank you so much for doing this," Mother said.

She was clomping to and fro in her knee-high boots and skirt and a high, cream-colored turtleneck sweater, leaving behind trails of her perfume. In makeup, with glasses off, a string of jade on her neck, I barely recognized her.

"It's my pleasure," said Tom Harris.

He sat like stone in our living room in a red velvet chair, his eyes half-shut in a semidoze. But I could tell he was watching me. Mom told me he had "jumped at the chance" to babysit me; now he was snoozing in the living room like the place belonged to him already. I glared. My mother fluttered between us, oblivious, lavishly scented, in high spirits.

"Isn't this exciting," she said to me. "This could be real money! Do you know how much these corporations pay? *Mm,*" she said—a familiar noise, her little grunt of envy. "Compared to what I made on my last translation. . . . *Mm.*"

"Who is this guy again?" I asked.

"Some consultant . . . to the *food* industry," my mother said dubiously, implying that both consultants and the idea of a food industry were suspect. This was the inverse of her envy grunt: utter disdain for commerce. ". . . who is trying to help his client launch Rogaine in Germany!"

Tom Harris chuckled.

"What's Rogaine?" I asked.

"Helps bald men get their hair back."

"Snake oil," added Tom Harris.

I ignored him. "Are you going to do the translation at dinner?" I asked.

"Translation?" It was as if she had forgotten what the meeting was for. Tom Harris cocked an eyebrow. "Oh. This is what you call schmoozing," my mother said. "Hobnobbing. Sniffing each other out. He wants to see if this crazy professor will be presentable to his client. Wonder if I'll pass the test? *Für aufsehenerregende Ergebnisse,*" she sang out, "*Wenden Sie sich mit dem Fingerspitzen an!*"

Tom Harris smiled slightly, gliding back into his faraway look. Maybe I would run away just to prove what a loser he was as a babysitter.

After finishing my homework, I came downstairs. Tom Harris was sitting in the kitchen. He was sipping a cup of coffee at the table. His hands were all tendons and veins, with a dusting of thick brown hair. Most people drink coffee with some kind of entertainment: conversation, magazine, television. He sat in silence at an empty table, his long limbs folded into the chair like a wire hanger bent the wrong way.

I stood in the doorway. He did not even look around.

"Have a seat," he said coolly.

I sat down, as instructed. "You're a weird babysitter," I said. "I don't need one anyway."

He sipped his coffee. "Your mother seems to think you do."

"She thinks I'm still a kid."

"You're not very mature for twenty-three."

"I'm only *eleven and a half,*" I corrected, scornfully.

"See what I mean?"

"I'm not a kid," I said. "For instance, I know something about you."

"Oh, really?" His eyes danced, his head bobbed. He seemed ready for a little playful jousting—until he heard what I said next.

"I know you like my mother."

He straightened up. "Your mother is one of my oldest and dearest friends, George. Of course I like your mother."

"That's why you're here all the time," I said sarcastically.

"What are you getting at, George?"

"You want to marry her."

A shower of clear laughter burst into the room and bounced around the walls. "If I want to marry your mother, what am I doing here with you?" he said.

Now it was my turn to hesitate.

"That wasn't it," I snarled. "I know something else about you." The bubbling feeling from Tom Harris's laughter faded, and in its place came the tingling thrill I had felt in the presence of my Friend. I felt a surge of adrenaline. This was my chance to find out the truth. "You know what happened to my father."

The laughter stopped. Tom Harris's eyes opened in surprise.

The feeling of exultation continued. Then something strange happened. I felt myself lean forward, grinning fiercely at Tom Harris. I could feel the muscles of my face tighten, grow hot from the intensity. I caught a glimpse of myself reflected in the panel of the kitchen window. The pane distorted my image. In the ripples of the glass, my lips seemed to have stretched themselves into a muscular furrow, baring my teeth from root to tip like a dog, and my eyebrows curled convulsively.

Tom Harris leapt to his feet as if I'd tried to scratch him. His eyes were wide. He seemed genuinely frightened.

"What's gotten into you, son?" he said with alarm.

"I'm not your son and I never will be!" I snapped. I touched my face. It seemed smooth again. "What do you know about my father?"

"What?" he stammered.

"You know something that you're not telling me or Mom. Don't you? About Daddy and why he went away. What is it?"

Tom Harris backed away from the table. He seemed disoriented, a boxer retreating from an opponent.

"George, that's a serious accusation."

"Is it true?" I shouted. "Is it?"

"George, your father was my friend for twenty-five years." He tried a stab at humor: "Fine, you can stay up for the late show. Just drop the angry act."

But he'd grown pale. If there were any need for proof of what my Friend had told me, it was written on Tom Harris's face as clearly as black ink. "I do know things about your father that you don't know," he said softly. "I do know things about how he died."

"You admit it!" I was shrieking.

Tom Harris stepped forward and continued in that soft, careful voice. "I asked your mother if I might come here tonight because I am worried about you, George. What you say gives me further cause for alarm. Not because you are wrong," he said. "No, because you are right. These are things that no one on earth could know—except a few friends, whose trustworthiness is absolute."

"Tell me!" I could not believe what I was hearing. The more I looked at Tom Harris's craggy, greasy face, the angrier I grew. "Why won't anybody tell me?"

"Because some things are not for little boys to hear!" he said loudly. He was angry now, too.

"Oh my God," my head was spinning. "You mean *murder!*"

"Stop saying that! Stop it!" Tom Harris towered over me and shook his finger. "How do you know these things, George? Tell me!"

But I could not. I ran from the room, with the hall, the stairs, swimming past in a blur. Tom Harris was close behind. I was near swooning. In my room, in the dark, I slammed the door and propped up a chair against the handle like I'd seen in movies. I heard Tom Harris's voice outside, calling my name, and I blocked it out, repeating, "Get away! Get away!"

Get away. Get away.

That scowling face.

It was quiet now. Dark in my room, but there was light under the
door, meaning that my mother was still out and Tom Harris was still in
the house. I was in my room, in pajamas, but roused into the heady,
world-warped atmosphere of my Friend. I felt like a patient under the
ether, when the tables and chairs in the operating room shimmy in
excitement and the fear hooks of surgery loosen and let go, amplifying
the delicious drumming in mind and ear and spine. My Friend stood at
the bottom of the bed. He was staring at me from out of the dark,
among the moonlit shadows. His face was vivid to me: he had hair like
straw, and a sooty face.

You scared me, I said.

I can't scare you anymore, he said into my mind.

Are we going into the night? I asked.

Yes.

Next I was floating unattached in the ethereal night, as before, and
the "upless" feeling passed almost immediately. The gray night swirled
around me, and this time, it caressed me. I felt a powdery, choking
sweetness at the back of my throat. All of it felt higher pitched than
before; it was musical, soaring, climactic. My Friend pointed, I followed.

We passed the great black shipwreck, the earth. All the little windows were alight, blazing, as if the shipwreck were aflame.

Why is it so much brighter?

It's not brighter, he said. *You just see it better.*

Am I a Beacon?

He grinned. *Oh yes.*

And then into my mind poured a whole new vision. It came into
me like music—richer, more complex than what I had felt before, serious and somber, like a cello sonata. I felt sorrow here. I began to feel
like weeping. The cello music was so passionate and sad, I trembled.
Grief was all around me.

What is this?

We're going deeper.

The very atmosphere began to take on words. It was my Friend
speaking to me: *This is what you wanted.*

Suddenly I was in a room.

It was a dry place, painted white, with bare floorboards. Muted daylight, as from an overcast day, radiated from a window I could not see. The room was familiar, and yet was not a room at home or school: it was some neutral space, like a waiting room.

My father was there.

He was just as he was before he left for Honduras. Sad, deep-set eyes, with crow's-feet at the corners, and thick brown hair. His nose was long, strong and pointed, and his skin was brownish, almost swarthy. To me, he was an Indian warrior: lean-limbed, tall, and grim. In life, when he was working or thinking, he stalked around the house in khaki pants and a ratty blue sweater, in forbidding silence. Now his dark eyes stared at the floorboards. He was garbed in pajamas. It felt like I was visiting him in a hospital.

George, he said.

You're tired, I realized.

Very tired, he said. *I've been carrying a secret.*

He placed a hand on my shoulder. I could sense the comfortable cotton rustle of his pajamas. Then he began to speak, his brown eyes blazing.

I am caught on a threshold, George, he told me. *This is a way station.*

I pictured a train station where the train does not come. There are no other travelers, no noise or movement, no clocks to measure the passing time, and no people. Just stifling silence. *It's a terrible high summer where I am, George,* my father said, and I could picture it. Like a southern mill town, choking on an August heat. *As still as noon. My memories never leave me alone.* There, in my mind, followed snapshots of situations: the chronology of how he died (*from his sickbed he stared at the opening in the tent, a mere patch of white daylight, where he hoped good news would appear, a medevac helicopter, or the supply truck that would take him away on rough, rutted roads, which it did,* the visions told me, *but it was weeks*). Through a flurry of dim pictures I saw some of my parents' friends, with names attached, *Clarissa, Freddie;* I felt the sad love he had for my mother, and I saw her face through his eyes on the day he left home for the camp—unreachable and unhappy, her sympathy for him so withered that even had he decided to stay, it would have made little difference.

Then he stopped, squeezed my shoulder, and said, *The worst of these memories, is this.*

What? I was desperate to know.

Someone hoped I would be killed down there. Tom Harris, whom you already seem prepared to adopt as a foster-father . . .

I protested. *I don't! I hate him!*

. . . he was the one who goaded me along, pushed me into going.

I knew it! I triumphed. *How?*

He played to my principles, convinced me I was unfulfilled, and dressed up this idea, this Catholic idea, of a calling. My father pronounced the word *calling* with the contempt he once reserved for novels he called *bogus* and *cheap-deep.* Instantly I shared his hatred. *It was an idea that he whipped up into a passion. He drove me to think I could accomplish something, by helping people endure a disaster that was far beyond me. Stupid and vain, do you understand, George? He manipulated me.*

I understand, I said.

Tom Harris, my father said, *is in love with your mother. He would come by afternoons when I wasn't home and talk to her, sometimes for hours. Made her resentful over my plans to go to Honduras—the same trip he goaded me to take! Sometimes he would still be there when I came home and would barely look at me as I came into my own house, as if I were a monster and he were ashamed to be my friend. Do you see what he did, George?*

I see! I said. *I remember that. How could you let him do it?*

I could not force him to stop. Your mother said she needed sympathy, and not from her own friends. She said it was better to have someone who understood me as well. She understood no better than I did that Tom Harris was as good as murdering me. I was outsmarted. Another wince of pain shot across my father's face. *Can you understand how this is agony to me?*

I felt a burning humiliation so deep it seemed to reach back thousands of years, to the epoch of tribes and chieftans—as if my father had lost in single combat with Tom Harris. He had believed Tom Harris's jaunty charms and had been duped by his intelligence, and now we both were shamed.

What can I do? I pleaded with him.

First, listen, he said. *Your godfather, Freddie Turnbull, was part of this scheme. Freddie has letters of mine. He keeps them for Tom Harris, letters they rescued from the house when I died. These letters prove everything I say.*

Prove? I asked.

But I felt the reality shift under me. That calm, cool room was jarred; distorted, like someone disturbing a reflection in a birdbath.

What do I do with them? I shouted desperately into the vanishing remnants of the waiting room.

Just find the letters. You'll see how Tom Harris twists the knife.

A howling rose around me as if tigers and dogs were held at bay behind the curtain of the warm night. I saw the gray mass, I felt chaos and motion. I heard my Friend whisper close in my ear: *They'll never tell you where they are. You will have to lie to them.*

Who are they? I asked desperately.

And then: a pounding and scraping.

"George," came a voice.

I rose in bed. The door: the chair I propped under it was still there. Someone was trying to enter. The door was shaking, jostling the chair aside.

"George!"

Finally the chair fell over. The door opened, and my mother's silhouette filled the bedroom door. Yellow light from the hall burned around her.

"George, are you awake? What is this chair doing here?"

She crossed into the dark bedroom.

"How was your night?" I asked, trying to be casual.

"I thought I heard you talking. Were you talking in your sleep?"

"I guess so."

She sat down next to me. She smelled of sweet perfume gone rotten with scotch and the faint mingled scents of cooking oil and bleach—restaurant odors. Her breath was tobacco-y. She began stroking my head, somewhat clumsily.

"I got the job. Isn't that exciting?"

"Mm."

She paused. "Tom Harris said you got upset tonight."

I was silent.

"Was everything okay?"

"Yeah."

She sat in silence next to me, waiting for more. "Why did you put the chair in front of the door?" she asked firmly.

"I don't know. I guess I was upset," I said, seizing on her word.

"Can you tell me why?"

I thought for a moment.

"When Dad went away," I said, "did Tom Harris want him to go?"

My mother turned aside, as if this question caused her pain.

"Sweetie, Tom Harris opposed your father's going for the same reasons we all did. It was dangerous down there." She peered at me in the dark. "Is that what this is about?"

"Did Tom Harris tell Daddy that? Or did he just *tell* you he told Daddy?"

"He told your father directly," she replied. "George, what's this about?"

"Are you *sure* he said that to Daddy?"

"George!" she said, exasperated. "What is all this?"

But I closed my eyes to make her think I had fallen asleep.

She waited for a time. Waited for me to stir and say something to ease her anxiety, something concrete and solvable that she could actually address with her ample combined powers of intelligence and love. But I didn't. Eventually she rose from the bed and crept out quietly. I heard the sink running, the aspirin bottle pop open, the pills rattling. Then

I drifted off for real, and, as I did, I recalled an image: a man with a thick mustache lounging on our sofa at Christmastime, bearing eau-de-vie and sweet dessert wines, telling outlandish stories, with fingers that fiddled and twitched with continual impatience. My godfather, I murmured to myself: Freddie Turnbull.

Hole

He was high up on the property, a little toy figure bending and bowing, seemingly dancing in an odd halting step—a kind of Electric Slide—all by himself. He was raking, actually. But the rake was invisible in his hands against the house, the yard, and the trees, all colored in the ash-brown hues of autumn.

Rosetta was the name of Freddie Turnbull's house. It was situated just south of town, on a hillock overlooking a quiet patch of Main Street past two hulking Presbyterian churches and an old hotel named for P. G. T. Beauregard, now a halfway house for local lunatics who on mild days could be seen lolling on rockers under the columned porch.

Rosetta was a broad-shouldered, brown brick house, with ivy crawling on every side, that wore, as it were, a Victorian lace cap in the form of a whitewashed, latticed widow's walk flanked by two chimneys. Its yard ran a hundred feet down to Main Street, and its interior was the pride of its owner: a shadowy place slathered in oriental carpets and antiques. Every year the house would be opened up for parties, and Freddie—Uncle Freddie, my godfather—would escort his friends around to show new acquisitions or restorations. Uncle Freddie had inherited a fortune from his parents, as well as Rosetta, so compared with his scholarly peers—he was a professor of art history at Early—he lived like a baron.

When he saw me coming toward him, the dance ceased. He leaned on the rake and watched me.

In summers Freddie would be seen in the same place, gardening. This is how I remembered him best: in great bloomer shorts, his bald head covered with a panama hat, trowel in hand, sweat pouring down onto his glasses. In summer he went bare-chested, and you saw he had the round belly and flat pectoral muscles of an aging wrestler, with tufts of hair growing from his shoulders. Now he was neatly packaged in pressed khakis and a flannel shirt.

"George! Well, what a surprise! What brings you to the pastures of the humble shepherds and shepherdesses?"

This was the way Freddie talked, in aggressive and mocking allusion.

"Nothing," I said.

"Nothing! You've come a long way for nothing. Shall I put you to work?" he said, gesturing to the wide yard littered with leaves. We stood near his terrace, a platform of mossy brick, furnished with black iron chairs and table. Evidently my face fell at the idea of raking, and he laughed. "I'm *teasing* you, ass! Boys prefer eating to working, isn't that right? Come, let's see if there's any gruel I can heat up for you. That's what we eat out here in the country. Or maybe you would like some lard?"

With that, we went inside.

What we had was a far cry from gruel. Uncle Freddie whipped together a wood platter laden with slices of blue cheese, pâté, corni-chons, and cracked wheat crackers.

"Just the simple food of shepherds and shepherdesses," he contin-ued, as he bustled around the kitchen. I tucked in hungrily. "How nice it is to get a visit from my godson."

"How is school?" I asked him.

"School?" he puffed. "My school? Back to the beginning, every year: classical architecture for undergraduates. The Parthenon, *agora,* Greek city planning. And grading papers. Grading *papers,*" he repeated with scorn. "There is no human achievement so great, that a freshman cannot reduce it to drivel."

I smiled. We sat in the shadows in his kitchen, around a little table.

"And *your* school?" he asked.

"I hate school."

"Of course you do," he said. "The school system has been ruined. Full of blacks and little inbred creatures from the county."

My eyes widened.

"Well, isn't it?" he said.

"I guess so."

"Of course it is," he said. "The civil rights movement destroyed education in this country. They had to *chaaange* the curriculum so that the little blacks would be able to get As, and they ruined it for everybody. The intelligent students fled for private schools, and the teachers they brought in were more ignorant *blacks.* And now it's just a god-awful mess."

Freddie sat despondently, as if his own speech reminded him of all the hopeless truths of modern times. My father told me that Freddie's family had once owned an Alabama cotton plantation but had sold it decades ago, *after the boll weevil,* and the property had been converted to a lodge for game hunters. It should have occurred to me that my godfather was one of the breed of curmudgeonly university homosexuals— bombastic, witty, overeducated—who fancy themselves the Socrates of their institution: the brilliant one, the one with taste, the True Protector of student virtue, saving young men from the mediocrity of *coaches* and *social scientists,* and God help them, *the impoverished, middle-class scrub that passes for Society in a town like Preston* (all phrases I'd heard him use at one time or another). Uncle Freddie's aristocratic nostalgia consti-tuted, in a way, his Platonic forms: the departed generation of great talkers; the ladies who wore hats and gloves to church; the gentlemen who held their liquor and never cursed or spoke about money.

I swallowed a cornichon and remembered why I had come. *They'll never tell you where they are,* my father had said. *You'll have to find them.*

"I want to see my father's old letters," I said bluntly. It was a childish opening to negotiations, but I didn't know any better way. "I want to know why he went away."

To my astonishment, Uncle Freddie glanced quickly at me, then stared down at his hands. A guilty gesture.

"I don't know what you mean."

Through the kitchen window I saw that the October sun was fading quickly and streaking the lawn with orange. In the unlit house, shadows fell everywhere around us. Uncle Freddie sat back in his chair, his face gone slack. Emotions swept his features like one of those time-elapse shots of weather streaking across a sky.

He rose. He picked up the now-empty platter and put it in the sink. He stood there, a silhouette, staring out the window.

"What prompted this line of inquiry, George?"

"I thought you had letters from just before he went away," I said.

"Hm," he grunted, evasively. "Why those letters?"

"I want to know about him. Why he left."

"I don't have them!" he shouted, turning on me.

His hands twitched violently. I had seen Uncle Freddie puffed up and bellowing in hot debates, but he had never yelled at me. I recoiled. My father had been right. Uncle Freddie wasn't going to tell me. Uncle Freddie could not be trusted.

"Maybe your mother has them," he sulked.

"She doesn't. I asked," I lied.

The house, by now, had descended into gloom. We literally sat in the dark. Finally he broke the silence.

"Come here," he said after a moment. "I want to show you something."

After unlocking a door with a skeleton key, he led me down creaking stairs to his cellar. Then he flipped a switch, revealing ceiling-high racks of wine, all gathering dust, some with chalk marks on them for turning, the floor scattered with cardboard boxes bearing images of châteaux, grapes, vines. More rooms spun out from this one; armies of glass bottles glinting in the dark.

"Have I never shown you the wine?" he asked. It was not *my collection,* or *my cellar,* just *the wine.*

"There must be a hundred bottles," I exclaimed.

"Altogether? Over two thousand," he said proudly. "There's more in the next room. Go ahead, take one."

I pulled a bottle from the wine rack gently, with two hands, afraid of dropping it. Freddie smiled. "Read it."

"Hermitage," I mispronounced.

"*Hermitage,*" he corrected, savoring the name. "A tiny domaine on the slopes of the Rhône, where the vines grow on such steep gradients, machines are useless and everything is picked by hand. Dirty fingers and paring knives. And the date?"

"1971."

"The year you were born," he said.

I looked at the bottle in my hand. It was covered with dust. I ran my finger along the top, wiping the bottle clear to reveal a glimpse of blood-red wine.

"We drank the first bottle of this with a lump of Parmesan cheese—your father, Tom Harris, and I." I flinched at Tom Harris's name. "Your father was happy then. Just as happy as he could be, that you were in the world."

I blushed, and looked at my shoes.

"Now this wine is ready to drink. Five cases, my friend. It's going to be my party wine at Halloween. You may have a glass—one only—if you think you're ready."

"I'm ready," I said.

"Wine matures faster than boys," he said drily. "Listen, George. You will learn about your father as you go—as you get older. He was a complicated man. You understand? No need for the private eye act."

I nodded.

"*Festina lente.* You know what that means?"

"Hurry slowly."

"*Bene.*" He smiled.

I was so deeply asleep I wonder if this one came purely from my dreams. Direct and potent, but so brief it was hard to analyze.

My Friend did not appear in my room to wake me. He did not take me on a journey through the nighttime ether. Instead, I dreamed of darkness. This might seem like an oxymoron, since sleep takes place in the dark, and since unconsciousness is itself a kind of void, or darkness. Dreaming, therefore, should be an illumination of that darkness . . .

If so, it explains why this was the worst dream of my life. In it, I am only awareness. I can perceive, but I cannot act. It's like I am sitting at the bottom of a well. When I try to speak, the effort dies before it begins. All I am is a stream of thought, a trickle of consciousness, a drip in the well. Constant, but weak, and hopeless.

Into the well enters another presence. It is my Friend. This surprises me, even in a dream. How could he follow me to this place? I am so deep, so remote, that his voice—soundless, though; better to describe it as his mind—is a shock. But it brings no relief. If before the well was a horrible, but neutral, place, my Friend's voice brings with it the element of pain. It speaks in long, gloating phrases that throb in my frail consciousness like a migraine. Finally the voice dies away into silence. Now I cannot stand the quiet.

I ask him if this is a prison.

It is an end.

Does that mean I am here forever?

Yes.

Terror ripples through me. I begin to wake up emotionally, as it were—even though moments ago such a thing seemed impossible.

I can't be here forever! I haven't done anything yet!

You are here because this is where the holes go.

At this point my Friend and I speak at cross-purposes; he seems to think of "holes" as people, I think of them as places.

Is this like a basement? I ask.

It is a state.

A state where? I am thinking of the South, or North.

A state of finishedment.

This odd word sets off a chain of thinking: finishedment; if I am finished, done with, over, then my Friend no longer wants me. I begin to wrestle with the dream. I begin to try and clamber out of it, like swimming to the surface when you're underwater. His voice comes to me. It follows me, so that I hear it as I gain the surface, achieve consciousness.

YOU ARE A HOLE. YOU ARE A HOLE.

Then I am sitting in bed awake, alive, breathing heavily, soaked and slimy with sweat, those words reverberating in my head. I could not go back to sleep, dogged by the hollow cruelty of that final voice. Its tone beyond mocking: hostile; an attack in itself. It was the voice of a Dean, or a Byrd, but a thousand times nastier: the voice of real hate. *But how could my Friend hate me?* I tossed and turned, becoming entwined with the bedsheets. A plaintive, whiny voice welled up inside me. *If he hates me, too, who do I have left?*

"How are you?" Richard asked, once we settled.

I shrugged, smirked, cringed all at once. "Look at me." I shrugged. I had not slept. Fear of descending into that dream well—that hole— kept me awake, and jittery, whenever I lay on my bed. I had started fighting to stay awake. For two nights running now, I had seen the sun rise. Now I felt like the walking dead. My glasses were greasy, askew on my nose. My eyes drooped, my feet dragged.

"What's the problem?"

"Tired," I answered.

"Have you been eating okay? Did you eat lunch?"

I had.

"What about sleep?"

"What about it?"

"Have you been sleeping all right?"

Have I been sleeping all right

The words seemed to drop into a chasm.

Have I been sleeping all right

I could almost feel them float and echo down the cold hole. Mud and sand and cold water below.

Have I been sleeping all right

I stood on the riverbank in moonlight—the spot where I had seen Tom Harris, down behind Revolution Hall, down among the intertwining paths and the pines overlooking the James River. Across the black water I saw a tree. Its monstrous silver branches stretched toward me.

Have I been sleeping all right

"George," he was saying.

"Yes."

"Can you hear me?"

"Yes, why?"

"George, where did you go just now?"

"Nowhere."

"You went away for a minute."

The office was the same as it was. Quiet, clean, plant in corner. But I had an announcement. "I don't like to sleep anymore."

"Don't like to sleep?" Richard said, surprised. "Why is that?"

"I have dreams."

"Tell me about them." I hesitated. "Are they bad dreams?" Richard suggested.

"Kind of."

"They scare you?"

"Uh-huh."

"You said they were 'kind of' bad. What makes them only *kind of* bad?"

"Not *kind of* bad. *Kind of* dreams."

Richard watched me carefully, processing this. "Okay," he said. What's a . . . *kind of* dream?"

"It's a dream where you hear real voices," I said.

"Your mom?" he prompted. "Neighbors?"

"No," I said.

"Then who?"

"I can hear my Friend."

Richard blinked a long, therapeutic blink.

"Your friend," he repeated, in a tone so soft his voice nearly vanished into the folds of his cardigan. "Really. And who is this friend?"

Outside the clinic, an unfamiliar car waited. A door opened, and my mother stood beside it.

"George," she said. She was like a stranger standing next to anything but the old Toyota. This was a sloping, amber Saab. "We're getting a ride today," she said. "This is Kurt."

A man climbed out of the driver's side. His blond hair twisted behind his ears and fell over his eyes in a shaggy, overgrown preppie haircut. He wore a standard, pale blue Brooks Brothers button-down, frayed at the collar and hems. His belly, arms, and—when he shook my hand, I discovered—even his fingers, bulged with a muscle-fat combination that created a uniquely masculine *solidity*. In combination with skin the tint of sand (from work under the sun? from good ol'-fashioned dirt?), Kurt carried the air of a WASP gone country. His lips were thick, but not sensual; his skull, large and blocky, like those bronze sculptures you see of Hercules where the figure's own strength seems to burden him. Kurt was a man who never needed to move quickly or talk loudly to make his point.

"George."

I decided he looked too intelligent to be a grown-up Early College bum: the kind who graduated and, addicted to reefer and the memories of undergraduate pleasures—inner tubing, bused-in Central girls, endless beer drinking—stuck around, maybe opened a store, or wrote a column for the *News Gazette*. Preston Lotus Eaters. No, there was another type that gravitated to Preston. Unlike their sensualist brethren, these were professionals, often out-of-towners, who quietly fell in love with Stoneland County's creeks and mountains and honeysuckle—and out of love with their white-collar jobs. They moved through Preston society with a gentle, almost monastic air, like they'd found something so special they didn't want to move too fast, or speak too loud, for fear of breaking it. Kurt, I reckoned quickly, was one of these.

"Hope you don't mind me picking you up," Kurt continued.

"I'm working on a translation project for Kurt," Mom interjected. "You remember."

"Yeah," I said. "Rogaine."

Kurt glanced at my mother. She shrugged.

"Those are corporate secrets," he said frowning. "But if you shake on it, I'll know you can be trusted."

I took his hand.

"Attaboy." His eyes crinkled into crow's-feet.

I settled in the backseat. Kurt walked my mother around to the passenger side. Their bodies pressed together; she pulled away and jumped in the front seat with a ringing laugh. She bounced around and turned to me and smiled with slightly smeared makeup and shining eyes. They had been kissing. My mother was unrecognizable. She wore the beaming countenance of a young, happy woman. Which I suppose, in that moment, she was.

The phone was ringing when we arrived. My mother rushed us into the house, throwing her keys down and scrambling to reach the phone in the kitchen.

"I'm fine, Richard, how are you?"

After a moment came a surprised yelp. *"Voices?"* my mother said.

She shut the kitchen door for privacy. If I strained, I could hear her—muffled but intelligible.

"But what do we do?" she said. *"Surely that's not necessary? Sending him to Charlottesville?"*

"So," Kurt drawled cheerfully, looking around, "this is a big old house. When did you move here?"

"Never," I said, only half-listening.

He blinked at me. "Never?"

Why couldn't he be quiet? "This is the only house I ever lived in."

"Never. I like that." He smiled easily.

My mind raced for ideas to keep Kurt occupied—and quiet.

"Do you want to see some pictures?" I asked. "Of my dad?"

Kurt blinked. "Sure."

I laid three large family albums on the floor. Kurt crawled down on the rug with me, while I flipped page after page, straining after the mutters I heard from behind the kitchen door. We were halfway through the 1970s—my phase of putting buckets on my head—when I asked him, just conversationally, "What's in Charlottesville?"

"Charlottesville? I guess UVa is the big attraction there. Why?"

"What's UVa?"

"University of Virginia. Great school." He smiled. "Already picking out colleges?"

"Somebody from my school is being sent away—to Charlottesville. I was just wondering what he meant."

"Sent away? I dunno . . . Maybe they mean the UVa hospital. Not good news for your friend, though. He having problems?"

My heartbeat in my ears, I flipped the plastic sleeves of the snapshots.

"Oh, no. He's kind of a faker."

My mother found us cross-legged on the living room floor with the drawers to the highboy flung open and photo albums and loose snapshots spread around us.

"George is showing me pictures of his father," said Kurt, deadpan.

"Oh, dear," she said. "I think it's time for Kurt to go home."

Tightness in her mouth told me other matters were on her mind. But she cooked my dinner, watched the evening news, helped me with my homework, as if it were an ordinary night. *Sweetie,* she said at bedtime, *how about you sleep with Snoopy tonight, like the old days? Crack the door?* But I told her, No, no, I wasn't a baby anymore, I wasn't afraid of the dark, so she tucked me in, lingering there awhile until I closed my eyes. Then I waited until she had gone, and rose, stripping my pajama top off and standing in the center of my room, fists clenched at my sides, to keep my body cool, tense, alert—to keep from falling asleep, to keep from falling in the hole.

Sick

I only got worse after that.

In fact, you could say I was getting sick. Not by the definition of any school nurse. In school, there were two things you went home for: fever and vomiting. Every student passed with envy that door by the principal's office where classmates could be seen in the nurse's chair, a thermometer poking from their mouths, minutes away from release. Less jealousy-inspiring were the astonishing acts of projectile vomiting I recall from grades K–5, especially the remarkable performance of one Tameka Jackson, a chubby girl with multicolored barrettes who one morning turned her head back and forth like a carnival game, alternately filling two industrial-sized garbage cans with a high-velocity fountain of brown vomit. The teacher's aides—babysitters, really; an underclass of school disciplinarians—protected us, or so they thought, by coining coy, redneck euphemisms for any biological function. To go to the bathroom was to "take care of your needs"; to vomit was to "upchuck" (ironically, a word that was pure onomatopoeic nausea).

I had not upchucked. I had no fever. But anyone looking at me could tell there was something wrong.

"You're yellow," said Dirk Hunsicker.

We were in the bathroom. I turned to the mirrors.

"Holy cow, look at him!" he exclaimed. Dirk was a military kid, son of a Fort Virginia colonel, with a shaved head and—standing next to me—peachy white skin. "Check this out!"

Earl Clemmer came over.

"Dag, boy," he said. "You should see the nurse."

"Stay away from me," said Dirk, dramatically moving away.

"Yeah, I don't want to get sick!" echoed Earl, and they left in a hurry.

I stared in the mirror. I *was* yellow. Sallow and waxy as a mummy, and my eyes were closing to slits, with a swelling around my eyes and throat. I wished I could crawl into a stall, wrap myself around a cool toilet seat and hibernate until I had changed back to normal. But a voice inside rebelled. *Oh no, no sleep for you.*

And it was true; the nights had grown worse.

It began the same way every time. With my Friend. What had been a name transformed itself into a kind of mantra that overcame me when the lights were out and I lay on my pillow staring at the cool light from the streetlight. I spoke the name and thought it and played with it and repeated it a hundred times to see if it lost meaning, like saying "umbrella" until you're convinced it's nonsense. Only for me, repeating it wove it more into my senses. My Friend was the answer to every question, and rose again at the end of that answer to pose yet another question; and so on, around and around, a question answering itself and asking itself. At first I listened to it like I did to the normal sound of a Preston night: a band playing a faraway fraternity party, the growl of a truck shifting gears on the street. Half interested. Somewhat curious. Then it was closer, louder, like hearing one-half of a telephone conversation, unwanted, yet irresistible, as the words *my Friend, my Friend,* kept coming, and I watched—I could feel my eyes moving!—the words go by as if they were on a ticker tape, *my Friend, my Friend, my Friend, my Friend.* The words came closer, in my ears, nearly touching. And at last, they were physical. I felt fierce fingers pinching my sides.

"Stop it!" I shouted. "Stop it! Stop it!"

I writhed on the bed. Everywhere I moved, hands gripped me and squeezed. I could not see them, but they came at me with terrific force, like birds plunging at me from a dozen directions. From their power I could almost sense the person they belonged to: a conniving, pinching child with sticky hands, gritting his teeth with the twinge of sadism. My mother rushed into the room. I had been crying out.

"George! George, what is it?"

"Can you see them?"

"What, honey?"

"The hands!"

What hands? she kept repeating, as she searched under the bedclothes for the unseen intruder. *What hands, Georgie?* For an instant, as if the sadism was catching, her confusion, her useless groping in the dark, seemed almost amusing. With a horrible wrench, however— stronger than the rest, a bully's last shot—I felt a great hunk of my flesh, just below my ribs, twisted in a knot. I yelped in pain, then grasped my mother around the neck, sobbing. The pinching stopped.

"What was it, honey?" she demanded, frightened herself now. "Is it fleas? Is there something in the bed?"

I sobbed. "I don't know."

"Are you hurt?"

"I don't know," I said. "I think so."

"Let me look at this." She turned on the lamp. Then she pulled back my pajama top.

My mother's expression of disgust and surprise at the sight of my middle frightened me again. I let her hold me for a long while.

❧   ❧   ❧

"Clarissa, thank you so much for coming," said my mother.

"Oh, listen, Joan," sang the queer, quavery voice of Clarissa Bing.

Professors make for tough company, since in any gathering, every single one of them assumes they are the most intelligent person in the room. But my parents—who were as prickly and competitive as any—held Clarissa Bing alone in unqualified esteem. Clarissa stood out from their tenured cronies. She was younger than my parents, in her midthirties. But Clarissa seemed an older soul than any of them. A dark-haired woman with a long, planar face, she wore in every weather the same clunky pilgrim shoes and knee-length sundresses that revealed her skinny, snow-white shins: oddball outfits typical of someone who had been isolated and brain-bound her whole life, who'd never noticed, or maybe never cared to observe, the habits of socialized folk. She drawled out her vowels, and fluttered her eyes as she spoke, in a kind of tic. She was pretty—a refined face, a rosy complexion—but somehow devoid of eroticism. She took no interest in classical music or literature (normally this disqualified anybody from friendship with my parents), but her burning interest in her own field, psychology, appealed to my mother's gender-is-destiny politics; and her status as a reader at the Episcopal church won over my father. Her defining moment for him came at one of my parents' cocktail parties, when she treated a room full of leftist humanities professors to a thirty-minute lecture about the clear indications in the Gospels, St. Paul, Acts, and Revelation, that the majority of people would, in fact, go to hell.

That's a little tough on those of us who aren't perfect, said one guest in a snide voice, clearly feeling he voiced the majority view. *I suppose you feel pretty sure of yourself.*

I reckon most of us have a little roasting to do before we're done, said Clarissa.

But hell or heaven—isn't that a typical male, black and white view? It was my mother speaking, her tone, urgent, argumentative—even a touch strangled, as if she felt nervous confronting her friend. *Women have been disqualified from virtually any role in the church. Why should I feel an obligation to submit to something that excludes me? Especially if it means . . . going to hell.*

A ripple of agreement passed among some guests. Or perhaps it was the excitement of a crowd at a bullfight—a sitting forward, a watching for first blood.

Clarissa defused it with an acquiescent gesture. *Joan is our hostess and gets the last word,* said Clarissa, without a touch of sarcasm. *And all this talk of hell has made me thirsty. How about another bourbon?* I remember my mother's face, smiling, gratified, but also tense—some conflict remained unresolved there—merely postponed.

I heard my mother ushering Clarissa into the hall. My door was open. I lay in my pajamas, under the window. Beside me sat a half-empty glass of water and a mostly depleted Tylenol bottle. The voices carried up the stairs.

"George is having some trouble," my mother whispered.

"What's the matter?"

"Can you take a look at him?"

"Does he need a doctor?"

"I'd rather start with you."

"A psychologist?" Clarissa chewed on this. "What about Richard Manning?"

"I'd rather Richard didn't know."

There followed a pause.

"I see," said Clarissa. Then: "Lead the way."

Clarissa appeared in the doorway a few moments later. In her hand she held a mason jar filled with water, containing a single cut flower: a parrot tulip of flaming orange-pink. She peered at me over her fine, long nose. She rested the flower on my dresser, then sat on the side of my bed.

"Hello, George," she said.

Clarissa's examination took only a few minutes. She asked me what had happened; I told her. She observed my back, stomach, and sides. Her reaction was somber, but terse.

"Put some ice on these," she said with a frown.

"Is that flower for me?" I asked as I pulled my pajamas on again.

"It is," she replied.

"Why?"

"I haven't seen you much since your father died," she said.

I did not reply; it was a statement.

"Thought I'd bring you something, George. Y'ever hear that song, 'a few of my favorite things'?" She reached out a hand and gently stroked the petals of the parrot tulip. "Grief," she said, "brings a little bit of twilight to everyone it touches. This is something to remind you of the bright days." Her eyes fluttered. "Get some sleep now."

Later, I heard them murmuring in the hall.

". . . serious bruises," whispered Clarissa. "You saw them last night?"

"They were welts," said my mother.

"I don't know what to tell you."

Their voices became inaudible, then moments later, sparked back to life.

"*Because,*" my mother was hissing, "Richard's talking about sending him to *Charlottesville.* I'm not ready for that."

"Well, the mind can't make bruises. Either someone did it to him, or he did it to himself."

"Well, I didn't do it. And there was no one else here."

Clarissa seemed to think about this a moment.

"Have you considered telling Tom Harris?"

My mother's tone became sharp. "Why would I tell Tom Harris?"

"He has had some experience with . . ."

"I know the stories. Why do you think it's relevant?"

"Just considering the possibility."

"No, I don't see that," said my mother, suddenly cold.

"Tom Harris has helped give advice to the church. He helped some suffering people."

"I said, forget about that," snapped my mother. Then in a conciliatory tone: "Let's not discuss it." Finally, filling a wounded silence: "I mean—thank you."

Moments later they were clumping down the stairs and saying good-bye. After the door closed, I heard my mother heave a deep sigh. That night, she cooked me a "sick dish," chicken soup with rice and lemon. The next day she wrapped me in scarves before sending me to school.

She debated whether to take me to Freddie's Halloween party. My mother had not missed a single Turnbull party in her entire time in Preston, she admitted, Uncle Freddie's parties being local legend. She considered the importance of "getting me out" and "cheering me up." I begged her to take me. It was the first Halloween party he'd given. Every seventh-grader I knew would be there. Finally, she relented.

"I'm going to do it," she said at last. "We need to get out, see people, do new things, refresh ourselves. We've barely seen another soul, besides at work and school, since your father." She omitted the word *died*.

"We're going to the Halloween party?"

"Yes, we're going to the Halloween party."

But even with the sickness, the sleeplessness, and the imposing presence of my Friend, I still remained focused on my father's mission. Discovering my father's letters. Keeping Tom Harris at bay.

All Hallows' Eve

Halloween day bloomed into a robust autumn afternoon with a broad sky. My mother and I walked together in Slopers Creek Park, kicking the hedge apples. She must have been thrilled. There was color back in my cheeks; I was practically romping through the yellow grass, picking up stones and throwing them into the creek. Back home, we made costumes for the party. My mother created a ruff collar out of a paper ornament, put me in a black corduroy shirt, rolled up some trousers to make knickers, and popped a black hat of hers on my head: a Dutch trader. She wrapped a scarf over her head and a patterned skirt around her waist, put on beads and a makeup mole: a gypsy. The sun went down. I counted the minutes.

Shivers went up my spine as soon as we approached Rosetta in the car, and the real blackness of night descended over a mild evening. Where we turned into the steep driveway, already crammed with cars, Freddie had placed jack-o'-lanterns on poles, hideous ones with long, stabby teeth and flaming eyes, and even elaborate earholes. "Only Freddie would think of art nouveau pumpkins," my mother laughed. The windows glowed gold, and promised, with moving shadows and shades of scarlet and white and black, many guests in wild disguises.

As the main entrance to the house, Freddie's kitchen was often the hub of the action. Tonight it swirled in chaos. A caterer with black and white cat whiskers noisily dumped a bag of ice into a punch bowl. More helpers, also in face paint, bustled around with trays of apples and nuts and dried fruits and cheeses. In their midst, Freddie, already tipsy, face florid, directed the staff and argued with the head caterer, Abby Gold, who was also his best friend, a diminutive actress in local theater with a sideline in canapés. She was yelling at Freddie.

"Herb chèvre and celery!" she insisted, in the overinflected voice of a thespian. Somewhere behind it, a slight speech impediment, maybe a lisp, had been covered over by careful training.

He boomed, "The theme, my dear, is American. Game meats and dried fruits and apples and nuts. Frontier food, corn—"

"There is no corn here, Freddie—"

"More's the pity. Creamed corn! Delicious!"

"It's fattening—"

"Oh, *Abby,*" he spat. "You don't worry about that at a *party!*"

Abby was obsessed with her weight: an actress's vanity, plus the sensitivity of a woman five feet tall.

"But these low-fat chèvres . . ."

Freddie filled his lungs and bellowed at the staff: "SERVE MY ENGLISH HUNTSMAN!"

They cringed, then produced a wood platter holding a gigantic wheel of layered cheddar, yellow, and blue cheeses, with a great wood-handled knife thrust into it like Excalibur.

"Beautiful!" he cried. "And push the Hermitage!"

Then he spotted us.

"Joan! George! Perfect timing—the real food is coming out."

Over the silk pajamas he wore, Freddie had wrapped a long, loose, oriental blanket that must have weighed thirty pounds, and on his head was a turban with a large costume jewel in the center. He was a typhoon of color.

"What do you think?" he said, raising his arms over his head.

"*Defies description,* is what Lizzie Beard said," chuckled Abby maliciously.

"Oh, *Abby.* Have some imagination."

"What are you?" I asked.

"What . . . ," he sputtered. "I AM A PASHA!"

"What you are is in my way," grumbled Abby, pushing toward the fridge.

"You're magnificent, Freddie," said my mother.

"Thank you, Joan; at last an intelligent woman in my house," he said, looking sidelong at Abby. "Let's get a drink in you. And I promised *someone* a sip of wine. Who are you, Hamlet?" he asked me irritably, regarding my costume.

On the way over it had dawned on me that I was wearing a lady's hat, so I had stowed it, sheepishly, in the car.

"Dutch trader," I said.

"'What a rogue and peasant slave am I!' " quoted Freddie automatically, and led us into the party.

Freddie Turnbull's manse must have been polished by an army of maids—every surface glimmered. Brass sconces shone under flickering white candles; above us a chandelier sparkled; and the curtains, fourteen feet from ceiling to floor, were drawn back regally from windows that reflected apparitions of every figure within. The dining room table and long marble-topped sideboard groaned with food: two whole roast turkeys and three poached salmon were laid out, partially picked at; bowls of stuffed mushroom caps; spaghetti squash; creamed spinach; roasted chestnuts with their skins cross-hatched and peeled back; carrot salad with raisins; mashed sweet potatoes; and candied apples for dessert. Porcelain plates were stacked next to baskets of napkins and silverware, alongside ice buckets and scotch decanters and scores of wine bottles in rows like artillery shells, waiting to be uncorked by the frantic waiters.

"Broke two red wine goblets already," he muttered to my mom.

"Should have used plastic, but what's the point of drinking good wine out of plastic cups? Should I use Dixie cups and serve wine out of a box? Hot dogs? Oreo cookies? Look at this provender," he beamed. "Perfect for a medium-bodied Rhône."

My mother laughed. Freddie whipped a glass of wine off a passing tray and handed it to me.

"I promised him, Joan," he said. "I chose this wine with Paul."

My mother's cheerful face sank at the name.

"One sip," she warned me. Then she forced herself to brighten again. "Freddie, the house looks marvelous."

"Don't know why I do it. Masochism," he said. Then he started. "Christ, the cake!" he moaned, and was off to the kitchen again without another word.

My mother handed me a plate. "Well, do you think we'll have enough to eat?" she smiled.

Mom and I piled up our plates and stood in the corner, under a seventeenth-century portrait of a fat, scowling burgher in a feathered cap, which bore a passing resemblance to Freddie and which he always jokingly referred to as his ancestor.

"Who's that?" I asked, indicating a tall man wearing green makeup and plastic Frankenstein bolts emerging quite realistically from his neck.

"That's Chaz Beaman," she said. "He's the director of the theater. Abby hates him."

"Why?"

"He's very arrogant," she said.

"In what way?"

"He thinks he's a genius."

"And he's not?"

"Maybe by Preston standards," said Mom. "Look at him flirt. Oh! Shameless."

We watched him put his arm around a red-haired woman in a white low-slung silk shift with angel wings. Next to them was Eddie

Pranz, Dean's father, squinting through his tinted glasses. He was dressed in tweeds and carrying a golf club. He, too, pawed the redhead.

"There's Dean's dad," I said mournfully. "Guess that means Dean is here. Where's his mom?"

All I knew about Dean's mom was that she was an exercise nut.

Mom took a bite of turkey. "She left."

"She left the party already?"

"She left Eddie."

"What do you mean, left?"

"She decided she didn't want to live with him anymore, so she went off, with some *guy*. She left him with Dean."

Left him with Dean. It sounded like a burden. Is that the way my mother thought of me? The way all adults viewed their children?

"You mean they're divorced?"

"I guess they will eventually."

"Wow," I said. "That's wild."

"It's very sad," corrected my mother. "It must be very hard on them. It might explain why Dean has been such a pill at school."

I thought about this. "I think he's just mean."

"Maybe so."

"Who's that lady with them, with the big boobs?"

"They're called breasts," Mom said automatically, more mother than feminist poststructuralist, "and I don't know."

Suddenly, what looked like a posse of shaggy G-men edged into our view. My mother gaped, then snorted with laughter and nearly choked on her turkey. One of four figures in black suits, with hair combed in a blowsy side part and carrying a toy guitar—whom seconds later I recognized as Clarissa Bing—also began cracking up. Lionel Bing followed, in little round glasses, his white hair swept in similar style. My parents never liked Lionel Bing, a medical doctor some twenty years older than Clarissa with a nasal voice and a pompous manner whom my mother referred to as *perpetually condescending* and my father referred to as *a great fool*. According to my mother, he kept control over the younger Clarissa with a string of phantom maladies, particularly a chronically bad back, all of which he worsened with erroneous self-diagnosis and gratuitous prescriptions. *How Clarissa puts up with him* was one of my mother's pet rants.

"Clarissa decided that since I already had the glasses, I could be John, which would leave her to be Paul," he explained in his lockjawed voice. Clarissa and my mother continued to laugh. "And here are George and Ringo," he said, indicating their daughters, Molly and Celia, also wearing black suits and trailing behind, mortified. I said hello to them. They rolled their eyes at their parents in reply.

A towering figure in a gray cloak joined us, appearing with a stick-on white beard and a plastic scythe. We all fell silent, then simultaneously recognized him and began speaking at once:

"Very ominous!"

"The Grim Reaper."

"Oh my God!"

"If my patients were here, they'd be having a field day."

I alone was silent when I saw Tom Harris. I wished he would stay away. Whenever he was absent, I did not think of him; but when he appeared, my veins filled with anger and adrenaline. I stared at him now, willing him to vanish. The fact that all these people—my mother, these friends—were pleased by his presence only stoked my hatred more.

"I am Father Time, not the Grim Reaper," he said. "Though with Abby's cooking, you never know."

"Oh, Tom," scolded my mother.

"I think you look evil," I said.

It was not so much my words as my tone—intense, angry, cutting—that brought the chitchat to a standstill.

"George," warned my mother.

"That's all right, Joan," said Tom Harris, drawing up and speaking in a creep-show voice. *"It is Halloween."*

A chuckle passed around, and conversation resumed. I drew aside to the table, sulking. I picked at the turkey, then spotted the wine bottles—the ones Freddie had shown me, the ones chosen by my father. I approached them reverently and fingered the labels. They were browning with age; the cursive letters seemed to have been inked with a calligraphy pen.

HERMITAGE
LA CHAPPELLE JABOULET
1971

I looked around to see if I'd been spotted—a boy handling the wine—and in the process caught sight of Tom Harris. As he stood in my mother's happily bantering circle, he stared back at me; in a few strides he circled the table and firmly took the wine bottle from my hands and replaced it on the table.

"I think it's time the two of us had a talk," Tom Harris said.

"What about?"

He lowered his voice to a whisper. "About what you said in the woods that day."

"What do you mean?" I said suspiciously.

"You said, 'Leave us alone,' George. But I only saw one of you. Who were you talking about? Your invisible sidekick? The little pal you keep in your pocket?"

"No. It's none of your business, anyway."

He turned me away from the party. In the folds of his robes, under the shadow of his enormous frame, it was like we were enclosed behind curtains. Tom Harris glared down at me.

"It's my business when you begin asking me funny questions. Questions about things you could not know about, like your father's secret reasons for going away. Then I find you in conversation with someone I can't see?" He leaned down and gripped my arm. "What's going on, George? Is someone—or something—telling you things?"

I wrestled away. "Why don't you stop pretending to be my father? You think if you pay attention to me I'll start to like you, and then my mother will like you, and then you can marry my mom or run away with her. But you're wrong. Nobody cares about you. And I can *talk* to whoever I *want*."

"You're messing with things you can't handle, George."

But I had already turned my back to him. Feeling his eyes follow me, I turned and ran into the party, grabbing on my way a full goblet of the 1971 Hermitage from the teeming sideboard.

I gulped at the wine. It tasted bitter, but I swallowed as much as I could. I was feeling the effects. I wandered through bodies and faces, and every few paces found myself bumping into someone or grabbing for furniture to stay upright. I was like a spacecraft moving in zero gravity: I couldn't get used to my momentum. I slung down more wine. My father detested parties, particularly Preston parties. He had despised the backbiting and the small-town jealousies, the idle wives who gossiped and picked at out-siders, the ones who once dressed down my mother at the country club because she said *dammit* on the tennis court, and who exhibited *none of the virtues of the real South, these Virginians,* he would say scornfully; *none of the conversation, the stories, the generosity of mind. Just old military families with their sterile Civil War nostalgia; Faulkner characters too boring to kill themselves, all golf and genealogies. Now they're being invaded by this California culture. People "trying to get in touch with themselves"— which really means destroying their children's lives with divorce.* With the rhythm and sway of bustling guests—the excitement of disguises; Chaz Beaman pawing the angel; two couples downing scotch together, Nettleman and Kilcullen, who'd lived across the street from each other and swapped spouses in a double divorce; Valerie Pranz and "some guy"; now my mother and Tom Harris—I understood my father's words. Freddie Turnbull's party was steeped in sex; it was not just a chance for small-town fellowship, but for small-town adultery, some-thing my father, religious in the old way, viewed sternly. Now, in his absence, the town was dragging down my mother and besoiling her with its groping.

Next to the entrance hall, near a crammed coatrack, I found Dean. He wore a flannel shirt and overalls with a straw hat and a piece of hay in his teeth.

"Hi," I said.

"Where'd you get *that*?" he said, pointing at my wine.

"Freddie said I could have some," I said.

"How come *you* get to have some?"

"He said my dad helped him pick it out."

"Can I have a sip?"

"Okay."

Dean took the glass and, naturally, gulped it down, so much that it splashed on his cheeks and dribbled down his chin. He grinned and wiped his chin with his sleeve. I took back the glass, now empty.

"Thanks," I said dourly.

"How could your dad help pick the wine? He's dead. No offense," he added.

"Freddie's my godfather. They bought it a long time ago."

"Freddie's a faggot," said Dean.

"No, he's not."

"Yeah, he is. Ask anybody. The man's a fudgepacker."

"He was my father's best friend," I said, naïvely not seeing where that would take us.

Dean did not keep me waiting. "Then your father must have been a faggot, too. Which makes sense, since you're a fucking fruitcake."

I pulled out my only card.

"At least I have a mother," I said.

"I have a mom."

"Then where is she? Not with you."

I took the wineglass and left him there.

In the corridor a cluster of adults—among them a magician, a Gerald Ford, and a fairy—laughed loud and wetly in a cloud of scotch fumes. I turned and climbed the stairs, toward sanctuary.

It was dark up there; in the corridor there were several doors. Only one light was on, a bedside lamp in Freddie's bedroom. I crept toward it. The room was yellowed and small. A pronounced crack in the paint split one wall. Laundry was strewn about the floor and unlike the luxurious furnishings below, here there was no decoration, except for a single painting of the Virgin Mary surrounded by a wide, shiny silver border, hung on a tack. A study lay beyond, a large desk at its center. I was drawn toward it. There, I knew, I would find my father's letters.

Debris—crumpled paper, old magazines and newspapers, notepads, pamphlets, coffee cups, pens, and erasers—littered the desk. A jack-o'-lantern glowed in the window. By its light I delved into the papers. The top ones were catering bills. I dug deeper. Insurance statements. Gas bills. And then my heart jumped: a note from Tom Harris—on personal stationery, the kind he relentlessly fired off, containing thank-yous, magazine clippings, afterthoughts; pale yellow with blue borders—handwritten, dated Wednesday, October 21.

> *Freddie,*
>
> *In response to your note: I said nothing to George about the letters. I'm as mystified as you are.*

"What are you doing in here?" came an outraged voice, in an unmistakable stage whisper.

I could hardly tear my eyes away—in my peripheral vision I read my name: *recent developments with George.*

"George!"

I turned. Of course it was Abby Gold. She stood in the bedroom—she had spotted me from the hall—and glared at me indignantly.

"You should be ashamed of yourself! What are you doing up here? Come away this instant!"

I put the letter down and followed her, face burning, brain clogged with adrenaline and alcohol.

"And you stink of wine! I'm getting your mother."

She marched me downstairs and headed toward the living room in a huff to find Mom.

"I'm going to get some water." I spun off in the other direction.

Now that I was in trouble, I should have sobered up, taken a chair, indeed drunk some water, and waited for the hell I would catch for drinking and snooping. But instead a kind of tremor began inside my skull; *the letters*. It sent off a chain of reasoning:

My father, in my vision, had been correct about the letters.

My father had also been right about Freddie keeping them, and lying about them.

Ergo, my father must be right about Tom Harris, and my mother. Tom Harris was my father's murderer.

I felt a vice close on my head. I knew I was powerless to change my situation, to change what my mother and Tom Harris had done.

It's a terrible high summer where I am, George.

In a slow, inexorable mutation, I felt long-fingered shadows squirm into the room and inhabit all the real shadows cast by the chandelier, by the Chinese lamps, by all the gold light of the party, turning those real blue shadows to varnish, to ocher, to insinuations and whispers I could almost hear.

Somebody knows, somebody wanted it!

I felt an echo of that total negation I felt deep in the well, in the hole of my dream; but here in the land of Abby Gold and roast turkey, of Rhône wine, of light, the negation could not be blackness; instead, it was ash. A film, a grit, covering everything when I thought of that coupling, of my mother and Tom Harris.

What I remember best is turning, slowly, dreamily, into the dining room, and seeing the great wheel of English Huntsman cheese, and the knife lying on its side on the platter.

⚜   ⚜   ⚜

I cannot tell how much time passed. If there are things I remember now, it is because I understand that certain things must have happened, with a certain kind of timing. But it is useless to pretend that they are actual memories. What I remember is this:

I stood in the midst of the party. I felt wild, delirious. I laughed loudly, my voice high-pitched and excited. I behaved even more drunkenly than before, now from adrenaline, not alcohol. My laughter turned heads and stopped a few conversations. It instantly drew the attention of my mother. She raced toward me.

"Where were you? What's going on?"

I threw my head back and laughed again, a free, volatile, kiddie giggle.

My mother looked me over. Greasy black flakes of dirt and something else—rust—stained my ruff collar. My black shirt was soiled.

"You're filthy, George! What were you doing?'

A strange sound outside brought conversation in the living room to a standstill. First, a car horn gave an unnaturally short burst. Just a blip—so short and interrupted, you almost couldn't register it because it didn't sound like a car horn should, which is *hoooonk*. This was a *ho*—

This unsettling sound was followed directly by another noise—more familiar. The hollow bang of two cars slamming together. You always imagine that car crashes sound like they do in the movies, solid crunching of steel on steel. Instead, they sound more like somebody popping a blown-up paper bag. Broken glass tinkled and skittered on pavement.

These noises broke over the party in a wave. Then came silence.

Before anyone else in Freddie's drawing room could speak, they heard the sound of me hyperventilating. I began breathing in and out rapidly, desperately. A few heads turned toward me with concern, but naturally people were more worried about the car crash, which was so close—the bottom of Freddie's drive—that it was likely to involve a guest, and therefore, a friend. Freddie was summoned, and with a few others he ventured down the drive. The living room thinned and people moved to the windows and murmured amongst themselves.

"That sounded terrible!"

"I've always told Freddie he should get the city to put up a stop sign down there."

"Does anybody know who was leaving? Was it someone from the party?"

"Hope it wasn't Ben Worth."

"Why?"

"He was a few sheets to the wind when I last . . ." Ben Worth entered the room. "Ben! You're alive!" Laughter.

My mother attended to me. A few women looked on with a mixture of concern, disapproval, and shameless curiosity. Mom got me a chair, but I wouldn't sit in it.

"Please, George."

I still wheezed away, heave, heave, heave, heave.

Abby bustled over.

"I better get him some cold water," she said, appraising me quickly, but stopped and turned toward me, as did everyone else, when a high-pitched voice, which I can only assume and understand came from my own throat, materialized freakishly into the room.

"He did it by cutting the brake line!"

My mother gripped my shoulders. Even my scholarly mother was not immune to the acute embarrassment I was causing her.

"George, sit down!" she hissed.

"He crawled under the car and sawed away the brake line!" I cried again, and this time, I raised my right hand into the air, in front of my own eyes, and looked at it. There was a smear of black grease across my palm.

I gave one more gulp of desperate, keening laughter, then collapsed into the chair under the pressure of my mother's full force. Abby escaped to fetch ice water.

The murmuring began instantly. My words and the car crash outside did not quite fit together yet—but some people already matched my words to the event and sensed something very wrong. Abby returned with the water. I drank it in gulps, and it did calm me down. I was lucid enough to remember pretty clearly some man in the gear of a Roman general come into the room and announce, distressed:

"Tom Harris crashed into another car at the intersection. They're sending the ambulance."

My mother let out a whimper. I remember most clearly of all Abby Gold saying to my mother and me, in a voice full of friendship but also of warning:

"I think you better go."

The Quiet Room

A handful of facts are for sure. We sat in the car, and my mother yelled at me, *What did you do? What did you do?* I did not answer. I was swimming on the verge of consciousness. We screeched out of the darkened clearing Freddie had commandeered as a parking lot—the other vehicles left behind us were chrome ghosts glinting here and there under the moon. At the bottom of the drive, pink lights glowed—flares set by a policeman in a broad hat, who waved traffic around the accident—along with red ones, rotating on the roof of an ambulance. Then we were gone.

The rest is a nasty memory, pictures jammed together like frames of film soldered into a continuous, confusing whir. First my mother drove us home, and I lolled on the living room sofa, where I heard my mother speaking urgently on the phone, stamping and gesturing, then slamming it down. I faded out, then she was rousing me to get in the car again. We passed the sign indicating a right turn for the A. P. Hill Hospital. My mother spoke to the attendant, a hick lady with curly hair, a potbelly, and white sneakers. Mom came and sat down next to me. Why are we here? I asked her. *Someone's got to take a look at you.* A doctor? I said. I feel fine. *You drank wine tonight,* Mom said. *I'm going to kill Freddie.* Dad chose that wine, I said, and she did not reply.

We saw Abby Gold and Clarissa. Why were they here? They huddled together by the mouth of the corridor leading to the treatment rooms and the ER. My mother gathered herself, traversed the waiting room and whispered in conference with them. She returned wearing a sad, lopsided smile.

"They don't know how he is yet," she said. It dawned on me she was referring to Tom Harris. "Mm."

Another figure crossed the room, coming for me. The social worker was forty, thin, in a hospital smock over blue jeans.

"Are you George?" she drawled, then gave a smile-at-the-child smile. "Why don't you come with me, now?" I followed her to a consulting room, sat on the examining table as she started asking questions, making notes with a ballpoint pen. Each question seldom seemed connected to the last.

"Have you been drinking alcohol tonight?"

Hermitage 1971, the year I was born, my father picked out the bottle, my father was dead.

"Is this your first time drinking?"

I had a sip of beer once (very proud—Miller High Life in a can, watching *In Her Majesty's Secret Service* on television one Friday night with Dad while Mom was away).

"Do you ever smoke cigarettes or any other substance? Sniff glue? Inhale paint fumes?"

No.

Then they got harder.

"Do you know why you're here?"

No. (Rather indignant: Why *was* I there?)

"A friend of your family's was in a car accident tonight. Do you know how he got hurt?"

No.

"Did you have something to do with him getting hurt?"

I don't know.

"Do you have a reason to want to hurt him?"

No—I don't know—maybe.

"Why is that?"

I don't *like* Tom Harris. (Petulant, childish.)

"Why is that?"

He killed my father.

"He killed your father, and that's why you want to hurt him?"

I don't know.

"Did you want to hurt him tonight? Maybe scare him a little?"

No. Well . . .

She waited, ballpoint poised.

My father told me to.

"Before he died?"

No.

A slight pause of comprehension before the ballpoint touched the page.

"Your father told you to hurt him," she said. "Your father who's dead."

I remember going to sleep on the examining table, rousing a few times. I woke . . . my mother huddled in the doorway, speaking with the social worker, who then came at me with a glass of ferociously cold water and a pill that she forced down my throat. I woke: I was at home, in my bedroom, my mother packing my underwear (white briefs, Fruit of the Loom) into a bag. I woke: a floodlit truck stop on the highway. When I woke up at last, a real waking up, it was dark, the middle of the night, and I had a headache and a desperate need to pee.

I was in strange pajamas, in a bed with a chrome rail. I found my way to a little bathroom, my feet padding on cold, hard-tile floors. I peed, went back to bed, carrying with me from the disinfectant-scrubbed bathroom an unmistakable smell: hospital.

I was in the Psychiatric Unit of the University of Virginia Medical Hospital. I had made it to Charlottesville after all.

❧   ❧   ❧

The windows had blinds with one of those chain pulls; I tugged them aside with a swish. I was on a high floor overlooking the hospital's utility outbuilding; beyond were more hospital rooms and some trees, gray and huddled together like naked prisoners. I sat on the heater (the boxy kind, set in the window). I touched the frost forming on the window with my fingers.

I sat there a long while.

They came slowly at first, like the first drops of rain when you're taking a stroll which you ignore, but which increase, suddenly, rapidly, even violently, until before you know it your shirt is soaked, your vision is blurred, and you a find a rainstorm thrashing you: the little details from the last week, two weeks, two months, which crept, then crowded and pushed into my memory. From my tantrum with Tom Harris in the kitchen, to the freakish, horrible phrases of the night before—*He did it by cutting the brake line*—all the nightmare clues came back to me. I dabbed a spot on the glass with my fingers, recalling facts suddenly available to me after a night of sleep uninterrupted by night noises or voices or visions.

I sat there so absorbed I scarcely noticed my bottom burning on the heating unit. And when I finally pulled away, I saw what I'd created: the window was a mosaic of smudges. I must have been at it for close to an hour, intent, placing a smudge for every day I'd "missed." I finally took in my surroundings. The green institutional paint. The heavy wire mesh over the windows (to keep people from breaking them? jumping out?). And a roommate.

He had swaddled himself in sheets, so that only his face protruded. The opened blinds allowed the sunrise to cast its dull blanched light onto his features. He was a black boy, younger than I, with an innocent face and rounded forehead, and pink fingertips poking daintily over the top of the sheets, which he held in a sleepy grip. But his face had been scarred. More than scarred—slashed. A long, pink wound disfigured him from the corner of his left eye, across his mouth, to the right side of his chin. It was ugly and quite fresh, a few weeks old. I later found out his sister had cut him in a rage; yet it was he, who, in the ensuing weeks, had tried to kill himself—out of shame about his scar, anger at his sister, who knows—and had been hospitalized, medicated, observed, and, occasionally, restrained. His name, I learned later, was Joe.

Joe had awakened, and was staring at me.

"Hi," I said hoarsely.

"Go away," he said.

After another hour alone with my thoughts—which came slowly, but with plodding clarity, like the words of a determined dumb kid who wants to make certain he gets it right—the nurse came, told me "the doctor" was waiting for me, and I went to see a psychiatrist named, with a comical aptness, Dr. Gilloon.

Tall, lean, with thick salt-and-pepper hair, he wore glasses, as well as a (then-unusual) set of adult braces. These gave his speech an unintentionally slack, couldn't-care-less quality. This was unfortunate, since, while clearly a bright man, Dr. Gilloon nonetheless strained to show any ordinary social warmth. He compensated for this by furrowing his brow often, no doubt wishing to convey sympathy and concern. But of course he only made you think you were crazy.

He first asked me if I knew where I was. I pointed out there was a black stencil reading "University of Virginia Medical Hospital" on his smock. He asked me if I knew my name, the current president, the day of the week. I did.

"George, I'm going to name three objects, and I'd like you to repeat after me: pencil, radio, butterfly."

"Pencil," I said. Words came with difficulty. "Radio, butterfly."

"Very good. Do you think you can remember those for me?"

"Okay."

"Okay. So, how are you feeling today, George?"

"I'm sort of melancholy."

"Melancholy," he repeated with a touch of incredulity. I guess he didn't hear that one too often on the children's ward. "Why melancholy?"

"Well . . ." My brain felt like it had been scrubbed with Ajax: clean, but chemical; stripped. No answer came.

"Do you know why you're here?"

"Because of the party?"

Dr. Gilloon pursed his lips. "Why don't you tell me what happened?"

"Car accident," I said, with effort.

"Do you remember that?"

"I heard it."

"What about before the accident? Remember anything?"

"Not specifically."

"Did you have something to do with it?"

"Not sure."

Dr. Gilloon furrowed his brow.

"Tell me about the man who was in the accident . . . Tom Harris." He consulted my chart.

"He's a friend of my parents . . . my mom's friend."

"Do you like him?"

"He's spooky."

"Spooky?"

"He thinks things he doesn't say."

"What kind of things?"

I shrugged. "He stares at me."

"Last night," said Dr. Gilloon, consulting my chart again, "you mentioned to the ER nurse that your deceased father told you things about Tom Harris. Does your father talk to you?"

"No."

"Then what did you mean . . ."

"Only once."

"How did he talk to you?"

"What do you mean?"

"I mean, did he show up and speak to you; did you just hear his voice . . .?"

"I was kind of asleep."

"Could you explain that a little more?"

"My dad," I said finally, "was sitting in a room . . ."

Dr. Gilloon waited for a moment, but there was nothing more forthcoming.

"George, do you sometimes hear or see things that nobody else can?"

The hands of the wall clock buzzed. The desk beside us had lozenges and prescription pads and gauze, just like a regular consulting room.

"George?"

"I guess so."

"Can you tell me about these times?"

"They're like dreams."

"Do these 'dreams' tell you to do things?"

"Not explicitly."

He furrowed his brow at my use of the word *explicitly*. "Can you elaborate?"

"He doesn't tell me. It's more like . . . information."

"Is this person, this 'he' you're referring to, your father?"

I shook my head.

"Is this the 'friend' you told your therapist about?"

"He told you?"

"He did, yes. He wanted me to be able to discuss it with you. Is that okay?"

I shrugged. It was hard to care. My mind was numb—emotions felt like paralyzed limbs I was dragging behind me.

"So this friend gives you information? How?"

"When I see him."

"In these dreams," he prompted. I nodded. "George, can other people see your friend?"

"I don't think so," I said.

"Do you see your friend right now?"

"No."

"When was the last time you saw him?"

"It isn't so much I see him, as I feel him."

"What do you mean by 'feel' him?"

"Even when he isn't saying anything, or doing anything, I can feel him. He's like . . . a cloud."

"A cloud hanging over you."

"Yeah."

"So he is more of a feeling than a person."

I shrugged again.

"What about now? Do you feel him now?"

I thought a minute. "No," I said.

"Does that make you happy or sad not to feel your friend?"

"Happy," I said—to my own surprise.

"Why does it make you happy not to have your friend around?" the doctor asked.

"I think he lied to me," I said, and I realized it was true. I recalled Tom Harris's anger from the party: *You're messing with things you can't handle*. "About people."

"What's an example of a lie he told you?"

"He told me that Tom Harris tried to get rid of my father."

"And you think that's not true."

Somebody knows, somebody wanted it. The notion had once seemed so obvious. It took great effort to overturn it. It was like rolling over a stone.

I must have drifted a long time. I found Dr. Gilloon staring at me. "George?"

"No," I said. "I don't think it's true."

He made a note.

"Let's talk about alcohol," he said.

He asked me a lot of questions. Was that my first drink? Why did I drink? It went on and on. Finally, I interrupted him.

"Is he okay?" I asked.

"Who?"

"Tom Harris. I mean, he didn't . . . he didn't die or anything?"

"No," said Dr. Gilloon. "No, I don't think there is any danger of that."

I nodded.

"Last question, George." He referred to his notes again. "I spoke to your mother on the phone this morning. She indicated your father had experiences similar to the ones you're describing. Seeing and hearing things. Were you aware of that?"

I felt my eyes go wide. My father?

"Mmm . . . ," I slurred, my mouth unable to catch up with my thoughts. "Mmm . . ."

Dr. Gilloon responded briskly, as if to show his complete comfort with my disability. "You may be experiencing some difficulty speaking and moving this morning. Last night you received 100 milligrams of Thorazine. Thorazine is a drug. It controls the impulses caused by your condition. We'll probably keep you on it while you're under observation. Okay? Best to give yourself a little extra time to do things. Like talk," he concluded flatly.

But I didn't care about the drug. I closed my eyes and concentrated, and the words at last popped out. "My father!" I exploded. "My father didn't see things."

Dr. Gilloon stared at me.

"Mmm . . . my mother said my father saw things?" I persisted.

"She said he experienced some hallucinations."

"No," I said. "No!"

"That's fine. I didn't mean to upset you. All I care about is the similarities between your symptoms, that's all. You can forget I brought it up."

"He didn't have . . . *hrm . . . hrm.*" The word *hallucinations* died on my tongue. But my mind whirled. That couldn't be true. Why would Mom say that?

Dr. Gilloon made a few notes. "Now, George, try and remember those three words I told you before. Can you do that?"

"Radio, pencil . . . butterfly."

He snapped his pen onto his clipboard. The interview was over. "Thank you, George. The therapy aide will show you where to go next."

A nurse scooped my clipboard from its shelf bracket on the examining room door. A heavyset white woman in her fifties, with artificially ash-blond hair in loopy, heat-curler curls, she moved with the certainty and swiftness of a sergeant. Her black name tag read PHYLLIS.

"Come on," she twanged, too loudly, as if I were hard of hearing. I rose obediently.

At first glance, the long corridor had the knockabout appearance of a regular hospital—bustling nurses, scuffed paint, hard-tile floors, foam-tile ceilings with fluorescent lights—but the paraphernalia of actual treatment were missing: stretchers, cardiograms, latex glove dispensers. Instead the place possessed the creepy feeling of a hotel, or dormitory, invaded by the sorrows and the sterile controls of medicine. Instead of brochures of local attractions, wall brackets held colored pamphlets on depression (green: stick figure with frowny face); speech therapy (orange: stick figure with open mouth); choking victims (red: stick figure clutching throat). A lanky teenage boy with shaggy hair walked methodically along the corridor. When he reached the end, he turned and repeated his course, as if he were circling a track—or pacing a cage. I wondered why the boy did not just go outside for a real walk. Then I saw a man in scrubs reach the end of the hall and yank from his pocket a jangling, five-pound ring of keys from a nylon cord. The great double doors at the end of the hall, I finally noticed, were the same bolt-locked, steel-plated kind you see on the *outside* doors at most institutions—only these just fed to another part of the hospital. We were securely locked in.

"School goes till 12 noon. Then lunch. Therapeutic community till three," Phyllis bellowed, still seeming to assume I was deaf-mute. "After that you'll have a shift of night nurses, an' medication. UNDERSTAND?"

"Yes."

The corridor opened into COMMON AREA A—as it was dubbed on a cork bulletin board in orange stencil letters—a broad room divided by columns. A television had been bolted to the ceiling on one end. It was surrounded by soft chairs. Next to it spread a play area: book-shelves crammed with old board games and ragged storybooks. Break-fast had been laid out. But the benches were empty, the tables deserted.

"Where in the heck . . . ?" exclaimed the nurse.

Then she spotted them: the children had crowded into a corner, in a kind of huddle. Their backs were to us.

"What is going on?" The nurse left my side. She charged toward the corner. *"What is going on?"*

The group turned. They were eight-year-olds to teenagers. Each of their faces bore an emotion ranging from boredom to thrilled curiosity.

"Kimberly's got something around her neck," one boy said flatly.

The nurse barreled through the group like an All-American fullback. The bodies parted for me to see a twelve-year-old girl, with blond hair cut in bangs, standing in the corner. Her neck and face had grown a shade of blotchy purple and had begun to swell. Her right hand hung in the air over her head. It took a moment to realize she held something in her hand—a thin cord—and that she was pulling this cord, and that the cord was wrapped around her neck. She wore a morbidly amused expression that is difficult to describe—a kind of vengeful, wry, *so there* face—rendered all the more uncanny for the fact that it was intelligible through her increasingly bloated features.

"Why didn't you say nothing?" raged the nurse as she dove at the girl. In an instant, the situation spun out of control. The girl dodged her. The nurse knocked into a table, its legs screeching against the floor. Kim-berly bumped into a bookcase. Whereupon Kimberly began to gag, loudly.

Two therapy aides and a nurse sprinted over. Each one grabbed a limb. My nurse went for the cord. Kimberly gurgled in protest.

"Oh lordy," groaned the nurse. "It's under the skin." She stepped away from the struggle and bellowed, "We gonna need shears!"

Soon a voice came over the PA: *"All available to House Four."*

Kimberly began to writhe—wild kicks, elbows cutting mean arcs. She caught one therapy aide in the nose and he buckled. He covered his nose and blood dribbled through his hands. More figures appeared—therapy aides in scrubs, nurses in smocks—from every direction. They surrounded the girl, multiple restrainers for every limb. But as they held her, she gained traction. Every twist lifted her higher in the air. Kimberly gasped and thrashed as if she were drowning in a sea of hands.

Then a stocky, white-haired doctor arrived, scowling, and bearing a needle.

"Hold her. Hold her please," he said coolly.

The crew now went about trying to tame the girl's flailing limbs long enough for the doctor to find a target of bare skin. Over the girl's white forearm the needle tip wavered—an uncertain, dripping stinger. The doctor took aim, then plunged the hypodermic into the flesh.

The girl stiffened. The shears appeared. They quickly snipped the cord.

"Get her to the quiet room," commanded the doctor.

Nurses began shepherding away the onlookers, but somehow I ended up opposite the other children—between Kimberly and her destination. The therapy aides carried her, now screaming, past me to a small side room whose official name—"locked seclusion"—I learned later. Its euphemistic nickname seemed more fitting. The quiet room's walls were white and scuffed; the fluorescent tubes above were covered with protective mesh; a layer of bare mattresses on the floor protected inmates from themselves. Into this place the therapy aides carried Kimberly and dropped her with the efficiency of a porter plopping heavy luggage into a suite. The door was locked; the stocky doctor placed himself at a small, mesh-protected observation window. He folded his hands behind him and gazed impassively.

"Go join the others," he said to me, with scarcely a glance.

But I stood immobile. I watched the doctor as the doctor watched the girl. A moment later, a nurse called him away to sign an incident report.

My heart beat loudly. True, he was only a few feet away—right there, really; he could return to the window in an instant—but the girl had been heaved into the quiet room in a suicidal rage. *Something might happen to her.* Terrified, I tried to speak: *Don't leave her alone.* But thanks to the medication, the message was never delivered. I moved to the door of the quiet room. I stood on tiptoe and peered in the window.

The girl had not slit her wrists or hung herself. But something was happening. It took me a moment to comprehend what I was watching. A maniacal game of tag? Some primal dance? Then I understood: like a modern-day Jackson Pollock feverishly circling a canvas, the girl had removed her pajama bottoms and now scurried from corner to corner of the quiet room in an attempt to smear all four walls with her own feces.

At 3:00 P.M. sharp came the passing out of medication. The children slumped around Common Area A. The therapy aides, or "TAs" as we called them, unhurriedly shuffled back and forth from the nurses' station to each child's seat. On each trip they bore a plastic cup of water and a small paper cup containing pills. The other kids—a porky white girl wearing hair scrunchies, a lanky black teenager sprouting, to my eye, the mustache of a grown man—swallowed the medication with dead eyes. My name was called. I timidly raised a finger. The aide, a woman with a mountainous bosom, approached me with the two cups.

"I don't think I was assigned anything," I said.

The TA turned to her friend, amused. "You hear that? *Assigned.* Hm. Ain't nobody ass-*iiigned* you anything. You take it like *eeve*ry-body else."

She handed me a small white pill and a drinking cup.

I held it in my palm, thinking cleverly that when she passed to the next patient I would throw the pill away. Apparently I was not the first to arrive at this brilliant scheme. She stood over me, eyes ever on the pill.

"Go on, it ain't poison."

I swallowed it. There were no words of praise or congratulations. She was already ambling back to the nurses' station to deliver the next dose.

"Activities" followed. For this, my fellow inmates, heretofore a sulky bunch, came to life. Each kid ran to a position. I guessed they had been waiting for this hour since they awoke and did not want to waste a moment. The most popular activity was cards.

"Hey, new boy," came a voice. A pasty boy with a massive space between his teeth and a Norman Rockwell crew cut beckoned me. "Hey, new boy," he repeated. "We need four for spades. You wan' play?"

"I don't know how."

"In fAAAv minutes I can make you a pro," he declared.

I was the crewcut boy's partner. It was established that my name was George and that I came from Preston. "My name Eustace," he replied. He savored the word: *Yoo*-stace. "I was born, raised, and I'm 'on die in Crozet, Virginia."

The rules were explained. Spades were trump. Jokers counted as spades. Each pair estimated the number of tricks they held at the outset. The object was to hit your minimum.

It seemed simple enough. But as Eustace continued, I sank in my chair. Sweat beaded on my lip and brow. My heart raced. *What was happening to me?*

"You got that?" Eustace concluded, after more explanation—all of which I missed due to the throbbing in my head.

"What?"

"Come on, let's go," snapped one of the other players impatiently.

A point of white light appeared in my vision and bored into my head like a drill bit. I closed my eyes against the pain. It was the onset of the Thorazine. I could not believe this was the effect of something anyone would call "medicine." The voices of the other kids echoed in my ears. Cards were dealt. I heard Eustace eagerly offering me direction, but it was hopeless. The drugs made me feel like a stowaway on a rocket ship, fighting to keep my head up and my lunch down. We lost hand after hand.

I felt their resentful glances. I felt fat and useless. With the sweat on my face I had trouble keeping my glasses on my nose. Eustace grew frustrated, began slamming his cards down and pouting. "What a fucking moron," said one of the kids with a glance at me, scooping up the debris of another Eustace-George defeat.

Afterward my dejected partner shook his head.

"George, boy, you are effed up. What they got you on, Thor'zine?" I nodded.

"Thought so," he said, morosely shuffling the cards.

"You," I panted, "you take it?"

"Me? Huh-uh."

"You're lucky."

"Lucky? Uh-*aw*. I cheek it."

"What?"

"Cheek it," he said, but it came out, *dtheek it,* because at that moment he gripped his cheek and yanked it to one side so I could see the space alongside his gums.

"Thut it light in theh," he crowed, snapping his cheek back triumphantly. "But you got to be careful. You stay off and you act up? After a couple weeks here they send you to State. State's for *long-term residence*. Compared to that place, this here's Mister Rogers' Neighborhood. I seen it. My daddy drived by one time? Staunton, Virginia? It's like a prison. Big buildings. Bob-wire fence. Grown men been in there they whole lives. I reckon they in there chained like a dog."

I nodded, pretending to understand while I gripped my chair to keep from sliding into a nauseated puddle on the floor.

"Now, I can cheek and I'm awright. That's because there ain't nothin' that wrong with me. I lit a couple fires. But they didn't hurt nobody—just property damage. If I didn't come here my daddy'd have to pay a fine. That's the only reason."

A voice interrupted us:

"George Davies? Your mother's here."

My mother waited in my room, in her boots and blouse and long necklace, with touches of blush and eyeshadow I knew meant she had come from work. For one second I saw her before she saw me; and for an instant, I caught a glimpse of her face, the one she wished to hide from me. She was pale. She fidgeted with indecision, agitation; lines had been deeply etched around her rigid mouth.

Then I took one step into the room. A maternal smile and an embrace jangling with jewelry swept aside the conflicted creature of a moment before. Wisps of rosy perfume overcame the hospital smell. She stood back and looked me over. She saw my hospital pajamas, bad posture, greasy hair, skewed granny spectacles, and my imploring face.

"Sweetie," she said, eyes full of pity, and she held me again, tighter. We sat down on the bed.

"I'm sorry to leave you here all day," she said. "They told me they needed to examine you."

"That's—that's okay."

"It's not okay. I feel terrible leaving you here. How was the doctor, Doctor—"

"Gilloon."

She smiled. I tried to smile back.

"Funny name for . . ."

"I know," I said. "He's okay."

"Just okay?"

"Yeah."

"Mm," she grunted, unhappily.

We talked this way a few moments, speaking softly, trading news. My speech slurred and slipped. I told her about learning spades. But I did not tell her about the girl, or the quiet room. I felt a strange need to protect her. Or maybe it was something simpler: shame, at having such children as my new peers.

"What did you tell them about Daddy?" I asked, at length.

She drew back. "What do you mean?"

"You told them Daddy was crazy."

"I said no such thing!" Mom was aghast.

I recounted the doctor's questioning.

She sat erect, her neck wavering—a bad sign, I knew, with my mother. "I was afraid of that. The moment I said it, he latched on to it.

Oh, George." She looked into my eyes then, and a bolt of terror pierced me. My mother—my parent, my protector—was afraid.

"What did you tell them?" I asked.

"About spells your father used to have," she said.

"He saw things?"

"It was no big deal," she said. "Nothing . . . *debilitating*." She shook her head. I watched her. "I can't believe it. Well," she sighed deeply. "It's too late now."

She squeezed my hand.

"Mommy?" I said.

"Yes, sweetie?"

"I don't want to stay here."

I volunteered to walk her to the corridor. She balked, then conceded. I wondered why until we reached the waiting area and saw that the cavalry had been called—I must have truly been in trouble. Richard Manning leaned on the doorframe, his hair more disheveled and manelike than ever, his eyes dark and mopey over his mustache. He waved. Kurt sat on one of the benches. He stood, grinning, and extended his hand. That lone gesture of respect, normalcy, camaraderie, nearly brought me to tears.

"We going to bust you out of this place?" he said.

"Tomorrow, maybe," Mom said. She was embarrassed.

Mom and Kurt were sheepish; they stood formally before me, shifting between one foot and the other, staring straight ahead, but never at each other, the pause growing deeper. Even at eleven, I could read these signals. They sent off a chain of reasoning in my head. I felt the mental circuits fusing.

Mom never really mentioned the translation she was doing for Kurt.

Kurt accompanied Mom on an important family visit.

And above all:

Kurt was kind to me.

This rolled and pounded around my head, the resonances flowing. The simple conclusion arrived at last. Kurt, not Tom Harris, was my mother's boyfriend. And judging from the way they instinctively touched each other—grabbing a finger, placing a hand on a back or elbow, then self-consciously pulling apart; two magnets alternately pushing away and snapping together—I saw that this was not the lechery I'd imagined at the Halloween party. This was vulnerable, tentative, teenage stuff. Even here, in a hospital waiting room, I saw that my mother was in love. I had been all wrong. I knew what I had to do.

"Mom," I said.

"Yes, sweetie?"

"When we leave," I said, "I'd like to see Tom Harris."

"They're ready for you," said a TA.

Dr. Gilloon sat on the swiveling desk chair in his examining room—the same I'd entered so groggily that morning. Dr. Gilloon appeared weary. He offered me the metal office chair. My mother and Richard stood.

"Pencil . . . radio . . . butterfly," I pronounced.

They all stared.

"Oh," said the doctor after a moment. "Right. We don't need to keep repeating that."

I opened my mouth to explain—he didn't get my joke—but the moment was lost.

"Okay," said the doctor. "Couple of things. I examined George this morning. I received reports from the nurses' rounds today. I consulted with Dr. Manning," he said. *Dr.* Manning? "I spoke to the Preston hospital, and police. About the car accident," he added quickly, when my mother began to break in. "Also, speaking to Mrs. Davies, I understand there's a history of mental illness here."

"Now, about that," said my mother, bristling. "I never said Paul was mentally ill."

The doctor nodded. "It's hard to call it that, when it's family."

"He was a *tenured professor,*" countered my mother indignantly.

"He was high-performing," acknowledged the doctor.

"They were *religious epiphanies.*"

"Accompanied by visual and auditory hallucinations," added the doctor. His tone was brusque, condescending.

Richard gently reached across to silence my mother. *Let him finish.* But she wouldn't.

"Do you classify anybody religious as mentally ill?" she demanded.

"Mrs. Davies, the point is not to judge anyone. Certainly not your late husband," he said. "But it's a factor in my diagnosis, okay? Not the deciding factor, if that makes you feel better."

My mother drew back, silenced not by his reassurance, but by the word *diagnosis.*

Dr. Gilloon tapped his pen distractedly on the clipboard. "Listen. These are difficult decisions. You've all been through a lot, especially in the last twenty-four hours. We need to work together. We're here to make the best decision for George."

The words had the intended effect: Richard nodded; my mother remained silent, her body language more acquiescent. I could not help but feel Dr. Gilloon had given this speech before. The grown-ups mollified, he turned his attention to me.

"George. You've had some problems adjusting, which is normal; had some emotional outbursts, which is normal, especially with a death in the family. And there's the family history," he said with a nod to my mother. "We're probably dealing with some organic factors, triggered by trauma, manifesting themselves as persistent command auditory hallucinations. But what really concerns me is the car accident. A person was injured—severely."

I gulped. What *had* happened to Tom Harris? I felt my palms grow damp.

"Our threshold, George, is whether you're a harm to yourself or others. That's the phrase we use: harm to yourself or others." His tone was bored, a recitation. "That means, Is it safe for me to release you? Right now, with these facts, it's hard for me to say yes to that. My recommendation is for you to be placed in a residential treatment facility."

"Which one?" cut in Richard.

The doctor's tone changed—calmer and flatter—when speaking to a fellow professional.

"I put in a call to Forest Glen," he said.

"Where's that, exactly?"

"Close to Lynchburg."

Richard nodded. Richard, in casual clothes—slacks, cardigan—suddenly seemed a powerless amateur next to Dr. Gilloon with his smock and clipboard and glasses. The doctor spoke to my mother now. "It's not as restrictive as an inpatient facility like this one—but George *will* have the care and supervision he needs. It's a better long-term solution, in my opinion."

"Long-term?" burst out my mother. "What's long-term?"

The doctor furrowed his brow. "Until he's ready, Mrs. Davies. Until he's no longer dangerous or violent."

"Are we talking about *keeping* him in Lynchburg?" she said, voice rising.

"It's a residential facility," confirmed Dr. Gilloon in his worst condescending voice.

"Jesus Christ," exclaimed my mother. "It was just one time." She held her hands to her head as if she were going mad. "Richard?" she said, appealing to him.

"It's his call."

"I'm not sure about this, Doctor," she said. "I'm not sure about this."

"Mom?" I said. "I-I'd be there without you?" The conversation between the adults seemed to happen at an accelerated speed: I had watched the three of them like they were a champion Ping-Pong game. Inside, I felt my heart, my guts, crumple into a little ball. I sat there, my feet cold in slippers, under that fluorescent light reflected off the green paint and medical supplies cabinets, knowing I would be lonely from now on. *Even my mother is sending me away.*

"You've got some time," said the doctor loudly, eager to head off more emotion. "We're waiting for a bed."

"A bed?" my mother asked.

"Sorry. That's the jargon. A *space*. They have a waiting list. Could be a month before Forest Glen is even ready for him. Maybe several months."

"Is it a top place?" she said.

Dr. Gilloon nodded—but without conviction. "It's good."

"What," I managed, "will the kids be like? At the new place."

"Like the children here. A real mix," he said, with satisfaction—as if the diversity between feces-smearing suicidals, pyromaniacs, and the plain-old brain-dead was somehow a great democratic virtue.

Until Forest Glen was ready, continued the doctor, he would release me into Richard's care for continued therapy and testing; he would prescribe a low dosage of Thorazine—*25 milligrams can be effective at George's age and size*—and would schedule a checkup in two weeks. "To see where we are," he said with a tight smile.

My mother knelt down next to me. She stared into my eyes, held my face in her hands. Whatever she read there—terror, betrayal, drug-induced docility—did not reassure her.

"I'm not sure I can do this, Doctor," she said at last, standing again. "I'd like to reconsider."

"Joan," began Richard.

"No," she stopped him. Her tone was resolute. She braced herself and faced the doctor. "I'd rather try to take care of him myself. Maybe take some time off work. I realize it's a challenge for someone who's not trained, but . . ." She cast a sorrowful look my way. "I don't think I can just . . . hand him over. I know I can't."

My heart swelled again. My mother would take care of me. My mother and Richard.

"Maybe I'm not being clear," said the doctor. "Mrs. Davies, the residential facility *is* voluntary. But if we deem a child dangerous . . . the hospital has a responsibility to the community."

"What do you mean?" asked my mother.

"We'll commit him," said Dr. Gilloon. "Involuntarily."

A silence descended on the four of us. At last the drugs came to my aid. If I had been fighting to stay abreast of the discussion—clinging to a grate with all my strength to hear the words spoken—I now let go, and dropped into the chasm. *Involuntarily committed. Residential facility.* A future of days staring out of windows. Sleeping alongside strangers. Children pacing, and pacing, and pacing, exhibiting all the tics of the confined. I dropped into the darkness below. A chorus sounded in my head as I fell: *I can't do it, I won't do it, I can't do it.* But behind all these incantations, a final phrase waited; an implacable killer behind a door, a certainty: *They're going to make me.*

February, This Year

The day my wife left me—the day she literally ran away from me—was a pale winter Saturday in New York. A late-rising sun exposed the dog walkers and the smokers making their tentative entrances to the weekend stage; ponytailed girls with fleeces and iPods strode to the gym. I leaned on the window, watching, willing my mind to drift.

"The blue one. The one with the booties."

Maggie's voice drifted into the baby's bedroom. I was alone with our son. I was supposed to be dressing him. Instead I ignored him, and he ignored me. This was not surprising. He and I were rarely left alone together anymore. In that sense, we had reached equilibrium, a tacit conspiracy. The baby babbled and gripped his tiny pink feet. I glowered from the windowsill. Both of us out of sight, trying to evade Maggie's Irish temper by avoiding a scene, a problem; staying on opposite sides of the room. Weekends were getting trickier.

"Okay," I called.

Minutes later Maggie bustled in decked out in blue jeans, turtleneck, down vest, sunglasses tucked into her mass of black hair. The baby lolled on the changing table—just as she had left him—only now he squawked impatiently.

"I thought I asked you to dress him," she said to me.

"Yeah," I agreed, still far away.

"So what are you doing?" she said, exasperated, moving quickly toward the baby. "You can't leave him on the changing table like that. He could fall! Jesus, George!" Seeing my lack of responsiveness, her voice chilled. "You know what? Never mind."

She grumbled as she squeezed him into an outfit and collected the bottles and the diapers and the wipes and the toys required for even a five-minute jaunt with a stroller. Sometimes the preparation seemed to last longer than the excursion, and if the baby pooped—*it's too cold to change him outside*—it would. I stared at the cabs in the street and laughed grimly to myself. *Booties,* I thought. *If you can't handle booties, what good are you?*

She stood scowling by the door with the stroller. Sunglasses down. "Are you coming?" she asked, without enthusiasm.

Outside was better. This was Fourteenth Street, loud, pushy, reassuring. Street vendors roasted nuts, sending up clouds of cloying charcoal smoke from their carts. Discount shops with names like U.S.A. IMPORTERS (with signage in red, white, and blue cursive) sold T-shirts, sunglasses, electronics, and toys by the heap, with, outside, ancient and eminently untrustworthy quarter-operated kids' rides—a scarred horse, a dingy helicopter wearing a chipped grin. The sidewalks thronged with pale denizens in black overcoats; leggy ladies on cell phones; whole families spread out across the sidewalk, strolling, eyeballing the shops, the sons punching each other and laughing.

Maggie pushed the stroller. Out here, we could forget the couple we were at home. We could revert to who we had been, a married couple with rapport, who held hands, who gorged on eggy brunches, and who sneaked into dressing rooms at the Gap and kissed. Out here, Maggie could speak in her usual weekend-errands patter: *Oh, you know what we need? X.* And X was always a surprise. Something I would never have thought of. *Heirloom tomatoes. A living will. An O-ring for the hose in the sink.* And I would respond mildly, *Sure, great idea, let's do it,* and we might acquire or accomplish whatever it was, but more likely, we'd stop for a pastry to indulge our mutual sweet tooths, drink a nerve-jangling gourmet coffee—while feeding the baby, nowadays—and soak up the energy and chaos of the city we both loved. Making envious remarks about the apartment buildings we wanted to live in, the cars we wished we could afford. Or—we could run into friends.

"Hey!"

"Hey guys!"

Another thirtysomething couple with a baby approached us. We pushed the strollers together and stood grinning at each other, a big people-island in the street. Pedestrians circumvented us with a frown.

The couple was Dominick—a software salesman with a shaved head and a cleft chin—and his wife, Tina, a wide-hipped woman with a flame-orange parka and big, soft, coffee-brown eyes, a stay-at-home mom. (*Dominick does well,* my wife had confided to me, significantly—not-so-subtle code for: *Tina doesn't have to work.*) We chatted about music classes, what we were doing with our Saturday. Maggie and Tina drew together and within seconds were laughing conspiratorially. Their daughter began to cry. Dominick dug out a pacifier quite calmly and plugged her mouth with it.

"George," called Dominick, "what do you say we take the kids to the dog run in Washington Square? Give the moms a break?"

The women perked up.

"I won't say no," beamed Maggie.

"She loves it," Dominick promised, nodding to his daughter. "Goes crazy when they chase the tennis balls. Don't you?" he said, bending over her, talking baby talk. *"You like it when doggie chases the ball?"*

Maggie put a hand on my arm. "You going to be okay?" she said quietly.

"Sure," I said, licking my lips.

Maggie took her hands from the stroller. I was supposed to take over now. Suddenly, we heard screeching tires from the street, followed by honking, shouting. Maggie and Tina turned their heads, made concerned *ooh* faces—a taxi accident, narrowly averted. Maggie returned her attention to me. My face felt numb. My palms were sweating.

A dream logic took over. I knew that if I put my hands on the stroller, something terrible would happen. Some connection would be made. *It would pass from me to the boy, like a fatal disease, a plague flea.* I could not let that happen. I should not hold the stroller.

Maggie's face was staring into mine. "George!" she shouted.

From a distance, I watched Dominick's jovial face, and Tina's sympathetic eyes, turn hard, suspicious.

That's okay. We can do it another time, they were saying.

What had I missed? Good-byes followed—markedly cooler than the greetings had been. A distant *See you, George* from Tina. A final, narrow glance from Dominick.

Maggie stood by the window of a Duane Reade. She held the stroller now. The sunglasses covered her eyes.

"What *is* it with you?" she said. Her voice broke. I realized she was crying. She wiped a tear from under her sunglasses. She stamped her foot in frustration, like a little girl. I always found it endearing when she stamped her foot, even though it meant I was in big trouble.

"What do you mean?" I said stupidly.

"Why did you *say* that?" she cried.

"Say what?"

"Dominick asks you to go to the park and you say, *The kids should stay away from me.* Like you're a zombie. It's *creepy,*" she hissed. "They think you're a child molester now."

"I'm not a child molester."

"Well, you're freaking me out," Maggie said, crying again. "Why are you doing this, George?"

"I don't know," I whisper.

The feeling returned to my face. I felt as though I were waking from a long nap. A tower of discounted moisturizer seemed ready to pitch over in the drugstore window.

"You don't even seem like you care about us! You just stand there!"

She was sobbing. A middle-aged woman with oversized glasses, walking a Chihuahua, slowed down to ogle us. Others—a couple in denim, an off-duty security guard—glanced over with nervous curiosity: open-air soap opera? Or opening act to a con game? You could never be sure in the city.

"I care about you," I protested, numbly.

I felt like I needed to say something meaningful. Answer her question. Solve the problem.

"But maybe it's better if you take care of the baby," I said, "while I work some things out."

A cataclysmic sob erupted from her.

"What?" she cried. She actually seemed to sway. "If that's the way you feel," she gasped, "then just stay away."

Maggie's lip quivered, her breath came in gasps—real weeping, tears streaming—and then, to my surprise, she started running. She pushed the stroller ahead of her as if she were jogging.

"Maggie!"

I started to give chase. But the stares from other pedestrians turned from curious to hostile. I slowed down. I realized how this looked. A man chasing a crying woman with a baby stroller. It had all the appearance of a crime in progress. Judging from the angry glares I was receiving, it seemed highly probable that someone would intervene, or even call the police, if I pursued her. I slowed—eventually stopped. Maggie looked over her shoulder at me, still crying. *My wife is actually running away from me,* I thought dully, as I watched her go.

Oversized yellow signs, faded to near illegibility, gazed down upon me from the windows of a wine store, gaily and unseasonably announcing *Le Beaujolais Nouveau est Arrivé!* Mr. and Mrs. Denim and the Chihuahua Lady had moved along. Others took their places. The sun peeked from behind its thin winter cloud cover. Vestiges of Maggie, of our family, disappeared; were trod on; became archaeological traces before my eyes.

I stood there, stunned. For some reason—maybe through a pre-
monition that, after a struggle, my marriage had entered its last
stages—I began to reminisce.

I remembered the moment when Maggie fell in love with me. I had
been in love with her for months. It was a sunny, clear June day. We
were lying on a hillside in Central Park kissing and talking about nothing. I reclined, gazing at the East Side apartments against a blue sky. She
rested her head on my stomach, hair spilling in curls down into the
bright green grass. I was teasing her—about what I don't remember—
making her laugh, provoking her. Then, at one point, she sat up. She
shot me a look. There was no revolution in her expression, no fireworks
or melty-gooey sweetness. Just a very, very sharp stare. As if, when she
had laid her head on my belly, some spark had jumped from me to
her—my pilot light—and I witnessed it, beaming back at me, out of her
eyes. We stayed on that hill until dusk. I took my time in asking her to
marry me—waited until Christmas, in fact. I was in no hurry. I reckoned that, once kindled, that light could not go out. *That's what all those
vows meant,* I thought; *the rings and the ceremony. It's a binding contract.
A one-way journey.* But a laconic voice interrupted these sentiments.
Marriages break up every day, George, it said. *Shit, you're lucky you made it
this far.*

I returned to the present. Fourteenth Street seemed suddenly to be
a grubby place, a place for drifters. The door to the wine store opened,
sounding a mechanical and irritating chime. A man with headphones
and sunglasses—giving him a space-alien appearance—sipped coffee
under the awning of a deli. Two men quarreled in Russian.

I was alone. My family had fled from me.

Where would I go now? I wondered.

Time for a Meeting

Tom Harris remained in the hospital. If I had spent three days among the mentally sick, here were the physically sick, with their own kind of desperation: ghostly cancer patients; the bedridden and bored staring at televisions, immobile for who knows how many days; and drifting among them, the reek of illness, of urine and—to my imagination—leprous decay, emanating from the hospital's many laundry hampers, bedpans, dirty pajamas, and brittle, starched sheets.

A cheery nurse bustled us down a corridor, carrying a yellow plastic water pitcher that rattled with ice. "He had another surgery, yesterday morning, so he needs his rest," she said, pronouncing it *ray-usst,* as she pushed open the door to Tom Harris's room with her bottom. "Visitors, Mr. Harris!" she announced.

Tom Harris lay propped in bed, face gray, pajamas blue. His legs stretched the length of the bedframe, and his horny feet poked out the bottom. An apparatus—an Erector set of bolts and wires—had been constructed alongside his left thigh. His jaunty energy was visible only in flickers, in his eyes.

My mother moved to his bedside, extended a hand gently to his arm. "Tom, how are you?" she murmured, face wrinkling in concern. I remained frozen by the door.

"They rebroke my fibia in order to set it," he grunted. "The plan, evidently, was: find the drunkest man in Stoneland County and ask him to do it with a mallet and a blunt wood chisel. At least that's what it feels like," he whispered, with a grimace meant to be a smile. "Not to complain."

"I'm so sorry," said my mother, gripping his arm.

"Not your fault," he said gruffly. His voice sharpened: "But . . . I see you have George with you."

My mother turned to me. "George wanted to see you."

Tom Harris's eyes went to mine. I felt ridiculous. What had I hoped to achieve by coming here?

"Is there something you want to say to Tom?" Mom prompted me. I kept staring.

"Maybe I should leave you two alone."

The nurse finished examining Tom Harris's chart. "I'll be back later with your medication, Mr. Harris." Mom followed her out.

Tom Harris and I continued to stare at each other. Finally, he broke the silence, summoning his old strength of voice.

"Well? Aren't you going to say 'I'm sorry'?" he demanded.

As usual, I could not tell whether he was teasing. "I am sorry," I said.

"And why are you sorry?" he intoned.

"Because you're hurt."

"But why are *you* sorry?"

I shuffled my feet.

"It's not a trick question. Custom dictates that when someone apologizes, he has something to apologize for. Am I right?"

I nodded.

"So. Are you responsible for this?"

He flung out his hand over his leg. My eye followed the gesture. Tom Harris's leg—bolted, bandaged, puffy flesh—seemed as tragic and shameful as a sacked city.

"I—I think so," I stammered.

"But you're not sure."

"It *is* my fault."

"Do you remember doing it, George?"

"I think so."

"What do you remember?"

"I remember being angry. I remember . . . coming into the party with grease on my hand." I struggled. "I must have been under your car," I concluded.

"When you came back into the party, you said something, didn't you?" Tom Harris demanded. "Do you remember what you said?"

"No," I lied.

"You said—according to Freddie—something about cutting the brake line of my car." He fixed me with a stare. "George, have you ever in your life looked under a car?"

"I've looked."

"But you don't understand cars, is that correct?"

"I guess not."

"Do you know where a brake line is?"

"By the tire?" I guessed.

"As I suspected, you wouldn't know a brake line from a chorus line. And you do *not* know how to find, and *cut,* a brake line. I don't suppose the psychiatrists in Charlottesville asked you that, did they?"

"No."

"No, they wouldn't," he muttered. "Do you have any notion how you might have acquired that knowledge—however temporarily?"

I remained silent, stumped by the question.

"Has anyone been giving you information about cars?" he persisted, testily. "About brake lines? When and how to cut them?"

I examined the floor—scuffed tiles, with beige flecks. A minute ticked by on the wall clock.

"I think we both know what we're talking about, don't we, George." I felt my face flush. "Look at me, son."

I did as I was told. His face had regained its full color, but its accustomed humor had been replaced by a fierce, interrogatory glare. Under that gaze I felt a sudden, intense pressure to reveal the truth.

"He took me to Daddy," I blurted.

"Who did?"

I stared at the floor again.

"Go on," said Tom Harris. "I think I understand."

"He took me to Daddy. And it was Daddy . . ." My lips grew dry. I had trouble continuing.

"Ye-es?"

"Daddy told me you *wanted* him dead," I blurted. "And that you want to marry my mom."

"Your father told you," Tom Harris repeated evenly.

"In a dream. Or whatever it was. He was angry that he couldn't do anything about it. *Frustrated,*" I recalled, "and incredibly sad." I paused, then spat out the melancholy kernel of this outburst: "Like he needed me to help him."

"Your father does need you," Tom Harris replied, in a softer voice. "He needs your prayers and your good memories." His voice hardened again. "But that was not your father."

"I know," I said. "The doctors said it was a command auditory hallucination." I had heard the term a dozen times in the past few days.

"I'm aware of what the psychiatrists said," he said.

"Mom told you?"

"She told me they are putting you in a home. She told me they think your father was mentally ill." He scowled. "The rest I can guess."

I stared at my shoes, face burning. "You know people who have the same thing I do?" I asked.

"You could say that," he said. "The fact is, I've had misgivings since I saw you scrambling in the dirt out there in the woods," he said. "My misgivings changed to concern, and now my concerns are outright fears."

"Don't worry," I assured him bitterly. "I'll be in Lynchburg. I won't be able to hurt anybody."

"That's not what I mean," he cried out, then winced—the effort had caused a twinge somewhere down in the construction zone of his thigh. He took several deep breaths, waved me off when I asked if he was all right. I noticed beads of sweat on his brow. "I want to help you," he pronounced at last. "It's what your father would have wanted. But you will have to trust me. And I will have to trust you. We have not exactly been pals these past few months, have we?"

I shook my head.

"Your mother, I should add, will not approve. It must be a secret from her. Do you understand?"

I had any dozen secrets from my mother, mostly minor infractions I had blamed on cleaning ladies—secret stores of cookies, a broken Chinese figurine. This would be my first secret with a grown-up. I nodded even before asking, "What secret?"

"For now, you must leave that to me. And Clarissa. And Freddie. Your father would have wanted us all to do what we could."

"But," I stammered helplessly. "Help me with what?"

"It, George," he said, fatigue creeping into his voice, and with it, exasperation. "That thing you saw. That you see."

"The command auditory hallucination?" I asked.

"Hallucination," he repeated coldly. "What you see is no mirage. And you do not belong in a home. You're no crazier than I am—and neither was your father. For what that's worth," he added.

Tom Harris sank into the pillows, the flesh in his cheeks growing pale again, his old liveliness dimming. I watched him rest. Hair greasier than usual. Face saggy and sallow. My new and unexpected ally looked terrible, and it was my fault. My mind swam. Could Tom Harris be serious? I did not harbor much hope that even Tom Harris—a Harvard-trained, well-known professor and author—could sway the judgment of the UVa doctors. Yet he made it sound as if he could cure me, and yet more thrilling, as if he did not believe I was sick at all.

The last few days had been grim, the worst since my father's funeral. Overmedicated in the children's ward. Two days of inpatient "school": kids who could barely read, picking fights out of boredom. Surly nurses; hospital food; steel plates on locked doors. And worst of all, my new and emerging view of myself. *Insane. Dangerous.* They were putting me away indefinitely. *I'm people garbage.* And I had inherited this from my father.

Now Tom Harris wanted to help me. He believed we were sane, my father and I both.

My stomach fluttered with excitement. I *knew* the things I'd experienced with my Friend were real. I had seen them, hadn't I? The doctors *thought* they were unreal—they merely diagnosed me—but I *knew.* I wanted to shake Tom Harris awake, quiz him on the spot. What did he know about my father? And why did he refer to my Friend as *it?*

Voices made him stir again.

"Hello?" called my mother, peering around the door. "Look who I found."

Clarissa Bing clomped into the room in her pilgrim shoes, unwrapping herself from a crocheted scarf—a vomit-y test pattern of orange, brown, and pink—followed by Freddie Turnbull, who, in his fuzzy herringbone jacket and his crumpled wool cap, resembled a great, waddling mountain of tweed.

"You look awful," ejaculated Uncle Freddie, before he could stop himself.

"Freddie," scolded Clarissa.

"Well, the way he described it on the phone—*just a simple broken bone*—I thought I'd find him dancing with his cane like Fred Astaire," Freddie sputtered.

"They broke his fibia with a mallet," I said.

Everyone looked at me.

"Can we do anything for you, Tom?" asked Clarissa, as if changing the subject.

"Joan can," spoke the voice from the pillows. "She can help George, too." Tom Harris brought himself to his elbows, straightened his hair—as much as he could—and suddenly spoke in an even, reasoning tone, as if he were piping up at a faculty meeting. "While there's no evidence that George has done wrong, he's just very graciously offered me his apologies—thank you, George. In addition, he's offered to make amends. I've accepted both offers. Joan, with your permission, I'd like your boy to come out to the house—a few times a week, at most?—and help spruce things up. *Some might say* the place could use a little sprucing," he added with a glance at Freddie.

"Far be it from me," Freddie replied, putting his hands together in a saintly pose.

"From what I understand, they're asking you to keep George on a tight rein these coming weeks. That right?"

My mother nodded, put her hand on my shoulder. "We need to keep an eye on him."

"Well, with you going to Foxcoe every day, and the three of us here in Preston . . ." Tom Harris look from Freddie to Clarissa. "These two can split chauffeur duty. It's a perfect arrangement. I'll be happy to pay the going rate for odd jobs."

My mother's grip on my shoulder tightened, and I was startled to see her eyes brimming with tears. She hugged Clarissa, then Freddie, and moved to the bed and gave Tom Harris a peck on the head, thanking each of them, saying she hadn't been sure what she was going to do, because while Kurt would help, of course, it would be different having old friends, people I knew, pitching in, being family, helping us.

"Good God, Joan, don't *thank* us," said Uncle Freddie. "Cleaning up that mess? You've sentenced him to hard labor."

⚜   ⚜   ⚜

"There are two key places to get a grip on."

"Key places?"

"Important places."

"Why do you say 'key'?"

Kurt made a face. "It's a consultant thing."

"Okay."

"The two *important* places," he said, "are the wrist and the ankle."

"Why?"

"Good leverage. I'll show you."

He grabbed my wrist, quick and hard.

"Ow ow ow ow ow!"

He laughed. "I didn't do anything yet!"

"Ow ow!"

He relented. "But you see how much leverage I had there?"

"I guess so," I said, rubbing my wrist. "That hurt," I whimpered. Then I dove for him.

We were sitting under the gloomy lamps of the "sitting room" as my father called it (a defiant southern alternative to the crass Yankee "TV room"), with the television jammed to a high volume on local news, which had suddenly turned to sports news, and as the voice of the hyperactive commentator rose to a "touchdown!" crescendo, Kurt grabbed me, I yelped, and we were scrapping on the sofa like a couple of barroom drunks. He took a wrist. I twisted to get it free. "You're only hurting yourself!" cried Kurt. I grabbed his knee and tried to pry it off the sofa. "Good leverage point," he said. "But you're open for the noogie!" Then he rubbed a knuckle in the back of my head. It was time to play dirty. I reached for his pressed shirt, found a pinch of skin, and twisted. "You little bastard!" We hit the floor, missing the coffee table by inches, and wrestled on the dusty rug.

"*Vorsicht! Vorsicht!*" scolded my mother in German, coming in with a bowl of salad. "Do you want to eat here or in the dining room?"

"In here!" I said.

"Okay," she said. But she just stood there.

The fact was, we had never eaten in front of the television in our lives. My father had disapproved of the television and had limited my intake of it. And my God: Wrestling in the house? I sat glowing at Mom, sweat on my back from the exertion, heat rising off my chubby body like rain off an August pavement.

Mom recovered and moved our placemats to the sitting room table. We watched the rest of the news. We watched the day's football highlights. When the sports news was over there was weather. When the weather was over, signaling the end of the news, *All in the Family* came on. My mother and I opened our mouths at the same time, both turning toward Kurt to say, *Change the channel.* But Kurt did not move. We looked at each other. We weren't sure what to do. Jean Stapleton sang "...SAWNGS that made the HIT PARAAAAAADE!"; Kurt lifted a forkful of salad to his mouth. He followed the show intro mildly, peacefully, as far as I know, unaware of the fact that we were staring at him, neither of us so much as breathing for fear of disturbing the experiment. *All in the Family* used to make my father apoplectic. *Contemptible* was his word for it. He would scramble for the *TV Guide* as soon as the camera panned across the working-class row houses of Queens.

Kurt continued forking salad into his mouth. He chewed slowly. The show intro ended—"Those were the DAAAAAAAAAAAAYS!"—and it went to commercials.

"George is a born wrestler," Kurt said cheerfully, turning his attention back to us.

My mother smiled at me. Something had changed in our house.

Mom came to tuck me in while I was rubbing my face in my soft, cool pillows, and lolling in the sheets.

"Glad to be home in your own bed?"

"Oh yes!" I said.

"I'm glad you're here, too." She sat down at the side of my bed and stroked my hair. "Have fun with Kurt tonight?"

"Yeah," I said.

"Would you like it if he came around more often?" she asked.

"Sure," I said. "When?" I thought she was asking whether I wanted to make some sort of playdate with Kurt.

"Oh, whenever," said Mom. Then she paused. "You might have mixed feelings about Kurt."

"Why?" I asked.

She hesitated.

"I know it's only been a few months since your father died. Maybe you feel the same way about him that you felt about Tom Harris," she said.

"It's different."

"Why?"

"It's like I imagined what was happening with Tom Harris . . . but in the hospital I realized I was wrong. That was imaginary. This is real." I shrugged. "It's okay in real life."

"You were furious at Tom Harris."

"Not anymore," I said. "He told me Dad and I were no crazier than he is."

My mother snorted. "For whatever that's worth."

"That's what he said, too."

"Did he?" She smiled. "What else did he say?"

Because I understood so little myself, I wanted nothing more than to confide in my mother, have her help to decode Tom Harris's cryptic comments, his unexpected gesture of friendship, his bizarre demand for secrecy. But something stopped me. I had injured Tom Harris, had seen firsthand the pain he suffered. If he asked me to keep a secret, didn't I owe him that much? Even more important: if I spilled the beans to my mother—and if Tom Harris was right that she wouldn't approve—she might stop Tom Harris from helping me. I actually opened my mouth to speak: *He said I wasn't supposed to tell you, but . . .*

"Nothing," I said, with perhaps too much nonchalance. I felt my mother's eyes on me.

"George," she said. "I want you to know I never said *anything* to the doctors to make them think your father had mental problems."

"So what did you tell them?" I said. "You said . . . something about religion."

She sighed. "Your father, even though he had a temper, was a sensitive man, and religious." She pondered for a moment. "He had some powerful experiences."

"What kind of experiences?"

"He only told me bits and pieces." She held her hand to my cheek. "I wish he could tell you himself." Then her voice hardened. "Let that be a lesson to us. Arrogant doctors. Making snap decisions that affect people's lives."

"Am I really going to have to go away, Mom?"

"I'm going to fight it," she said, straightening. "But *you* need to be on your absolute best behavior. No rough stuff at school. Homework on time. I can't argue that you don't belong in a home if you're out there making trouble. Understand? I want you perfect for a month."

"Nobody's perfect."

"Give it your best shot," she said drily. "Which reminds me . . ." She held out a tiny white tablet. "Every night, remember?" she said.

"It makes me stupid."

"Dr. Gilloon said this is the lowest dosage they give anybody."

"So I'll only be *mostly* retarded."

"Better than all the way miserable. Consider this part of your new perfection."

I drank it down. She rose from the bed. Our business was done.

"Mom?"

"Yes, honey?"

"Will you pull the shades when you go?"

She went to the window and gave both drapes a yank. They slid into place across the moonlit window and the room went dark.

"Okay?" her voice said in the blackness.

As her footsteps faded, creaking down our stairs, I realized how accustomed I had grown to the hospital. The place never fully got dark. Banks of fluorescent lights were bolted in every possible location. Even after lights-out, a rim of cold fluorescent sunshine penetrated through the crack under the door; and the rattle of laundry carts and phones ringing never quite ceased. Here, I lay in my own tomb of blackness and silence. The sheets covered me. I closed my eyes, anticipating the nauseous onset of the drugs.

Instead I heard a rustling in the corner of my room. I sat bolt upright, squinting into the darkness, expecting to make out the shape of a mouse chewing paper. But the noise shifted eerily. The papery crinkling I heard mutated into the rustling of leaves, the sound broadening until I thought I heard, and felt, currents of cold air blowing in an open sky. Were my senses playing tricks on me? Another sound wove into the others: *George,* it said. *George.* I froze, questioning: Had I really heard that? Then it came swiftly, growing in volume like an approaching missile: *George George George George.* I threw myself on the bed again and only caught a glimpse, as my head hit the pillow, of the walls of my room falling away to reveal a deep blue night sky; cold stars; freezing air pouring in over me. I clenched the blankets around my chin and shivered violently. Now it surrounded me: *George, George.* My own name circled the bed like a fringe of grubby fingers, prodding and poking for an opening. I squeezed my eyes tight. *No,* I kept repeating, inside my head, hoping I could resist. I saw a point of hot white light. For once I was glad to see it. It built and built until the great wave of medication reared up—sickening me, dampening my upper lip with sweat—and crashed over me, sweeping away stars, voices, fingers. My grip on the covers loosened. My mind buzzed, numb again. I slept.

I returned to Julius Patchett Middle School with a new schedule. Walking home by myself and passing the afternoon unsupervised was now forbidden. Two days a week—Tuesdays and Fridays—I was to have a regular therapy session with Richard. Two days a week—Mondays and Wednesdays—for at least two weeks, I was to return to the clinic for testing. A psychologist named Rachel was to give me a series of tests. On the off day, Thursday, Clarissa had agreed to drive me home, or to Tom Harris's, after dropping her daughter Celia off at band.

And so I moved back into ordinary life. I was back on the rails. Or, thinking about it another way—maybe I had never been off the rails. On medication, my thinking, my reactions, were slower: none of the bursting impulses to share a quirky sentiment; none of the bubbly need for attention in the halls. I spoke slowly and clearly to head off the Thorazine stammers. I raised my hand once per class. I went from daily scoldings about messy handwriting to tidy homework. I watched more television. TV and Thorazine, I discovered, were a classic combination—and as an added bonus, when I ate lunch with the hicks, we had all seen the same shows. Ironically, I had become precisely the type of student teachers loved. Orderly. No extra trouble. I received secret pats on the back, private smiles of fatigued gratitude. *Thank you for making my day a little easier.* Dean, Byrd, and Toby ignored me. It was an experiment in personality physics: I no longer created friction. This was an excellent way to get by.

That Thursday, the afternoon schoolyard was nippy. I stood outside in a windbreaker and jeans, my fingers white and chilled gripping the handle of the French horn case. The wind blew; the metal stays rattled on the flagpole. A familiar figure appeared in the corner of my eye. She hailed me, then slowly made her way toward me in her boots and shaggy blue dress. The Bing family vehicle—a massive and muddy four-wheel-drive GMC—hulked in the parking lot.

"Well," said Clarissa. "Ready for the twelve tasks?"

The GMC rumbled. The French horn lay on my lap.

"And how are you?"

I knew she meant more by this than a greeting.

"Better."

"Oh?"

"I don't have those problems anymore."

"Went away, huh?"

"Yeah."

"Just like that?"

"They give me drugs now."

She grunted. "Psychiatric medication," she lectured in her qua-vering voice, as she tugged the wheel of the enormous vehicle around a turn, "is intended to suppress the unwanted symptoms of your condition. Not cure it. And there's more to what happened on Halloween than your behavior—you can't just put a cork in it. There's the spiritual side. Your father died—what's an eleven-year-old sup-posed to make of that? There's the emotional side. How are you cop-ing? I don't suppose the doctors in Charlottesville talked about any of this."

I shook my head.

"No," she snorted. "Ever hear the expression, 'If you're holding a hammer, every problem looks like a nail'?"

I shook my head, puzzled. "Who's holding a hammer?"

"Your doctor. It's called a prescription pad." She sighed. "How do you like the medication?"

"I *hate* it."

"It was a trick question," she said. "Nobody *likes* Thorazine."

The GMC growled out of the intersection near our church—the Jubal Early Memorial Episcopal Church, hewn in rough stone—where my father had been a lay reader. I had not been inside since he died.

Rain was falling now, and droplets pelted the windshield. The sky had gone heavy gray.

"Is there something wrong with the fact that I feel better?" I said. "I'm *supposed* to feel better—right?"

"You're supposed to feel how you feel. If you feel better, fine. If you don't, there's more work to do."

"More work," I reflected. "Like cleaning up Tom Harris's house. Only it's my house. My brain."

"Don't sell your brain short," Clarissa snorted. "Wait till you see this place."

Pure Sense

The drive to Tom Harris's farm flew past in a roar, with the GMC spitting gravel on Route 17. We passed the truck stop with rows of eighteen-wheelers that had been parked, or propped on jacks like stilts. We passed the combination fireworks store and souvenir shop hunkered at the bottom of a creek dell, with a yard full of concrete swans and lawn jockeys and a billboard bearing a Confederate flag and the boast LARGEST RATTLESNAKE IN THE SOUTH. (Once I forced my mother to stop there to buy Snap 'n' Pops; the snake *was* pretty big, a coiled wet sack in a filthy aquarium.) We passed the Howard Johnson, a deserted body shop, a drive-in movie theater, the latter a forlorn whitewashed structure like one wall of a temple ruin.

The landmarks fell away, and we came to the pastured landscape of Stoneland County. Rolling fields spread out on either side of the highway, punctuated by limestone slabs rising from the turf like the backs of dolphins. Tin-roofed barns built of weathered planks dotted the fields. A clay-bottomed creek split one pasture in a jagged red line. Billboards advertised the few area tourist attractions, like the caverns and the threadbare zoo off Exit 9.

At last a left turn brought us to a gravel drive. Ahead of us, forest crawled down from the hills. After a twist or two, a house came into

view. I don't know what kind of a place I had expected Tom Harris to
live in—maybe a log cabin to match his Abe Lincoln appearance—but
his real home was ominous and strange beyond my expectations.

The gravel drive curved around the perimeter of a meadow, under
a line of scrubby cedars, and along a barbed-wire fence. Atop the hill, a
grove of mulberry and cedar trees hovered like a cloud bank, the leaves
casting blue shadows. As we approached, what appeared to be a many-
cornered house with various tin and copper roofs turned out to be several structures: a long central building of brownish ivy-eaten brick with
a great paneled window; and two squat outbuildings, walls and chimneys crumbling and only intermittently restored with patches of jar-
ringly pristine mortar. The tools for repair—hoes, trowels, and
wheelbarrow—were lying nearby in the grass, as if they had been
abruptly dropped mid-job. Finally, away on the left, a smokehouse
lurked in the weeds: a tiny wood shack, no larger than a toolshed or a
large outhouse, with an open, slanted roof. Its upper quarter had been
blackened by years of use, and I could almost see greasy smoke lapping
at the paint in black curls.

Clarissa parked the car behind Tom Harris's tiny Mazda coupe.
Another car was parked under the boughs of the scruffy mulberry: a
cream-colored Mercedes. The air was still, close, and fragrant with pine
needles and a mash of wet leaves and mud.

Clarissa held the door for me, explaining, as she led me to the
house, that it had been restored from an eighteenth-century farm-
stead—the sheds and shacks visible from the drive had been slaves'
quarters—and the current kitchen had once been a group of store-
rooms where fruits were dried for winter consumption. I made my way
into a house that seemed to be built on a slant, and for a burrowing
mouse: the kitchen, into which the side porch entered, was split into
three inconveniently tiny rooms. Despite its historical interest, the place
carried the present-day whiff of bachelorhood: pots sat soaking in the
sink; *Time* magazines, telephone bills, and Pepperidge Farm cookie
wrappers were piled up on a little table; the linoleum looked fuzzy and
distinctly unmopped. As the living room came into view, there came

also the musty but comfortable odor of books, old sofas, and mothballs, reminiscent of the few but precious times my father, in a genial mood, had allowed me to stay in his study while he worked. I would burrow in his graduate-school couch and doze, and wait for him to shake me gently awake for supper.

"George!"

Tom Harris hailed me from an armchair. His face had regained its former color, and his voice its full power, though his eyes seemed shadowed and more deeply set, as if they, at least, had not forgotten the worries of his hospital stay. His leg, encased in a cast, rested on an ottoman.

"I'm in one piece again," he said, "thanks to the brilliant surgeons of the A. P. Hill Hospital." He winked at his friends. "I may walk with a slight limp . . . if I do walk again . . . because one leg will be four inches shorter than the other . . ."

Clarissa snorted with laughter.

". . . but that was an arithmetical error. Nothing to do with medicine. Not my doctor's fault."

"What anesthesia did they give you, Tom?" said another voice: Uncle Freddie's, explaining the presence of the Mercedes. He reclined in a beat-up antique chair—its upholstery once a plush yellow velvet, but now a scuffed fabric reminiscent of my worn-out stuffed animal toys—flipping pages in a picture book. "Corn mash?"

"You'll go blind, but you won't feel a thing," interjected Clarissa, laughing.

"Bite down on this rope."

Their chuckles rose to a crescendo, then faded. Clarissa and I took seats on a long, lumpy sofa under Tom Harris's picture window, which looked through warped glass panes—some rose- and some gold-tinctured, bound in soldered iron—onto a tangle of bush, then down the sloping meadow.

We sat there. I assumed they were waiting for me to start my chores, but were too embarrassed to put me to work.

"Did you," I hesitated, "did you want me to start with this hedge?" I pointed out the window.

This gave rise to another round of snorts and jibing: *Yes, is that where you wanted him to start, Tom? He won't need shears, he'll need an axe.* But again the teasing faded, and I quickly found myself sitting in an unlit room under the weak glow of daylight, waiting for three adults to speak. The cheer now felt brittle and forced, a thin cover for nervousness. I wasn't used to this in grown-ups.

"Tom is joking," said Clarissa at last—the only one of them, I recognized, who had children, and who might be inclined to understand my bewilderment. "You're not really expected to clean up."

"Apparently no one is," muttered Uncle Freddie.

I blinked at Tom Harris in relief. I had spotted fierce-looking thorns in the bracken outside.

"Okay," I said, not sure what *was* expected of me.

"Rather, as I understa-and it," continued Clarissa in her odd, tremulous voice, "you're going to help *us* work."

"We'll help each other," offered Tom Harris. "I wasn't fair in the hospital. I asked you questions, made promises, but explained nothing. Today, we'll explain. I told Freddie and Clarissa what we discussed. Between the three of us, we have some expertise in these matters. Very few know that Clarissa, in addition to being a psychologist . . ."

"Tom," she scolded.

". . . is an ordained deacon, from a previous life. I am a medievalist. And I have a good knowledge of the mystical canon, thanks mainly to your father. Freddie, in addition to being a scholar, is your godfather, with an interest in your immortal soul." Here I might have expected Tom Harris to smile wryly, but he did not. "A long way of saying, we're not complete cranks. And we want to help you."

"The doctors are helping me already," I said, glumly. "I'm seeing a therapist. A lady's giving me tests. I have my medication. And I have a checkup in Charlottesville in two weeks."

"The doctors know some things," said Tom Harris. "We know others."

"You know about my father," I guessed.

"That's part of it."

"Can you help keep me out of Forest Glen?" I asked. "The home?"

They exchanged wary glances.

"We want to keep you from harm, George, put it that way," said Tom Harrris. "We can't make promises."

"But . . . ," I said, perplexed by their seriousness. What was it they knew? And why did they *care*? These were grown-ups, with families, careers . . . houses to clean. "What do you want to do?"

Tom Harris laughed. "To start, just talk! To be more specific—to hear you talk."

Clarissa cut in. "We'll need you to tell us everything, George. *Everything.*"

"About what?"

Uncle Freddie spoke up. "Those visions you're having, sonny."

"Visions can be dangerous for people who don't understand them," said Tom Harris, reading my puzzled expression. "Your father understood that. He would have wanted us to help you if he knew you were going through this, on your own."

The intensity of their gazes magnified. I felt a collective pulse beating in the room, bump, bump, bump, as they waited for me to respond. Through their continued silence, I understood the implication: *those people are treating only one part of you; we want to help you with something else.* What was that something else? They needed my approval, my sanction, before telling me more—that much was clear. And they wanted it from me now. Their faces hovered in the half-light as if carved in soft stone: statues gazing down from an archway, either warning me, or welcoming me, to pass through. A few months ago, I realized, my father would have been a fourth face in this group. *Your father would have wanted . . . your father would have wanted . . .* Tom Harris had said it twice now. How did he know so well what my father would have wanted? They had been close friends, I knew; but I now felt sure this strange club of grown-ups had shared more than the bond of friendship. And because of what had happened to me, I, too, was being offered initiation.

"What do you want to know?" I whispered.

"Tell us about what you've been seeing," said Clarissa. "Whatever it is, we've heard a lot worse, I promise you."

"What about Mom?" I asked. "I haven't been saying anything to her. Do you think she'll be mad if I talk about it?"

I thought I noticed Clarissa freeze.

"Joan wouldn't approve," muttered Freddie.

Tom Harris jumped in. "Your mother wants to help you, just like you said."

"Okay," I said, willing to be convinced. "One more thing."

Tom Harris nodded. "Go ahead."

"If I tell you, you have to promise to tell me about my dad."

Tom Harris's eyes softened. He nodded his long shaggy skull. "We will, George. I promise."

"Okay." I meant to sound upbeat, willing, heroic; but it came out hoarse. A little boy's voice, afraid.

I began at the beginning. With the first night, the feeling of swimming through space.

Clarissa sat back with hands folded in her lap, as she might, I presumed, sit with a patient. Uncle Freddie fidgeted in the background, fingers tapping out a phantom piano piece on his thigh, sometimes standing and pacing, his lower lip pouting from beneath his mustache, eyebrows furrowed. Tom Harris merely sat and stared at me, immobile, as if I were a complex math problem scratched on a blackboard.

With my Friend it had been, I struggled to explain, a *thought* space, a place where I felt welcomed and at home and accepted. I told them about the strange images: the undersea battleship; the Beacons.

At mention of this Tom Harris sat up as if he'd been electrocuted. *"What did you say?"*

Freddie and Clarissa started.

"Take it easy, Tom."

"Please, George . . . just repeat that," he said urgently, waving them off.

"He told me Beacons were . . . people. Someone who's interesting. Any . . . anyone," I stammered, feeling strange quoting back these odd, private phrases, "who takes an interest."

"Good Lord." He fell back in his chair.

"Tom, are you okay?" asked Clarissa.

"Yes. Of course," he said. But his face remained pale, his expression distracted.

I hesitated. "Should I go on?"

"Please do, George," said Clarissa.

The next encounter: seeing my father. The conversation so real, I told them, I could have been as close to him as I was now to Clarissa on the sofa.

Then I described the voices in the night—whispering, tantalizing, bewildering—and the pinching fingers.

"I saw the welts," said Clarissa to the others.

"They're still there!" I raised my shirt like I was showing off a cool scab in the playground and pointed out the now yellowed bruises on my ribs. "Here and here."

Uncle Freddie drew a breath.

"Thank you," said Tom Harris coolly.

"There's not much else," I sighed. "You were there on Halloween."

"Is there more you can tell us about that night?" Clarissa probed.

"I don't remember much," I said. Then I remembered the anger I felt, the shame. "I didn't want my mother to . . ." My voice trailed away again, but my eyes shot involuntarily to Tom Harris.

"No one wants to think of his mother as having a romance," he recited evenly, as if reading my mind. "The vision painted me as a lothario," he explained to the others, rolling his eyes. "Not an especially credible idea."

Clarissa and Freddie looked at me in surprise. Then the room fell silent.

"That's all, George?" asked Clarissa, as my testimony came to an end.

I considered telling them about the voice in my room, the one I heard while the drugs kicked in. But no, I remembered what my mother told me—I would need to be *perfect for a month*. I needed to help my new allies keep me out of Forest Glen—not make their job harder.

"All of this could be explained as wish fulfillment," Clarissa declared, after a moment. "Paul giving George a reason for his death— children need a reason. The friend, so-called, a replacement for real friends at school."

"I have friends," I said, defensively, lying; but I was ignored.

"But those marks," said Uncle Freddie. "I hadn't known."

Tom Harris then asked some questions. Had my mother mentioned my father's letters to me before? Specifically the ones that had been sent to the three of them? I shook my head.

"In your kitchen," he said, "when I was babysitting, you made . . . a kind of a face. Do you remember?"

"Mmm. Maybe."

"If I asked you to, could you make that face now?"

"How can I if I don't remember?" I pointed out.

"Fair enough," he smiled. "On the same night," he went on, "you claimed I knew why your father went to Central America. Do you remember that?"

I nodded.

"What did you mean?"

I shrugged. "My Friend told me to say it. He never said what he meant."

Finally, continued Tom Harris, those phrases I had mentioned. The ones with references to "beacons." Had I heard my father use those phrases before?

"Never." I shook my head with certainty.

"Ahhhh," said Tom Harris, with a long sigh. He closed his eyes, reclined into his chair, folded his hands across his stomach. Clarissa and Freddie, puzzled by his behavior, prodded him—*Tom, what's going on?*

Are you awake?—but he remained silent. Slowly a smile crept over his face—not a happy one. A one-sided smile of resignation. "How about some tea?" he said at last, opening his eyes. "Anyone who can walk without pain feel like putting on the kettle?"

After the bustle of boiling water and finding mugs (clean ones) and tea bags and discovering who wanted what type of tea and sweetener, Tom Harris announced, "You're not the first in your family to have visions."

I was sucking on my teaspoon when he said this—I had just finished swirling a dollop of honey into my mug of hot water. The steam misted my glasses.

"You mean, my hallucinations?"

"That's the doctor's term," interjected Clarissa heatedly. "A judgment out of context."

"My father had them, too, didn't he?"

"He never told you? No reason to, I guess. And you're young. But he had them. Potent ones. Your father, I'd venture to say, was a real mystic." He looked to the others for disagreement, but they were nodding.

I blinked, imagining my father in dark purple robes and a wand. "What's a mystic?" I asked.

"A mystic is someone whose faith in God is more intense than most people's," offered Clarissa. "It's personal, emotional. They love God so much, they are *in* love with him."

"More to the point," broke in Tom Harris, "mystics *see* and *feel* spiritual reality, the way normal people see and feel material reality. Sometimes with visions. Hallucinations," he added drily.

"Sensitive, creative people, generally," added Clarissa.

"Joan of Arc was sensitive?" interjected Freddie.

"I said *generally,* Freddie."

"There are mystics . . . in Preston?" I asked with such sincerity they all laughed.

"Why not? It's a long tradition, going back centuries, George," said Tom Harris, "John the Apostle wrote the book of Revelation . . . in the

Middle Ages, there was Julian of Norwich, Catherine of Siena . . . but there are hundreds of others, thousands, in other places, all over the world—and in other religions, I should add. Mystics—people who have religious visions, who see and feel spiritual truth—are among us everywhere. Step into any church, and two or three may be kneeling there, who knows?" He shrugged. "Why not Virginia, or Preston?" He paused. "None in the Early College faculty, I think."

"No," piped in Freddie. "They'd have to be creative or sensitive." Clarissa made an exasperated gesture.

"You're right to point out, George," continued Tom Harris, "that it's not an accepted thing to discuss publicly. Smacks of poor mental hygiene. Instability. You see what happened when Joan told the doctor about your father? *We* trust one another to discuss it because we have a common intellectual interest, and a common faith."

I looked at the three of them in turn. This was the special bond, I guessed—this speaking freely about secret things, or things that caused suspicion. It was hard to imagine a discussion about *being in love with God* at the country club, or Fort Virginia.

"Your father trusted us," added Clarissa. "We helped him when he needed us."

Once again I felt my father's presence in the room. I saw him pacing before this window in Tom's house, gesturing with his long, sinewy hands, his long nose and his deep-set eyes downcast, searching to interpret some troubling image or dream as his three friends sat in shadow, just as they did now, listening intently. For an instant I perceived Tom Harris, Clarissa, and Freddie as three lonely students before an empty podium.

"But what about me?" I said. "I didn't have visions of God. At least I don't think so."

"No," agreed Tom Harris, growing somber.

"Your father's visions," Uncle Freddie spoke now, in his lecturing tone, "were what tradition would call visions of the *intellect*. An awakening of the head as well as the heart. Instead of painting him a picture, his vision gave him an idea, deeper understanding. And, as such, he could apply his own critical faculties to it: Is this truly holy? Is this something I believe may be divine in origin? *Do I believe it?*" Freddie boomed. "The true mystic must ask all of these questions before *beginning* to accept what his vision is telling him. I should add, this is easier when the vision is an idea—when it's a vision of intellect."

"You make it sound like there are different kinds," I said.

"Two, in fact. The type *you've* had are called 'visions of pure sense.'"

"Pure sense," I repeated. "Pure. That sounds okay."

Uncle Freddie winced. "Think 'pure nonsense' or 'pure balderdash.'"

"Oh."

"Generally Christianity is friendly to the senses," said Freddie, now on a roll and pacing alongside an old rustic table laden with papers and magazines. "A divinity who is human, who physically dies, with blood and bodily pain. But with mysticism the relationship to the senses is trickier. It's a matter of optics."

"What do you mean?"

"If I come up and whisper in your ear, 'Your house is on fire,' how would you know whether I'm telling the truth or not?"

"I don't know," I answer.

"Right! All you have is what you've heard, through your senses—which ain't much. Now if I were the chief of the fire department and said the same thing, you would believe me. You'd go running off to pull the fire alarm. Correct?"

"Sure."

"But what if all you have is sensory information. I put on a fire chief's hat, *then* tell you your house is on fire . . . would you pull the alarm then? I *look* like the fire chief. But how do you know? Who is *really* sending the message?" Uncle Freddie's eyes were bright. I saw the pedagogue at work as he paced.

"George," joined Tom Harris, "it's very important you understand this. Answer Freddie's question."

"How do I know who's sending the message?" I struggled. "I see them."

"Precisely, George! But it's just an image. And there's the danger. In a vision, you only have sensory information. *Pure sense.* Can you trust the information? 'Your house is on fire'? It's just data. The man in the fire hat? Just optics. How do you know *who* is sending you the message? What's their identity, their intent? Do they mean you harm or good? Should you do what they tell you before you know the answer to that question?"

"I—I guess not," I stammered.

"Of course not! That's why the mystics view visions of pure sense with *gre-eat* skepticism," intoned Uncle Freddie warningly. "Especially when they're being told to do things." He leaned in toward me. "*You never know who's on the other end of the line.*"

"But what does that *mean?*" I pleaded, almost whining now, my comprehension stretched to the breaking point.

"It means," said Tom Harris, slowly and calmly, "that if you see or hear the visions again, you are to view them with suspicion. You are not to listen to them. Do you understand?"

The three friends now watched me intently. The sun had sunk into the hills on the far side of Tom Harris's rambling home, leaving every windowpane black, the warps in the glass reflecting the single light in the kitchen.

"This is scarier than when they were hallucinations," I said, in an attempt at levity. No one laughed.

"Visions are a window into things beyond our understanding," said Tom Harris in low tones. "Your fear shows uncommon good sense."

I felt suddenly cold. I shivered in the dark.

Click. A golden glow illuminated the room. We startled. Clarissa withdrew her hand from the neck of a table lamp.

"Abracadabra," she smiled.

Tom Harris rose and thumped on his crutches—their rubber caps squeaking—to a far corner of the room. He bent over one of his many bookshelves with a grunt of difficulty and retrieved something from the shadows. He turned it over in his hand, examining it.

"Your father and I had a professor at Calhoun. A gentleman—and a gentle man," his eyes twinkled, "who took a special interest in us. Finley Balcomb. He loves ancient things. Finley gave this icon to your father. Your father left it to me when he died," he said. "But I think it's better if you take it."

I rose and received from him a small rectangular box about the size of a playing card crafted from a soft, coppery metal. It sat lightly in my hand. Sculpted crudely on the front was a figure with halo and wings, carrying a sword. In the place of a face, there was a hole in the metal, revealing features carved in wood underneath. The image had worn down, leaving only a few ridges.

"What is it?" I asked.

"An icon," said Uncle Freddie. "An artistic representation of a holy figure, from the Eastern church. "You're holding Saint Michael the archangel. It's very old."

Tom Harris's tall figure bent close, placing a long, strong hand on my shoulder. I smelled his herby tea breath as he whispered: "Keep it with you." I placed the icon in my pocket, and he smiled.

"Can you tell me more about my father?" I pleaded.

He patted my shoulder. "That's enough for today."

⚜   ⚜   ⚜

"What about my mother, then?"

Uncle Freddie made a face. "You're relentless!"

His Mercedes purred through a pool of highway light as he drove me home, plunging over a hill with yellowed, winter-dry cedars on either side. The lights along Route 17 strobed across Uncle Freddie's glasses.

"Well," I said, "you keep saying, *it's got to be a secret* . . . or, *your Mom won't approve.* I just want to know why."

Uncle Freddie chewed his lip. "It's no secret. Your mother's not exactly old school when it comes to religion. She got a bellyful of Marxism at Columbia. Very trendy. Very lit crit. She's a brilliant woman. But scrape the surface and she'll be calling Christianity a *patriarchal construction* or some other nonsense," he said, taking flight now in his accustomed mode—a melancholy, yet somehow combustible, state of disapproval. "Liberals. They want to think of religion as a *metaphor!*"

"And my father was a mystic," I said, recognizing the conflict at last.

"Oh yes. I think he enjoyed the challenge your mother offered. I'm not sure the feeling was mutual. Your father became quite absorbed in theology," said Uncle Freddie, pronouncing it *ab-sawwbd,* "in his work *and* his life. If you ask me, your mother rather resented it."

"Why?"

He shrugged dramatically. "Wasn't *modern.* Found it distasteful."

I thought of my mother, with her stacks of jargony journals, her knee-high boots, and her slender collection of pop records that leaned up, so modestly, against my father's miles and miles of Mahler and Wagner and Beethoven. Why shouldn't she have her tastes, too?

"And then there was the book," Freddie said.

That book again. The one that people hated. "My mother didn't want him to write it?"

"The academic establishment—which your mother is always very keen to penetrate—*viciously* attacked your father."

"Why?"

"He had the temerity to claim evil existed. That there is a devil. He wrote eloquently about Christianity being the foundation of our civilization. All of it unassailably true. Naturally, they treated him like a pariah."

"Who did?"

"Oh, *everybody.* Reviewers. Faculty. The president of Early snubbed your father publicly. Called him *dangerous to the reputation of the college.* But bring in a *Leninist,* someone spouting Chomsky, and people fawn. Ah, me," he groaned, volubly. "What a world we live in."

"My mom agreed with them?"

"Not at all! Your father would have fallen to pieces if not for your mother. But by the time it *had* blown over . . ." He turned to me with a crooked smile. "Your momma had had enough of religion."

Your mother will not approve. I fully understood now Tom Harris's injunction to keep our conversations secret.

"There's nothing wrong with skepticism, in itself," continued Freddie. "If someone walked up to you and told you they have hallucinations sent from God, how would you react?"

"I guess I'd think they were weird."

"You'd have every reason to believe they were crazy, or a fool!" he boomed. "Even if you are a practicing Christian. Don't misunderstand Tom Harris—true mystics are very rare, very special. Plenty of people fake it. Plenty are crackers. So if you're *not* especially religious, well . . . it's a bit hard to swallow." He sighed. "Your mother loved your father very much. But . . ."

"It was a bit hard to swallow," I finished.

Uncle Freddie looked over at me. "That's right."

We rode in silence.

"So I shouldn't tell Mom?" I said.

Uncle Freddie fidgeted, no doubt dreading the reaction my mother might have to the afternoon's discussion.

"Mm. Best to be discreet. Or we'll all be in trouble."

"Discreet?"

"That's the *fay*-ncy way of saying, yew keep your mouth shet, boah!" he said, with a country twang and a mirthless laugh.

But a prolonged inquisition did not await me at home. Kurt did. He leaned against our kitchen counter, elbow crooked, holding a beer in a foam rubber cozy, beaming as I told my tales of Tom Harris's ramshackle home, about the slaves' quarters and smokehouses, interjecting in a kind but highly unrealistic way that I could learn a lot about *restoration* in a place like that. Over supper my mother added a story about Tom Harris: *how his housekeeping was so notorious . . . during a dinner party Abby Gold saw a bowl of brown slop in the pantry near the bathroom, and she assumed it was you-know-what . . . so she flushed it down the toilet! She had a hard time explaining herself when it turned out to be dessert!* After supper, as we did the dishes, the kitchen radio played a song my mother loved. She wiped the dishwater off her hands and bounded to the living room, lifted the velvet cover off my father's hi-fi, found the station (the dial still set at the local classical station, a short, violent burst of organ music blasting through the speakers when my mother pressed the power button), and began bopping mildly around the living room rug to *ooooooooooooohhhh . . . how do you like your loooove* as Kurt and I stood in the doorframe, both mortified and excited by the blasting disco tunes. Kurt leaned to me, saying in my ear, *You know she's going to try and get us to dance,* milliseconds before my mother started exhorting us in an endearingly square way to *Come on,* and she came and took Kurt's hands, forcing him to stand on the rug and shuffle in a self-mocking version of the twist as he shrugged at me, grinning. As I watched, I felt the primitive and overwhelming pulse of the song—*more more more*—and was seized with the urge to escape. I ran upstairs.

The Ruin of Souls

W ell," said Richard. "You look much better than when I last saw you."

We were both in heavy sweaters: Richard in a knotty brown cardigan (replacing his usual yellow), me in a Scottish wool one. The weather had turned crisp. His office seemed smaller, cozier than before.

"What did I look like?"

"You had what grownups call a hangover."

"A hangover?" I smiled.

"A headache from drinking alcohol."

I stopped smiling. "Oh."

"I'm glad to have you back," he said. "Can you tell me about what happened that night?"

I shook my head. "I lost control. I lost myself."

"Do you remember what you did?"

I found myself unexpectedly angry. "Are you going to tell them what I say?"

"Who?"

"The UVa doctors."

"What we say in here is confidential."

"You told them about my Friend," I said, accusingly. "Now I'm going to a home."

Richard, taken aback, spoke carefully. "Dr. Gilloon is recommending you receive long-term treatment. That's because of what happened on Halloween, not because of anything I told them. Everything is still between the team of people treating you, and you and your family—still confidential."

"I don't want to end up one of those kids in Charlottesville," I blurted. "You should have seen them. They were like animals." I remembered the uncanny smile on Kimberly's face as she choked herself with a cord. *"I don't want to go to a home,"* I said fiercely.

"You don't think you belong there?"

I gripped the chair handles—realized I'd been picking at the armrests with my fingernails. *I started to become like them,* I thought, *to understand the urge to pace up and down the long hallway. When my mother came for me, my face—accustomed to that limbo of a place, built to contain, control, and deaden the wild things within us—did not remember how to smile.*

I only managed to whisper, "No."

But he read my expression. I saw him absorb it all: the misery, the fear. His jaw set with determination.

"All right," he said. "Then I'm going to help you stay out."

I know it was transference, or whatever term it is that Freud coined a hundred years ago to describe the attachment patients feel for their therapists, the host of admiring, attention-craving, even lustful impulses generated by that strange, special relationship; but I'd swear that as Richard said those words, he sat up straight in his chair, lifted his chin, maybe even puffed out his chest; he was resolute as a warrior on the threshold of a besieged city, saying, battle-scarred and defiant, *I give myself.* I melted in hero worship.

"But let's be clear, George," he continued. "Things are going to be different now. The tests you're taking . . . the medication.

These are all pieces in the puzzle. We will have to work harder," he
warned.

"Okay," I said. "I want to."

"All right then," he said. "There's something very important we
need to explore now, directly. And that's your father's death."

"We already talked about it."

"I'd like us to delve deeper."

"What do you want to know?"

"Well . . . you can start by telling me how you first found out he
was sick."

It was late July.

Summers I went altogether barefoot, over the grass and green
walnuts in the yard and over our hot, prickly graveled sidewalk. Inside the
house the floors were as cool as a cellar, and the shades would be pulled
until evening, or until a late afternoon storm rumbled over the valley,
turning the light gray-green. In former years my father might have taken
his place on the porch swing, cradling me under his arm, to watch the
storm as if it were a tennis match, the winds whipping the trees and flipping their leaves pale-belly side outward and bending their branches. This
summer I sat alone on the swing and felt the spray of the rain on my knees.
I shuddered when thunder rattled the windows. I wrote my father letters
in my head, a few of which I committed to paper. The relief organization
returned them to me when they shipped his effects home.

That had been our means of communication. Crinkly blue airmail
letters stenciled POR AVIÓN, posted fat and full of hope, the replies arriv-
ing battered and bent. My father answered my first two letters. My
third reached him too late, and he never replied. My mother received
more—usually one per week. She would take the letters to her bedroom to read. Once I came home when she was alone, reading them,
and I found her sitting on the edge of the bed, sobbing, holding the
baby blue airmail envelope torn open in her hand, her face broken up
and miserable.

• • •

"Why was she crying?" Richard asked.

What does he say? I asked her, and she said, *It's nothing important.* I tried to grab the corner of the letter to peek but she took it away firmly. *What is it?* I cried. *Is Daddy okay? I hope so,* she said.

"That must have worried you," said Richard.

"The handwriting was in . . ."

"Yes?"

"It was in blue . . . blue . . ." The word stuck—the effects of Thorazine. "Blue ink."

"Is there something wrong with blue ink?" asked Richard.

"There was something funny about the handwriting."

"Funny, how?" asked Richard.

"The handwriting was all wrong," I said. "It was horrible."

In a week, I received one myself. The day was a Thursday, a golden summer afternoon I passed on the Fort Virginia parade ground watching summer-school cadets play softball alongside Civil War cannons. When a teammate left, they let me play catcher, and the time vanished into foul balls and base hits, and when our side batted we watched from iron benches under the shade of a buckeye tree. As the seven o'clock cannon fired—a summer tradition at the military school—I pulled myself away from the game, dusty and sunburnt, and wandered home in no rush to enter the house when, on our porch, I saw the lip of the mailbox raised— no one had removed the mail. I noticed the blue airmail envelope immediately, and my father's handwriting. The letter was addressed to me.

Letters can be hard to read; people omit punctuation, words are unintelligible; my father's penmanship at its best spiked and squiggled hieroglyphically. But this was a letter to be lost in. It would speed along for paragraphs with conversational notes on the heat, the water, and the reek of the latrines, and then, somehow, several sentences, paragraphs, or possibly pages later, it was as if the subject of the sentence had gone missing, the way a friendly, well-marked road fades into a strange turning. I flipped back and forth between the leaves, in search of what I'd missed; the pagination got confused; I scrutinized passages repeatedly, hunting for references that I was certain belonged but were not there. I grew flustered, then breathless and angry. The post office had removed a page, I determined. The letter had been censored by the Honduran government (my parents had joked darkly about this). Someone had done something to the letter. It did not occur to me that that someone was my father, or that some terrible flaw had been embedded in his mind, and that it was this defect that allowed the letter's logic to zigzag like a spider across a tabletop. I turned, and returned, the pages, and squinted, and cursed, sure that I had missed something, and *where was it,* suppressing a sickened feeling I did not understand. *What is wrong with this letter?*

And that's the way my mother found me. It was dusk. She emerged from the house, looking for me, and hesitated on the verge of saying something to the effect of *Dinner's almost ready* or *I've been waiting for you* or *You're late.* But she saw the letter, took in my expression quickly, and dashed across the porch, snatching the letter from me as if it were a bottle of Drano I had put to my lips. She read a little in the light of the window. *I don't understand it!* I said. My voice trembled. My mother flipped the page, read more, and emitted a sob, so sudden it was nearly a burp. *Oh, George,* she said. I began to cry. She sat beside me and I pressed my face to her chest, wetting her blouse and apron. *What's happening?* I wailed. She rocked me and held me. Amid the fear and misery, one part of me reflected: This is how things happen— summertime and excitement and play and then you come home to the shock and the lightning bolt, and find your life has become an undesirable story, the one people hear about and feel glad they're not in, and you never realized how lucky you'd been the moment before. We rocked back and forth on the porch swing. I asked her questions, but none of the answers were good.

"Your father was already sick," Richard guessed, "and it affected his mind?"

"I think so," I said.

"Did your mother know, then, that he might die?"

I shook my head. "She said she couldn't find out anything about him, she couldn't reach him," I said. "She said she was scared." I thought a moment. "She didn't have to tell me. I knew."

Then I remembered.

"It was the last time I cried," I told Richard.

⚜   ⚜   ⚜

I spent the week interpreting line drawings and inkblots for Rachel. Rachel was a psychologist with a hint of cool. She sauntered in and sauntered out of a special testing room, all elbows and knees in long, tight, worn hippie jeans and embroidered linen tops, and honey-blond hair she combed down her back in a rippling cascade. When I told her once that a Rorschach blot reminded me of "a peninsula, maybe in the Aegean," she made a note and cooed, "Ooh, I love the Aegean," as if I had suggested we jet there for supper. In these sessions, I felt the effects of the drugs most. My mind moved flexibly enough, but as if it were making tiny motions in a wide, echoing chamber; thoughts and intentions didn't "take," didn't move to the lips or limbs. There were some days when pulling on my socks required effort; where I could not taste my food; where I stumbled in my speech. As a result I had quickly exchanged the school label "in-tell-ectual" for "Mr. Special" (as in Special Olympics), courtesy of Dean. Did I need to fail my own psychological testing as well?

I told Rachel I thought I was not performing very well on the tests—maybe I could take them again, without the medication. "Oh, you need your medication," she said in her singsong cadence, ever smiling.

"George Davies?" said the receptionist.

A winter evening had descended: though it was just four o'clock, I could see only streetlights, like weak stars, beyond the clinic's tinted glass walls.

"Yes?"

"Your mother work in Foxcoe?"

I nodded.

"She called. She said you should walk home, 'cause she'll be late." The woman smiled. "She said she's sorry."

I stalked home in the dark, counting my paces over the brick sidewalks. *Working again. Working late.* The normal kids had normal moms waiting for them at home to cook them normal suppers, or to force them to do chores, which they would complain about in their normal way. My mother lingered late in the office to teach Feminism, and telephoned me, at my therapist, not to wait for a ride. No wonder I was going to a home. *Maybe they're right,* I thought angrily. *Maybe I'll be better off there.*

I fetched the key from the windowsill and unlocked the front door. The rooms within throbbed with dark silence. I stared inside, stretching out with my senses, but I heard and saw nothing. I punched the light switch. The sickly yellow overhead bulb somehow made it worse. If the Thorazine had not been dragging through my circulatory system—the dry mouth it gave me forcing me to swallow constantly—I would have dashed up the stairs, sprinting to make it before whatever was going to get me, got me. Instead, under the influence of the drug, I plodded up the stairs one by one, while inside I screamed *go up go up go up go up faster it's coming.* Terror and immobility combined.

I stood at the end of the second-floor corridor. A string dangled from the ceiling. This cord pulled down a wooden staircase leading to the attic. I had been forbidden to touch it as a little boy. I had not even thought of this string for a long time. But I also had not been alone in the house for a long time, not since Charlottesville.

Dragging over the hallway chair, I reached up for the string, and tugged. I unfolded the wooden steps. Carefully, I ascended into the narrow attic.

A gust of stale air and dust struck me as I climbed. The attic had been filled with my father's suits after he died. They hung in plastic zipper bags under the beams, like cocoons. From the bags seeped the pungent, chemical odor of mothballs. I pulled a chain hanging from the ceiling, and in the light of a bare bulb, I saw that not only my father's clothes, but all his possessions—shoes, framed photos and diplomas, letter openers and personal knickknacks—had been stored here in boxes and on shelves. They mingled with my own baby clothes and toys, my boyhood sled and board games.

A bookshelf on my right drew my attention. Pulling aside a velvet drape hung over them for protection, I found shelves of poetry, mythology, art books, cookbooks; and finally, on the bottom, a shelf containing some dozen copies of a single title. *The Ancient Prayer,* it read, and at the base of the spine, *Davies.* The cover was silver, bearing a photo of a medieval ivory carving of devils clawing at naked bodies. The subtitle read, *Early Church Doctrine and the Problem of Evil.* I knew it by another name: *That Book.* I flipped it open. It was dedicated to my mother. The epigraph was ancient Greek, but below it the translation read:

> *Holy Michael the archangel, defend us in the day of battle;*
> *be our safeguard against the wickedness and snares of the devil.*
> *May God rebuke him, we humbly pray;*
> *and may the prince of the heavenly host, by the power of God,*
> *thrust down to hell Satan and all wicked spirits,*
> *who wander through the world seeking the ruin of souls.*

Michael the archangel . . . I felt in my pocket for the icon and pulled it out. The low relief figure caught the attic's lightbulb, and I saw again that he held a sword. *Defend us in the day of battle.* I lowered the drape and yanked the bulb and quickly descended to my room, holding *The Ancient Prayer,* carefully folding up the staircase behind me. Then I crawled into bed and began to read.

The book analyzed heresies, doctrines, points of theological debate (many, many pages on Manicheanism), social history, and political history of fourteenth- and fifteenth century-century Europe, with endless boring footnotes. Eventually I began to flip. The book lay ten years beyond my grasp at least, and with the medication, I watched it more than read it. I nearly lost interest or hope of interest in the book by the time I opened chapter nine, with its unpromising title, "A Case History." But within minutes I found my hands shaking. My father's voice—not the analytical, painstaking scholar, but the one I recognized, the spinner of tales about strange and arcane legends—rang out of the volume so clearly my eyes filled with tears. I read the story of a convent in the fifteenth century where many nuns began speaking in strange voices, going into angry fits in the presence of the Eucharist, claiming to be "the Enemy," and jousting with priests in Greek and Aramaic (languages they did not know); then how they wore down the priests who tried to save them with sudden physical attacks, endless debate, and attempts at seduction. *The few who stood up to their enemy did so alone, with only their mind and their faith to defend them,* wrote my father, *and risked everything.* His commentary chilled me: *If even within the walls of a convent, souls may be subject to the invasion of the devil, how could any be safe?* Then came a sweeping view of the ancient world, in my father's voice, like urgent testimony from a witness stand: Pliny's belief that the "upper airs" were thronged with demons who pluck people's prayers as they rise to heaven; in the saints' lives of the *Golden Legend,* record of people killed outright by demons; early church fathers' conviction that Christians must be engaged in constant prayer as *our struggle is not against enemies of blood and flesh, but against the spiritual forces of evil;* how the monastic tradition of morning, midday, and evening prayer, combined with vigils through the night, represented nothing less than a constant spiritual defense against the devil, by solitary monks, on behalf of the world; and finally how our world had changed: *Protestantism and modernity brought with them so-called progress and reform, but with these came anxiety. In past ages, the heroic nature of the Church was not in dispute; angels and human saints formed a protective ring around their flock. But with empirical knowledge on the ascendant, revelation, and God's power with it, seemed to weaken . . . and Satan's presence seemed never to be stronger. Protestant countries such as England and the Netherlands abounded with unresolved case histories of demonic possession, greeted by authorities as the "rantings of the rustic few" and condemned by Calvinist propaganda. In much the same way, contemporary psychiatry conspires to undermine the belief in God today, and to render superstitious, lower-class, and backward those claiming to have brushed against something as mythic and obsolete as evil. Such people must be either beneath our concern (uneducated, fanatical) or abnormal—in need of fixing.* This almost bitter view of the modern world echoed the sentiments I'd heard Uncle Freddie give voice to, but something different lay beneath. An immediacy; not just argument or opinion, but the voice of someone who may have been himself labeled backward, who understood the monk in his lonely vigil. And the reference to psychiatry fell like a blow.

A sudden crash sent vibrations through the house. I jerked erect. Slowly, cautiously, I set down the book and made my way downstairs. The yellow light still buzzed in the hall. I listened to the silence. Then I inched my way to the kitchen. A splay of brooms and mops lay on the floor. I stared at them. They had flopped out of a closet—their weight must have shifted and pushed the door open.

Nothing, I told myself. But I did not touch them. I returned to my room and picked up the book again with trembling hands.

The next passage shocked me as much as the others thrilled and frightened me. My father recounted a tale told by the French jurist Jean Bodin. It described an encounter with a man he knew who had become *afflicted by a spirit who appeared to him in many shapes, sometimes in the guise of an evil-favored dog, black in color . . . a familiar which would haunt his steps.* Bodin's friend at first welcomed these encounters with the spirit. *It promised to tell him secrets which might make him rich and respected . . . but at length, the imp only plagued him, and pinched him, and talked to him of nothing but avenging himself on his enemies or bringing about some malicious trick.* It was accurate, in all essentials, to my encounters with my Friend. The pinching, the promises of secret knowledge, and the wreck of Tom Harris's car were nothing if not malicious tricks. *I never heard of or saw this gentleman again,* concluded Bodin, *so know not whether he rid himself of this misery.* This, my father concluded, with the somber assurance of bedside clinician, typified the lure of Satan: the simple proposition; the lure of fact mingled with fiction; and then the maze with no outlet.

I held the book in my lap. I felt the whole house pulsing as the facts and fragments slowly coalesced in my mind.

The nuns who knew languages they could not know. *You said I knew why your father went to Central America.*

The nuns' angry fits. *You made a face I'd never seen before.*

The prayer about Saint Michael the archangel—who thrusts evil spirits down to hell—and the icon of his image, of which Tom Harris told me, in all earnestness: *Keep it with you.*

The clock said 5:11 P.M. My mother would be home within an hour. *I want you perfect for a month,* she had said, and my appointment with Dr. Gilloon was only a week away. But surely this was too important to be ignored. I needed to tell Tom Harris I understood.

I snapped the book closed. I rose from the bed, opened our front door, and walked out into the cold night by myself.

A row of massive, whitewashed columns fronted the main campus, where most Early College classrooms and administrative offices were housed. Under the narrow porch of these columns ran a narrow walkway, paved unevenly with centuries-old brick. The students had gone for the day. I walked alone, an undersized figure in the twilight. I stopped at a warped stone stoop—flanked by iron cleats for demucking the boots of the college's eighteenth-century founders—and entered Massie Hall, home of the English Department. Most lights had been extinguished. A pug-nosed secretary sat alone behind a desk, tidying papers, preparing to leave.

"Excuse me."

She jumped. "Yes?" she said curtly.

"Where is Tom Harris's office, please?"

"He's on the third floor. But office hours are over," she warned. "May I ask what your business is?"

I ignored her and climbed the stairs at my accustomed, sluggish pace. I passed a corkboard covered with exam schedules, framed posters of Ireland and Shakespeare, and finally reached a door with a black plastic plate reading TOM HARRIS in white letters. I knocked. Next door, the brass knocker my father had screwed to his office door—a lion's head—remained. But the nameplate had been changed. I could not read it in the dark.

A voice boomed. *"Lasciare ogne speranza, voi ch'entrate."*

I pushed open Tom Harris's door and blinked in the yellow glow. "Can I come in?"

He had propped his cast on the desk, where it gave the impression of being a small cannon ready to fire five toes into the ceiling. He read a stapled composition and held a red felt-tip pen poised over it.

He took a beat to recognize me. "Have you come here to complain about a grade?" he drawled. "The seventh grade, perhaps?"

I placed *The Ancient Prayer* on the desk beside Tom Harris's cast, and sat. He glanced at the book, touched it, recognized it. Very deliberately, he set down the composition.

"Reading this?" he asked.

I nodded.

"Why?"

"Uncle Freddie mentioned it."

"Did you read all of it?"

"I read chapter nine," I said.

"Refresh my memory," said Tom Harris. Then he rubbed his forehead as if he'd suddenly acquired a headache. "No—don't."

"It's the one about being possessed by demons."

"I know," he said. "Your father got in trouble over that chapter."

"So?" I said. "Are demons real?"

The question lay at the heart of my father's alienation from the college; his public humiliation by peers, reviewers, and readers; maybe even unhappiness in his marriage. I expected an explanation worthy of the subject.

"Yes," Tom Harris said flatly, then he scowled at me over his plaster foot. He seemed to be wishing vehemently that I would go away.

"Demons are real," I repeated. "How do you know?"

"Your father and I helped the Diocese of Virginia diagnose true cases of possession," he said, shifting uncomfortably. "We would visit people. See if the case met the three tests set by the medieval church." He paused, then seeing my expectant face, counted off: "Knowledge of things it is impossible for the subject to know. Doing things impossible for a human being to do. Revulsion at Christian tokens or rituals."

"Why did they need you and Dad?"

"Even the church needs help from time to time."

"Why?" I persisted.

"There are not as many medievalists in the state as you'd think," Tom Harris said testily. "Now, shouldn't you be home? Wandering around, unsupervised, at night," he said, rising to his feet and grasping the crutches propped behind his typewriter table. "I don't remember that as part of your treatment."

"I thought you didn't believe in the treatment."

"Who said so?"

"You did!" I said.

"Well, maybe I was mistaken." He circled the desk and towered over me now, glaring menacingly. "That's enough of this. I don't care what you've read. I'm taking you home now."

"Why are you getting angry?" I cried.

"Because these are not things for children!" he erupted. "Your mother would murder me if she heard me discussing demonic possession with you. Even *she* doesn't know what I just told you. Imagine the doctors' reaction if they got hold of that, George? Hm? They'd seal you up in a fruitcake tin with a label that says 'Do Not Open Till Xmas.' Let's go."

I rose, feeling a hot blush on my cheeks. Tom Harris ushered me out like I was a wayward three-year-old being escorted back to bed. I stood forlorn in the dark hall, waiting for him. His lanky form filled the doorframe in silhouette, slapping pockets for his keys.

"When were you going to tell me?" I asked weakly.

"Tell you what?" he replied.

"That my Friend is a demon?"

He stopped. I could not read his expression with the light behind him.

"You think I passed the three tests," I continued. "That's why you brought me to your house, right? To ask me questions and find out?"

Tom Harris sagged against the doorframe. "How did you figure that out?" he said, after a moment. "Not more 'pure sense,' I hope?"

"Just reading the book," I answered. "I—I don't really even know what a demon is," I added.

He leaned back, summoning a quotation from the air. "*Then war broke out in heaven*," he recited softly. "*Michael and his angels fought the dragon, who is called the devil and Satan, who leads the whole world astray. And the dragon was hurled down to death, his angels with him.* The rebel angels," he continued, "who fought alongside Satan at the beginning of time. That's what demons are."

"You think my Friend is one?"

"It's possible."

"So I'm not crazy," I said. "I'm really seeing something. Not just visions . . . but *something*."

"It's possible," he repeated.

"Then why didn't you say anything?" I asked. "You're the expert. If the church believes you, why shouldn't the doctors?" I grew insistent. "Tell them my father had real visions, and so do I." Tom Harris shook his head. "Why not?" I cried.

"The reason why not is in your hand"—he pointed at *The Ancient Prayer,* symbol of my father's social exile. "People don't understand, George."

I thought about this. "Maybe you're afraid," I challenged him. "Maybe you think what happened to my dad will happen to you." I felt a swell of righteous indignation. "Well, it's not *you* who's being put away with the other *retards.*"

"George . . ."

"You've got to tell them! You can't let them put me in a home. *I'm not crazy! You said so!*" My voice echoed down the granite stairwell and bounced around the empty corridors.

"For goodness' sake, come inside," he hissed. He pulled me back into the office, but not before poking his head around the corner to see if we'd been overheard. He shut the door behind me. Then he circled his desk to stare out the window into the ivy-lined courtyard. For the first time I took in Tom Harris's office—small, ringed with seemingly inside-out cabinets, with the filing and the papers heaped on top of them. Pens and paper clips were sprinkled liberally over the whole mess; bookshelves rose to the ceiling. The sole decoration hung on a nail: a four-foot-tall charcoal rubbing of a medieval knight, hands together in prayer, sword at his side.

"I have another quotation for you, George: *Solicit not thy thoughts with matters hid,*" he said. "Ever hear that one?" I shook my head. *"Solicit not thy thoughts with matters hid,"* he repeated. *"Leave them to God above; him serve, and fear!"* He turned, dark eyes zeroing in on me. "You agree with Milton, George? Or are you more of a Romantic?"

"I—I don't know," I stuttered.

"Your father was a Romantic—for a seventeenth-century man. He and I assisted in exorcisms. Those are the rituals in which priests cast out demons. Participating in a few of those can change someone, George." He turned back to the window. "The reality or unreality of demons becomes irrelevant because you watch them work on their victims: ordinary people, *vivisected* by evil." He paused; I saw him frown in distaste, as if reliving a nasty memory. "You see this once or twice," he continued, "then five or six times . . . you want to do something about it. Write a book." He turned to me and smiled. "But how does that help anyone? No, your father wished to take action. But how?" Tom Harris raised his eyebrows. I shook my head. "Use his special gifts, of course. Use his visions to see into their world—the demons' world." Tom Harris watched me carefully. "He wished to make the proverbial trip to hell and back. He may have succeeded."

My mouth hung open. *My father tried to see into the world of demons.* I found a chair and sat, head swirling.

"Mystics help the faithful, George, by illuminating the mystery of Christ," he said. "Why not shine that same bright light on evil? That was the reason your father went to Honduras. He had a vision of evil. He saw—*felt*—that there is more evil in the world than can be explained by human depravity. Mass murder. Modern tyrants who twist and torture whole peoples. Through his vision he understood that men are drawn to great evil by demons. He felt a responsibility," Tom Harris said. "*If* your father could reveal how demons find us, choose us, *habitate* in us, he felt he could help stop them. He would go to Honduras, where such things were happening; find demonic influence, understand it, and *act.* Heroically. Romantically. Now, was this *wise?*" He cocked his head ruefully. "Given the outcome, most would argue unequivocally no. Because here we are. No Paul. *Solicit not thy thoughts with matters hid.*"

"But what did he find?" I probed.

"In Honduras, he told me in a letter, he found and interviewed a demoniac." He leaned on his crutch, seeming tired suddenly; an old bent tree of winter. "Your father followed him . . . into deep places." Tom Harris's voice trailed off.

"And what happened?"

"To your father?" he said. "He discovered strange secrets. Saw things no human being has ever seen."

"How do you know?"

"His letters. The ones, incidentally, your Friend had you chasing."

"Where are they?" I asked.

"I burned them," he answered offhand. "They were a little intense, even for me."

"And what happened to the demon?" My pulse beat so loudly I was surprised Tom Harris couldn't hear it.

He shook his head again. He picked up the composition lying on his desk—as if the student essay had suddenly become compelling reading. "Who knows," he murmured.

"Tell me, Tom," I said, licking my dry lips.

"Hm," came his reply.

"Tom? Please tell me?"

He suddenly slapped the composition back onto the desk.

"Did you ever wonder," he snapped, "why a demon would concern himself with a little boy?"

"No," I said, quelling a sense of rising panic. "Not really."

"Demons aren't termites, George. You don't chase them to their holes and try to stamp them out. The apostles didn't. No one but Jesus has actually harrowed hell. But your father did, or tried to. No one can do such a thing," he said sternly, "and expect to walk away, free of consequences!"

"Consequences?" I squeaked.

"Think about it," he said.

"You think the demon is coming after me now," I concluded. Terror pulled me to my feet. "Out of revenge?"

"God knows," he grunted.

"Can't you *do* something?"

"What do you think I've been working on," he muttered. Agitated now, he seemed to wish very badly to pace. Since he couldn't, he tapped his rubber crutch-tip distractedly on the floor. "You need an experienced practitioner."

"You said you were an expert."

"No, I said I was a medievalist. A practitioner is a different animal. Our church has deacons, priests, bishops. No office of exorcist. As a result, the ones available tend to be a little . . . homegrown." He shrugged. "However, I've sent word to the friend I mentioned—Finley Balcomb. When he has seen you, then we can take action."

"Will he be here in time?" I said. "Before they take me to Forest Glen?"

"Forest Glen?"

"The *home,*" I said, exasperated. "If we get rid of the demon, the doctors will see I'm not crazy!"

"Forest Glen?" Tom Harris repeated, puzzled. "That's what you're worried about? There's more at stake here than the doctors, George!"

I opened my mouth to speak, then shut it. I sank heavily into the chair again. More at stake than being locked away? I slumped miserably. "What do I do until Finley Balcomb comes?"

He thumped around the desk with two strides. He leaned forward, towering over me, brows and black eyes glinting. "You can't beat the devil on your own. Don't fool yourself that you can, no matter what gifts you possess as a visionary. They are fallen angels, with all the powers of an angel. They have power over matter. Bodies, faces, furniture. They can make a heart . . . *stop.*" He snapped his fingers. "They are not to be trifled with."

"Tom," I whispered, my throat now completely dry, due either to Thorazine or fear, "are you going to help me?"

He raised an eyebrow, teasing. "I thought I *was* helping you. With all this wisdom."

"I meant . . ." I could not say the words. We had entered a place where only Tom Harris knew the way. I wanted assurance that he would not abandon me, or leave me to the doctors and my mother. They meant well; but they weren't my father. They did not understand that thing, that element—was it mysticism? or something else: the lonely, strange, and unenviable heroism that went with *seeing evil*— which bound my father and me together.

"I know what you meant," he said. "And don't worry. I owe your father that much, and more." He paused. "George, if you see it again," he said, "say your prayers. That's our best defense when we're alone."

I nodded.

"This is a lot to digest before dinner." Tom Harris yawned suddenly. "Shall we?"

He thumped to the threshold and removed his coat from a hook. Tugging on the brown corduroy lump, shoving the ungraded composition in his pocket, he opened the door onto the dark corridor.

"I think," he said, his accustomed ironic smile returning, "office hours are over."

❖   ❖   ❖

That night I made my first attempt at "cheeking."

I wanted to be cured—really, truly cured, not *treated* or *rehabilitated*. And if my Friend was a demon, then what could the drugs do to protect me? They could only stop me from understanding the truth, or suppress the mysterious gifts my father and I possessed. Tom Harris may have been concerned with my immortal soul; my mother may have felt that taking the drugs, being orderly, punctual, nice, would help me pass whatever tests the doctors had in mind; but I wished, now, to understand my Friend. Was he a demon? What link to my father did he hide? Only when I learned these things could I be free of him; free of the label crazy, strange, or special; and free of the threat of Forest Glen Residential Home for Children, forever.

My mother came to my bedroom as she had since my visit to Charlottesville—in that time around ten o'clock when I dithered with my leftover homework and teetered on the edge of either a second wind, or sleep.

"Time for your pill. Do you have water?"

I did. This should have tipped her off. I never had water.

"Okay, down the hatch."

She handed me the white pill, like a tiny, powdery egg. How did Eustace accomplish this, I wondered, as I stared at the pellet in my hand. I tried to conceptualize the lingual movements that would tuck the pill safely away before the water hit. They would need to be lightning smooth, quick.

"Everything okay, sweetie?" said my mother.

"Yup," I said, and placed the pill gingerly on my tongue. The bitter taste swam across my palate. I tried to turn my tongue into a scoop to deposit the pill in the red gum space Eustace had showed me. It took several tries. I was sure I was making faces like a clown. My mother would notice any instant. But she was busy neatening my dresser. I lifted the glass and drained it.

"Okay, sweetie," said my mother. She kissed my forehead. "Go to sleep." A moment later she was gone.

I spat it into my palm. The pill swam in a sticky pool in the cup of my palm. I climbed on the bed, reached behind it into the dusty corner where the carpet met the wall, and with a little force, stuck the pill to the molding.

From my sock drawer I retrieved the icon and clenched it in my hand as I turned off the light. *Be our safeguard against the wickedness and snares of the devil,* I quietly repeated to myself in the dark. *Thrust down to hell Satan and all wicked spirits.*

Man of the House

In the morning I awoke with the icon in my hand. Its lightness again surprised me, its hue seemed more golden, the worn features of Saint Michael in the wood, more sad. I brought the icon to my lips and kissed it. The gesture came to me naturally; I had no idea that I had discovered for myself the ritual gesture of millions of Orthodox Christians; nor did I understand that I held the symbol of the church's warrior archangel. I only guessed that if the devil appeared to me as my Friend, or as an evil-favored black dog, Saint Michael could help.

My mother called me. I dressed hastily, one of those times when, in search of clean clothes, I dug deep in the back of the drawers. I retrieved a red-and-blue-striped shirt that had slumbered at the bottom of my drawer like a rotten log in a woodpile. From the same zone, corduroys that did not zip all the way. But I did not stop and check; I grabbed my schoolbooks and ran. When I at last arrived at school and recognized the extent of the sartorial damage (my underpants were exposed by the defective zipper and my belly stretched a broad horizontal hole in the striped shirt, like a run in a stocking), I was forced to walk the corridors with my crotch to the wall. By noon I was twisted up like a piece of taffy.

I carried my lunch in a brown bag, my first time doing so. It had not occurred to me, before, that the cool kids carried their lunches in brown bags, and only the oddballs used lunchboxes, which smacked of Mommy and back-to-school shopping. It was an early version of slumming it; the hicks also carried brown bags (though often the outsized grocery-sized brown bags rolled from the top, not the slim, stylishly crumpled ones that Byrd and Dean brought to school). So perhaps it was my new accessory, a brown paper bag, that emboldened me, against all reason, to join Toby, Byrd, and Dean, gathered at one of the Formica tables. Trouble started before I even sat down.

"Uh-oh, here he comes," said Dean, loud enough for me to hear. This did not deter me. I sat.

"Hi guys," I said weakly.

"Wooooooooooo!" Dean said, waving his arms.

"What's your problem?" I said in as cool a voice as I could muster.

"It's not my problem you need to worry about," said Dean, darkly.

"*Guys,*" protested Toby.

"Wooooooooooo!" Dean said again.

"I shouldn't have said anything," said Toby.

They watched me quietly then. Dean stared at me with his ferocious, narrow eyes.

"What," I demanded, but halfheartedly, smelling disaster.

"Toby heard a rumor that you went to the hospital," explained Byrd.

"Byrd!" squeaked Toby, like a scolding spouse.

"Cuckoo, cuckoo," said Dean.

"I did not!" I protested.

"It was only a rumor, Dean," Toby scolded. "God, I just said I didn't *know.*"

"It's not a *rumor.* Your mom *told* you," Dean replied.

"How does she know?" I demanded. I had forgotten that Toby's mom volunteered at the hospital two days a week and probably saw my name on an ER admission list, kindly checked up on me to see if I was okay, and stumbled on the information that I had been referred to the psychiatric unit in Charlottesville. This would have become dinner conversation, passed from parent to child, and so on. Thus flows the news in small towns.

"See? He admits it," said Dean.

"I do not!"

"Yes, you do. You just did. I wish they'd kept you there," Dean continued morosely. "So I wouldn't have to look at you. Every-fucking-day!"

"Dean," I said, trembling with anger, "why don't you just shut up."

Byrd and Toby's eyes shot to Dean.

"Ooooooooh," Byrd said.

"Burn," pronounced Toby.

"You're telling me to shut up. You. You," Dean repeated, nodding his head in scorn, as if to say, you of all people, you the mental patient, you the pathetic.

Girls descended. Tiffany Struggles, another fatty, who diverted abuse from herself to others with an obsequious grin and a tendency to gossip; Holly, the prim, blond, freckled, sullen dentist's daughter seemingly destined to date Byrd; with one or two others in tow, including a tiny girl with a sardonic manner, named Violet, whom I had grown to like. They bore hot lunch trays and brown paper bags. When they sat, we ceased the conversation. But this could only arouse interest. Only something juicy could reduce four seventh graders to silence.

"What's going *on?*" Tiffany's eyes darted around the table, foraging for news.

"Nothing," said Dean moodily, suddenly disgusted with the whole topic.

I tucked my half-eaten sandwich back in the paper bag and left. I threw the bag in the garbage.

"Going on a diet?" Dean called after me. Then the whispering began.

It would not have been Dean to tell them. Dean despised girls, after a fashion; he might flirt or crack jokes to impress them, but gossip was beneath his countrified manly code. No, it would have been Toby to crack under the social pressure. I was only halfway to the door when Tiffany's voice burst out:

"MENTAL hosp—" before she theatrically clamped her hand over her mouth and changed to a stage whisper, "*Mental* hospital?"

"Oh my God," said someone. "Is that true?"

My heart beat with shame. I stood and looked back, hoping to see a table filled with sympathetic stares. But they were engrossed in this delicious development.

By the end of the day, my locker had the word *psycho* scratched into it. Only it was misspelled, fortuitously, as "sicko" (a redneck passing my locker, seeing my confusion, translated it phonetically for me). Because of the misspelling I knew it was not Dean, but more likely one of the hicks—the ominous Tex with the patch over one eye from a firewood-chopping accident, or his sidekick, the malnourished, scrawny J. J. Sweet, a pale boy in the ill-fitting clothes of the dirt poor who walked his phlegmatic, retarded sister to school every day. This was worse than Dean doing it, or Byrd, because if the news had traveled from one social group to another—middle-class kids to the hicks—it meant everyone knew.

Richard's office was freezing.

"I'm sorry about the cold," he said. "Something wrong with the boiler. You going to be okay?" He was wearing his cardigan, with a tartan scarf wrapped around his neck. "Keep your coat on, if it will be more comfortable."

He asked me how things were going in school. I told him about the mental hospital revelations. He was sympathetic; he nodded and did some modest probing; but as always, he steered me away from the present and into other areas, dim areas, the shaded places where I did not want to look, forcing me to describe, enact, revive the painful moments: to set the clay figures in my mind to life.

But what good were all these words? I could string them together, along with the feelings they described: *powerless, impotent, wounded, defeated, crushed, unloved.* But would revisiting all my unhappy scenes put me at peace? I wondered, dispiritedly, whether a simple exercise in an office could make make me a normal boy, a citizen of the active world, like Dean who explored the bumpy back mountain roads with his father in a truck, or Byrd with his endless hours of father-son weekend golf. The painful truth beneath it all is that the shock and shame of my father's death only served as the final snap for my brittle personality. If my father had lived to be a hundred and won the Nobel Prize for Literature, it would never redeem us; we would never belong to the world. That haunted man, in our grubby house, lived in a world of his own imagination. He viewed people over a chasm of bitterness, spiritual isolation, untreated depression; a marriage made of career compromises; and maybe even, who knows, a share in the pain of the Old South, passed down like a bloodstained deed with hereditary memories of Sherman's march and the boll weevil. My grandparents' modest Greenville, South Carolina, home, whose decor boasted a few grand heirlooms—a giant mahogany secretary, a silk-tasseled Civil War cutlass wrapped reverently in felt in an upstairs chest—betrayed the failed hopes of a postaristocratic household that stood awkwardly at the sidelines of a suburban, television-driven culture. Aca-deme provided a refuge, but not a haven, for my father's particular brand of gloom. A proud colleague whose piercing silences intimidated depart-ment chairmen and university presidents alike; a tale-spinning host; a quarrelsome friend to Uncle Freddie, Abby, and the Bings; a confessing melancholic to his old friend, Tom Harris; and a father and husband who paced the floors of his own house like a prisoner. In the end, my father left me a kind of treasure—the many phrases of Byzantine shine and bril-liance that arose from his intellect and his nonconformist views—and I was the dragon atop the pile. I could never be a citizen of the world. My inheritance lay in that musty, poisoned, ephemeral heap. Richard sensed this, maybe; maybe he did not. He was doctor enough to sniff out the wound, however, and treat it, by asking the simple questions.

"When your father died," he said now, voice scarcely a whisper, "what was that like for you?"

•   •   •

After the phone call I stalked the halls like my father in one his funks. A voice inside me said, *You will be man of the house.* My father himself had said it when he was picked up by the van from the Catholic relief organization that would take him to the airport. *Take good care of Momma. You will be man of the house.* But this was no house to be man of, anymore. Not after the phone call. My mother hovered in her bedroom, or threw herself into household chores like laundry and ironing, a prisoner for seventy-two hours while we waited for the insurance company to call back and explain why they had telephoned to ask if this was Paul N. Davies's residence and if he was traveling in Honduras. Why were they calling? But it was a flunky, some woman at a desk drinking coffee from a Styrofoam cup and rubbing the industrial carpeting with her toes. *We had an inquiry from the Ospitale Santa Maria in Te—Te—Te—* (Tegucigalpa, my mother had interrupted) *which we are checking on— someone was carrying an insurance card with that name.* Is it my husband *I don't know* Is he sick *I don't know* Well what's going on you must know something what kind of treatment are they requesting to be covered *I don't know this is just a verification call ma'am we do it when we get a request from countries the state department has issued warnings for is your husband traveling in Honduras?*

The frantic calls began. Consulate, embassy, the relief organization, Mother in blue jeans and a pink work shirt, unsmiling, bent over the phone. I was her witness—no chores, even, to perform—just a pair of unblinking eyeballs and sharp ears, alternately eavesdropping and tuning out the keening silence of the house with play. But while I played I was ashamed. *Man of the house.* My stuffed monkey, on a sword-fighting adventure; Asterix books; my mother's phrase, repeatedly overheard, penetrating my summer idleness: "something seriously wrong." *Oh Abby, we don't know if something is seriously wrong. Sir, I'm trying to find out if there is something seriously wrong.* I sat and waited. Mealtimes rolled around like another grinding turn of a mill wheel, and my mother, a slow eater in normal times, ate so slowly as to eat nothing; and I gobbled, cleaned my plate, and knew it was wrong to do so, but did it at every meal.

"How did you feel?" asked Richard in his freezing office.

Powerless, I told him. Helpless vulnerable wounded.

When my father came back he was a skeleton, a series of angles wrapped in hospital sheets, yellow.

"He had jaundice?"

"Yes."

He could not speak. My father lay mute, nearly unrecognizable—so long in absence, the contours of his face were strange, gaunt. His eyes rolled. My mother rode with him in the ambulance from the Roanoke airport. I sat with him in the hospital and stared at him but he never saw me.

"That must have been very hard for you not to be able to communicate with him."

"The doctor said the fever was so high he was most likely hallucinating."

"Were you able to say good-bye?"

"No."

"Did he ever recognize you?"

"No."

"Were you able to say good-bye? I mean, for yourself? Say good-bye to him in the hospital, even if he couldn't respond?"

"No."

He died with his jaw set at a humiliatingly wrong angle, off to one side under the sunken, translucent cheeks, as if the body no longer protested against gravity and time, and I thought, *There can be no heaven, look at my father, he's just bones, there is no heaven, no soul, we're just energy boxes, and when the energy stops, the jawbone hangs off at an angle, and the body stops pretending to be a person.* I told the priest at the funeral, I tugged his robes and he nearly shoved me automatically along as a child holding up the procession until he recognized that I was the bereaved, and when he took my shoulder, pulled me aside, and leaned over, I told him I didn't think there was a soul since my father died like an animal, unseeing, unspeaking, just stopped energy. The priest replied, *Scripture prepares us for this, George. It says we go from "dust to dust." The soul is what makes us different from animals. That's what was in your father. And when it left him, he did change, you are right.* He was gentle, and whispered this to me as if it were a secret between us, then held my shoulder until someone came for me; I don't remember who.

"Do you think maybe your dream about your father," Richard said, "the one your Friend showed you, might have been a way of saying good-bye to him?"

I shrugged. We sat for a long time.

"It's freezing in here," I said.

"I know," said Richard.

When we were finished I walked alone into the corridor, flush with garbled memories and oddly grateful for the hot and present pain. So this is how you lift a dragon's curse, I thought. I turned to thank Richard, but the door had closed, cutting off the warm lights, and plunging the hallway into darkness.

The Practitioner

Saturday came unseasonably cold. Mom said a jet stream had brought the low temperatures from Canada, and I imagined a kind of lateral tornado, like one from the Wizard of Oz, twisting down to touch Virginia with crackling hands of frost.

Still, the sun shone brightly. I sat in my room in a sunbeam, reading, when I heard voices from the hall.

"Tom, it's too cold for that kind of work, isn't it?"

"I'm making a giant pot of coffee. He'll be toasty warm."

"You don't give boys coffee, Tom."

"Hot chocolate, then."

"Does it have to be today?"

"I've got my worker, Reval Dumas, there in the car." He pronounced the name *ree*-vull *doom*-ah. "He's got jobs the next three weekends."

"Reval?" my mother reacted to the name. "I see."

I was summoned. I found Tom Harris leaning on his crutches in the hall. He had dropped by because he needed my help to fix his smokehouse, he said—the odd jobs were beginning in earnest. Along with the laborer Tom Harris used to "fix things up" around his dilapidated property, I would be engaged in exciting, character-building activities such as mixing mortar in a wheelbarrow in the freezing cold, slathering it onto broken sections of wall with a trowel, and patching up that same wall with bricks, acquired at a very reasonable price, secondhand, at the farmers' co-op. That's what his words said. His eyes lingered on mine, however, making a point—*you want to do this job.*

I peered out the front door. A boatlike Pontiac idled on Piggott Street, frost obscuring the windows.

"I'll get my coat," I said instantly.

"George is becoming quite the Boy Scout," remarked my mother, a little drily.

"Would you want a cripple doing the work, in his place?" said Tom Harris, holding out both hands with exaggerated self-pity.

A few minutes later I found myself bundled in two sweaters, a winter coat, a hat, and gloves, making my way across grass so frozen it crackled underfoot, while Tom Harris took up the sidewalk with his splaying crutches. He kept his head low and whispered to me conspiratorially.

"There's someone I want you to meet."

"Who? Your worker?" I said dubiously.

"I told a white lie," responded Tom Harris. "Reval Dumas is here to do a job . . . but of a different type. He's our practitioner," he said, with a flash of his eyes.

"An exorcist?" I whispered excitedly.

"Not officially," said Tom Harris, hobbling toward the car. "Not a Catholic. Reval is an *ee*-vangelical missionary. In town just for the day, on his way to Chicago. Going home from Sri Lanka, if you can believe it. Flies out at nine tonight."

I saw my mother, leaning on the glass of the front window. I waved. Tom Harris waved, too.

"Keep walking," he said.

"Is he going to help me?"

"Not you. We're all going to help someone else."

I stopped. "Then why am I coming?" I whined. "*I* need help."

Tom Harris halted, too. He wore only his long black overcoat, no scarf, leaving his neck and shaggy head bare. When he spoke, wisps of frost curled from his lips; and with the pale November light blue-white on his craggy features, he looked like Old Man Winter.

"I told you we needed to understand your Friend before we acted. This is going to help," he said. "And you want to know more about your father. Yes?"

"Yes."

"Well, this is what we used to do," he said. "Now, if you're no longer interested . . ."

"I'm interested," I said quickly.

"Oh, good." His mouth twitched in a smile and he resumed his way down the walk. "Do you remember the woman I told you and your mother about several months ago?" he said. "The woman who spoke in tongues?"

I remembered: the tale about going to the Pentecostal church. The Asian languages professor who got spooked. "Yes," I replied.

"She got herself in some deep trouble," said Tom Harris. "Her husband had the good sense to ask for help. Reval Dumas is who they found. Lucky for them."

As I circled the car, I saw my mother's figure still in the window, watching us. I imagined her watching my father from that same spot, in similar circumstances. I felt a tingle of adventure, and of pride—*I was doing what he did.*

I realized I was also seeing what he saw: my mother's face, full of concern, watching from the window. I got in the car.

"Hi George," said Reval Dumas. "I'm Reval."

The hard accent hit my ears like a different kind of music—the first Midwestern accent I'd ever heard. I half-expected it to shatter the ice layering over the windshield. Each "r" ripped at the ear like a fish-hook, and each phrase rose at the end, in a manner that both ingratiated and posed a prim challenge, as if to say *Yes, you're George, and yes, I'm Reval, but what are we going to do about it today?*

The owner of the voice surprised me as well. Since I had at first expected a worker, a local, I had imagined a heavyset, smoke-smelling redneck, in worker's boots and a wool-lined coat, maybe missing teeth. Instead, Reval Dumas was a small man behind the wheel of a vast car. He wore a white shirt and tie, like an insurance salesman, and his hair—yellow-blond—stood on end in a spiky crewcut. His face, however, was pudgy and pink, showing signs of sunburn on the nose and cheeks, giving him a boyish—even babyish—air despite his true age, which I guessed to be midforties. He fixed me in a squint. His full lips pulled around crooked teeth in a small, amused smile.

"Hi," I answered.

"Tom didn't mention what a young fellow you are," he said. "Tom" came out *Taaam,* that single vowel bold and flat as a quack.

"I'm eleven."

Reval turned back to give Tom Harris a nervous glance. "Tom . . . if this woman is going through what they say she is . . . George should be at least sixteen. We're not going to mow a lawn here."

"Or mend a smokehouse." Tom Harris winked at me. Then to Reval, meaningfully: "This is Paul Davies's son."

The round face turned to me again. The smile disappeared, and the squint deepened.

"Paul Davies," he repeated. His eyes were glued to me for what seemed like minutes. "I'm sorry about your dad."

"You knew him?"

"Knew him a little. Knew *of* him." Reval shook his head. "He was a special person, God bless him."

"Reval," said Tom Harris, "George here, young as he is, has been experiencing visions of his own. Not necessarily the good kind. I want him to appreciate the full spectrum of what he may encounter, if he's not careful."

"Deep end of the pool, eh? Well, sometimes it's time, and you're ready . . . and sometimes it's just time." Reval scowled. "Are you ready to step into your father's shoes, son?"

I quailed at his diamond-hard gaze: he wanted me to enter the demon world—pursuing them with visions. I was only eleven! How could they expect me to take on that kind of responsibility . . .

"Oh ho ho, you should see your face," laughed Reval. "I'm just kidding ya. It will be fine," he said. "It always is." And with that he started the engine.

We swerved onto Route 40, dipping under the overpass of an unused trestle bridge, which marked the boundary between Preston and the county on the town's western side. We passed a development of homes on crisp, treeless lawns, then a fancy horse farm with whitewashed latticed fence. Some miles later, the land rose to a crest, where a Moose Lodge squatted over a gravel parking lot and some incongruous streetlamps, as if marking the last outpost of Preston's meager urbanity. We cut sharply left, down into a dell.

The road descended and curved, following a creek bed. The trees and bracken grew closer to the road here; brown tresses of winter willows brushed the warning signs and guardrails on our left. The houses stood close to the road, as if huddling against the flat ground.

"Tom says you're a practitioner," I ventured.

Tom Harris patiently explained our private lingo.

"Oh," Reval laughed. "Well. I had a lot of practice in the East. Performing the rite. I borrow one from the Catholic Church." *Catholic* came out *Kaaa*-tholik. He reached into a bag by his lap and handed to me a mimeographed, stapled set of pages: prayers typed in a big font. "They know what they're doing. More of a tradition, am I right?" Tom Harris averred that he was. "It's important to have the script. When the demons of confusion come, your brains turn to scrambled eggs. You need that anchor. I've seen a lot . . . *weird stuff* since I been out there," he said. "Done a lot of special blessings. I wouldn't say it's *fun*. I don't need to tell you, Tom. When you see kids in that condition . . ." He shook his head sadly. "Couple of months ago, I saw a young girl— white girl, a diplomat's daughter—take the shape of one of their gods," *gaaa*ds, "with her arms waving, teeth bared." He shook his head again. "She claimed she was the goddess Kali," he said. "The goddess of death."

We slowed, then bumped over a bridge. We crossed the stony creek and turned onto a one-lane road that hugged the creek, its turnings tighter.

"I think before Christianity, those ancient religions set root out there," he continued, "and among the good stuff . . . and there *was* some good stuff . . . the demons snuck in, set themselves up in the place of gods. But are they *tenacious,*" he exclaimed. "Part of the religion, too, the meditation? It's about saying yes? That's how this particular girl got lost. Opening the mind. Now I'm all for being open-minded," he chuckled. "But not to the enemy. Some people can't tell the difference." He frowned at the road. " 'Course, easy for us to say sitting here, eh, Tom?"

"Nothing easy about it," said Tom Harris.

"Nope," said Reval, "I think you're right."

I watched with interest how Tom Harris, a professor at a respected college, treated this itinerant, evangelical minister with perfect respect. An unspoken fellowship seemed to pass between them. I imagined my father—and possibly, one day, myself—being a part of this fellowship: a network of quiet practitioners that superseded country, education, accent, age.

"This is it," pronounced Reval, squinting at the number on the mailbox.

We slowed to a stop. To our left, in the floodplain, a few houses were set at roughly thirty-yard intervals. The one in question—number 179, of what road I never learned—was a common kind of house in Stoneland County: painted white wood with dark-green trim, but dirty, with mud spattered along the walls and a dejected look; a torn screen door; the front porch scattered with toys—a Big Wheel, a wagon, many dolls.

"Gosh, the kids aren't home, are they?" said Reval with sudden concern.

"Away with the grandmother," said Tom.

"Okay then," said Reval, taking a deep breath. "Ready?"

•   •   •

Reval led the way. Our footsteps—and Tom Harris's crutches—made a tumult on the wooden porch. We rang the doorbell, then Reval called out, waited, shrugged, and opened the door. Tom Harris seemed too tall for the front door and stooped down on his way in. Despite the fierce cold, the house felt close and damp, like it had not been opened in some time. A staircase filled the cramped hall. To the left lay the living room—a matching sofa and chair with checkered dust ruffles, and a big TV. On our right, voices. We followed them, Reval first. I watched him enter the room, absorb the scene quickly, then begin speaking: an unhesitating continuation of his good-natured patter. For a moment I felt oddly jealous, hearing his friendly banter focused on someone else. *Hi there. We let ourselves in. Hope that's okay. I'm Reval Dumas. Your pastor called me. This is Tom . . . and George . . .*

I bumped up against Tom Harris and his sweeping overcoat, and together we walked into a long, cramped, train-car-shaped bedroom adorned with some homey, womanly touches—a dresser top with a lacy shawl thrown over it, flower-embroidered potpourri cushions. On the dresser: a red and white heart-encrusted frame featuring a dated snapshot of two teenagers in prom gear—corsaged girl grinning, overexcited; guy stiff in a rented tuxedo. Next to it, another frame, the snapshot equivalent of a movie jump cut: a family of four, with the prom couple older, more tired, and with them two smiling children, a brunette girl in barrettes and a black-haired boy with a well-reconstructed harelip.

On the floor, next to the dresser, lay a thick curtain rod—more of a pole, really—with gauzy white curtains on either end. It had been ripped from the wall and flung to the floor. The screws were still in the fixtures. The pole was bent, twisted in the middle.

Disturbed, I drew my attention to the people in the room. A man—heavyset, round jaw, balding in front, exhausted circles under his eyes—was introduced as Bobby, the husband, whom I could almost recognize as the teenager in the tux; and a woman in a purple and somewhat battered ESPRIT sweatshirt, with the edgy manner and skewy, poufed-up hair of someone who had not been to bed. This was Denise, the sister. A woman lay asleep on the bed. The hair-sprayed teenager at the prom, with baby fat and a tan, had transmogrified to a pale, slender woman whose long, refined nose gave her a kind of drained yet dignified beauty even lying in pajamas on a tousled bed. This room felt even closer than the front of the house, locker-room pungent, as if Denise and Bobby had been doing calisthenics in here all night and were now taking a much-needed, if joyless, break.

"We need some relief," Denise announced with an air of resentment, as if we were somehow responsible.

"You the minister?" Bobby asked Reval, then began telling the story, working backward from recent details.

Been getting really bad at night, like she's trying to wear us out. Had to take the last two days off work. Called in sick, 'cause, well . . . what can you tell 'em? Where do you work? Reval asked. *I'm the sales manager at Preston Rent-Alls on Route 17,* he said, the words flowing automatically, confidently, conjuring an atmosphere of commerce and normalcy at odds with our steamy surroundings, and the heavy breaths of the sleeping woman. *We had her looked at, but she was fine at the hospital, like someone flipped a light switch. Just told 'em she'd been feeling tired.* Bobby pronounced it *taaard. They did some tests, and sent us home. Then . . . same night . . .* he shook his head. *Back where we started.* A pause; Bobby's eyes welled up. *I don't know what gets into her.*

"Has it been talking to you, Bobby?" Reval said. Bobby looked up at Reval, alarmed, as if he had guessed at something secret, and intensely private. "You know what I mean," Reval persisted. He asked what "it" had been saying, a distinction Bobby caught and flinched at, himself sticking with the "she."

When she gets going she never stops, Bobby answered. *Half of it nonsense, and half of it . . .* he shook his head again. Denise screwed up her face in disgust and joined in. *It's nasty,* she offered heatedly. *I can't stand it no more. Never used to talk that way, I can tell you that.*

"Oh, it's not her," declared Reval. This set Denise back a bit; her face twisted, as if it were trying to digest this bizarre idea.

Tom Harris drew Bobby aside, began asking him about the Pente-costal service, about their attendance at that church, and when the "change" began, but my eyes were drawn to Reval. He approached the sleeping woman. Laid a hand on her forehead, felt her pulse. Inter-rupted Bobby and Tom Harris to ask about her general health. Then laid on a chair a gallon-size plastic Ziploc bag that he had been carrying, which I had not noticed until now. From it he removed a white stole—made of felt, with crosses, chalices, and other emblems sewn on it with brightly colored felt pieces—a small Bible, additional prayer mimeo-graphs, and a tiny crucifix. He draped the stole around his neck.

Reval moved quickly from this point, making sure Tom Harris and I held prayer printouts. Then he sent Bobby and Denise away to rest.

"We'll call you when we need you," he said. "And don't worry—we'll need you."

After they obeyed gratefully, Reval turned to us. "Her name is Grace," he said, a sad twinge of his mouth showing he was not unaware of the irony. "We'll start with the prayers, see what kind of response we get. When we hit a sore spot, we'll know." I had noticed that Bobby and Denise—even Tom Harris and I—whispered when in the woman's presence. Reval spoke in a normal, confident tone. "That's the cue to keep at it. Okay?"

I moved to stand near the door.

"Save your servant," began Reval.

Tom Harris leaned lightly on his crutches and read along in a strong voice. I struggled to keep up at first, but finally found the lines for the responses: "Who trusts in you, my God."

"Let her find in you, Lord, a fortified tower."

"In the face of the enemy," I mumbled from the purple mimeo-graphed type between my fingers.

"Let us pray," intoned Reval, and pray he did, in an easy, collo-quial manner—more a nice dad saying grace around a Thanksgiving turkey than a Holy Roller. *God, who consigned that fallen and apostate tyrant to the flames of hell,* Reval began mildly, *who sent your only-begotten Son into the world to crush that roaring lion; hasten to our call,*

*and snatch from the clutches of the noonday devil, this human being made
in your image . . .*

"Amen," we said, and so it went. I watched Grace as she lay, her
hands folded near her face, her breathing slow, her face pale and slack,
like someone laid up with a rotten flu. Every few minutes, Tom Harris
shifted his crutch-borne weight to a different armpit, but otherwise the
drama, or lack of it, rolled on. I glanced out the window. A winter scene:
a fence and grass glazed in frost. A tan pickup in the neighbor's drive. I
followed with the responses. *Amen*s and *who put their trust in you*s. The
novelty wore off, and after an hour, I began to drift. Tom Harris sensed
this and leaned over to whisper, "You can take a break if you want."

I retreated to the living room. Bobby had gone upstairs to the kids'
room for a nap. I found Denise sitting on the sofa. She held a magazine
in her fingers and faced the television—which was off—but looked at
neither one. Her hands moved continually. Folding the magazine.
Placing it on her lap.

"She all right now?" Denise asked aggressively.

"I don't know," I said, unhelpfully.

"I ain't never seen her like this," she said. Then, as if finally taking
notice of who I was, asked: "You the preacher's son?"

"No," I replied.

I felt her eyes bore into me questioningly.

"The preacher," I said, "was friends with my dad." Denise kept
staring. "My dad died," I added.

She nodded, not really hearing.

"My dad did this," I ventured, tossing my head toward the bedroom, watching Denise for a reaction. "Special blessings."

"Kind of in the blood, huh?"

"Kind of," I said, pleased by this association with my father.

"Hope this don't go on too long," said Denise, after a time. "I got
dogs to feed." She licked her lips distractedly. "Don't know what Bobby
needs me for. It's his wife. I don't see why they can't treat her at the hospital. That's what they have nurses for, idn't it? They should take her
back there. Can't send people home that kinda condition." She picked

up the magazine. Opened it. Shut it. Her manner gave evidence of a mind overloaded with unhappiness, but with only one mode of coping: irritability. "Don't know how she got herself into this anyhow. She calls me the slut queen of all Stoneland County for partying eight days a week. HUH. Look at her."

A few awkward moments passed. I didn't want Denise to feel I was unsympathetic.

"Yeah," I said. I picked up another magazine, opened it—but also found it impossible to read. The prayers in the next room continued.

Evening came early, and true to Bobby's observations, Grace seemed to stir at sundown. Outside, the weak yellow sun sent a parting volley of beams through the willows, then disappeared. Soon I heard Reval's and Tom Harris's voices rising, and Tom Harris leaned his shaggy head out of the bedroom, calling Bobby and Denise in. "You stay there," he said to me coolly. Denise rousted Bobby, who came downstairs blearily, and the two of them went into the bedroom. Soon Reval had them chanting neatly as a choirmaster.

Lord, hear my prayer.

And let my cry be heard with you, came the three voices in response, booming through the wall. It was too loud to think of, or do, anything else but listen. I stared at the blank television. Reval's voice continued, the words inaudible, but the tone more urgent than before.

And also with you, came the chorus.

Then came a loud bump against the wall. I heard shuffling, and orders given, and in my mind I saw Tom Harris, flung to the floor, cast cracking, pain across his face . . . I ran to the door.

Grace had awakened. Her body gyrated spasmodically. Bobby, behind her on the bed, locked both arms in a grip to keep her from flailing freely. She had apparently just pushed Bobby backward into the headboard, making the noise.

Denise ran to help steer them. Grace moaned and her hands flapped.

"I command you," came Reval's voice, louder now, "unclean spirit, whoever you are, that you tell me by some sign, your name, and the day and hour of your departure!"

My eyes widened. Something was happening now in the room. Tom Harris felt it, too, and waved me back through the door. But I stood mesmerized. Grace was trembling, her brow furrowed, troubled; her body sagging briefly, then tensing ominously—not going rigid, but more coming to consciousness, as if she were moving her limbs intentionally now, after mere sleep-thrashing. Denise, feeling it, too, took a step back.

Suddenly I felt a blast of cold. I checked behind me, in the living room, to see whether the front door had blown open. But it had not. The cold came from within the bedroom. Chaos descended. With controlled movements, Grace crawled out of Bobby's arms. Bobby tried to grasp her back, calling, *Honey c'mere . . . c'mere*. Reval repeated his phrase, now shouting, *I command you, unclean spirit!* Denise blew on her fingers, feeling the freezing temperature, and assuming, as I had, that the front door had opened onto the arctic chill. She yelled at me angrily, *Shut the door!* But before I could respond, all our attention was drawn to the figure on the bed. Grace turned to face the room full of people, kneeling and swaying back and forth. Bobby still followed her, trying to rein her back. But she turned quickly backward to face him, her movements so sharp and attack-fast that he reared back as you might from a cornered animal. Grace had come fully awake, and whatever was in her—possessing her, you could see why the word fit, now—had, too.

"I command you," Reval said, "to obey me to the letter, I who am a minister of God despite my unworthiness."

Grace, in her pajamas and bare feet, stretched her spine with a yogalike movement—hands on the mattress, fists clenched, back arching—but the movement took on a strange, languorous quality. As we watched, she extended herself to an unnatural length, as if she were suddenly capable of adding inches of space between her vertebrae. We stared transfixed, even Reval silenced by the unnaturalness of what we saw, as Grace's back and neck coiled into an S shape. Her face slack, her eyes unfocused, her physiognomy seemed entirely bent on the transformation at hand, until her torso hovered in the air at a seemingly impossible forty-degree angle, scarcely supported by her knees resting on the bed. Her head then swiveled menacingly. Her eyes refocused. They beamed at us, fiercely. Cold and hateful. I recognized what I was looking at and felt a trickle of urine warm my underpants. It was a thirty-year-old woman in the shape of a snake.

"I command you, unclean spirit," Reval began. But before the last word left his lips, Grace shot her body forward. She extended her frame in a straight line, like an arrow. Reval ducked to one side. I heard her jaw snap shut with a hard *chak* on empty air, and she wriggled, twisted, in that ugly, instinctual, break-the-victim's-neck twist, her teeth bared and clenched in fierce pleasure on Reval's imagined flesh. Denise crawled away in terror on hands and knees. But Bobby, determined and unfazed—an owner controlling a wild dog—grasped Grace by the waist and hauled her back onto the bed. Now Grace thrashed wildly. She shook him with an inhuman speed and ferocity, a lizard or snake slapping and wriggling for life. But Bobby held. After a few moments of this, Grace gave up, exhausted, her chest heaving.

To my astonishment, Reval approached the bed. He made a sign of the cross. He stood over Grace—so close to that dangerous creature I almost called out, *Don't!*—and placed a hand on her head with perfect calm.

"See the cross of the Lord; begone, you hostile powers!"

She sat up with a jolt. Reval stepped back. Grace appeared human again; she wore an expression of annoyance.

"I was *asleep,*" she complained.

The sudden normalcy of her tone struck me as comical, and I found myself giving an involuntary giggle. Grace's head snapped in my direction. I felt Tom Harris move toward me protectively. But rather than pounce, or make any other violent motion, Grace, instead, grinned at me. I felt relief flood through my body. She wasn't angry— she was happy to see some humor in the room, someone who could cut through all this sickroom silliness and see her charm, her strength, the fact that she didn't need all these men to nudge her around the room like a cow . . . these thoughts flitted through my mind until my eyes, as it were, woke up to what they were seeing. Her smile was more terrifying than a pointed gun. Toothsome, warm, ingratiating, it seemed to charm and welcome, but glinted with a chilly knowingness. Then one eye closed in a wink. Conspiratorial—that was the only word for it. I felt the others staring at me.

I fell backward onto the carpet and raised my hands to cover my face so I could no longer see her. *She can see it,* I said to myself. *She can see the demon in me.*

"Tom," I whimpered. "She knows."

"Quiet." Tom Harris spoke fiercely.

Reval stepped to his left, blocking the visual connection between Grace and myself, and pointed his finger accusingly. "Strike terror, Lord, into the beast now laying waste your vineyard," he declaimed. "Fill your servants with courage to fight the dragon."

"Stop it," said Grace, again in that *quit-it-you-guys* tone of impatience.

Denise sat up and responded. "Grace?"

"That's not your sister speaking," warned Tom Harris. "Let Reval continue."

Denise made a sour face. "Sounded like her," she grumbled. "Comin' out of her mouth."

"Professor Expert is here," taunted Grace, her voice suddenly light and airy. She sounded like a flirt at a party. "But you came all alone. Where's your friend? Not *this* guy. The one you *usually* come with." She gave a ringing laugh. "Professor Expert and Mr. Mystic. Professor Expert and Mr. Mystic."

I looked up and saw Tom Harris go white.

"What did you say?" Tom Harris asked.

"Where's your friend? The *real* deal?" she said, maintaining the light tone.

"Who are you talking about?" demanded Tom Harris.

"You know who I mean," she said.

"I don't. If you have the courage, say his name."

"Tom," said Reval warningly.

"I said it already. Mr. Mystic. And you're Professor Expert. The one, the only, vainglorious second fiddle." Then, cold and dismissive: "You're nothing on that guy."

"Who do you mean?" Tom Harris seemed to have lost all sense of where he was. Reval's printed prayers hung at his side, forgotten; he had taken a half step forward; he was about to put weight on his cast.

"Boo hoo, now he's gone, big deal," continued Grace in that same, familiar, sarcastic tone, so evocative that, in hearing it, I could have believed she was just an old friend, an old gal pal; maybe she and Tom Harris had dated once upon a time; but now she was beyond being impressed, and in fact, felt it was her role to keep him honest, to remind big, intimidating Tom Harris that he shouldn't get too big for his britches.

"How did you know that?" said Tom Harris. "What do you know?"

"We didn't hurt him, if that's what you mean," she answered. "He came to us . . . and we took him."

"What did you do to him?"

Reval's voice rose. "Tom, we're here to pray."

"I want to hear this," he said, taking a step toward Grace. "Tell me: Who are you speaking about?"

"Tom, *get out of here,*" said Reval. He crossed over to Tom and gripped his shoulder. "Come on."

Grace made a funny face, then spoke in a mockingly deep voice, as if she were doing an imitation. "I . . . buried . . . Paul," she said, then smiled—an open, self-deprecating laugh—a lady at a party sharing in the fun of her own goofy impersonation.

Meanwhile Reval had shoved Tom Harris's crutches into his hands and was ushering him from the room. With a crooked finger he summoned me as well. "Come on," he commanded, his pudgy, pink face distorted with anger. He shoved us through the living room. Tom Harris hobbled along quickly. Reval, with his comparatively tiny frame, boxed him against the front door angrily.

"You know better than to enter into . . . *conversation* with it, Tom," Reval sputtered.

But Tom Harris had gone white again and seemed to hear nothing.

"*Taaaam.*" That flat midwestern timbre stripped Tom Harris of his reverie. His eyes snapped back into focus. "I want you to get outside and get some air. It's cold, but you need it. Go on. Both of you," he added to me, eyes flashing.

And before we knew it, we found ourselves standing on Bobby and Grace's porch. I stumbled over the Big Wheel's big wheel. The dusk was silent and ice-blue.

Tom Harris paced the porch, agitated, walking on only one crutch.

"Should we go back in?" I shivered.

The curving road, white with frost; the neighbors' houses; the trees; the patches of grass, thin as worn carpet, all faded rapidly as one last corner of the sky glowed weakly. I did not want to be left outside in the dark. After what I had seen, every shadow seemed to hide a threat. I reached under my coat and touched my trousers front. The urine had soaked a patch into one thigh on my pants. My coat would cover it, but it felt icy.

"No," murmured Tom Harris. "We're finished."

"What happened?"

"I made a mistake," said Tom Harris. "Reval was right to throw us out. Or me, anyway." He gave a rueful chuckle. "My first time being expelled." His voice teased, but his eyes searched the floorboards, agitated; and he didn't meet my gaze. "You shouldn't talk with it. It draws you in." He hunched up his shoulders, moved to the porch railing. "Caught me by surprise."

I plunged my hands into my pockets to stop them from trembling from shock and cold. My teeth began chattering instead.

"What was she talking about?" I said, unable to assume the practitioner's use of "it." "Did—did she say my dad's name?"

"You caught that?" said Tom Harris quickly.

"Yeah. She made that funny voice."

"It's from a Beatles' song," said Tom Harris. "'I buried Paul.' Part of the nonsense talk in one of their records. Which song was it?" His voice trailed off, then he muttered, almost to himself: "Means nothing."

"Then why did you get so upset?"

I wondered whether Tom Harris heard me. He stared up the road, his long, black back to me.

"Was she talking about my father?" I persisted. "That Mr. Mystic stuff?"

"It would certainly seem so," he answered, his voice thick.

"What did she mean when she said they didn't hurt him?"

"I don't know, George." Then, after a moment: "That's not true. Guess I'm through with all the polite and appropriate cover stories for you, George. I do know."

I waited. "So?"

"Your father's letters from Honduras made it sound like his sickness was a kind of losing struggle. A spiritual struggle for his own life. I confess I didn't really believe it before."

My mind, only two days clear of Thorazine, fused two points together. "Now you think my dad was telling the truth," I said, suddenly not feeling the cold. "You think the demons killed him."

"Killed him," Tom Harris repeated. "Killed Paul." He drew a ragged sigh, a sob in reverse. "My God," he said. His long black back convulsed once, twice. He bent his head, pressing his eyes with thumb and forefinger. Then he exhaled a cone of frost.

"I, er . . ." he cleared his throat again. "Didn't know I had that in me," he said. "No wonder it came after me. Sitting target. They smell it on you." He sighed. "We must get you to Finley Balcomb immediately."

"Why?" I asked.

"It's clear now, at last," he murmured to himself. He turned to me and spoke in a clear voice. "Demons possess, George. But they also kill when they can. Like any enemy, they first target the real threats. Priests are often injured. Here I am, 'Professor Expert,' with a broken leg. Paul, it now seems likely, was murdered. Next on their list . . ."

He did not say the name, but I knew what it was.

"You think they want to kill me."

"As you said—for revenge," he replied. "Your mother may be in danger as well."

I felt a sudden yearning to be home again—in our warm kitchen with the smells of potatoes frying in oil, and of baking chicken—to hug my mother and pretend I was a little boy again, to be given a glass of milk and be told what to do. Instead I shivered. The night sky deepened. Other than the bedroom light that spilled in a trapezoid onto the lawn, the dell lay in inky black.

I saw one ray of hope. "Can Reval help us?"

"If you haven't noticed, he has his hands full." Tom Harris sounded dubious.

"Before he leaves?"

"With you not properly 'diagnosed'? Without any visible signs? Even if I gave Reval my word, he would still need to satisfy himself. Perform the tests." He shook his head. "There isn't time, George. His plane leaves this evening."

We pulled our coats more tightly around us. I fought an urge to burst into frustrated tears.

"Let's wait in the car," he said at length. "Before my testicles shatter in this cold."

I sat brooding in the backseat. Tom Harris had finished speaking for the night, it seemed, and I contented myself with watching his cowlicks silhouetted against the house lights. My father had died, a victim of demons. His best friend remained miserable and impotent over his death. My mother believed none of it. And I was alone. I wished to dissolve right then into the cheap upholstery of the Pontiac. I was ready to let go: surrender to the drugs, the treatment facility, the psychiatrists, the creeping horror of my Friend, whichever would have me first.

The porch light flicked on. Reval Dumas's unprepossessing figure appeared in the doorframe. He pulled up his collar and trudged to the car. Tucked under his arm was the plastic Ziploc bag.

"So?" asked Tom Harris, when Reval got behind the wheel and slammed the car door behind him.

Reval said nothing. His head hung a few inches lower than it had just a few hours earlier on our drive here. Weariness and the stale odors of the house rose off him. He sat for a moment in silence, hunched over. Then he drew himself up and turned to give Tom Harris a fierce squint.

"Sorry ta kick you out, Tom," he said. "You understand."

"I do," said Tom Harris quietly. "Thank you, Reval."

Reval shoved the key in the ignition and started to turn it—then hesitated. He looked at both of us, seeming to read us and our dejection for the first time. His pudgy lips broadened into a grin, revealing crooked front teeth—and a glimmer of something I would not have expected from such an odd, yet holy fellow: self-satisfaction. The cockiness of an athlete who has just trounced an opponent—and at an away game, too. He enjoyed the moment, and played it out, holding the key in the ignition while we waited to learn the outcome.

"When the enemy leaves them, they open their eyes like a newborn babe." He turned the key and the engine growled to life. "Feel like an OB/GYN sometimes," he said with a laugh, over the noise. "Wasn't so bad."

Then he gunned the Pontiac and, with a gravelly crunch and a roar, drove us back to town, around the curves of the twisting, unnamed road.

T.A.T.

It happened this way.

Rachel was administering a new test. We had spent the entire last session doing an incredibly boring IQ test. She seemed giddy not to have to hear my solutions to geometry puzzles anymore, and she unveiled the new test like it was a chocolate cake. From a manila envelope she pulled out a deck of outsized index cards.

"Each of these cards shows a situation," she said. "I want you to tell me a story about what you see."

Usually I asked a half dozen questions before we began any game, to make sure I understood the rules, especially when the Thorazine slowed my comprehension. But today I said nothing. She waited for me to leap in. But I didn't. So she jumped ahead and answered a few questions—the kind I would normally ask.

"The stories don't have to connect," she said.

Then, after a moment: "And they should be based on what you see in the card."

Finally she gave up and began flipping the cards.

The first was a picture of a little boy gazing sorrowfully at a violin, which sat on a little table. I stared at the card.

"So," said Rachel, smiling at me good-naturedly. "What do you think?" she prompted. "What's the situation?"

"There's a violin," I said.

"Riiight," said Rachel.

I stared at the card some more.

"Anything else?"

"No."

"Why do you think the boy in the picture is sad?"

"I don't know."

Rachel explained the rules to me again: I was supposed to make up stories about what I saw on the cards. "This should be right up your alley," she said, with a hint of impatience.

She held out the next one. It showed a car, with a man in it, driving away from a family. The family—a mother, daughter, and son— waved to him.

"What about this?" asked Rachel.

"He's driving away," I said. And that was about all she could get out of me.

"Okay," she said. "Let's try the next one."

She placed another card on the table. I stared at it long and hard. I felt the air pounding in my ears. I turned to Rachel.

"Are you kidding?" I demanded.

"Sorry?"

"Did you put this here as a kind of joke?"

She held the card up and examined it. "No, that's the real card."

She placed it on the table again.

"Get that away from me!" I shouted, and flicked it off the table with my fingers. "What the hell!"

Rachel stopped dead. I had never cursed in front of her.

"George, there's nothing wrong with that card," she said, recovering. "It's just part of the test."

"Who told you, anyway?"

"What?"

"Did somebody say something?"

"About what, George? What are you referring to?"

"Never mind." I crossed my arms and slumped in the chair.

"George," said Rachel carefully. "Is there something about this card that upsets you?"

She picked it off the floor and placed it in front of me again, keeping her hand on it.

"GET IT AWAY FROM ME! I *told* you!" I screamed. I rose and slapped the card out of her hand.

Rachel gave me one more searching look, then got up quickly and left the room. I heard her speak to someone just outside.

"Is Richard free?" Rachel asked her.

"I think so." The receptionist peered in at me with a worried expression.

"Would you get him for me, please?" said Rachel. She gingerly shut the door again, then placed the remaining cards, facedown, on the table. She folded her arms and waited.

"Can you explain to me why this card upset you?"

I sat in Richard's office. He wore a tie. A stack of paperwork cluttered his normally clean desk. Evidently this was not his day to see patients.

"No," I said, surly now.

"George, it must have upset you for a reason."

"You're going to tell."

"Who am I going to tell? We talked about confidentiality," he reminded me. "Are you nervous because your checkup with Dr. Gilloon is tomorrow?"

I stared at the floor.

"George . . ."

"What."

"I need you to talk to me. Are you afraid something's going to happen to you if you talk about it?"

I nodded.

"Okay," he sighed. "Now *I'm* going out on a limb here. I promise whatever you tell me—unless it's a matter of life and death—I will not mention to the doctors in Charlottesville. Okay?"

"You promise?"

"I promise."

"Okay," I said. Then I continued in a hushed voice, as if we might be overheard. "He can do whatever he wants to me. I'm like Job. Everybody is, so are you. You can get . . . boils," I said, remembering my Bible stories. "He can kill me, or my mom. He can stop your heart."

Richard gave me a hard look. "Dr. Gilloon?" he said with surprise.

"No."

"Then who? Who does these things?"

I muttered a reply.

"Pardon?"

"The *devil*," I said.

He turned this over a moment. "You're afraid of the devil?"

"Aren't you?"

Richard blinked this one off. "I'm more interested in why you are. George, did this card remind you of the devil somehow?" He held it up.

"Yes," I said definitively.

"What about this card made you think of the devil?"

"The . . ." I hesitated. "The dog."

"What about the dog?"

"Because that's how he appears. He can come as an imp, or he can come as a dog. An evil-favored black dog."

Richard leaned in toward me. The dark creases under his eyes seemed more pronounced than ever.

"Have you been talking about this with somebody?" he said. "Kids at school?"

"Why?"

"'Evil-favored black dog.' Doesn't sound like you. Did you read that somewhere?"

"My father wrote it," I said defiantly (and somewhat inaccurately).

"Your father wrote about the devil?" asked Richard.

"Yeah, a book called *The Ancient Prayer*. I've been reading it."

"Okay," said Richard, absorbing this. "But surely your father didn't mean that the devil comes and kills people like you and me."

"Yes, he did," I declared.

Richard retrenched. "Your father was a professor. I'm guessing this is a book of scholarship—of history."

I nodded.

"So . . . what you read might have been out of context." I shrugged. He changed tack. "Why are you reading it, George? I mean, why now?"

"It was in the house," I blurted, defensively. "It's not like they told me to."

Richard held very still. "They?"

That was how I came to tell Richard about my discussions with *them*—Tom Harris, Uncle Freddie, and Clarissa. Even under the protection of Richard's promise, however, I omitted mention of Reval Dumas, and Grace, and the trip to the country. I had an instinct that that might push the limits. Instead I spoke about my father's visions, his book, the fact that I was experiencing *visions of pure sense,* and how it was possible my Friend was a demon. I explained that this *proved* I was sane—since I was not really hallucinating—that I was therefore exempt from the proposed one-way trip to Forest Glen.

When I finished, I had the foolish notion that I would somehow be congratulated for single-handedly diagnosing the problem that had eluded the medical professionals. Instead, when I finished, an angry fire lit Richard's eyes.

He started from his chair and picked up the phone.

"Clarissa, this is Richard. Would you come in here for a minute?" He hung up.

My mouth fell open. "Oh my God, what are you doing?"

He stood there, his jaw clenching and unclenching. "I'm sorry, George. This is going to be rough."

"But what about confidentiality?" I cried.

"I told you those rules don't apply if we're talking about life or death. Given what you've told me, I have to take action."

"But I'm not going to hurt anyone!" I pleaded. "I won't endanger anyone!"

He frowned. "Son, that's not what I'm worried about."

"Then—then I don't get it."

"It's that someone's endangering *you*."

Before I could even formulate the next question, a soft tap came at the door. At Richard's word, the door opened, and in its frame stood Clarissa in one of her knee-length dresses—purple mixed with a brown—with a home-knit wool sweater for the cold.

She looked from Richard, to me, back to Richard again.

"George," she nodded at me, in her accustomed, fluttery-eyed greeting. Then, "Richard, what's going on?"

❖   ❖   ❖

Half an hour later my mother arrived at Richard's office.

She stood pale in the doorway, not sure what the lay of the land was. In the room before her, Richard, Clarissa, and I sat in an awkward and cramped semicircle.

"I apologize to everyone for calling you in," said Richard, as my mother sat down to join us. "The circumstances require a little explanation."

He went on to describe the flash card incident with Rachel. Mom's face grew a shade paler as Richard talked, and she threw a probing glance my way. Clarissa sat with her head hanging. She would not look at my mother.

"I asked George what had set him off. He told me it was the card that depicts a black dog barking at a little girl. This is a standard picture in the Thematic Apperception Test, or T.A.T. The patient is supposed to project their feelings onto the picture. George said he associated the black dog," he hesitated, "with the devil. He told me he had read about this in his father's book."

"Good gracious! Where on earth did you get that?" demanded my mother.

"The attic."

"Why did you go rooting for it there?" asked my mother.

Silence.

My mother scanned our faces. "What am I missing?"

Richard continued. "George was referred to the book by his god-father. Apparently, George's godfather, Clarissa, and another professor have been meeting with George. This other professor is in possession of some letters, written by George's father, in which he claims to have had encounters with the devil."

The details were not exactly right, but nobody bothered to correct him. My mother had gone white.

"Am I okay so far?" he said to me.

I nodded.

"When I inquired whether the adults were inclined to believe the letters, George told me they had were—that they had discussed the devil at some length. They warned George about the powers the devil wields over people; and further, they told George that the hallucinations he experiences are akin to his father's religious visions—implying George might be communicating with the devil."

A groan erupted from my mother.

"What are you *doing*?" she said, turning to Clarissa.

"I guess Tom Harris and Freddie must have said some things," Clarissa said helplessly. "All we wanted was to warn George about the hallucinations."

"Warn him? About what?"

Clarissa reddened. "Not to listen to them."

"But why? Because they're the *devil*?" my mother's voice rose incredulously. She covered her eyes with her hands. "This is a nightmare."

Richard took a deep breath.

"George, I apologize to you. You have every right to be upset, angry, disappointed . . . because this," he gestured at the four of us sitting in the room, "violates everything we've established together here with some very hard work."

We sat in silence for a moment. My mother seemed overwhelmed; then she straightened.

"Thank you, Richard," she said.

"I hope I did the right thing."

"Oh you did," she exclaimed. She turned to Clarissa. "I would like some sort of explanation."

Clarissa's head bobbed with emotion. "Joan, we have differences on religion. Paul and I were more in agreement there. I tried to do right by both sides." She pursed her lips. "I'm sorry it worked out like this."

"What about your *professional* responsibility?" persisted my mother.

"In my view I have gone over and above what was called for, both as a professional and a friend," said Clarissa haughtily. "Though I understand it is hard to see it that way right now."

"Yes, it is," said my mother fiercely. She turned to Richard. "Richard . . . what do we do? We're seeing the doctors tomorrow. George has been behaving so well. I have notes from his homeroom teacher. I mean . . . is this going to set us back?"

Richard shook his head. "I view this as a problem with the adults, not with George," he said. "You need to rethink whom you trust with your son's care."

Clarissa stood, her face burning scarlet. She glared at Richard. He stared right back, also flushed, but impassive. Clarissa clomped from the room without a word.

My mother leaned forward. "You're not going to tell the doctors about this?"

Richard looked at me full in the eye, emphasizing his meaning— he was honoring at least this part of his promise. "I don't think it needs to come up."

· · ·

Out in the lobby, Mom knelt down and searched my face, as if looking for scratches and bruises.

"Poor baby," she said. "No wonder."

"Did I do something wrong?"

"I wish you had told me."

"I thought you'd be mad."

"You're damn right I would have been! I'll be calling every one of them."

"Is Clarissa in trouble?"

"I don't know," Mom said. Her voice hardened. "I hope so." She took me by the shoulders. "George, is there anything else?"

"Like what?"

"Has there been anything else like this? Anything you've seen? Anything they've told you?"

I froze. If one discussion about dad's visions provoked this uproar, what would happen if I revealed I'd taken part in an exorcism?

"You know why I'm asking, don't you, George?"

I shook my head.

"Sweetie, this kind of talk . . . about devils and demons and visions . . . this is the kind of thing that gets people *put away*. If we mention any of this to the psychiatrists, it could ruin all your hard work. All those days taking stupid pills for nothing." I blushed, guilty that I'd been sticking them to the wall under my bed. "We've got everything we need for tomorrow. Perfect attendance at school, perfect reports. Richard called me this morning and told me the tests were good. Don't let them take you, George. You're too good for that. You're too good for that." She clenched me to her. I felt her warm breath on my neck. "Please promise me," she whispered in a hoarse voice.

I opened my mouth to speak, but no words came.

"Let's go," she said, suddenly pulling away.

Clarissa had entered the lobby and had drawn up short in the mouth of the corridor, carrying her briefcase. My mother pulled me through the glass doors. Outside the air was inky blue and freezing. Snowflakes were beginning to fall—the tiny hard kind that make *pit-pit* noises when they land. Clarissa emerged from the doors of the clinic behind us.

"Joan!" she called.

"Mom, she's calling you."

"Joan, wait!"

"I hear her," Mom said.

"Joan," Clarissa called again.

"George, get in the car."

I took my seat on the passenger side and glued my eyes to the rearview mirror. As our headlights swept the trees and driveways and the increasingly thick curtain of snow, Clarissa remained a small, forlorn figure under the lights of the clinic vestibule. When we turned the first corner, she disappeared.

My mother kept patting my leg, referring to my *perfect performance,* my grades, the reports from my teachers; kept repeating, *I knew you could do it,* until finally I asked her nervously to please watch the road. In the summertime, the highway over the mountains to Charlottesville afforded splendid views of the lush green valley and the purplish mountains beyond. That morning, a dense fog had settled over the landscape of snow-encumbered firs, and the highway climbed steadily with nothing but white mist on either side and red taillights ahead. At last my mother, sobered by the dangerous driving, dropped the overexcited patter and focused on our journey to our checkup with Dr. Gilloon.

At its peak, the road cut through gulleys of limestone that had been blasted out of the mountainside, leaving long scars. I watched the silent stone walls as we passed. Snow clung to their crags like moss.

When we arrived, however, Mom seemed sprightlier than ever. *What a drive! I need a beer!* She babbled with nervous excitement about taking the afternoon to sightsee, to visit Monticello. Earlier she had drilled me, repeating how I was not to mention Tom Harris or Clarissa or Freddie. I was especially not to mention *that book*. Richard would fudge the fact that I was retaking the T.A.T. Today, everyone agreed, would be the last time in my life I heard the words *residential treatment facility*. If Mom and Richard thought the visit would go smoothly, who was I to disagree?

We sat in the long, white waiting room. A palsied youth repeatedly bellowed a phrase: "*Ta' it off!*" (take it off) as he tried to yank a snow boot from his foot. "That's enough," his mother snapped. An octogenarian man, waxy and spotted, sat in a wheelchair while his middle-aged daughter stroked his hand in silence. My mother was called first. After a time, the nurse in blue scrubs returned. "George," she said. I passed my mother, who stood at a nurses' station filling out forms.

I sat on the examining table. Dr. Gilloon—lean, dark, and brow-furrowed as ever—whipped my chart from the door and scanned it, then peered at me, scrunching his nose to keep his glasses on.

"George Davies. Taking your medication?" he asked brusquely. He face and voice conveyed no recognition. He had rubber bands on his braces. "How are you feeling?"

A battery of questions followed. Seeing anything? Voices? Thinking constantly about anything, anybody? Scribbles on the chart. Did the nurse take blood pressure, weight? No? She can do that afterward. Running behind today. Lots of patients. Therapy helping? Did I like my therapist? No scribbles on that one. Just a nod. "Good, good." Mumbles about my tests. Check, check, with the pencil. "Okay," he said finally. "Let's get your mom back."

My mother returned. We watched the back of Dr. Gilloon's salt-and-pepper head while he hovered in the hallway, momentarily engaged in a whispered conference with a resident—a mole-covered twentysomething fellow with large, perplexed eyes. At last the doctor extracted himself from this conference, and in a single motion, shut the door, and flung himself into his chair.

"Davies, Davies," he said, again fixing on the chart. "He's responding to the Thorazine," pronounced Dr. Gilloon. "Tough doing homework with the medication?" he asked me, a little loudly.

"No, I like homework now," I said.

He shook his head. "Haven't heard that one before. No problems
in school?"

"He's fine. The teachers said so in his reports," broke in my
mother impatiently. "I gave all those to the administrator. He's been
getting As. Perfect attendance."

"Tests from therapist . . . all okay," nodded the doctor. Finally he
pulled his nose out of the chart and spoke to us. "Well. That's the good
news."

"Does that mean there's bad news?"

"Well, yes," said the doctor, double-checking my chart for confirmation. "There's still no spot for him at Forest Glen. I have to
apologize," he said. "Usually they give us an indication of when a
bed's coming available. Makes it easier for everyone to plan. But," he
shrugged, "they have a new director. He's probably bringing old
patients with him and giving them priority. That's how these things
work sometimes, unfortunately . . ."

"Doctor," my mother interrupted. "You said the tests were good."

"That's right." He nodded. "This is the kind of follow-up we hope
for. Means we have the right dosage, and reasonably attentive parents,"
he added, with a clinical callousness.

My mother ignored this. "So why do we care about . . . *Forest
Glen?*" She made it sound like a cheesy air freshener.

"I'm sorry?"

"I can just take George home," she stated.

"Sure. Of course," said the doctor, standing up. "Like I said, I
apologize. You shouldn't have much longer to wait."

"But," said my mother, struggling to clarify, "he doesn't have to go."

Dr. Gilloon's mouth hung open for a moment and his adult braces
stretched their rubber bands. He and my mother faced off now, finally

understanding that after speaking at cross-purposes, they were each confronting an opponent.

"You must have misunderstood," said Dr. Gilloon, in surprise. "George has improved—but due to sedation. He still has to be treated."

"He's practically a star pupil," fumed my mother. "What do the C students get, electroshock?"

"Mrs. Davies," began Dr. Gilloon, controlling a rising impatience. "George's behavior is what we're monitoring—not his skill at long division. He's impulsive and unpredictable. If we don't treat him, there's no telling what could happen."

"So why put us through this?" cried my mother, standing now, agitated and pale. "Why drag us back here just to rub our noses in it?" Her voice cracked with emotion.

Dr. Gilloon's brow furrowed, for once without seeming calculated to make himself seem nicer, or someone else crazier.

"It's Forest Glen or an involuntary solution. I told you that on your last visit." He lowered his voice. "I didn't want to mention this last time, because I didn't foresee how far you would take this. But . . ." He removed his glasses. His eyes peered out at her, green, close-set, and watery; tired eyes; all-nighter eyes. "Do you know what that means for a kid his age? We're talking about juvenile detention. Is that your real preference, for a kid like George? A juvie home?"

My mother recoiled. "He hasn't broken the law."

"The people in the car accident he caused would beg to differ."

"No one's pressed charges."

"*Mrs. Davies,*" he said, exasperated. "You're missing the point."

"*You're* missing the point," said my mother, her voice dry, tense. "I'm not going to let him go."

The argument dragged on. Nurses interrupted, poking their heads in to call him away, but Dr. Gilloon dismissed them curtly, seemingly determined to make my mother understand. He stood, he sat; he cited standards, procedure, medicine, and finally ethics. My mother grew angry. Their voices rose. At last the door opened. It was the young resident with the perplexed eyes, who jerked his thumb over his shoulder. *Time to go.* Dr. Gilloon's shoulders slumped as he took a step toward the door.

"I'll call Richard Manning," he said. "Maybe he can explain this better than I am right now."

"Oh, I understand perfectly," said my mother. "You're supposed to be helping us, but you're telling us we have no options."

He turned back to stare at her.

"*Doctor,*" insisted the resident.

Dr. Gilloon left, shaking his head.

In a few moments my mother and I found ourselves on the cement-and-brick plaza outside the hospital, free of that strange environment which combined airless sterility with the entropy of scuttling caregivers and complaining patients. The cold breeze bit our faces, our fingers. Snow flurries were falling again. A dozen paces from the entrance my mother stopped, as if one last line of argument had struck her, and she was contemplating charging back inside. Her coat hung on her arm. She had forgotten to put hers on. I had never taken mine off.

Hospital workers passed us by. Snowflakes melted on my face and glasses. I waited for my mother.

"Still want to visit Monticello?" I asked weakly. She did not reply.

Racket Ghost

My eyes opened, but I lay rigid. I wondered whether I was being summoned out of sleep by my Friend rapping on the window with a terrible force. No: too far away. It came, a regular, rough banging, from somewhere inside the house. Maybe some pipes had frozen and backed up. I rose from bed and tiptoed to the doorway.

The noise was a scraping sound. It was followed by some form of contact—the banging noise I had heard. The combination made a kind of *swish-boom*. Regular, or semiregular. *Swish-boom. Swish . . . boom. Swishboom.* I stood and peered into the obscurity, toward the bathroom.

My mother's light flipped on. "George?" came her voice. She appeared in her own doorway, bleary and without glasses, wrapping a robe around her. "George? What are you doing up? Is that you making noise?"

"No, Mom," I said.

She stood in confusion for a moment.

"It's coming from down there," I said. I took a step toward the bathroom. The noise grew louder. I reached the doorway and extended my arm into the darkened room and switched on the light.

I saw it first; Mom was still putting on her glasses. The shower door—a glass one in an aluminum frame, the one through which I had first beheld the face of my Friend—was sliding back and forth on its track. *Swish,* it slid; *boom,* it struck the side of its frame. The hundred-watt bulbs in the overhead light burned brightly over this scene. The cheery shade of lime green on the walls smiled down upon it. The dimpled glass of the shower door shimmered in the bulb light as it slid back and forth. *Swish boom. Swishboomswishboom.*

My mother and I simply stared. Then she moved toward me and swept me up in her bathrobe.

"Get in here," she said, and hustled me into her bedroom. She had the sour smell of sleep on her. As she pulled me in, I realized all my limbs were shaking. She slammed the door and locked it.

"Call Tom Harris," I told her. "Call Tom Harris."

She picked up the phone. Her hands were trembling. She dialed once but screwed up.

"Hurry!" I told her.

"You're not helping," she snapped.

She dialed again.

"Hi, it's me. I need you to come over here. Yes, now. It's an emergency. No, right away. Kurt, I can't explain now." She shot a look at me. "No, it's not George," she said more softly. "Come as soon as you can."

In the movies the noise would have stopped after the phone call was made, and the boyfriend would come over and say, *Now now, little lady, what's all this?* thinking we were crazy. But the sound went on and on. The shower door kept sliding and slamming, sliding and slamming. It was a fifteen-minute drive from Kurt's place to our house. We waited in the bedroom listening to the noise, Mom in her big blue chair, me on the bed. With the light from the bedside reading lamp, I noticed the framed prints on Mom's wall: a series of seashells, and one of a Vitruvian façade. Some stockings were laid over the arm of her wicker rocking chair. In here the sound was muffled and persistent like a prisoner digging his way out of the next cell with a pick. We both sat, ashen. But eventually we made conversation. Our words were clipped; the sentences seemed to die in the charged atmosphere.

"Did it wake you?" Mom asked me.

"Why do you think I was *up*?" I said. "Didn't you hear it?"

"Yes. But I was deep asleep. Tired."

Swish boom, swish boom.

"What do you think it is?"

"I don't know. I guess we have some sort of poltergeist." Her lips were very dry.

"Poltergeist means 'racket ghost,'" I volunteered.

"Yes, it does."

We were silent for a time then.

"It's getting worse," I said.

The sound had changed. It was no longer *swish-boom* but *boom . . . boom . . . boom.* The door was slamming itself against the aluminum frame with increasing violence. We could feel the impact through the wall.

"Should we stop it?" I asked. She shot me a sudden suspicious glance, as if to say, *You know how to stop it?* For an instant I was George the mental patient again. "You know, put some towels there so it doesn't break."

"You mean the glass could shatter," she said, understanding me.

"Yeah."

"That's a good idea."

Neither of us moved.

"I don't think I want to go in there," Mom said.

"Okay," I said. I stayed seated—I sure wasn't going in without her. Mom came and sat next to me on the bed and put her arm around me.

Finally the doorbell buzzed. Mom leapt up and tied her robe around her. "You stay here," she said. She took a deep breath and opened the door. *Bang, bang.* The noise sounded like a team of workmen with hammers.

"I'm coming, too."

"No, stay here."

A minute later I heard footsteps, then a soft knock. I cracked the door open and saw Kurt, my mother behind him.

"Hiya George," he said. He wore his usual smile, but his eyes were puffy and his hair was tousled. He was bundled in a flannel-lined jacket, and he wore pajama bottoms with snow boots. "Anything going on in here?" he said looking around, meaning the ghost.

"No, 's quiet here," I said.

"Okay."

I held the bedroom door open to watch. Kurt faced the bathroom, transfixed. *Bang*. The shower door jerked again. My mom peered at him anxiously.

"Never seen anything like this," said Kurt with a nervous laugh.

He advanced toward the bathroom and the shower door.

"Don't!" my mom shouted. But in my head I urged him on. Someone had to cope; Kurt was the man; Kurt was coping. He inched forward—perhaps half expecting the shower door to attack—until he stood a foot away, my mother and I trailing behind him. Then, slowly, he leaned forward and extended his meaty-fingered hand to catch the door.

The shower door stopped.

Kurt stood upright, puzzled, but pleased. I think he was about to make some joking remark like *Problem solved!* the way you do when a radio "fixes" itself the moment after you've given up fiddling; but another sound stopped him: the creak of glass on chrome. He took a step closer.

"Come away from there, honey," said my mother. It was the first time she'd used a term of affection for Kurt in front of me. But I had no time to dwell on it. Kurt moved a half step back. The door was banging again now, but not along the traces. It slammed against them. Invisible hands rocked it back and forth with increasing force, pressing it outward from the center of the glass, giving it a convex belly.

Suddenly the glass exploded like a starburst into tiny fragments. Before I closed my eyes to duck away from the flying glass, I registered an image, a snapshot of Kurt, big belly and back nearly filling the door frame, one arm crooked around his face as the glass pellets flew and stuck to his hair and clothes, bounced off him and scattered across the tile, making a hundred tiny scratches.

Like people fleeing a tornado, we hastily dressed and packed socks and toothbrushes and a day's worth of clothes into bags. We piled through the front door, with me in the lead. Crossing the front porch in the cold dark, I noticed Kurt and Mom stop and spin around sharply.

"Come on," I said. "What is it?"

They frowned.

"Nothing," said Kurt firmly.

But I didn't take orders from Kurt yet. "What *is* it?" I said, and pushed past him back into the house. "What . . .?" I was about to ask again, then stopped, because I heard it. The aluminum frame of the shower door was sliding again, without the glass, regular as an industrial machine.

Kurt set down his bags. "I'll take a look . . ."

"Leave it," said Mom. "Just leave it."

Kurt's place overlooked the green and sluggish James River. Sycamores curved over the water like white stalks. From one of them—a thick-trunked monster that jutted over the stream at a forty-five-degree angle—dangled the frayed end of a rope swing. Planks had been nailed to the tree's skin as crude ladder rungs. In summer a tire would be tied to the the rope. County folk would park their trucks along the roadside and line up to leap from a hump in the tree trunk, swinging out over the river and splashing into the deep water.

But now, in wintertime, the river formed the frigid border between county and town. On the county side lay floodplains of brown grass, then fences, then a hinterland of sandy-colored hills. On the town side rose the machicolations of Fort Virginia, protected by a sheer, lichenous cliff face.

Kurt's home was a split-level, sleek and modern with a vaguely Frank Lloyd Wright hill-hugging sprawl. The entry hall was hung with photos: Kurt skiing with pals, grinning under black goggles. A collie. A collage of nephews. An older woman—his mother?—with a hair-sprayed white coif, pearl earrings, and a frown.

The hall gave way to a vaulted living room supported by beams. Sliding glass doors looked onto a shallow backyard. We dumped our bags on the floor, peeled off our coats. My mother went upstairs to change.

"George, you'll be okay on the couch down here, won't you?" asked Kurt.

The sofa in question smelled new, with oversized beige cushions that seemed commodious enough for three. I eagerly accepted and quickly prepared to bunk down.

Then it hit me.

"Where are you guys sleeping?" I asked.

"Your mother and I are sleeping upstairs," Kurt said evenly.

On the way over, we had chattered excitedly about the shower door. My mother joked that she would call the historical society in the morning to have them add our place to the local ghost-story tour; Kurt sent shivers up our spines suggesting, in a dramatic voice, that a prior resident had hanged himself in the basement. We shouted him down— *No, stop it! Too scary!*—and giggled with nerves and late-night excitement. Now I felt a sense of dread.

"No ghosts out here, that's for sure," Kurt was saying. "This house was built just ten years ago. One owner. A tax lawyer. Ectoplasmic reading of zero."

My mother padded downstairs in robe and slippers. She shooed Kurt away, fished in our overnight bag, and produced the pajamas I had started the evening with—blue flannel with fire engines. I changed. She bedded me down as only a mother can, with tender efficiency.

"You okay?" She stroked my hair.

"Mom?" I said tentatively. "Do you believe it now, too?"

"Believe what?" Her voice dropped twenty degrees.

"About the demon?" I waited, heart beating.

Her stroking stopped. She seemed to drift into reverie, reliving the instant the door shattered. "This would get me to believe it, if anything would," she said.

"It would?" I sat up on one elbow, excited. "Tom Harris says they have power over matter," I said. "*Bodies, faces, furniture.* That's what he said."

"George, we talked about that," she said warningly. "You're not to mention that again."

"But—but you saw what happened," I pleaded.

"We've got an old house. These things happen," she said crisply. She patted the pillow. "Come on. Sleepy time."

"But Mom." I lay back down. "I thought I could talk about demons. I'm going to Forest Glen anyway."

"Exactly," she said grimly. "And I want you coming back from Forest Glen, too."

She dimmed the lights. After a time I drifted to sleep in the clean, new-furniture smell of the pillows, thinking of her parting words to me: *We're okay, now,* she said. *Kurt will protect us. We had a scare, that's all.*

When I woke it was some time later—a few minutes, an hour—and I heard them. First, my mother giggling warmly, then Kurt's deeper tones in a murmur, then the wet smack of kissing. I strained to hear, fascinated, my heart beating. But soon the sounds changed. I put the pillow over my ears. I couldn't stand to listen. *She doesn't care that my father's gone* was all I could think. *She doesn't care.* I tossed on the sofa, trying to get comfortable; attempting, impossibly, to find a position where I could not hear the sounds of their lovemaking; hoping they would hear me tossing and turning, that they would stop and realize the shame of what they were doing. But it seemed to last forever. Their gasps, the bed creaking, grew louder. Finally I threw the bedclothes off me, determined to do something. I would scream. I would turn on the brightest lights and accuse them, to their flushed and sticky faces, of how rotten they were, how my father, my father . . . I stood in the center of the living room, trembling with anger.

In the sliding glass doors I saw my reflection: heaving chest, disheveled hair. But there was something wrong. A malevolent grin spread across the face in the reflection. I touched my face. My reflection did not.

You left Saint Michael at home came a familiar voice. *Poor George.*

"What are you doing here?" I said aloud.

What are you *doing here?* he echoed mockingly.

"We're here because there's a poltergeist in our house."

My Friend seemed to grow at these words and become more vivid. I saw him no longer as a reflection, but as a flesh-and-blood child—ragged and dirty in his pajamas. He stood in the frost-covered grass, just beyond the glass doors. I no longer heard the moans of the two grown-ups upstairs. I only heard the shimmering, ethereal voice in my ears. I stared at the figure standing in the moonlight in Kurt's backyard, an inch from the glass door, his breath making fog on the glass.

I meant what are you *doing* here? He shook his head sadly, pityingly. *They don't want you, George. Listen to what they're doing.*

I knew what I was supposed to do: say your prayers. But the one I knew best, the Lord's Prayer, seemed remote, fragmentary, only guessable: the phone number of a friend who had long since moved away.

They don't want you, he said.

Suddenly he stood next to me. No longer separated by the glass, he reached over with his hand—fingers grubby, nails bitten and bloody—and clutched his fingers over my chest. I could scarcely breathe. Tom Harris's words returned to me. *They can make a heart . . . stop.* My forehead broke into a cold sweat.

I will die here, I thought. *I will die here and they won't know because of what they're doing.*

They don't want you, my Friend whispered close, in my ear.

I searched in one final frantic effort for a prayer, but merely swooned. His lips kept moving next to my ear, hissing long, circular, hypnotic phrases. I listened, I argued and defended, but I was swimming against a tide. The circuitous debate lasted until finally, too exhausted to remember when or how, I crawled back under the covers, trembling and chilled, and fell into a bleak unconsciousness.

March, This Year

The fluorescent lights in our corridor flickered. Odd, how in only a month our apartment building could change. The striped carpet was the same. The unreliable lighting was the same. It was I who had transformed into an interloper. When I saw our neighbors—the roly-poly Wall Street couple, the gay mountain-biking fanatic—I grinned and waved, but they held up a cautious hand in greeting, offered a dubious smile. They knew Maggie and I had split. They appraised my two-day scruff, my change from suit-man to sweatshirt-guy. They thought, *trouble.* Now I stood in the hall, outside my own apartment, holding a thick manila envelope. I saw the locked doors and the empty hall from the point of view of a delivery boy, an exile, a thief. And I waited.

Maggie turned the corner. When she saw me, she came to a full stop.

"What are you doing here?"

"I wanted to talk to you," I said.

"There's nothing to talk about," she said. "You should go."

This resolved, she withdrew her keys—a big tangle in a red leather pouch—and charged the door, studiously picking out her key to avoid eye contact.

"Listen," I said. "I'm working with the psychiatrist, like we said." But she plunged the key into the door. "I'm just not going fast enough." She turned the bolt. Started to pick out key number two. "Stop it!" I said.

I grabbed her hand. She jerked it away, face white with fury. I often wished she would go red like the other Irish—her livid anger spooked me.

"Get off."

"There's stuff you don't know about me," I said. "I'm staying away from him for a reason."

"I'm glad you're gone," she said spitefully. "It's better."

I stepped back, wounded. She fumbled for the second key, hands shaking now. This violent separation from the past was too much to bear. Maggie and I opening this door together hundreds of times. Giddy. Grumpy. Drunk. Stamping snow off our boots. Sun-baked and sweaty. Maggie bending at the waist, *Hurry, I gotta pee so bad.* With shopping bags. With new furniture. With friends. With her gentleness and patience and beauty, Maggie had redeemed me once—from the rootless misery of a volatile, self-loathing youth. Why couldn't she pull that trick again? Yet here I was, stale-smelling and red-eyed, pulling at her like a beggar. I was Grendel, a monster gazing longingly at a campfire from my place in the woods. The past seemed so close. I wished to reach out, dip my hand into that other dimension, be her husband again, rewind back to our first date at an East Village bar, drinking dirty martinis and swiveling on barstools like kids.

I gripped Maggie's face with both hands. I forced a kiss on her. It worked. The sensations returned: her full lips, her scent—same perfume, I noted—the nearby jangle of earring, the tickle of her curly hair, her presence, her aura, the slight clamminess from a ride on the subway, the end-of-day fatigue . . . it was all still there—a destination in itself, a place where I'd been happy.

But Maggie jerked away with a cry of outrage. She bumped her head against the door, hard. Almost instantly, the door popped open—the babysitter must have heard us arguing and had been standing there waiting for some signal to intervene. Maggie staggered backward. The babysitter drew her in. Then the door banged shut. It was over in three seconds.

Our neighbor—the Merrill Lynch broker—opened her door to peep. I hung my head and said nothing. I dropped the envelope on Maggie's doorstep. *Let her send me another set, if she wants it so bad.*

⚜ ⚜ ⚜

"I got the papers in the mail. I'm the defendant in our divorce," I explained. "I've hired a lawyer." I sighed.

"I'm sorry to hear that," you said, with feeling. "Are you okay? You seem a little run-down."

I had hit bottom, I told you. My wife had kicked me out of the house. I had hoped that the situation would be temporary. Now I commuted to your office from my friend's couch in Brooklyn, shuffling to the Q train in the frigid, predawn dark along with the Mexican day laborers heading to construction sites in Manhattan in their jeans and workboots. I regarded them guiltily. They were poor, didn't speak English, and worked like horses to send money home to family. I was white and college educated, but something invisible prevented me from holding my child and sharing a bed with my wife who lived in the same city. In the subway that morning I had rested my head on the window and with burning eyes read the ads for cheesy dermatologists (*Call Dr. K!*) and personal injury lawyers (*Work Injury? Fleischer & Dietz Will Get You $$*), and next to them, a public service ad called Poetry in Motion, presenting a few lines of Dante's *Inferno* for the edification of commuters, embedded in decorative computer graphics:

> *When I had journeyed half our life's way*
> *I found myself in a darkened wild,*
> *for I had wandered from the true road.*

This was my fourth visit in our new "early slot." You handed me coffee in a big colored mug. You always gave me milk, which I don't take, but I never corrected you. It was our new ritual.

"Well, I'm glad you manage to come here," you said. "It shows you're still working toward your goal."

"I think," I said, "I've forgotten what that is."

"To reclaim your family," you said firmly, "and your right to reenter it."

"It's too late!" I groaned. "And I have no energy to fight it. No . . . *will.* I'm going to lose them, and I'm immobile. Exhausted."

"Maybe you're exhausted because you're doing heavy emotional work," you said. "You need to be realistic. These journals you're giving me—there are serious incidents here. Going to a mental hospital? Possessed by demons?" You stared at me. "You weren't aware of any of this?"

"I told you," I said lamely. "I hadn't thought about it in a while."

"And you thought you were just going to muck the stables in your journals, but keep wearing your nice neat neckties during the day?" I didn't answer. "People don't come here to use the tissues, George. They come here to work. It's going to exhaust you."

"I thought it was supposed to make me happy."

You blinked, then without a hint of irony, said: "Not necessarily."

"Great."

You fidgeted a moment, as if conflicted over your next words.

"What do *you* think about what you're writing, George?" you said at length. "Do you believe you were possessed?"

They were the facts as far as I knew, I told you—memories recollected, as if seen through a camera, with the film already beginning to fade around the edges. How could I know what had caused those facts to happen?

"You're presenting the thesis about demon possession as if you believed it."

"I did at the time," I said carefully.

"Okay," you said. "What about now? Do you believe what you're writing in your journals?"

"I'm writing what happened," I said.

"You're writing what you remember," you corrected.

"Fine, sure," I said. "It's a memory. Subject to interpretation."

"Sometimes a new interpretation is what's required to move forward."

"New interpretation of what?"

"Of you! George Davies and the universe he lives in."

"George Davies, divorced washout," I grunted. You blinked in annoyance—you had grown severe about these self-deprecating asides. "Okay," I conceded, "help me out."

"Am I a victim?" you persisted, rhetorically. "Did a *demon* make me miserable? Or do I take responsibility? How can I expect my family to forgive me, if I can't forgive myself?"

I threw up my hands. "Forgive myself for *what*?"

"Ah," you said, with your sphinxlike smile. "For starters ... inducing psychosis in others. *Folie à plusieurs,* if you prefer the French."

I shook my head. "Remind me how this helps with my divorce?"

"Hear me out," you persisted.

I sighed. "Go ahead."

"*Folie à plusieurs* means madness of many. It's when a dominant figure forms a delusional belief and imposes it on others. I see this in the stories from your journals."

"We're talking about me? When I was eleven?" I asked skeptically. "A dominant figure?"

"Children can be powerful inducers of delusion," you retorted. "For children, imagination and reality intersect. When a kid offers you an imaginary ice cream cone, he expects you to take a lick. Get the flavor wrong, and he'll correct you. Sometimes you see children get the upper hand over adults this way. The child's imaginative belief is so powerful, it makes the grown-ups doubt where the boundaries are."

At last your reasoning became clear. "You're saying I manipulated these people," I said, incredulous. "Around the demon idea."

"You created a shared delusion."

"Why would I do that?"

"It would have been preferable to the alternative."

"Which was?"

"Accepting that you were angry and destructive. That maybe you still are . . . a danger to yourself or others. Your feelings of guilt would explain the repression. But why is it coming to light now?" you asked. "Who are you afraid of endangering, George? Your son? Is that why you're afraid to touch him?"

"I don't know," I said. I found myself short of breath. "I'm afraid I'm a danger or afraid I'm still . . . a link to the demons."

You took this in. "If you were afraid of demons, you would take him to a priest," you said. "Instead *you're* staying away. Can't touch him, be near him. I'd say you were more afraid of *you*."

My heart thumped in my chest.

You tapped your finger, ruminating on something. "Would it change your point of view," you said, "if you believed demons didn't exist? Or no—scratch that. If you believed *you* had never been possessed? When you were eleven?"

I raised my hands in frustration. "My father's friends—they were the ones to make the demon interpretation, not me," I said.

"I'm not so sure about that."

"Well, whatever. These were adults. Scholars. An eleven-year-old can't lead a bunch of PhDs around by the nose."

"They were predisposed to believe you due to their religious and intellectual convictions. As a gifted child, you perceived that." You watched me for a reaction, but I merely blinked. "Your father was their friend, too. And even adults want explanations, George—for grief, for loss. Someone's got to set the rules. Would you rather live in a universe of ambiguity, or one where your ice cream cone is *strawberry?*"

"This went on for months," I objected. "People were hurt."

"The greater the commitment to the fantasy. 'If I turn back now, all this suffering would have been for nothing.'"

"So you think I was a rotten kid. Is that what you're saying?"

"I've treated eleven-year-old rape victims who become eleven-year-old seductresses," you said. "Trauma and loss of innocence can have unpredictable effects. Children are not always weakened. They learn to protect themselves."

"No," I said, shaking my head in frustration. "I loved those people. They were family friends."

"Then ask yourself: Why am I struggling so much?"

You waited for me to answer, but I had none to offer. You spoke clearly but urgently, like a teacher speaking to child.

"If you hurt someone you hate, there's no conflict. If you hurt someone you love . . . there's conflict. Conflict in here," you said, pointing to your head. "In here," you said, reaching across the gap between us and making a fist to represent my heart. "It causes people trouble, makes them seek help. Do you understand?" To my surprise, you gave me a lopsided, apologetic smile. "I see it in all my patients, George. Getting at that pain is harder than anybody imagines."

I said nothing. I felt dizzy.

After a moment, you relented, reclined in your chair. "I'm being direct with you, George."

"I know. I asked for it."

"I want you to be direct with me."

"Okay." But there was suspicion in my voice.

"I want to go back to my original question," you said. And then you repeated, emphatically: "Do you believe what you're writing?"

Now I understood what you were asking. All I had to do was confess that the demons weren't real, that I had manipulated the grown-ups, done all the deeds myself; and then renounce any religious claim to an overarching, defining force in all this. *I believe in one God, the Father, the Almighty,* I began reciting, mischievously, in my head. But I knew: that wouldn't go over in here. In the presence of your enlightened, sympathetic prying, even I wanted badly to surrender my faith and my memories; just release; let go; say to myself, it was all a dream; it was all

folie à plusieurs. Your expression implored me to join you: the wilder-
ness guide, reaching for the client who's tumbled into the drink.

It's nothing but a sophisticated superstition, that expression seemed to
say. *You've internalized the religious logic, George, and my slightest suggestion that you "give it up" could rack you with guilt—and destroy my credi-
bility. But can't you see how, as a doctor, it's my obligation to free you from
this? There are no monsters out there, George. There is only human kindness, and the struggle against life's troubles. You've got it hard enough. Don't
complicate things.*

How could I resist? I was seeking your help, your skills.
These were founded on medical science, medical training—secular
knowledge. Your world (as I perceived it in these sessions) represented
the Enlightened Good Life—education, competence, prosperity—a
French garden of secular virtues. My religious beliefs, on the
other hand, splashed on the walls a wild spectacular of fear and hope.
Christ heaving and bleeding on the cross. Demons feasting on souls as
they plunge into hell. The ecstasy that might one day lift us from the
grave.

Between the two, a lonely vacuum yawned, where neither set of
rules applied. Depression. Lousy marriages. The conformist game of
corporate life. That baseline throb of anxiety in a city where you fought
crowds for every job, every apartment, even a spot near the pole on the
subway.

If you keep fighting on both fronts, you seemed to say, *the physical and
metaphysical, you will lose. Choose your real life.* Your hand reached for
me. I wanted to take it. Did it come to this—that if I were to accept all
the good you could offer me, I must also accept, as a whole, the world-
view that supported it?

"My father used to quote Shakespeare on this one," I said, a
conflicted smile torturing my face. "And I never heard a better way to
put it."

"Let's hear it," you said.

*"There are more things in heaven and earth, Horatio, than are dreamt
of in your philosophy."*

I watched for your reaction. Would you attack me with more debate? Delight in my choice quotation?

Instead you nodded, without smiling. You had been expecting this. Your eyes fell to the floor . . . you were looking away. Why? With shame? In defeat? More, I think now, with resignation. Another client drowned.

The Letters

Kurt and my mom puttered and babbled in the kitchen. They were still excited from the events of the night before. Our midnight escape from a fixture-smashing ghost now seemed more like an adventure than a nightmare—at least it did from the perspective of Kurt's kitchen, with steam licking the rim of his shiny black coffeemaker, and amid the cheerful clank of their breakfast preparations: Mom sifting flour, Kurt cracking eggs.

"Where's the baking soda?" asked Mom.

"Cabinet," Kurt said, and moved to show her. His hand went to her lower back. "Pancakes, George," he said. "How 'bout it?"

I stood in the doorway glaring at my feet, unable to face them after overhearing them the night before.

"I want to go to church," I declared.

A final egg smacked the side of a bowl, and their patter ceased. They turned to look at me—a small, angry boy with circles under his eyes—and exchanged a glance.

Preston scarcely stirred awake at 10:00 A.M. on a winter Sunday. We sat at traffic lights alone. My mother turned on the radio, but I snarled in a nasty way, and she punched the button off. My eyelids felt red and itchy from lack of sleep. Sensing my foul mood, she said nothing until the car at last came to a halt at the end of Early Avenue.

"Why do you want to go to church all of a sudden?" asked my mother. "Is it because of the ghost?"

Before us stood the Jubal Early Memorial Church. Its blocky, rough-hewn stone walls seemed almost to fade into the gray day, as if the building had risen out of the ground and its front were the mouth of a cave. This forbidding place seemed nearly as ominous as the appearance of any poltergeist.

"I hope it's not because of what Clarissa and the others told you," she persisted. "Remember, I want you to keep your distance from them. Do you hear me?"

We sat in silence for another moment in the pale morning light.

"Will you come with me?" I asked finally. *If she says yes, and comes, I told myself, everything will be okay; it means she still loves my father; it means the poltergeist will go away; it means my Friend will leave me alone because everyone in our house believes in God and we will be like a tight, well-defended fort. It will mean my mother can believe me, if she tries.* I hoped all this fervently, recited it to myself like the prayer that had failed me the night before.

My mother wavered. "Kurt offered to help move some of our things out of the house," she said at last. "He needs help."

I slumped. Always the good reason.

I glumly received my mother's kiss and her reminder, *I'll pick you up at 12:30,* and entered the courtyard. As I climbed the familiar steps, I took a program from the usher. *Last Sunday of Pentecost,* it read, with a spidery line drawing of the Jubal Early spire.

The habitual mix of church folk made their way up the broad stone stairs. Widows in hats and elbow gloves, clutching the cast-iron rail; professors in herringbone jackets and khaki pants, their wives' graying hair cut in sexless mop-tops; their daughters behind them, self-conscious before the eyes of their friends, some fluffed and hairbanded, others chunky, in braces, praying for invisibility. Fort Virginia cadets marched to their seats in a dress uniforms with black-billed officers' caps under their arms; and alongside them, the Early students in their own uniform: blue blazers, pale blue Brooks Brothers shirts with button-down collars and red ties. Some were slim-waisted, lacrosse-y, heroic figures from a Housman poem drawing glances from their professors' daughters; others were red-eyed and puffy with beer fat, carrying an air of smug debauchery as if they were even then hatching their first white-collar crimes. Finally came the Episcopalian oddballs, the loners: Uncle Freddie, hulking in a thick tweed jacket, fidgety and formal; Mr. Newton, the languid and asexual organist; Dr. Patricia Burke, the first lady medical doctor of Preston, prematurely widowed (car accident) but beatifically kind; and giant Tom Harris, laboring in cast and crutches under his greatcoat, assisted by Clarissa and Lionel Bing, whose daughters, already bursting with boredom and underutilized IQ, trudged behind with shifting eyes and fingers like radicals searching for something to bomb. We all stood.

The Lord be with you.

And also with you.

Lift up your hearts.

We lift them up to the Lord.

Let us give thanks to the Lord our God.

It is right to give him thanks and praise.

It is meet, right, and a joyful thing, always and everywhere to give thanks to you . . .

So it began, and warmth and relief spread through me. Was it enough to banish the lingering sensation of my Friend's fingers on my chest? I was not sure. The church's vault of dark beams rose above us, the choir sang, and the messy-haired acolytes shuffled at the rails. I had missed the ancient and mysterious movements of the clergy, *passed down,* as my father had told me, *from the first days of the Temple in Jerusalem. Actual cattle were sacrificed back then,* he told me; *slaughtered behind the screen. Their blood ran into a gutter at the priests' feet.* Our rector, a high-church Anglican, made certain the altar was draped in some rich fabric every week—embroidered, my father told me, by two sisters in Blacksburg—that was studded with ornamental beads and scales, and stitched with Latin formulations, VENIAT REGNUM TUUM or simply GLORIA GLORIA GLORIA, on top of which shimmered the silver Eucharistic plate. The priest and assistants, arrayed in the same fabric—today a warm, silky pink with gold lining—prepared the altar for the Eucharist. They trundled in a row, from one end to the other, the rector in the center carrying the censer and bathing the altar in sweet smoke, the assistants on either side holding his robe. Then an acolyte took the censer and gently swung it toward the rector, three times; to the assistant priest, twice; to the deacon, once. The assistant bowed to the choir; they bowed in return; then he swung the thurible toward them on its long chain. The motions were repeated for the congregation, and the clanging censer left a cloud of smoke whose pungency lingered, crawled under the pews, and faded. The grandness and nobility of this exchange again reminded me of my father, and the incense seemed to carry with it another set of smells: powder, shaving lotion, and mothballs. These were my father's Sunday odors, the whiff of pocket handkerchiefs and stored suits. I felt indescribably lonely. I had never been to church alone before. I turned and spotted Uncle Freddie just a few rows away and got up and pushed my way into his pew.

"Whew!" he said.

"What?"

"You smell to high heaven," he said. "Have you bathed?"

"I need to talk to you," I whispered.

But Uncle Freddie frowned, then shushed me. "You can't sit here," he said. "Your mother's forbidden it—*no contact*. She called all of us."

I drew back from him. My mother had telephoned everyone? She meant it, then, about staying away. I cast a nervous eye around the church. It held two dozen folks who knew both my mother and Uncle Freddie—and Clarissa, and Tom Harris—who might report us. I fought back a frantic, weepy feeling. Now who could I turn to? I looked for Tom Harris, whom I saw in the back, next to the Bings. He appeared to listen to the service attentively, but I sensed a deeper scowl on his face than usual. My mother had called him, too.

"But something's happened," I said. *"The visions came back."*

Uncle Freddie ground his jaw—his way of digesting unwelcome information. "Wait for me in the side court after the service. We'll talk then." Then he scrunched up his face. "You really are ripe, sonny," he whispered, fanning himself with the program.

The courtyard, a twelve-foot circle of slate paving stones between the church and the church office building, had been speckled with the rotten remains of horse chestnuts and ginkgo leaves. I sat waiting on its single bench, an ornate, cast-iron affair under the black boughs of several trees. My watch read 12:11. Only a few minutes until my mother returned for me. Where was Uncle Freddie?

At last he appeared, cheeks puffing, as if he had been growing more and more flustered about my news over the past hour.

"As I say, I can't talk to you," he declared. "I've been expressly forbidden."

I opened my mouth to tell the story when Tom Harris appeared on his crutches, followed by Clarissa. They soon surrounded me—a wall of wool coats and somber expressions.

"Is it true Mom called you?" I asked them.

"It's true," said Uncle Freddie. "And if we interfere again, there will be consequences."

"She's going to punish me?"

"Not you, ass," boomed Uncle Freddie. "Us. For one, she's talked of calling the state agency that oversees licenses for clinical psychology. That is no laughing matter."

I looked at Clarissa and my heart sank.

"I'm a grown-up and I make my own decisions," remarked Clarissa stolidly, eyes fluttering in her usual way.

Tom Harris spoke: "Freddie tells us the visions have returned."

I nodded.

"Tell your doctor right away. And Richard," said Clarissa. "That's the way things have to be now. Promise you'll do that?"

"You can't help?" I said, incredulous.

Uncle Freddie shook his head. "It's impossible."

My eyes shot all around the courtyard—anywhere but into the eyes of the family friends who could no longer speak to me. I had put Clarissa's job in jeopardy. My mother had forbidden my own godfather to speak to me. It was worse than being unpopular at school—it felt like exile. I looked up and saw Tom Harris studying me.

"You'll be all right, George. Your mother's a smart woman."

I nodded, miserable.

A pause followed. They shuffled in their places. But no one left.

"Is there more to it, George?" asked Tom Harris.

"Yes."

He sighed. "Go on."

Reluctantly, haltingly—was I breaking rules even now by telling them?—I recounted our clash with the poltergeist.

"Your mother saw this, too?" inquired Clarissa, when I had finished.

I insisted she had.

"Then it's up to her to deal with it," interjected Uncle Freddie.

Tom Harris eased himself onto the bench alongside me, as if suddenly weary. "Freddie," he said, "you know what a poltergeist really is."

Uncle Freddie turned red. "It doesn't matter, Tom. It's no longer our affair."

"You don't believe that."

"A poltergeist is a racket ghost," I offered.

"That's just a translation," said Uncle Freddie impatiently. "A translation of a misnomer. What does a poltergeist do?"

"Breaks things."

"Is that what ghosts do?"

I thought about this. "I don't know."

"Ghosts are apparitions. Echoes of the malcontented dead. They don't smash up your bathroom," he exclaimed. "Only a demon can do that."

I looked to Tom Harris for confirmation. "Don't you remember?" he said patiently. "They have power over matter. No ghost has that. Freddie's right."

"Of course I'm right," huffed Freddie.

"We've got to do it."

The three of us looked at Clarissa. She wore an odd expression: chin in the air, lips in a tight line, face pale, but firm.

"Do what?" Freddie asked her.

"The exorcism," she stated.

"Are you *mad*?" said Uncle Freddie. "You'll lose your license—at best. At worst, we'll lose our souls, or get shredded with a mattress spring like that young priest in Manassas. When is your friend, Finley Balcomb, coming?" he demanded of Tom Harris. "George needs someone experienced. Not *us*."

"Finley, I've discovered," said Tom Harris archly, "is on a cruise in the Turks and Caicos with members of his conversation club. He is unreachable. And when it comes to experience, speak for yourself."

"Well, we can't ask the rector here, or any priest for that matter," continued Freddie, undeterred. "Any clergy will ask for Joan's permission. And quite rightly."

"Why do I need an exorcism all of a sudden?" I asked, controlling the tremor in my voice.

"Because the demon wishes to kill you," said Tom Harris evenly. "This is how it happens. The obsession, the visions, the penetration of the mind. Breaking physical objects. Then . . . breaking the body."

I thought of the twisted curtain rod in Grace's bedroom. Her body transforming into a snake. Sound seemed to drain out of the air. All I heard was the echo of Tom Harris's voice in my head: *kill you.*

"That's enough," snapped Clarissa, tough again. "It's a simple solution. We do it or we don't. And we have to do it. Right now."

"The time is right," Tom Harris said quietly.

"Isn't there a practitioner available?" I squeaked.

"Reval Dumas is in Chicago. We can't go through the church. But we do have Clarissa," he smiled. "Our personal deacon." He reached over, put a long finger under my chin, and lifted it until I looked him in the eye. "We're all in this together now, George. Will you trust us one last time?"

My breath made a mist in the damp winter air, then faded among the blue-gray stones of the church and the stink of rot from the ginkgo leaves. I looked from face to face: pale, puffy, and, except for Tom Harris, frightened.

"George?"

Someone was calling my name. The others heard it, too. I rose, passed between the three friends, and peered into the churchyard. Kurt stood there, in baggy blue jeans and a wrinkled cotton shirt, among the congregation's stragglers. They eyed him curiously. He couldn't see me.

"George."

I wanted to run to him: my hero and my buddy. Kurt who was brave enough to touch the shower door before it smashed. Kurt who had rescued us from the poltergeist. But then I remembered last night: the sticky smacking of kisses. The murmured phrases: *You're a beautiful woman.* My mother's giggle. I felt the boil of a jealous anger: they didn't want me anyway. They didn't need me. Maybe Kurt was searching for me because the call had finally come: it was time to take me away; a bed had come open at last at Forest Glen. Or maybe the game had changed. Maybe my mother's arguments had cost us my spot— Dr. Gilloon was punishing us—and our sights were now fixed on Commonwealth Juvenile Correction Center, where I would see my mother once a week, during a sixty-minute visiting period; where I would be limited to five-minute calls home; have no personal property; and where I would certainly no longer have contact with Tom Harris, Clarissa, or my godfather. And if my confinement was not today— well, it might be tomorrow, or the next day. Clarissa was right. The only time to do this was now.

"We'll leave the back way," I said. "So no one sees us."

Tom Harris held out his hand to me. He did not smile, but his eyes shone bright and clear. I took his hand, helped pull him to his feet. Then we turned away from the street and walked among the blackened trees and soggy, snow-covered leaves, down the slope to Uncle Freddie's waiting car.

We sat in a circle in the musty, dim living room at Tom Harris's. Our host sat on the sofa; Clarissa, in her Sunday dress—a long, paisleyed hybrid of sundress and frock—poised on a stool like a prehistoric bird. She held a crucifix that Tom Harris had rummaged from a desk, but unlike Reval Dumas, she wore no stole. Meanwhile Uncle Freddie paced by the bookshelves, scanning the titles nervously. Tom Harris chewed his cheek distractedly as he reviewed the stapled pages of a leftover Reval Dumas prayer packet. *I asked him to leave these,* Tom Harris had said with a wink. *Had a feeling.* We sat in awkward silence; four friends with big plans, embarassed now that the moment had arrived.

"Come on," burst out Freddie at last. "It's getting late."

"Should we postpone?" I said hopefully.

"Working tomorrow," said Clarissa, shaking her head. "Family in town next weekend."

"Oh, perhaps they could join us?" joked Tom Harris.

"This is ridiculous," broke in Freddie. "Are we going to do this or aren't we?"

"Clarissa?"

"We're doing it," she said. Then, casually: "Gentlemen, I need a moment alone with George."

The two men exchanged a look, then in unison headed toward a back room, Tom Harris throwing off an afghan and creaking to his feet with the usual crutch theatrics. "Whenever you're ready," he said, thumping out of the room.

"I've done these before, George, as an assistant," said Clarissa, still perched on her stool. "I'm not a neophyte. You don't need to worry about that. What you need to worry about is holding tight to your brains, and staying cool."

"Okay," I said. So much adrenaline coursed through my veins, my muscles practically jerked of their own accord. My fingertips were ice cold. Clarissa's body language, however, told me the conversation had not concluded with this pep talk. She seemed uncomfortable—a little girl caught in a transgression, squirming.

"*When* I've done this before," she continued, "the enemy has a way of . . . drawing out uncomfortable secrets. As a way of humiliating the priest. Distracting him."

I nodded. I'd seen it happen to Tom Harris.

"I just wanted you to know something," she said, with difficulty. "Namely, that I loved your father very much."

"Thanks," I said gratefully. "Y'all were good friends."

"I mean," she continued. "A little . . . more than that."

I started to respond, then stopped.

"Nothing specific. Nothing to be ashamed of," she said quickly. "Nothing that he even knew about, or at least, acknowledged. Just . . . something I carried around. It was a good thing," she concluded, with a slight smile. "A nice thing." She added, as an afterthought: "Life and marriage aren't always what you hope they will be, George."

Thunderstruck that Clarissa Bing, my parents' friend, married and mother of two, was telling me that she had been in love with my father, like a schoolgirl with a crush . . . I struggled to respond. What on earth did she expect me to say? "That's—that's okay," I stammered.

Clarissa regained her clinical tone. "I wanted you to hear it from me. The good side. In case it got perverted, or *used,* once we got started. No sense you doubting your practicioner halfway through."

"Okay."

"Okay, then."

We sat there another moment.

"Are you ready?" she asked.

"Think so."

"Let's give 'em hell." She winked, and, without waiting for Freddie and Tom Harris to rejoin us, she immediately began the prayers.

"Save your servant," she intoned.

I knew my lines. "Who put their trust in you."

The three of them encircled me, in mismatched chairs, reading the rite in unison, but with a different mix of accents—none of Reval Dumas's midwestern voice this time, but all southern, of different flavors: Uncle Freddie's aristocratic Alabama pomp, Clarissa's hint of Tennessee twang, and Tom Harris—a house of many colors, painted over with Ivy League, and the local Old Virginia, but underneath, very deep, an earthy, hillbilly burr. These voices made a strange kind of music— reciting prayers full of images of terror and battle, yet with three varied and beloved instruments.

As before, I found myself lulled into distraction, following the voices, not the words. I felt funny being the object of this exercise when so clearly—I now considered with confidence—I had absolutely no need of the rite. Here I was *participating;* how could I, if I indeed had a demon inside, join in on the very prayers to get rid of one? The pol- tergeist, the vision, must just have been a hangover; farewell blips from my pre-Thorazine, pre–Reval Dumas consciousness, which would be erased by a wrestling match with Kurt and a few nights' sleep. It was precisely when my mind turned to these pleasant thoughts that I felt a sudden spasm of dizziness, as if the room had shifted. I wondered, troubled now, whether I needed lunch, and whether this sensation sig- naled a hungry faint . . .

And then I saw myself. I was sitting on the far end of the sofa. Upright, alert, listening. And then I looked down at myself—saw my thighs where they should be, my feet touching the floor, belly protruding slightly in a slump—on the near end of the sofa. I looked up again. There I was: spine straight, pleasant, congenial, prepared for a discussion. I was sitting on both ends of the sofa. How could this be happening?

Tom, I started to say, but found my voice died quickly away, inside my throat. Myself, the Other George, turned to me with a patient, indulgent smile, and put a finger to my—his—lips. *Shh.*

I recoiled in horror and saw the others, too, had detected this sudden shift in body language. I saw Clarissa tug at her frock and Freddie shiver, and I realized that the room had grown cold—though I could not feel it—and knew that the moment of possession had come, just as when I had seen it take over Grace in her bed.

"Its name," instructed Tom Harris.

"I command you . . ." read Clarissa. But her voice seemed flat, hollow, with none of the relaxed power and control that Reval Dumas showed. I felt a chill of terror shoot through me, as one might from the sidelines of a sporting event—a boxing match, one where people get hurt, shed real blood—watching a loved one, slack, unprepared, unconditioned, get into the ring with a pro. *No, stop it!* I shouted, but my voice died again, and this time Other George did not bother rebuking me. ". . . unclean spirit, whoever you are," Clarissa's voice seemed to squawk, she sounded birdlike now, weak, awkward, a joke, "that you tell me by some sign, your name . . . and the day and hour of your departure!"

Other George drew himself up, languid. "Why don't *you,*" he said, indicating Tom Harris with a nod, "just ask me what you want to ask me."

The experience was bizarre. I heard my exact voice—touched my own throat to make sure there were no vibrations there—come out of the apparition's mouth. But I also saw a strange and subtle difference in demeanor and inflection. Just as Grace had taken on personas to suit her purpose—a snake, a party flirt—so did Other George assume the height of bored arrogance: a chilly upperclassman interrupted by freshmen, eager to be rid of them so he could return to more sophisticated labors elsewhere.

"Keep up with the rite," exhorted Tom Harris.

Clarissa continued praying.

"You shouldn't be doing this," said Other George, with a sneer.

Clarissa faltered.

"I mean *him*," he nodded to Tom Harris again. "*Solicit not thy thoughts. Mm mm mm,*" he tsked. "Are you *probing* into the *secrets* of the *universe?*" His voice dripped with oh-wow mockery.

Clarissa resumed the reading. Other George sighed with boredom. "I said: Why don't you just ask me what you want to ask me. Someone's got to take me home. George's mommy is waiting."

I shook my head, trying to clear it. I focused all my concentration on my lips, my voice. "You're not me!" I challenged him.

My voice broke out into the air. The others reacted. Tom Harris pointed at the text, excitedly.

"George is there," he said. "Read!"

They pronounced, in unison: "Tell me by some sign, your name and the day and hour of your departure!"

I crossed my legs testily, agitated. They were upsetting me. Or they were upsetting Other George—it began to be confusing.

"*Shut up,*" I—or he—snapped. "You want to know the secrets? Fine." He drew a deep breath, with a regretful air. "The first is what I know. I'll begin with that."

The others paused, listening.

"First . . . okay, follow me here and I'll make it understandable. The first thing is, what I can tell you. And that thing is this: How can it jibe? If I know and you know, that's what makes you and me tick. When we click, you'll have a first glimpse of the thing I've been trying to tell you. Underneath all of it—follow me now—underneath it is, first things first, all of the secrets combined—names, hours, days, *history,* above all—what you're really asking. I know, I understand; and first, I want you to understand, so, that's why, I'm making it, simple, for you . . . to follow my *follow my words follow me I'M ANSWERING YOUR QUESTION SO PLEASE PAY ATTENTION these notions are mysteries and cannot be simply explained first but rather first no first no first NOW no NOW no NOW no NOW I want you to understand that's why I'm speaking at your request of course but clicking and glimpsing are more to it than that I WANT YOU TO FOLLOW ME . . .*"

Clarissa's prayers slowed to a halt under this battery of speech. I watched as her face pinched into the expression a child makes just before it bursts into tears. Tom Harris squinted, as if in pain, and instinctively raised a protective hand to his ears. Uncle Freddie's cheeks puffed out. His face went scarlet. Sweat broke out on his forehead. I— my body, my own inconsequential, seemingly weightless body—rose from the sofa in alarm. Uncle Freddie was having a heart attack. I had to stop what was going on. I had to stop the speech, that infuriating garble, and save my godfather . . .

Uncle Freddie's face swelled like a hyper-ripening tomato. But it was not a heart attack that was building. It was a typical Uncle Freddie expostulation.

"THIS IS NONSENSE!" he bellowed.

The fear and confusion blew instantly from the room like air from a balloon. Uncle Freddie dabbed his face with a monogrammed handkerchief, still puffing with annoyance, as if that onslaught of speech had been something he objected to grammatically above all else. The others stirred. The spell was broken.

Tom Harris recovered first.

"Tell me by some sign, your name and the day and hour of your departure!" he shouted, alone this time.

Other George slumped—a mix of disappointment and fatigue— and his eyes went dull. He reclined on the sofa now, seemed to drift into sleep.

The three regained their unison, voices stronger now, on the offensive: "*Tell me by some sign, your name and the day and hour of your departure!*"

Other George made no motion. I saw my chance.

"Just get up and leave," I said. Other George and I seemed to be alone now, locked in some kind of seal of sound, together on the sofa. I heard the prayers, but they drifted to us as if through a closed door. "Just go away," I said. The phrases were pure middle school. But I didn't know what else to say. I moved closer to him on the sofa. "Go away!" I said, with more conviction. I inched closer, then reached out and grabbed him. His soft forearm sank under my touch. Clammy, warm. *Is that what I feel like?* Other George flopped over toward me, as if I'd shaken someone in a dead sleep. I removed my hand, shocked. Had he passed out, somehow? Had we won? On instinct, but terrified, thinking of Reval Dumas's brave hand-on-head blessing, I reached up, took his cheeks, turned his head toward me. The eyelids parted. The eyes beneath were a void. Empty. *It.* I drew my hands away in horror. No sympathy or character or even dead tissue lay there. Just shadow. *It.* At last I understood.

Other George flopped back to his corner. I saw its upper lip break out in a cold sweat. It mumbled, as if delirious. But I heard the words clearly, because its voice, I realized, came clearer to me than theirs did. It was half in my head. *Just ask me.*

They paused.

"Just ask me," it repeated, quietly. The three of them stared. "That's what we're really here for, after all. *Tom.*"

Tom Harris went pale again, the way he had at Grace's. Something caught my eye. A tiny white light, flickering behind the couch. A firefly? A reflection? I had a sense of foreboding. *No, Tom!* I shouted again, uselessly.

Other George's voice hissed in my head, commanding, even as his figure lay sickly on the sofa: *Let him speak!* it hissed. It lolled its head toward Tom Harris, eyes opened now, and spoke aloud. "Go ahead," it said softly. "Ask me."

Tom Harris's pallor deepened. I thought he might faint. The others seemed to draw back, leaving him to face the demon alone.

"Did you kill Paul?" he asked, hoarsely.

Other George smiled.

"You want to know what happened to Paul?" it asked.

Tom Harris's eyes narrowed suspiciously—too late.

"The best way to understand what happened to your friend Paul," said Other George, faintly bored now, but still superior—the upperclassman had become a campus tour guide for clueless parents—"is to see it."

That tiny drifting point of white light suddenly began to grow, from speck size to stamp size, from stamp size to hand size ... then it rushed toward me, a crashing wave. The bottom dropped out of the sofa. I fell onto my back. I felt a choking heat. Sweat broke out over my forehead and back, even across my arms. The white light overwhelmed me. A voice spoke then, clearly. No longer fogged in, as Freddie, Tom Harris, and Clarissa's voices had been.

"Mister Paul," it said. "I'm ready to continue now."

I looked up. A teenage boy had entered the tent, closing the flaps behind him, shutting out the blinding daylight beyond. He was speaking to me. He did so with respect—I knew, the way you do in dreams, that it was not eleven-year-old George whom he addressed. My arms were full, hairy. My body, fevered as it was and stretched out on a hot floor, felt like a long, lean instrument. *Mister Paul.* The boy was addressing my father. Me.

The boy seemed fresh, alert, if a little pale. He was fourteen, and gaunt, with shaggy black hair, dressed in a T-shirt and shorts. The odors of latrines and unwashed urine-y clothes filled my nostrils. I felt a wave of revulsion looking at him, despite his bright eyes and pleasant smile. He looked Mexican.

Everything caused pain. The daylight. The heat and the sweat. But most of all, that voice.

"Just a minute," I said. I licked my lips. Even whispering required effort. "I need to rest."

In Honduras, in his sickness, your father interviewed a demoniac. Followed him into deep places.

The scene jumped.

The same tent, but nighttime now. I sat at a table with a lit kerosene lamp at my elbow—a new one, with a green hood, a dirty price tag still affixed to its base—producing an orange glow. I must have fallen asleep. I was bent over blue sheaves of airmail letters. They stuck to my sweaty arms. I had to keep unsticking them and laying them down again. *Distractions. I needed time to write!*

I felt them for the first time, I wrote, at last placing pen to paper. *It was a horrible sensation. We all wish from time to time, abstractly, for the experience of someone else's mind, mostly out of curiosity. But now that I have had this wish fulfilled, it seems I will never be rid of the feeling. I gripped his hands, which were deadly thin, pale and clammy even in the heat—dead man's hands—and shut my eyes, and prayed. At first there was nothing, then, slowly, I realized that I was listening to the trail of a voice. It was like someone passing behind me, speaking softly, but with purpose. I nearly turned around. Then I realized this voice led to another voice. This went on for a time, as I tried to catch one phrase after another. It was like someone waving a hundred perfume bottles under your nose. Only then did I realize that the voices were not consecutive as I had thought, but were simultaneous, some of them soft and wheedling, some bold like a stump speaker, others rising in a sort of fury, raging with real rage, shrieking, animal rage, like grief or loss that has turned to vengeance. I opened my eyes, and I saw his face staring at me, and his expression chills me even now. I tried to pull away from him but he gripped me tighter and he leaned close and his eyes bored into mine. I lost track of time. I am not sure how long I lay there, the boy by my bed, ever patient—as if he were the one ministering to me.*

Perhaps I am sick. I have been feeling tired lately and prone to cold sweats and dizziness. These physical sensations have been accompanied by what feels like a thinning of the world—the colors of trees and grass seem grayer; I feel weak; and daily, sometimes hourly, I will "come to" standing somewhere arbitrary, where I have evidently passed into a brown study and stopped in my tracks, emerging exhausted, on the same spot, studying the ground at my feet, my mind following an insidious, circular path. I feel that my body and my senses are going dull. Even my soul, if it is not a sin to say it, seems to be shutting down, out of self-preservation, or irrelevancy. My prayers now feel automatic. I suppose that is better than no prayers at all.

I stopped writing. I was gripping the table to hold myself upright. I felt a sickly swoon coming on. It rose, became a tightness in my belly and then a roar of nausea. I bent over and vomited.

When I righted myself, I found I gripped something soft. I had returned to Tom Harris's living room. The sofa—I felt its worn fabric under my fingers. But something was not right.

I looked over and saw Tom Harris, Clarissa, Freddie, peering at me, with expressions of revulsion and pity. Then I turned my head and saw myself—Other George, now awake again—beaming proudly, and with genuine pleasure. Other George seemed to glow, as if filled with sunlight, while my friends appeared dreary, dingy. I shivered violently, from puking, from the fever. But none of it mattered. At all costs, I knew, I must continue writing.

I put my pen to the paper again. My fingers trembled. So I spoke the words aloud. That helped. Kept the mind focused, kept the ink flowing.

"They came for me again last night, Tom. The villagers think I am *perdito*—their word for the boy, so now I am lumped with him. Not a good sign," I laughed grimly. "The relief organization leaders are trying to persuade me to medevac, since there's no proper hospital. I tell them no. I don't want to be moved. Because fighting them off requires all my concentration. I lie still all afternoon. At evening, as the horizon dims, I feel a sinking dread. I feel them muster, as if I'm in a beleaguered fort, a doomed captain on the wild frontier. It begins with the whispering. Then I begin to see their world again.

"Tom, I am cursed with sympathy—I see it all the way they do. First the interminable racket of their talk, their thinking, like a hundred, no a MILLION souls, shouting at a bazaar. There is no distinction between beings. All arguing, all fighting, all insinuating and insulting and damning, the air is full of curses, and it is maddening. Here is the comedy: they are trying to get away from it. They are like ambitious assistant professors angling for a trip to the MLA, trying to get out of Idaho State University, get a job, go away, leap into some other sensibility the way I have leapt into them. But what they are looking for is a human. They are all looking for holes, holes into human beings and into materiality. They want us because the violent motion and incessant noise compels them. Their search is like that of an animal looking for a tree to scratch itself on. And I am a target, I am handy, so they pound me like mosquitoes. But something about me keeps them back, and though I should be gratified, and I am, when I return to my bed, I can still feel them buzzing about me, and feel weak. I just lie and lie and cannot move for hours and days. When I see the boy I ask him about this. 'They are looking for us, aren't they,' I say, and he lies there staring at me as if I were already dead, a smile on his lips."

I shuddered so violently that the pen fell from my hand. I reached down for it. Grasped it. But I touched the floor—so cool, and solid—it felt welcoming. I lay down on it, and slept.

In my sleep, an angel came to me and placed soothing hands on my cheeks.

"*Our Father, who art in heaven,*" she said.

Gray streaked her dark hair. The angel had a Tennessee accent. Her eyes were as cool as drinking water and full of mercy.

"*Hallowed be thy name.*"

I opened my eyes. I saw Clarissa. I was seized by a jolt of animal fury. I jerked upright with a sudden, violent movement. She stepped back.

"Leave him!" I heard Other George's voice scream. "Leave him or he's dead."

She must have come down to help me, I realized. I yearned for the feel of those hands again. *Keep on with the prayers, you idiots,* I wanted to shout. But that desire to speak disappeared, quick as amnesia, and was replaced by another. *I must write.*

It was an overwhelming compulsion. I had to let the others know what I'd learned. It's what I came for. I knew I was going to die, but I had to tell them *this*. Or it would all be for nothing. I groped my way to the table.

I must tell you this, I write. *I have seen something so terrible it has taken my sight. Among them, it is called the kingdom. Are you laughing? They are, it is a mockery. Thy Kingdom Come. Like a placenta, only gray, ethereal. I was there and I had a guide like Dante, I think it was the boy.*

He said spirits had a means of identifying souls who are open to them. He said there are ways into a human's soul, the foremost of which is tricking them. How can they be tricked, I asked, since the decision to do good or ill must be made with free will? The answer is, they are tricked, because they ask to be tricked. "They create a gap," he told me. "It is as much as saying into the great emptiness, Where should I go? There is always a voice ready to respond. They have wandered out to the fringe and may fall."

A light appeared above us. I knew it was a soul. It was very bright, but the warm, sickly grayness crept over it like a lichen, only unnaturally fast. Then the light vanished. I heard a whimpering, like a child feeling sorry for itself and moaning. Then I realized, that was the characterization of all their noises, a sound that tugs at you as potently the last moment as the first, without diminishment, because it is circular: self-pity so deep it is nearly grief, grieving over the soul that self-pity has destroyed. It is unbearable. Then the boy uttered a phrase I would like to forget: "All of these souls shine out of the world and into the Kingdom like beacons." This is what they name them, beacons. "The world is full of them," he said, "and in hell they light the night sky like stars." Surely you see how important this is . . .

The pen fell from my hand again, but this time, I knew there was no hope of picking it up. I had no strength. I scarcely had strength to reflect—only to feel, only to be, only to sense the pain in my head and limbs and feel the beating of my own heart, and my breathing.

I was taken away—away from the tents and the danger, and back somewhere, back home.

I opened my eyes. My arms had grown bone-thin, just sinews, and knobs where the joints were, yellow in tint—*jaundice.* My hands were long, ghastly, tendons exposed, fingernails long, and pale yellow, all pigment faded except for the color of sickness and corpses. I was in a hospital. I shuddered. I drew the sheets around me, feebly, but the cotton chafed and stung.

I saw myself again—Other George—only this time, it was the real George, *my* George, standing beside the hospital bed, wearing a worried expression, too mature in depth of sadness for such a small boy, and I felt my heart break. *Oh honey,* I said, *oh sweetheart, please don't be sad.* Only I was not strong enough to say the words out loud. *Oh please God, let me tell him,* I thought, *let me tell him not to be afraid or sad,* but I couldn't, and that thin pulse that drew out breaths from me, and heartbeats, and even pain, stopped. My vision closed. It all went silent.

The Birthday Card

Wool and mothballs.

Strong, thick arms.

My father has come back to me.

"Get him on the sofa," said Tom Harris.

A grunt, up close, and then a sniffle. I opened my eyes and saw Uncle Freddie's face—his puffy cheeks, mustache, and wire-frame glasses—inches from my own. His tweed coat scratched my face; the odor of mothballs, just like my dad's, tickled my sinuses. He propped me up on the sofa. His cheeks were slicked with tears.

"He's awake," Uncle Freddie announced. He withdrew a hand-kerchief from his pocket and blew his nose loudly. "Oh thank God. He's awake."

"I can see that," said Tom Harris, also hovering nearby. Clarissa appeared, too. I was lying supine on the sofa, looking up at them.

"George, can you hear me?" asked Tom Harris.

"I hear you," I said.

"And it's you?"

I sat up. The three of them crowded around me. There was a bucket on the floor. Clarissa's sleeves were rolled up. She wore elbow-length rubber gloves and had been sponging my vomit from Tom Harris's rug.

"You turned yellow," said Uncle Freddie, weeping again. "You turned yellow and shrank down like a skeleton. Or maybe it was just my eyes." *Muh eyes.* "Oh, God in heaven, I never want to see that again." He wiped his cheeks. "You sure you're all there, sonny?"

I sat up a little. "Yes," I said. I trembled and felt chilled, but recognized the sensation: postvomit tremors. "Sorry I barfed."

Clarissa knelt down with a glass of water.

"I didn't realize . . . I didn't know what would happen," she whispered. "That sounds so stupid now, doesn't it?" She shook her head. "I'm sorry."

"S'okay." I gulped the water gratefully.

Tom Harris towered over us, face livid.

"Do you remember anything?" he demanded.

I returned his gaze, with a dead feeling.

"I saw what my father saw," I said. Then I curled myself into a ball in the corner of the sofa, nursing the water and a sullen silence.

The three of them watched me for a stunned instant.

Then Tom Harris emitted a groan, collapsed into a chair, and placed a hand over his eyes. "What have we done," he said.

We sat like that for a long time, a clock ticking somewhere measuring the time and the silence. Dusk crept over the meadow outside Tom Harris's picture window. After a stretch, we heard a distant grinding noise—a car on the drive.

Clarissa stood and squinted out the window.

"Someone's coming," she said. Then, after a moment: "It's Joan."

None of them moved. They slumped where they sat, waiting for the inevitable. We listened to the car crunch to a stop. Heard the parking brake creak; then the sound of the screen door swing open, and bang shut. My mother appeared in the doorway.

"George!" she exclaimed, coming to me without a word to the others. She knelt down, stroked my hair, examining me. Her face was drawn with worry. I saw her nose twitch; she turned and saw the bucket. Sniffed again. Then she stood.

"What happened here?" she said. "Is that vomit? Did you do that?" she said to me.

I nodded.

She knelt again. "What happened?"

"I didn't feel well."

"Why didn't you come home?"

I said nothing.

She stood again, hands on hips, and looked around at the others. "What have you been doing?"

Uncle Freddie ground his jaw. Tom Harris sat glumly. Clarissa adopted that same, odd, look-at-the-wall response that she had in Richard's office.

"Someone answer me!"

"We made a mistake," said Tom Harris dully. "One that Paul would never have made."

"Don't you use him," hissed my mother. Then, with growing apprehension and anger: "My God, you've been doing some ritual. Did you perform an exorcism on my son?"

"Not a successful one."

Tom Harris's joking did not help. My mother grabbed my wrist— tight—and yanked me to my feet.

"Come on."

She marched me across the living room until we reached the threshold between the twilit living room and burrowlike kitchen. Then she turned and addressed the three of them.

"If I see, or hear of, *any of you* near him again . . . I'm calling the police." Her mouth tightened into a white ring of anger. I could feel her hands trembling. "And if you don't believe me, try me."

"Joan . . ." began Tom Harris.

"I'm sure the police would love to get their hands on a couple of *bachelor* college professors who find little boys at church," she said, voice shrilling, "to take to their houses in the county."

She waited for this to sink in. The three of them sank back into their defeated slump. This seemed to frustrate my mother even more.

"Do you hear me?" she shouted. "I don't want you near him!" Her breath came quickly. "Our friendship is over!" Tom Harris put his head in his hands. Still, no one spoke. *"Do you hear me?"*

My mother did not even look at me in the car. We pulled up Kurt's drive. She got out of the car and walked into the house without me, without a word.

I sat for a moment. Snow dusted the dead leaves and saplings around Kurt's drive, and the tree trunks stood gray, cold, and dry. I unbuckled my seat belt and followed my mother into the house.

The sound of a TV football game erupted from the back den. But another, closer sound drew my attention. I followed it into the kitchen. My mother leaned against the counter, weeping. A tear dripped onto the tile with a little splat.

"Did you know how worried I was?" she said to me, her face a shadow in the weak winter light coming through the windows. "Don't you know what I thought had happened?" She wiped her eyes. "We thought you . . ." she shook her head. Then broke out crying again.

"Thought I what?" I asked.

"People who are unhappy, taking medication . . . sometimes they kill themselves, George."

She ripped off a paper towel and wiped her face.

"Oh Christ," she said, heaving a ragged breath. "You don't know what I went through today."

I stood watching her, dumbstruck.

"Is that why you wanted to go to church?" she said finally. "So you could meet with them? Or did they take you?"

"They didn't *take* me," I said, defensively.

"Then why did you go?" The anger returned. "I told you that *I didn't want you seeing them!* Why did you do that?"

" 'Cause," I said sulkily.

"What?"

"Because they're the only ones who believe me," I said, louder.

"Believe you?" repeated my mother, incredulous. "Honey, I've listened to everything you've told me. I, I brought you to Richard. I took you to the hospital . . ."

"Yeah, thanks a lot."

"*Do you think this is easy for me?*" she erupted.

"They know what it is, Mom! What it *really* is."

"Don't you say it," she said warningly. "They put that in your head!"

"It's a demon, Mom. The door to our shower smashed *by itself* ! What other proof do you need?" I shouted. "They have to help me before I go to Forest Glen. Otherwise I'll be stuck there . . . with *this*." I pointed to my head. "*Possessed.*"

"Oh, God, honey," she cried. "Do you know what you sound like?"

"What—*crazy?*" I challenged.

She shook her head, bit her lip, trying to maintain control. "Listen . . . George . . . when your father wrote that book, he meant it, he believed it, but it was *commentary, criticism*. He didn't believe demons were things you could reach out and touch, that actually *enter* you."

"Mom," I began.

"You don't have a demon, George," she said. "It's not possible. They're not real."

"That's where you're wrong!" I shouted, raising a finger and pointing at her like a prosecutor. "Dad and Tom Harris helped the church when people were possessed by demons. And Daddy had *visions*. A vision of evil," I said. "That's why he went to Central America."

She stood back, as if I'd slapped her.

"Who told you that about your father?"

"They did," I pouted. "Tom Harris and them."

She did not correct my redneck grammar. "What else did they say?"

"They said he went away, because he wanted to do good. Because he had a vision that told him to help people against evil."

My mother's eyes moved away into the middle distance. I watched as she stood mesmerized by some internal videotape, her expression flickering, absorbing and responding to the images on a fast-forward screen.

Abruptly the fight drained out of her. Her face transformed from an angry pucker to a mask of sadness.

"That's not why your father went away," she said at last, her tone low and even. "He went away because of me."

I waited. My heart pounded in my chest.

"We were having problems when he left. I . . . I didn't see any reason to tell you before."

Having problems?

"I know where Tom Harris and Uncle Freddie get their story," she continued, quietly. "Your father did have a vision. He had a few. But . . ." her voice trailed away. "That's not the reason he went." She smiled bitterly. "His vision of evil was me."

"Mom," I said, the anger melting away, seeing her dejection. "No. How could that be?"

She remained silent, the pained smile still on her face.

"It was nothing bad, though, was it? Your problems?" I pleaded. "You weren't going to get divorced, were you?"

"Your father and I loved each other very much, George," she said. "When he died it was the worst thing that ever happened to me. I've suffered more than even you know, Georgie. There's one thing I want you to understand." She knelt down, coming close to me in the dark. "Parents do things," she said, "because they have stories in their own lives. Those stories have nothing to do with the children. The shitty thing is, the children have to suffer because of it. And it's not fair."

She reached out to me. I knew that the hand she extended would be warm and soft, and that she ached to embrace me, to reassure me, to make up, to restart a cheery evening the way only my mother could, with a lilt in her voice, a suggestion that we all eat ice cream or watch TV or do something silly.

"George," she said. "Please come here." Her voice thickened. "Honey, I'm sorry that all this had to happen to you."

"What do you mean?" I said, puzzled.

She opened her mouth to speak. But at that moment the room flooded with yellow light and noise as Kurt emerged from his den, striding toward us, football game and lamplight following him along with a cloud of scotch fumes.

"Everything okay now, guys?" came his low, appealing voice. He put his hand on my mother's shoulder.

Seeing them together, I recoiled. Something instinctive came over me. I took two steps back.

"Honey?" came my mother's voice.

I turned and ran.

I pounded up the stairs, down the dark corridor, into the only lighted room on the second floor. I slammed the door behind me, pressed my back to it, sank down onto the floor.

I closed my eyes. The voices in my mind rose to a roar—*my father and mother had problems; my father wouldn't have gone away if it weren't for their problems; there are no such things as demons; my mother says it has nothing to do with me*—until I gave vent to them in a howl, *Rrrrrrrrrrra,* punctuated by my pounding the floor with both hands.

The noise died, tinnily, in the little room in which I squatted. For the first time, I noticed where I was.

I had stumbled into the spare room—a nooklike study, an after-thought with a slanted ceiling—tucked in between the main rooms on Kurt's second floor. A small chest stood in one corner. The floor had no rug. The only reason it stood open, with the light on, I realized, was that Kurt had been storing boxes there—the ones he and my mother spent the day packing at Piggott Street. There were three large cardboard boxes in the center of the room: one filled with my clothes and school textbooks;

another with my mother's work clothes; a third with items from my mother's desk—picture frames, correspondence rubber-banded together, manila folders with my mother's neat penciled cursive on the tabs. Our things from home. I hung my head over one cardboard box and sniffed: must and dampness, with the faintest whiff of my mother's perfume, and clean clothes from the dryer. Home. I curled myself around the box, pressing it to me like a teddy bear on a stormy night.

I had been lying there for some time when I heard noises in the hall. The door bumped my back. I scrambled to my feet.

"Don't move, don't move," said Kurt, poking his head into the room. A bead of sweat swam down his nose. "I need to . . . I just . . ." He took in the clutter. "Okay, you're going to have to move."

"What are you doing?"

"Straining my back," he deadpanned. "I'm bringing this cot in here for you to sleep on."

He nudged the door open with a shoulder and dragged in the oldest, heaviest iron bed frame I had ever seen—two giant metal jaws with a mattress sandwiched inside.

"You're bringing that for me?"

"You didn't think I was going to keep you on the sofa, did you?" he grunted, as he tugged the monster past me.

"I didn't think you'd want us here anymore."

"What?" Kurt wiped his brow with a forearm. "Why would you say something like that, George?"

"Because we're too much trouble. Because I run away. And my mom yells."

"If you think that's yelling, you haven't seen yelling," he said. "My mom used to drink schnapps in her bedroom, come down at three in the afternoon in a nightgown screaming murder and police." He grasped each half of the frame with his thick, sandy hands and squeezed the two together until they creaked. The latch came loose.

"My big brother would carry her back upstairs in his arms. Like a bride over the threshold. Catch this, for me, would you? It's heavy," he warned, lowering one half toward me.

"Did you come from a bad neighborhood?" I asked, with such earnestness that Kurt burst out laughing.

"Court End, in Richmond," he said. "One of the worst for lady drunks."

I caught the frame and lowered it carefully to the floor.

"Attaboy," he said.

"Was your mom mean to you?"

Kurt leaned toward me, tugging at the skin by his right eye, indicating what looked like a long pockmark. "See that?" he said. "Diamond ring."

"You're kidding," I said suspiciously. Kurt shrugged.

"Gotta move these, too, if you're going to sleep here," he said, seeing the cardboard boxes. "Whew. Mind if I sit down?"

He eased himself to the floor and let out a sigh.

"You know, it's one of the best things about growing up, when you realize you're pretty much as smart as anybody. Learn to trust what you think. Listen to the voice in here." He tapped his chest. "Your mom says you ran away to see your friends, because they believe in demons. I guess that means you believe in demons, too."

I nodded slowly—cautiously.

"Okay," he said. "Just be sure it's you who believes it." I watched him. His shrewd eyes drilled back into me—no redness or vagueness despite the whiff of scotch. "Not them. Not your dad." His eyes did not move from mine. "Not your mother, either. Though I know she doesn't believe in that stuff."

"She doesn't believe in anything," I said, and added: "She's a liberal."

Kurt's mouth twitched in a smile.

"George," he said. "Christian. Liberal, or whatever. They're not camps. Not teams. You don't need to pick a side."

I considered this. Sometimes, hearing Uncle Freddie talk—even reading my father's book—you did begin to think there were teams; and that it was vital for you to choose the right one. I looked at Kurt with renewed interest.

"You can be your own side," he continued. "Or we can be a team. When everyone else gets a little too wound up. You know what I mean? Too excited. You just pull me aside, we'll watch a ball game. Go for a drive in the country. That's what I love about this place," he said, grinning a lopsided grin. "Get out in the car, take that turn you never took before, end up finding a spot that looks out over the whole valley . . . with sunshine pushing through the clouds." He splayed his fingers and made a swooping motion. "That's what I do when I get upset: client yells at me . . . my brother got real sick last year. Clears your head." He nodded, gently, to himself. "The side you pick doesn't have to be your mom, or your dad, or your dad's friends. It can be . . . just you. That's part of growing up, into a man."

I found, almost by magic, that as I sat listening to Kurt, all the noise in my head had indeed ceased.

"Okay." I nodded.

"Okay?" he repeated, louder now, jolly.

"Okay."

We exchanged a smile.

He heaved himself to his feet, groaning. "All right, now clean this place up, it's a mess," he joshed me. "What're all these boxes doing here, anyway? Somebody movin' in?" He winked.

That night, dinner dragged. My mother, seemingly exhausted from her anxiety and our fight, did not cook. Kurt warmed up frozen pizzas. My mother did not touch hers, but allowed Kurt to refill her glass of red wine many times. I ate my pizza mechanically, tip to crust, and just as mechanically reached for more. Kurt seemed to be watching us.

"Your ghost," he said, in the midst of a silence. I raised my head from my plate. "Your ghost might actually help me," he said.

My mother looked at him in disbelief.

"I was telling George today how much I like having you around." Kurt placed his hand on her arm. "Might be nice to *keep* having you around."

My mother said nothing. Clearly, Kurt was pleased with himself for some reason and wanted to get something off his chest, no matter what the emotional climate.

"Thing is, I've been offered a job in Cincinnati," he said.

My mother lit up. "The one . . . ?"

He nodded. "They met, and exceeded, my salary requirements." He grinned. "And, I gotta tell you . . . I'm not kidding . . . my *first thought* was: I can't do this without Joan, and George."

"Kurt . . ."

He raised a hand to silence her. "Now I thought to myself: I can ask Joan to come. But if I ask her *before* I accept, she'll feel responsible for whatever decision I make. So I got crafty. Decided to keep the company dangling till I got Miss Joan in my clutches. My good friend the ghost helped me there. Because look who's here in my house?"

He made a blinking expression, as if he'd just woken to find us at his table. My mother and I managed a laugh.

"Meanwhile the company thinks I'm playing hard to get. So what do they do?" He paused for effect. "They up my offer fifty percent."

"Fifty percent!" exclaimed my mother.

"That's what I said," he laughed. "So now it's an easy call for everybody. Right? I accept. Got plenty of moolah to go around. And I swoop in for the kill with you all." He grinned. "Joan. George. I'm going to Cincinnati. I want you to come with me." He pounded his meaty palm on the table. It made a startling bang, rattling the silverware. "Who's onboard?"

"Kurt," my mother said, shaking her head. "You're crazy."

"Did I mention the signing bonus, the moving expenses? Enough for a down payment on a big place in Cincinnati. Plenty big for three. And now," he said, "with the ghost keeping you out of Piggott Street; George having some troubles...I figure it's a way to get everyone excited about moving." Then he whispered coaxingly to my mother: "Plenty of schools there with women professors, Joan. Not just German 101, either. I checked."

My mother rolled her eyes. "You checked?"

"I checked something else, too." His face grew serious. He rubbed his finger on the tabletop. My mother and I waited, puzzled. "A minor who's been involuntarily committed to psychiatric treatment in one state and moves to a different state...will not have his status follow him. Not transferable," he said quietly. "Never, under no circumstances. There's no federal law. That minor would have to repeat his actions in the new state and get a new evaluation to see if they fit that state's criteria." He lifted his eyes. "Understand me, guys?"

My mother and I looked at each other. I felt a thrill rise in me: it shook off every drop of misery that clung to me. I was happy. My mother was happy. I'd forgotten what it felt like. Glee and surprise and fancy all at once brightened our faces. We looked at each other, at Kurt, at each other again, unable to pick which question to ask first, which feeling to give vent to.

"So?" he said. "You coming?"

And suddenly it all came out at once, the yeses, the thank-yous, the thousand questions: have you been there, what is it like, where will we live, when are you going. This last Kurt corrected.

"When are *we* going," he said. "Listen. I wouldn't have done this if it weren't for you. And I don't mean I did it *for* you, or *because* of you, or as a favor, somehow."

"Then why?" said my mother playfully.

No more Forest Glen, I thought with growing delight, no more miserable house, no more demon, no more slamming and splintering shower door . . .

"I just think," said Kurt, "we need to get the hell out of here."

. . .

Mom let me stay up late, to celebrate, so it was after ten when she came to my room to observe our new bedtime ritual, the pre-teeth-brushing-pill-taking.

"Are you excited?" she asked me, when we were finished. I had become so adept at cheeking I could even hold a conversation with the pill wedged in my gums.

"Yes."

"Good. Me, too." She paused. "It's good to have something good happen."

"It's like Kurt said." I smiled. "Maybe the ghost helped us."

"Maybe," said my mother, with effort.

I thought for a moment. "Does Kurt like me?"

"Of course!" she exclaimed. "Kurt adores you. Why do you even ask?"

"It seems like a big step to have a . . . ," I hesitated, "a kid move in with you, too."

"Kurt's a grown man, who can make decisions for himself," my mother replied. "I think he's the kind of person, who, once he makes up his mind, doesn't change it. That's one of the things I like about him."

I nodded, satisfied. "That's one of the things I like about him, too."

Once alone, I looked for a hiding place for the pill. I settled on the top side of my sock and underwear drawer—the pill stuck to the wood nicely. Then I undressed and tried tossing my balled-up socks into the cardboard boxes. I missed the first try. Hit the second. I retrieved the sock-ball, and stood back to "shoot" again, when the reality struck me: we were moving. I would never live in Preston again. I went to the box, the one containing Mom's office stuff, and gingerly pulled out the picture frames.

My mother in her doctoral gowns. My father, bundled in a winter coat and wearing Watergate-era sideburns, carrying me as a baby. A portrait of my mother from decades ago: a black dress, white pearls, a broad smile. No marriage, no child, no worry lines. I started to dig for more photos, hoping selfishly to find more of myself, and to spur a nice nostalgia session.

And then I saw it. The ripped fold of an airmail envelope, like a lick of blue flame.

My mother's words echoed in my mind: *I think he went away because of me.* What did she mean? I remembered the letter she'd read that day, in tears. Could this be it? If so, could I find out the truth? I tugged the remaining picture frames from the box . . . I dug deeper, searching for the slip of blue I was sure I'd seen . . . found bills, payments . . . and only one blue airmail envelope, addressed in my father's spidery writing. It seemed thin, light. I opened it—no pages inside. None of the crinkly thin paper that stuffed his other missives to me and to my mother. I deflated. My mother must have taken this one by accident. Indeed, a card seemed to have fallen inside the blue envelope. I shook it out. A single, oversized, cream-colored stationery card, with some boyish, handwritten letters in black ink. Not my father's writing. I tossed it aside and searched the rest of the box. I found nothing. I emptied it to the corners, placing the contents to one side, like an archaeologist excavating a site. No more airmail envelopes. No more personal correspondence. No hidden secrets.

Discouraged, I placed the objects back into the box, one at a time, until I reached the airmail envelope once again. I searched it for any useful hints. The post date—June. The first few weeks of his trip. Why would my mother choose this envelope to bring with her from the house? Nervous about upsetting the order of the box in any way, I reached for the cream-colored card to place back inside. The card was crinkled, battered. There were brown and green fingerprint smudges on its sides—odd, since its thick stock, embossing, and fountain-pen script gave it an elegant air.

To go with your beautiful blue eyes, it said. *Happy Birthday.*

Had my father sent this to my mother? She did have blue eyes. But how could he, since it was not his writing? I held the card another moment. Who had written it, then? I cocked my head, looked to the ceiling for an answer. Three letters under my fingertips, in blocky Deco capitals, raised from the paper: K M A. Kurt Moore. I had scarcely known his last name until seeing it on the mailbox when we arrived.

My mind puzzled over this again and again, until it grew dizzy and seemed to drift off on its own, leaving me slumped against the door in the tiny room while some other, subterranean part of me—the wiser part, wearing an eyeshade and willing to slave over a handful of contradictory clues—did the work.

The Hiding Place

In Kurt's guest room, my mother stood over the chest of drawers, which was now stuffed with my underwear, pj's, and jeans. The top sock drawer was pulled open; her left hand held two or three balled-up pairs of socks: she held her right open as if cradling a baby bird.

My heart dropped.

"George," she said slowly. "Come here please."

While Kurt traveled to Cincinnati to meet his new "team" and look at houses (*in Covington, Kentucky, just across the river,* he said; *we can still be southerners*), my mother and I remained in his house by the James River. No one wanted to return to our place on Piggott Street.

"Probably nothing would happen," Kurt had said.

"Probably not," agreed my mother.

"You're not going back there," Kurt dared her.

"Not until I run out of blouses."

"Washing machine's downstairs," Kurt said. "Leggett's is open late."

This seemed to satisfy everyone. Major decisions appeared to have been made offstage: my mother and Kurt shared a bedroom; they shopped together; my mother pored over Cincinnati real estate listings in a newspaper from the public library while Kurt expostulated on economic factors affecting interest rates for mortgages; and yet the issue of marriage never arose, nor, for that matter, did the fact that my own father had died only months prior. My mother, liberated from my father's old-fashioned mores, seemed to ease quickly into the seventies-flavored ethics of the time. Kurt was a new world for her, far removed from the one she and my father had circumscribed, where command over the great ideas, and wit, were sufficient to define and fulfill any person; and where deviation from these virtues—to show a lack of seriousness, or ignorance—was to deserve contempt. Kurt's bookshelves contained thick volumes on art and architecture, and a whole shelf of broken-spined classics. But he also liked fishing. He listened to bluegrass. He read—actually read—the stock tables in the *Washington Post*. He liked television and the homestyle food he could find in bar and grill joints in the county, and he was friends with his garage mechanic. His house—modern, airy, luxurious—reflected what I later learned to be the virtues of the upper class, the nonscholarly affluent: an expectation of quality, pleasure, *fun*. On the one hand, the wine cellar; on the other, the trippy Peter Max poster my father would have winced at.

And if Kurt's house defined his ethic, my mother and I were mighty glad to be in it. As soon as Kurt pulled out of the driveway for his flight to Cincinnati, we began to play around like two teenagers left alone in a swank hotel. Mom raided the wine cellar (a green bottle of Riesling chilled at fifty-four degrees; *cellar temperature,* she said), and I sat in front of the giant television set with *a remote control* (this was cool in 1982), flipping between a football game and a kung fu movie. I padded around, feeling the clean, new wood under my feet, smelling the mildew-less carpets and furniture and pillows, and flicking light switches—ones not linked to cruddy overhead lights or antique standing lamps with yellowing shades, but lights with dimmers, museum-type lights, track lighting. Cozy, delighted, we watched the intermittent snowfall. I did homework at the kitchen bar. Mom

read from a tourist guidebook about Cincinnati. From her hungry flipping of pages, you'd think it was Tuscany.

I had just pulled on my pajamas when Mom knocked at the bedroom door carrying a load of laundry.

"Mind if I put these away?"

"Nope." I crawled into bed—clean sheets—and opened a new fantasy paperback with a Tolkienish cover and illustrations. Mom loaded
my pants drawer. Then my shirts. So full of contentment was I that I
didn't realize what was happening. When she reached my sock drawer,
she stopped.

"What's this?" she asked.

"What's what?"

"This." She poked at something in her palm.

"George, come here please."

I crossed to her. In an instant all my equilibrium vanished. I knew
what she held in her palm.

"Can you tell me what these are?"

"No."

"George."

I hesitated. Then, sulky, trapped: "They're my pills."

"Can you tell me why they're in with your socks?"

"No."

My mother waited.

The fact was, in the new environment, I was far from perfecting
my new cheeking-and-hiding methods. After I affixed them to the top
of my drawer, the tablets must have dried, and after a day or two, fallen
onto my socks.

"I don't like taking them," I protested. "I told you. I'm like the
walking dead."

My mother regarded me. "George, how long have you been hiding
your medication?"

"Just since we came to Kurt's," I lied. "I didn't think I needed it
anymore."

"This is very serious."

"I know."

"No, you don't. These pills may be what's preventing you from having more episodes. You don't want to go back to the way it was, do you? You were very sick."

"I know."

She stared at the shaggy white dots in her palm.

"How have you been hiding these? I watch you take them."

Reluctantly, I pointed to the spot on my gum—the hiding place.

"Where is your pill for tonight?"

I produced it.

"Let me see you swallow it."

I downed it.

"Now let me see your gums."

I showed her.

She heaved a great sigh and slumped down on the bed. "Oh, George," she said. "What are we going to do?"

"We're going to go to Cincinnati," I gushed. "No more medicine, no more Dr. Gilloon, no more Dean. I'll go to a new school. Kurt says he'll buy us season tickets to the Bengals."

"Moving away will not solve problems, honeypie. Every school has its mean kids. And the problems you've been having," she said, stroking my hair, "they're not going away 'cause we move."

I thought about this. "Maybe they will."

"Maybe," she said, and that word hung in the air a few moments; it was like watching a particularly beautiful bubble rise on a gust of wind. One thing is for certain: sitting in Kurt's house made our craziest hopes seem possible. But Mom the Freudian popped the bubble. "Working through deep unhappiness takes time and effort. That includes taking your medication."

"But . . ."

"And I'm going to call the UVa hospital," she said. "If the pills are bothering you that much, maybe you're ready for a lower dose."

I panicked. "But we're moving!"

"Not for a little while," cautioned Mom. "Plus," she added grimly, "I want to hear the doctor's point of view on what's happened—with those guys." She was referring to Tom Harris, Clarissa, and Freddie. "Maybe that will change his diagnosis."

"But I don't want the pills! I don't need them!"

"George," said my mother, surprised by my vehemence. "I had my doubts at first, but I must say, they've helped you tremendously. Ever since you returned from Charlottesville, you've . . ."

"*I haven't been taking them,*" I blurted. "*At all.* Okay? So that proves they don't work."

"What do you mean, you haven't been taking them? Since . . ."

"Not since the hospital. So the doctor's wrong and Tom Harris is right. If you think I've improved because of the pills, it *proves* you're wrong. I'm not mental. It's not me. It's *in* me. It's not going to stop until we leave!"

"George, oh honey, listen to me . . ."

"I saw him *here*. He's following me, Mommy. We've got to leave. It's the only thing we can do. We've got to go to Cincinnati, *now*. Don't you get it?"

"Who are you talking about?"

"You know who. The boy . . . that I see." I explained, with a whisper: "The demon."

My mother's voice dropped an octave, to the calm, commanding lull of a hostage negotiator.

"You're going to take another one of those pills, right now," she said. She rose and took the bottle from the dresser. "Where's your water?" She disappeared and reappeared a moment later with a full glass. She twisted the bottle, shook a tiny tablet into her hand, and handed it to me. "Take it."

I swallowed it. For the second time, she checked my mouth and gums.

"Now it's time for bed."

"Can I read?"

"Ten minutes," she snapped. "Then lights out. In bed," she commanded.

"Are you still going to call the doctor?" I asked.

"Don't worry about that," she said. "You just get to sleep." Then she crossed the room, and kissed me as if it were any other night. "Ten minutes," she said. "I'm checking."

Her footsteps disappeared. I had only moments to take the trash can from the corner and lean over it while I stuck my finger in my throat. My guts wrenched. I went to the corner of the bed and covered my head with the bedspread so that my mother wouldn't hear me. After a few tries I heaved into the trash can. Recovering, I wiped my mouth, and turned my attention to hiding the foul odor of stomach acid. I shoved the trash can under the bed, to the center of the space under the springs, then draped the bedspread over the sides like a curtain. The trash can would remain unseen, unsmelled. I returned to bed, sniffed, and opened my book. As an afterthought, I jumped out of bed, rummaged under the socks, and pulled out the little icon of Saint Michael. I stashed it under my pillow. A few minutes later my mother apppeared in the door. "Lights out," she said.

Later I heard my mother's voice on the telephone downstairs. I knew who she was calling.

⚜   ⚜   ⚜

I awoke suddenly to a noise like whining, and an irregular thumping. I stood straight up out of bed, nearly tripping on the sheets. On instinct I snatched the icon from under my pillow and charged out of my room, down the dark hallway, following the noise to the room Kurt and my mother shared. I pulled open the door. Pitch blackness and noises awaited me.

The first sound was the rapid swishing of the bedclothes, as if they were being tossed about. The second reminded me of when my mother made veal cutlets, when she would cover the meat in wax paper and beat it with a kitchen mallet—a short, solid, punching noise. The third was what I had heard from my room: a kind of confused whining. This was my mother. I called out her name, and for an instant her crying ceased as she listened to my voice, but then the punching resumed, and so did her groans. I ran to her bed. There was motion all around in the dark, and violence—I could feel the bed shake.

My eyes adjusted. I saw a scruffy, angry-faced boy with smeared cheeks and wild hair standing straight up on the bed, rearing back with his fist and slamming it into the bedclothes, and then, with his other hand, rearing back with a long staff or rod and pounding with that, too. My mother had self-protectively burrowed under the blankets. I wanted to lift the icon and thrust it at him, but I could not move. I could only listen to the horrible sounds. The boy stopped striking long enough to turn to me. It was my Friend. He smiled. Then he reared his fist back in a wide, mocking arc and brought it down onto the bed. I heard the blow land with a crunch. My mother cried out.

With a yell I dove for the bedside table, whimpering in fear, until I found the light switch—the frustrating kind built into the power cord as a little notched dial. I fumbled with it. At last the light came on. I leapt to my feet. There was no sign of my Friend.

"Mom, Mom, Mom," was all I could say. "Mom, you okay?"

I wish I could forget what I saw next. My mother's face emerged from the blankets. It was red and raw, swollen as a boxer's around the eyes and mouth. You realize what a difference expression makes. Boxers emerge from fights deadened, beaten, but patient—they take their punishment willingly. My mother's lips trembled. Her eyes were wide with animal panic. She flinched at the sight of me, then curled up on her side.

I crawled to her over the mounds of yellow blanket, got tangled in them. I had no idea what to do. I scrambled for the phone, and with a dry voice asked the operator for the number of a hospital or ambulance or something, *something,* and could she please help me, my mother was hurt, she was crying, please.

Like Steve Garvey

My mother was visited by the sole on-call doctor, was injected with copious pain medication, and fell asleep. I slept in a pull-out chair, under a starchy sheet provided by the nurse.

A few fitful hours later they woke us to begin the X-rays to determine if bones had been broken.

Soon a policeman arrived, summoned by the staff to inquire about the attack. His hair was bristly white-blond, his face ruddy and weather-beaten, and he wore the brown Stoneland County sheriff's uniform and a revolver in a holster. He asked me a single question. *Tell me 'bout the inc'dent.* He held a leather-bound notepad open, but made no notes. He listened with dead eyes to my answers as I babbled excitedly, and when I ran out of steam, he rose slowly, muttered one more word—*rright*—and eased from the room. If I'd been older I might have identified the vanilla whiff of booze on his breath.

A nurse wheeled my mother back to the hospital room. The entire left side of my mother's face had swollen into purple mush. Her lips had swollen. The rims of her right eye, and the white of it, were stained with thick streaks of vivid red blood. I stood over her, and whispered some questions, but the nurse told me she needed to sleep.

. . .

I awoke. Afternoon light—white, wintry, and weakening already—glared in the windows. Kurt stood, still and monolithic, with the window behind him, his great blocky head bent in a somber attitude over my mother. She murmured to him. Their voices had awakened me.

When he saw me stir, Kurt approached me.

"Hey, buddy. How you doing?" He spoke with his normal cheer, but in a scratchy, fatigued voice.

"What are you doing here?"

"Last night I got a call from the hospital. Got a 6:00 A.M. out of Cincinnati and drove straight down from D.C."

I took this in. "How's Mom?"

He grunted. "Not great. Broken wrist. Two broken ribs. She's beat up pretty bad." I rose and stood next to my mother. Her eyes stared out of the puffy flesh surrounding them. Her expression had grown hard.

"Hi, Mom," I said.

"Hey, buddy," said Kurt's voice behind me. "How about a trip to the cafeteria? You must be hungry for breakfast, right?"

I turned and waved to my mother over my shoulder. She did not speak.

We sat over green plastic trays holding Styrofoam bowls of milk, cereal in cardboard boxes, and plastic utensils. A few families sat at other tables, speaking in soft tones. They looked poor, and sad—county people with anxious faces. Kurt snapped the tab of a Coke. He popped a can for me. Then drummed his fingers on the table.

"George," he said. "I want you to tell me what happened." He leaned over, close to me, and whispered. "What *really* happened."

I was surprised by this. I told him what I told the nurses: an intruder had beaten my mother, and that the intruder had fled when he heard me.

"That what really happened?"

"Why?"

"Is it?" he persisted.

I hesitated. "You remember what you said? About us being a team, sometimes?"

"I remember." But his eyes were hard.

"I'll tell you what really happened, if you promise not to tell anyone. Mom, or anybody."

Kurt shuffled in his seat. "I promise I'll listen to what you have to say, George."

That was good enough. He was my only ally now. "It was the demon," I whispered.

Kurt lifted his Coke can and drained it, shook it to see how much was left, finished it off, setting it down hard on the table with a hollow bang. When he took his hand away, I saw his fingers trembling.

"I went home this morning before I came here," he said. "I checked the closet downstairs where I keep my sports stuff. You've seen that, right? Where I keep my old lacrosse sticks and gloves . . . baseball mitts, and all that junk?"

I nodded.

"I couldn't find my aluminum bat in there. Baseball bat." He eyed me. "I also spoke to your mother. She's hurt, George, but not just in her body." He broke off. Looked down. Laid his hands flat on the table. Gained control. "Your mom says it was you who beat her. Did you use that bat on your mom?"

"*No.*"

"Why would your mother say that, then, buddy?" His great sandy-colored hands rested on the table. I felt like his client.

I, too, spoke in a whisper now. "Because he looks like me."

"Who does?"

"The *demon.*"

"Aw, man." Kurt shook his head sadly.

"I heard them, and I ran in there and I saw him! He was standing over Mom—standing on the bed—and he *was* holding something! It could have been your bat!"

"George, demons are imaginary. They can't beat somebody up in real life."

"But you saw it!"

"No, I didn't," Kurt said, taken aback.

"What about the shower door? Have you ever seen anything like that? It smashed, and there was nothing there! Wasn't *that* real life?"

Kurt held my eye.

"George," Kurt began. "I'll grant you, that was weird. I know plenty of ghost stories from Richmond. Every old house's got a young lass who appears at midnight waiting for her Confederate sweetheart. But this is different. Your dad's friends have got you talking about the devil." He shook his head. "Your mom has got to get you help."

"What does that mean?" I demanded, cold suspicion in my voice.

Kurt fixed me with a piteous stare.

"She told me she said something already."

"The hospital."

Kurt winced. "Soon as she's discharged and on her feet, we're taking you up there for treatment, buddy. And after last night . . . it might be more than a checkup."

My ears rang. I gripped the sides of my chair, picking at them with my fretful tic.

"She said she was going to call about the pills. She didn't say anything about treatment," I argued.

"Well, now it's treatment."

"Who says so?"

"George, you saw your mother."

"Yeah? So?"

"She's in no shape to make a tough decision like this. And believe me, it's as tough as any I've made."

"So you decided for her," I said fiercely.

"George, you're missing the point," he said, his voice rising. "You need help, buddy. The kind your mom can't give you."

"I'm going to the juvie place?" I said, licking dry lips.

"The other one."

"Forest Glen?"

He nodded.

"What about getting me a bed?"

"Your doctor twisted a few arms. For an emergency."

Rather than jumping to my feet and screaming, I responded to this catastrophic bit of news quite coolly.

"Before I go, I want to see Richard," I said. "At the clinic."

Richard—tall, careful Richard, with his baggy eyes, mustache, and ubiquitous cardigan—was summoned, and while I sat in the scooped chairs in the Mental Health Clinic waiting room, Kurt stood next to Richard in the corridor and explained in soft tones and a few hand gestures what had transpired. Richard listened, wearing a poker face and nodding. Kurt approached me. He leaned down, looked me in the eye.

"Okay, George, go ahead," he sighed.

We sat next to each other, as before. Same room. Same view of parking lot and trees. Richard and I faced each other grimly like co-conspirators, one of whom was about to do hard time. Evidently Richard's viewed it the same way.

"You probably don't think much of the treatment you received here."

"Why's that?"

"Well . . . I was forced to break your confidence. I may be getting your friend's clinical license revoked. And now you're being committed to psychiatric care despite my best efforts. Not exactly an A-plus."

"It's not your fault," I said.

"You're kind to say so. I'm glad you wanted to see me. After the last time . . . I wasn't sure."

"Kurt told you what happened."

"He told me his version. Do you want to tell me yours?"

I lapsed into silence. "What does it mean," I said at last, "to have a demon come after you?"

He smiled thinly. "It's not my area of expertise."

"You must have some patient, somewhere, who thought *something* like that. Right?"

It was his turn to shrug. "When I worked at a hospital, yes."

"So . . . when those patients told you about demons, what did you think?"

"I thought they needed help very badly," he began. "And I tried to find ways the demons fit into the story of their lives." He warmed to the exercise. "Why those voices came when they did. Did they represent a person or event they'd had trouble coping with? In your case, for instance, I'm sure they are connected to your father's death."

I reflected on this. "Maybe it's all happening because my father is trying to tell me something."

Richard shifted in his chair. He saw an opening and was trying to hide his professional excitement.

"If your father *could* say something to you," he said softly, as he always spoke when he felt he was close to the point, "what would it be?"

"'I'm sorry,'" I blurted. "That's what he would say."

"Why would he say 'I'm sorry'?"

I shrugged. But Richard waited me out.

"Because," I admitted, "because he didn't take much of an interest in me."

"What makes you say that?"

But I shrugged again. Such plain words. *My father didn't take much of an interest in me.* Telling Richard the truth flushed my brain with the warmth of embarrassment and relief. Just as these feelings were curdling into self-pity, Richard rescued me.

"Put it this way: What do other fathers do that your father didn't do?"

It was a mouthful, but it helped.

"I don't know," I said. "Toby's father takes him fishing. They have a cabin down by the river. They go out there, and cook out."

"What else?"

"They play basketball. His dad built a hoop." I thought some more. "On holidays his father comes in and gives him and his sister Torture Sessions, where they wrestle. I know because I was there on Thanksgiving one year."

"You don't feel you and your father did things together?"

"Some things."

"Like what?"

I told him about the walks.

"Anything else?"

"Not really," I said. "My father was in his study a lot. He was doing research for another book."

"What about?"

"Milton."

Richard laughed. I tried to.

"That was hard for you to share," he said, serious again.

"Yeah." I felt gloomy now.

"So you think your father would want to apologize for that?"

"Maybe."

I slumped over. I was wearing a thick wool sweater my father had brought back for me from England that never quite fit me properly. I felt ugly and tired.

"You said you felt your father didn't take much of an interest in you. It's possible that you could not spend much time together, but he could still love you very much."

"I guess," I said.

"Were there other things that made you feel that way—like he did not take an interest in you?"

"It's like those meetings," I said. "I know I'm not supposed to talk about them. The ones with Clarissa and Tom Harris and Uncle Freddie."

"You can talk about whatever you want."

"I learned about my father from those guys. Things I never knew. My father had visions. He wrote a book so brave and different that people turned on him. And for me, listening to them talk, it's like I'm hearing about this great person. They looked up to him. They talk about him like I talk about Steve Garvey." Don't ask me why, but I was a Los Angeles Dodgers fan and owned a shoe box full of little cardboard Steve Garveys.

"Heroic," Richard nodded. "But?"

I frowned, suddenly struck silent.

"But he wasn't heroic toward you," Richard offered.

I shook my head.

"How was he toward you?"

"He was either lecturing, or he was gloomy, or he would yell."

"Would he yell at you?"

"Oh yeah."

"When?"

I went blank. It was hard to capture a hundred little moments in a phrase.

Richard understood. "He had a short temper," he offered.

"He used to tell me I was awkward when I would drop things. He would come home from class talking about his students, how they were brilliant. And I would say I was smart, too, maybe even smarter. And he would say I would never be as smart as them."

"Why would he say that?" marveled Richard.

I shrugged unhappily. "Maybe they were smart."

"But you're only eleven," he said.

"That's what I said. I told him I'd be smarter than they are, *one day*."

"And how did he respond?"

"He laughed."

"Because you were being funny, and defending yourself."

"No," I said despondently. "He was laughing at me."

Richard pursed his lips. "How did that make you feel?"

I thought hard. "Small."

"Small, because he had belittled you." I nodded. "Did you also feel betrayed because your father, who is supposed to stick up for you, was putting you down?"

I nodded. "I guess so," I said. My voice was hoarse.

I suppose sometimes therapists decide you're ready, and just come out and give you the answers.

"Your father sounds like a very conflicted person who held himself to high standards. Probably too high. When he couldn't live up to them, he forced himself to pay a price. For instance, his trip to Central America. That sounds like a penance. A cruel one, even," he added. "He held deep religious convictions, so he forced himself to try to become a saint. If *you* couldn't operate on his level, he was dismissive and harsh. He made you pay the price. But it wasn't fair. Even if it were possible to live up to those standards—which is unlikely—you were too young. It wasn't fair to you."

I nodded. The tears started to flow. Richard said everything for me. I felt the oceanic crush of emotion; Richard translated it into the beautifully neutral language of psychotherapy. Richard performed with athletic skill in those moments.

"But then I hear about all the things he did," I said, my face wet, "the book he wrote, and the people he helped, the way he talked, making anything interesting," I said, "and I think about the good things . . ." Here my voice cracked. "I miss him so much!"

I bawled. Great big heaving wailing sobs. The way my mother had cried, I realized, the day she found out he died. It had finally arrived. During the dry months since his funeral, I had not cried over him. I had not even realized I needed to. My mother and I were so intent on moving ahead, keeping up with school and work, we had forgotten the grief. I lost myself in the hot tears and pressed the heels of my hands against my eyes. I moaned deep in my chest and found myself shaking. I wiped the tears and snot on the sleeve of my English sweater and tried to stop; through the watery film over my eyes I saw Richard, an expression of cool sympathy and understanding on his features. But

I kept crying, and crying, until the walls of the room seemed to fade away, and I rose out into the cold, blue dusk, over the sleepy houses and the black-boughed trees and the rolling frozen ground hidden by snow, and I hung there in the sky, eyes shut tightly, listening to whispers on the cold breezes and wishing I could disappear among them.

An Unexpected Visitor

I gazed out the window all the way home, memorizing details, storing them as visual postcards for later, like a prisoner on his way to the clink.

Preston decorated in Christmas gear. The wreaths hung across Main Street. Twinkling lights and spray-on frost in the windows of the bank. The life-size, and somewhat bizarre, painted crèche in front of the white Baptist church. Christmas generally pumped a lively and sentimental spirit into Preston. But today the sky hung heavy and low, like the belly of a bomber about to dump its payload. Only a few people trudged on the twilit streets, all bundled up, one man in a hunting cap with earflaps.

At East Preston, we turned onto Kurt's road. Kurt took the curve gently for my mom's sake. She sat in the front seat; her pain medication, and a few effects from the hospital, lay on the seat beside me in the back.

On the bald-headed hill, on the right, yellow grass pricked the surface of the thin layer of snow. On the left, the river seemed immobile. The enormous rope-swing tree hung dolefully over the water.

We crunched up Kurt's drive, headlights bumping as we maneuvered over the ruts—then came to an abrupt halt. A strange car blocked the way. A nondescript, newish red sedan.

"Does that car look familiar to you?" Mom asked. Her voice slurred through her swollen lips.

"Nope," muttered Kurt, shifting into first gear. "Should put up a no-parking sign here."

We inched forward. As we came round the circular drive, we saw two figures standing by Kurt's kitchen door. One was a familiar figure, tall in a long black overcoat, standing with the aid of crutches. The other was smaller. A pair of glasses reflected our headlights.

"Who is that?" asked Kurt without killing the motor or turning off the lights. The little man raised a hand to shield his eyes.

"Tom Harris," said my mother. "Paul's friend."

"Ah," said Kurt, and turned the key.

"My plans for burglarizing the house are foiled," called a hearty voice as we stepped from the car. "I'm Tom Harris," he said to Kurt, limping toward him and extending a hand. "I don't think we've met."

"I've heard a lot about you," said Kurt, shaking hands. "Excuse me." He circled the car.

"Goodness gracious—Joan!" exlaimed Tom Harris when she emerged. "What's happened?"

It took several minutes to help my mother out of the car. Her right arm hung in a sling; her face had been padded with gauze. Moving her torso, though, required the most effort—she could not bend without pain due to the broken ribs, so we had to, in effect, slide her out of the car and to her feet.

"Broken ribs, broken wrist, lot of bruises," said Kurt, taking her arm. "Been a rough few days on Miss Joan, here."

"But what happened?"

My mother murmured something. Through the gauze, and the swelling, it came out unintelligible, "Krrrr rrr."

"I—I'm sorry, Joan?" questioned Tom Harris.

"Car accident," said my mother, louder.

I looked to my mother's car—as, on instinct, did Tom Harris—and saw it parked, whole and scratchless, in the drive.

"I'm sorry to hear it," Tom Harris said soberly.

He and his guest watched in silence as Kurt helped ease my mother across the drive. She kept her head bent, watching her feet to avoid slipping on the snow. I followed, carrying the bag and the pills. When at last she reached Kurt's porch steps, she stopped, sighed with relief, and straightened.

"Tom," she said, slowly and carefully, intent on maintaining her dignity. "I think you understand why I don't ask you in."

"I do understand," he began, but hesitated. Clearly Tom Harris had come prepared for a fight. Finding my mother in this condition threw off his plan of attack. "I came . . . I wanted to discuss something with you. Ah . . ." He gestured to his guest, an elderly man, who waited patiently with hands folded. "Joan, this is Finley Balcomb. He was my professor at Calhoun and knew Paul very well."

Our attention went to the man next to him. He was around seventy, stood a full head shorter than Tom Harris, and seemed underdressed for the wintry weather: he wore a light trenchcoat with a jacket and tie underneath, and his trouser bottoms were wet from dragging in the snow. His shoes—leather wingtips, in contrast to the bucket-sized galoshes Tom Harris wore on his good foot—were dead wrong for the weather, and dirty and damp from the gravel drive. His nose was sunburned. Finley Balcomb smiled sheepishly at us and raised a hand in a tentative wave of greeting. Wisps of white hair blew in the wind, and with a finger he pushed up his most noticeable feature: a pair of large, black-framed glasses that continually slipped down his small square nose. His features were doughy, collected in folds around an apologetic mouth. It was as if his whole physical being—frail little body, head like a large pea, face, clothes, glasses—had all been issued to him at random that morning, and he was trying to communicate that he knew how ridiculous he looked, and was willing to share in the joke.

"Joan," he said, his head bobbing slightly as he spoke. "I find it hard to believe we've never met. I have heard so much about you. So many *lovely* things." His voice was a halting tenor, with a southern accent that turned *r*s in to rich, resonant *y*s—*heyd so much about you.* "I'm sorry we have to meet like this. I wish you a speedy recovery."

"Finley," said my mother, surprised out of her pain momentarily. "We met at the funeral."

"Yes, we did. Thank you for remembering," replied Finley courteously, with a little bow.

Tom Harris indicated me. "This is George Davies."

Finley turned his attention to me, and his deep brown eyes suddenly came into focus. They brought back a memory: a face at my father's funeral; turtlelike, curious, mouth drawn in a mournful frown, peering at me from a back pew.

"George," he said. "How wonderful." He approached me, shook my hand. His palm was warm and dry.

My mother watched us with alarm. "It's time to get inside, George."

"Of course! We were just going," blustered Tom Harris. He frowned at Finley, as if to say, *Forget what we said before—this will not work.* He turned his crutches toward the red car. A chorus of cheerless farewells ensued.

To my surprise, it was the courtly Finley who cut through the patter.

"We just wanted to have a few words about, about our friend here," he persisted, not releasing my hand.

I felt a thrill pass through me.

"Tom has made his views well known on that subject," said my mother icily. "And I'd rather not discuss it anymore." She gestured for Kurt to help her climb the stairs. "Good night. I'm sorry you came out here for nothing."

"Ah . . . well," Finley looked to Tom Harris nervously, and shuffled like someone called upon to make a speech unexpectedly. "Tom Harris contacted me at Calhoun, very concerned about the troubles young George has been having."

Mother continued her slow ascent to the house. Finley resumed with more determination.

"I was very close to Paul. I corresponded with him right up to the end," he said. "Naturally something that affects his family so deeply is of concern to me."

Only traces of dusky blue remained in the blackening night. The snow glimmered faintly on the ground. My mother halted, halfway up the stairs, gripping the rail with one hand and Kurt's forearm with the other.

"We have everything under control." She spoke without turning around. Her voice cracked like a teenager's, audibly straining between anger and self-control.

"*Ahhhh,*" said Finley suddenly, an unexpectedly passionate noise from the little man—part sigh, part groan. "No, Joan," he said, "there's no chance of that."

My mother stiffened.

"I think this conversation can wait," Kurt said firmly, smelling danger and not wishing my mother to upset herself. "Goodnight, y'all. You okay getting back down this drive?"

"I—I don't mean things *won't* work out," stammered Finley, as if Kurt had never spoken. "Just not on their own. The timing is *crucial.* Will you accept my help, Joan?" He pushed his glasses back up his nose. Something about Finley's bewildered apologetic manner allowed him to address a wounded woman so directly, when no one else would have dared. "Tom and I have taken the liberty of speaking to the rector of the Jubal Early Church," he said, "and we have arranged an interview, for this evening, at eight o'clock. The rector was willing to make special arrangements. Given . . . given the urgency of this case. Though I must say, just seeing George now gives me a great deal of hope."

"*Hope?*" said my mother. I could hear the polite façade rip. The cold chilled her; her injuries ached; the bruises on her face made speaking painful and difficult. All she wanted was to sit down for a few minutes and eat some nonhospital food before thinking about the long, painful trip with me to Charlottesville, and then Forest Glen, the next day. "Mr. Balcomb, I have spoken to Tom frankly, and I will speak frankly to you. You are not welcome here. I would like you to go."

"Joan," said Finley softly. "You were not in a car accident."

My mother whirled in anger. "We are . . ."

The pain stopped her. She curled over, grasping at her side. Kurt wrapped himself more protectively around her. Through her bruised lips, the words came out *mmee err.* Still clutching at her side, she spoke again: "We are," she breathed, "taking George to get treatment tomorrow. We will not need your help. That," she said, "is final."

She turned, slowly, and resumed her climb toward the kitchen door. I stood, mesmerized by Finley's voice, his certainty, his odd appearance; I was strangely thrilled to be center of so much attention; and above all, I clung to anything that might prevent me from entering Forest Glen.

"Finley's had experience with such things," boomed Tom Harris to my mother's back. "We can take action. I *wish* you would come with us to the rector's tonight, to talk things over."

At those words my mother abruptly burst out crying. It began with a gasp of frustration and continued in a sob. She leaned against Kurt.

"I think you'd better go now," Kurt growled.

Tom Harris and Finley wavered for a moment. Their faces bore the conflicted agony of well-bred men who have just made a woman cry—should they stay and rectify the situation, or cut their losses and go? Frowning, Finley turned and shuffled silently toward their car. Tom Harris stood his ground for another moment, forbidding despite his plaster cast and his greasy, tousled hair. He and Kurt stared at each other. In his great black overcoat, Tom Harris stood like a tower against the white, snow-dusted drive. I watched them wide-eyed, like a spectator at a boxing ring.

"George," Tom Harris said at length, not taking his eyes from Kurt's. "Remember what I gave you?"

"What's that?" I asked.

"Your father's icon. Keep it with you," he said. "Do not let it go, not even for a moment, over the next few days. Do you promise?"

"I promise," I said.

"Let me see it," he said, "so I know you have it."

I fumbled in my pocket, and retrieved the Saint Michael icon. It was small and felt warm from being near my skin, despite the cold.

"What is that?"

A voice rang out, clear and angry. My mother's voice.

"Bring it here."

She laboriously made her way down the stairs again. I crossed to her and held out the icon, helpless before her commanding tone. With a surprisingly quick motion, she snatched it from my hand. And before I could say a word, she tossed the icon into the woods. It disappeared in the darkness. We could hear a tiny *pip* as it fell—somewhere. My mother groaned in pain. Kurt ran to her and wrapped her once again in his thick arms.

She hung her head, breathing heavily, regaining a grip on herself. Then turned to Tom Harris. "Now, go."

"No!" I cried. "Ma, no!"

Tom Harris trudged toward the car. But not before a glance over his shoulder at me. His expression held pure sorrow. It was like he was pitying me for something in advance. I shuddered, full of foreboding.

I ran to the perimeter of the woods, looking for the icon.

"George, come back here," said Kurt.

"Where is it?" I cried. "Where is it?"

"George!" Kurt said in a warning voice. I was on my hands and knees, scrabbling at the snow. "George! George!" But I ignored him, searching frantically. *Holy Michael the archangel, defend us in the day of battle.* I could hear the prayer in my head. I kept burrowing in the snow. I would be locked away with the demon, all alone, no Tom Harris, no Finley Balcomb. *Be our safeguard against the wickedness and snares of the devil; may God rebuke him, we humbly pray.* I was on my knees now, and my hands were freezing, numbed by wet snow. But I had to find it. The demon had killed my father, it was coming for me. *By the power of God, thrust down to hell Satan and all wicked spirits, who wander through the world seeking the ruin of souls.* The ruin of souls! Oh God, oh God, I thought, I knew it was coming, I had to find it, the last and only item of protection I could take with me. But finally Kurt, exasperated, appeared beside me and grabbed me around the waist. He lifted me into the air and began carrying me bodily to the house. I cried, desolately.

This was the tableau Finley and Tom Harris's retreating head-lights revealed as they backed down the drive. Their own faces were pale and gloomy with defeat in the country dark.

Running in Darkness

Kurt bathed my mother. Splashes followed by murmured instructions, and the tinkling of water dripping from a raised arm or sponge. Warm white light spilled from the cracked door. Heat and steam and all the fragrant odors of intimacy, gentleness, and care.

My bag was packed. Kurt had supervised me. He worked from a list dictated by the administrator at Forest Glen: socks and underwear mostly; books, but no belts. In the morning we would make the journey. The bag sat by my bedroom door. I stared at it. Then I stood and strode past it.

In the guest bedroom closet hung my winter coat, with its blue waterproof shell and wool lining. In the laundry closet downstairs, I had noticed, Kurt stored a utility flashlight. Quite calmly, I collected these items. I exhibited none of the haste of flight. I would need to move silently and precisely in order to find the icon before it came time to take my pill.

I passed through the kitchen. The dishes had been put away. A television program whispered lonely in the den, its flickering blue light reflected on the snapshots in Kurt's hall.

I opened the kitchen door and stepped outside. The cold punched my lungs. I descended the steps and made my way to the woods where my mother had thrown the icon—a mess of ivy, brambles, and skinny trees that fell away on a sharp slope. I swept the ground with the flashlight but found nothing. Heavy, drifting snowflakes caught the light. It was snowing again. How far had the icon traveled? In which direction, precisely? The search might be wide and impossibly difficult in the dark; and the snow could easily hide the icon even if I were to stand right over it. The icon, and the protection it afforded, would be lost, maybe until the spring, when it would be far too late.

The hair on my neck stood on end. I felt a strange rumor in the air—a ripple, a warping of reality, which meant only one thing: the approach of my Friend, of *it*. I would have to hurry. I dropped to my knees, frantically sweeping the snow cover. My bare fingers reddened with the cold.

Down the hill, a car hummed at a cautious pace, its snow chains jingling. Suddenly I stood erect, puffing clouds of frost. An idea struck me. I estimated times and distances, staring at the driveway that curved its way to the road, and recalled what Finley had said. *I have arranged an interview.* Finley, the practitioner. I knew where he would be, and at what time. Without the icon, they were my only hope. I jumped to my feet, ready to make the journey to town, on foot.

Light flicked on in the kitchen. One second later Kurt burst through the back door in a heavy coat, pounding down the stairs and scattering the new-fallen snow as he went. I froze.

"George!" he called. He reached the bottom and turned around in a circle, deciding which way to search. "George!" he called again. Snowflakes gently drifted past his nose.

Snow. He remembered to look at his feet. The prints I'd left showed a clear track—not down the drive, but up the slope, into the woods. I followed his gaze as they traced these steps, my heart beating. He raised his head. Our eyes met.

"George!" he bellowed.

I turned and ran.

Tree trunks blocked my way. Bracken caught on my shoes, causing me to stumble. I fell headlong into a wet mix of snow, leaves, and mud. I scrambled down the slope.

Kurt gained on me quickly. "George, stop." His voice was at my back. I felt him reach out, grab my coat with his fingers. But just ahead the ground fell away to the road. I jumped. His hand grabbed air. I slid—a baseball slide in the freezing mud—and hit asphalt.

I gained my footing. I stood there, chest heaving and burning. But Kurt still followed. I turned, and holding the cramp in my side, started off again down the road. I'd put twenty yards between us before he called again.

"That's enough, George," Kurt huffed. He, too, had reached the road. "That's enough. I'm a fat old guy, but even I can catch you on flat ground," he said, leaning on his knees. "Come on back home."

I came to a halt and turned. City streetlamps were not installed this far into the county. We stood in near blackness. The only light rose from the inch-deep dusting of snow at our feet, which seemed to cast a faint blue glow of its own.

"Where are you going?" he said, walking toward me.

"What do you care?" I called bitterly.

"It's cold, it's late, and your mother's hurt," he said. "Don't you want to see her before you go away?"

"When you drop me off tomorrow, you'll be jumping for joy," I yelled. "Then you'll pack up in a moving van for Cincinnati and that's the last I'll hear of you. So why should I stay?"

"George, are you kidding me?"

"Oh, like you would never do that?" I backed away, but Kurt started closing the distance between us with long strides. "Like that's *above* you?" I continued, spitefully. "You and mom already killed my dad—why not flush me down the toilet, too?"

"What?" said Kurt, incredulously. "George, I never even met your father. You're talking nonsense now. Just—come on." He stood two paces away and held his hand out for me to take. His fingers, like mine, were bare and red. His breath came heavily, making puffs of mist.

"Look atcha," he said. "Look like you've been dragged behind a truck. I think you're the next candidate for a hot bath." He grinned, but his eyes remained somber.

The air rippled, and I felt a pulse of white-hot hatred. "I found the card," I said.

"What card?"

"The one you sent to Mom," I said. "The one for her birthday. The mushy one, that says *to go with your beautiful blue eyes.* My mother's birthday is in March. *March!*" I repeated. "My father didn't leave until *June.*"

I let this sink in. Kurt's features grew troubled. His hand slowly dropped to his side.

"You've been together all this time—since before he left," I continued, venomously. Then I drew a deep breath and screamed at the top of my lungs: "You and Mom broke his heart. That's why he went down there. He didn't care if he lived anymore. *You killed him!*" My voice echoed across the water and under the tall, white-fingered trees.

Kurt drew back. Fear flickered over his face. I saw him shudder. Suddenly I shivered, too. Even in the frigid air, there was something new now—another level of chill, one that reached the bone. Something caught my eye, and I turned to see a figure dressed like me, with my angry posture—balled fists, chin jutted forward in an accusatory glare—right next to me. It was me. It was Other George. Instinctively I touched my throat. Had it been me to say those things, or him?

Kurt held his ground. "I think you'd better talk to your mom about this," he said.

My mother. Something clicked in me, spurring me on.

"You hurt my mother."

"George, I was hundreds of miles away. We need to stop this. Please, just come inside." Kurt's voice seemed less certain now—unnerved.

"Not you," I said.

Kurt opened his mouth to speak, but only gaped. "Excuse me?" he said finally.

"Look at me," I said.

Other George, with a bored roll of the eyes, turned away from Kurt. In its sullen boredom it reminded me of Dean Prantz: that superior and dead-eyed cruelty. We faced each other. A gust of wind blew snow from the trees. It dusted my cheeks and eyelashes. The figure did not stir.

"Go away," I said through clenched teeth.

"*You* go away," it replied, unruffled.

"What's going on here?" said Kurt.

"He wants to lock you away—are you going to let him?" said Other George, nodding at Kurt.

"You're the reason," I challenged. "If it weren't for you . . ." Then I caught myself. Don't argue with it, don't engage, Tom Harris would have warned me. *Say your prayers.* But what prayers? Something about daily bread. Or Hail Mary, full of grace. *I'm not even Catholic,* I thought. Did it count if you didn't know the whole prayer? Did fragments have the same effect? Quotations?

"Now I lay me down to sleep," I said aloud, "I pray the Lord my soul will keep."

Other George stared at me, dumbfounded, then erupted in laughter. *You may as well not bother* came a voice in my head.

Instead I took a step toward the figure. Its expression changed, to one of surprise. "I'm not afraid of you," I said aloud. "I know what you are. I saw your eyes."

And what am I?

"A demon."

Other George's face transformed to an expression of scornful anger. I felt a blast of chill air.

And you're nothing, the voice roared in my head. It shook me—its impact was skull-shaking—and I fell over backward in the snow. Another gust whipped snow from the trees. I raised a hand to shield myself. Each snowflake seemed to carry a message. *Your family is nothing here,* the snow said. *Your father died—one layer stripped away. You and your mother move from town—another layer. You go to a home—did it say a home, or a hole?—and all that's left is scraps. Just vanish,* the voice commanded. *Just run, and never stop.*

Snow filled my eyes. *I won't, I won't,* I repeated. I knew if I did not resist, I would slip away, lose myself in its myriad voices.

I felt strong hands on my jacket. I opened my eyes. Kurt was pulling me to my feet. Over his shoulder I saw Other George, ten feet away, smiling indulgently. *Poor kid, just look at him,* its expression seemed to say. *Lucky he's got someone to take care of him.*

"No!" I wriggled from Kurt's grip. "Now I lay me down to sleep, I pray the Lord my soul will keep. And if I die before I wake, I pray the Lord my soul will take."

I marched to the figure. I raised my hand to strike it. But my fist locked in the air. It was a bad dream: one where you're falling off a cliff, paralyzed, or cannot strike at your mortal enemy. *You killed my father,* I said, through angry tears. *It was you, not Kurt.*

I didn't do it, said Other George, assuming a pouty, innocent voice. *It was mosqitoes, malaria, madness.*

Kurt's voice came faintly to me—"George, what are you doing?"—but Kurt didn't matter anymore. The demon and I had entered that strange vacuum where voices could not reach us. I needed to be rid of him, to free my mind and soul; when I had freed my mind, I would also be free of Forest Glen. But I would have to do it without the help of Tom Harris and my friends—I was all alone.

You know how malaria works, don't you? Other George continued, warming to its story. *The sickness makes its victims smell sugary sweet. That brings more mosquitoes. They come to suck at the victim, and they come, and come, and pound at him, so that he's swatting them away, a cloud of them, for hours, unceasing . . . it drove your father crazy!* Other George laughed gleefully. *It wasn't demons. He died. He just died. For no reason. Wah, wah, wah,* he mocked me with baby-crying sounds.

I dove for it, and this time, my body obeyed. My hands gripped the demon's shoulders and I pushed it to the ground. We hit the road with a hard thud. *You can't hurt me that way,* it said, but its eyes were doubtful. We struggled.

Our father, I recited in my head. *Who art in heaven. Hallowed be thy name.*

Kill Kurt, the demon hissed. *Not me. He's the one trying to lock you away! He's the one who killed your father!*

The demon pinned me against the snow. We had rolled under the guardrail, on the far side of the road. I lay there, heaving, looking up at its triumphant face—the superior upperclassman, sneering.

It wasn't Kurt, I thought. *I don't believe that. It was you.*

A tide of fury rose up in me. The demon had killed my father, the demon had cursed my family, cursed us with a sickly existence on Piggott Street, laying the reek of unhappiness in our house and on our skin, so badly that those with noses to smell the worst in people, the Deans, the unforgiving gossips, would say, *Your house smells,* and what they meant was, *There is something wrong with you.* My mother, lonely in a suffocating town; my father, isolated by visions others couldn't see or understand; me, their creature, their awkward, unlovable son. The demon, the vision of evil, had done its magic, twisted time and fate and collided all our failings, so that the conclusion was death. My father, alone in a camp. And other endings: hope for my freedom outside the animal cage of psychiatry. My mother's love for me.

I grabbed onto the guardrail with both hands. I strained, dragging myself from under Other George's weight. Gravel scratched my back. Pulling free, I rolled to the far side of the guardrail, and stood, arms out—exhausted from the effort, but ready. In a blink, it stood beside me. *You can't win,* it whispered, but I seized its jacket—identical to mine—and pushed from my legs, just as Kurt had taught me. I shoved it along the narrow riverbank that sloped steeply into the freezing water. All the while I recited the prayer in my head. *Thy kingdom come, thy will be done, on earth as it is in heaven.*

Stop it, it said, casting a fearful glance back over its shoulder. *Stop it, enough. Enough!*

But I kept pushing, stretching myself into a wrestler's pose, shoving it backward. I felt sweat on my face, felt the movement warming my chilled body, and with that heat, the fear and humiliation—all the sniping, picking voices—melted away. *I am Jacob wrestling the angel,* I thought, *wrestling the fallen angel.* I heaved. The demon gave way, and we both toppled over and slid down the gravelly slope, our feet splashing in the water.

The demon recovered. It pulled itself up, gripping the roots of a vast tree for assistance, and scrambled back up the slope. I chased him. Sweat drenched my hair. I continued praying. The words came fast and clear now. *Give us this day our daily bread,* I panted, *and deliver us from evil.* Other George reached the top and began climbing the tree like a cat. Surprised, I looked for a way to follow, and saw rungs nailed to the bark. This was the rope-swing tree. I tested the rungs—they were firm—and followed it, my arms burning, muscles depleted, scarcely able to squeeze my fingers around another plank. The demon reached an upper limb. I climbed two rungs, three . . . but could not climb anymore. I saw its face smiling down at me in delight, eyes glinting. *I'm still here,* said a voice in my ear. With a grunt, I forced myself to climb. At last I reached the top. We faced each other.

I stood on a branch. He was farther out, bobbing on it—just as he had been when I had first seen him, outside my window, a scruffy Huck Finn, an ally.

A friend. And I had needed a friend so badly.

I felt the full fury of its betrayal. Another surge of anger filled me. I took a breath—and leapt.

The demon grinned. It was a stupid move. One foot landed on the branch. The other swung out in midair. I clutched at the branches. My fingers grasped a fistful of twigs that bent, bunched in my hand, and steadied me, but could not hold my weight. The river heaved black and silent beneath me. My head reeled.

I heard a soft laughter. The demon now appeared above me, leering. It had climbed to a higher branch, and stood there, weightless, bobbing. *I'm still here,* it said.

I felt my legs quiver with fatigue, felt sweat dribble down my legs, my back. I knew I could not last much longer. I swung my arm around. Not to punch him—to grab him. My fist closed on the jacket. *Get away,* he said, shaking me fiercely. I held tight, swinging precariously over the water.

My thrashing left hand hit something soft. Instinctively, I seized it. I pulled it toward me. It was the rope-swing rope, thick and furry under my palm, anchored on the trunk above our heads. I tugged it once, trying my weight on it. It held. I knew what I had to do. With one hand firmly on Other George's jacket, I put all my weight on the rope. My body pulled downward—taking the demon with me. It lost its grip on the braches overhead and toppled toward me with a cry. It fell against me—now clinging to my jacket for support.

I let go of his jacket and gained purchase on the branch below with my legs. Now our faces were inches apart, mine heaving hot breath, the demon's odorless, a living chill. I gazed once more into its eyes and saw the void. *Do it,* I said to myself. *This is what killed your father.* I wrapped the rope around its head and yanked.

Other George's eyes popped. Its fingers clutched at the rope. But its hands had been holding on to me for support—when those hands let go, the demon fell. The rope tightened around its neck. Its feet desperately sought out the branch. It began pulling itself back to safety. I looped the rope around its neck a second, a third time. I put both hands against him and pushed.

But I had gone too far. My feet slipped from under me. I flailed, then dropped into the freezing water. Shock numbed me and stole my breath. In the thigh-deep water I managed to steady myself, my sneakers sinking into algae-slimy mud. With my last strength, I tipped myself forward, my chest landing heavily on the sandy bank. I lay there too exhausted to stand. I used my elbows, chin, fingernails, to heave my legs and feet from the river. My face came to rest on gravel and snow. I closed my eyes.

If you have never run outdoors in complete darkness, the experience is difficult to imagine, or even to process logically while you are doing it. You feel that somehow, some streetlight, some star or moonbeam, *must* be able to penetrate to wherever you are. But sometimes it cannot.

A tree canopy, and heavy clouds, kept me enveloped in blackness. I ran on snowy pine needles. Broke through bushes. Finally, I reached asphalt again—a parking lot. I ran, stumbling, unaccustomed to the even ground. I felt snowflakes on my face.

Then ahead I saw them: one red pinprick, and then a silver. Then a cluster, like frozen fireflies. Christmas lights on dogwood trees. Joy burst in me. *I would be saved now! I would be saved!* I veered toward the house—its windows lit yellow, warm, welcoming—feeling the sensation of treading on an even lawn.

The lights came closer. The shadows turned to shapes: a great wooden door, some eight feet high, curved into an ecclesiastical arch.

My breath came noisily. I rang the bell. The *clunk* of a thrown bolt shook the door.

A crack appeared in the darkness, and warmth—almost steamy to my bone-chilled frame—poured forth. I heard voices, the tinkling of glasses. A figure stood in silhouette.

"Hello?" he said quizzically. Then he looked down, and saw me. "Goodness!" he exclaimed. He stood apalled for a moment, taking in my appearance, before he squinted at my face. He grasped my shoulders and pulled me inside.

I had never visited the rector's before. I was herded through a vestibule thick with hung coats into the middle of the living room, a Victorian confabulation of whitewashed walls, robin's-egg carpet, and muscular antique chairs. And in those chairs, in a circle, around a spitting fire, sat Uncle Freddie, Tom Harris, and Finley Balcomb. They were sipping sherry out of silver goblets, wearing jackets and ties.

"Good Christ!" boomed Uncle Freddie, when he saw me. He dropped his drink and cursed as he mopped sherry off the table. "What the hell is going on?"

No one flinched at Uncle Freddie's use of bad language in the rector's home. They all stared. A pool of dirty water gathered at my feet. My trousers and jacket were soaked from the waist to the cuffs. Mud smeared my face; grit and sand clung to me; leaves still flecked my hair. My jacket had a tear across the right shoulder—the wool liner hanging like a flag in defeat. My hands and face stung scarlet from the cold, and from the branches I'd run through. My breath came in painful waves. I kept turning from face to face, waiting for someone to understand. "It's over!" My voice came out louder than I intended, a shout.

The shocked silence continued.

"What's over, George?" asked Finley finally.

"The exorcism!" I said. "I don't need it."

No one moved. I felt a burst of teeth-clenching energy. I grasped with both hands the lapels of my jacket, and like a superhero revealing his true identity, ripped the jacket off my body in one motion. I laughed—it seemed like the funniest thing I'd ever done. It was then I began to shiver violently.

"Well for frig's sake, let's get a blanket on him," blustered Freddie. The rector charged from the room, calling for his wife to put tea on, and where were some spare blankets, and did they have any of the children's old clothes. Uncle Freddie followed, running to look for towels. Finley Balcomb pulled my soaking shoes and socks from my feet. All the while Tom Harris peppered me with questions, bending awkwardly with his crutches so he could look me in the eye. How had I gotten there? Had I walked? Run? I was soaked, he said. *It's snowy out,* I babbled. *Dark, too. It's dark when it snows, because of the, because of the cloud cover. Aren't you proud, Tom? I did it by myself. I got tired of waiting.* Tom Harris exchanged a look with Finley. Did my mother know where I was? he asked. I shrugged. *Didn't you hear me? I did it!* I said. *I must be better than my dad. If I could do it, no prac-titioner.* Tom Harris frowned and stumped from the room, bellowing to the rector for a phone. Clattering and motion filled the rooms beyond. I found myself alone with Finley Balcomb, who removed his jacket and wrapped it around my shoulders. I shuddered violently again.

"Come over here," he said softly. "Come sit closer to the fire."

He guided me to an ottoman near the hearth. Then he drew back the fire screen. The full heat of the flames roared out at us—my frozen skin felt like it was cooking. Finley bent down, and with his small, pink hand, he placed a log on the bed of flame. Then he dragged over a stool to sit next to me.

"Ah, thank you, Ruth," he said, as the rector's wife passed him several big, woolly, mint-green towels and a quilt.

She clucked at me. "Those pants are ruined, *and* those shoes." Then she muttered, "And so is my ottoman." She began to savage my hair, legs, and arms with the towels. "He's going to get hypothermia. How long were you wet?"

"I'll take care of him, thank you, Ruth," said Finley firmly. When she withdrew, he methodically wrapped the towels around my legs and draped the quilt over my shoulders. "I was in the war," he smiled, "in the Pacific. I know how to treat shock."

"Not in shock," I said through clenched teeth.

"You're shaking," he corrected.

A shudder seized me for a full minute. I felt my lips quiver and heard an *uv-uv-uv-uv-uv* sound escape my lips. Finley placed a hand on my back and frowned. "Quiet now."

"I fought him," I said, smiling through my chattering teeth. "Just like my dad."

Finley's eyes met mine. But instead of beaming back at me proudly, his eyes registered deep concern.

"What do you mean, George?"

"Just now," I said. "I don't need an exorcism after all. I got rid of him. I don't feel him." I shivered again. "He's gone. I'm sure of it."

"You've hurt your hands, George," said Finley quietly. He took one. My knuckles and the back of my hands were scratched, speckled with fresh, ruby-red scabs. He turned my hands over. Three thick rope-burns intertwined on my palms, turning them the color of raw steak. Finley started.

"What happened?" he said.

"I told you," I said triumphantly. "I fought him."

Finley's brow furrowed, and he raised his eyes to mine. "You got these . . . fighting a demon?"

I nodded.

He returned his attention to my hands. "The scars we receive from the enemy are not of the flesh," he murmured. He turned my hands over and placed them back on my lap. "What have you been doing, George?" he said quietly. "Please tell me."

All the character in Finley's unimpressive face—the folds of pale and liver-spotted flesh, his pinkish scalp with its wisps of hair—seemed suddenly pinpointed in his tiny brown eyes. They drilled into me. They seemed to sweep across my mind, like a remorseless searchlight. I shrank away and pulled the quilt closer around my shoulders.

"I did something my father never did," I whispered, staring into the fire. "I killed one of them. I got revenge."

Finley's gaze softened. He took my trembling hand again. His own glowed with a comforting, dry warmth. He stared into the fire alongside me, patiently, as if we were an old couple holding hands, watching TV.

"Always remember, George," he said, pushing his glasses up his nose. "Christ is ever and always with you. No matter how far you stray from him."

"What are you talking about?" I snarled.

"Just remember," he said. "Will you promise me? It is the devil's worst snare, to make us think our sins are unforgivable. But none of them is, not one."

In the baking heat of the fire, my hands enclosed in Finley's soft pink mitts, my maniacal energy slowly drained away. Terrible fatigue, worse than the Thorazine at its dullest, replaced it. I slumped.

❧   ❧   ❧

When we arrived, my mother—even with her arm in a sling, even with me wrapped in four layers of towel, blanket, and coat—clutched me to her in a grip of life and death. At last she pulled away and greeted Tom Harris, Finley Balcomb, and Uncle Freddie, with a strange, distant formality, as if they had not been in an argument that same day. Kurt, she explained, noticed me missing as soon as I left the house. There was a burglar alarm—of which I was ignorant—that went off as soon as I opened the back door. Kurt ran out to look for me. That had been at seven-fifteen. It was now nine-thirty. Kurt had not returned.

"Did you see him?" my mother asked me.

"Yeah," I said, raising my head. "But I ran away."

"I called the police an hour ago," my mother continued. "They don't begin a search before a person's been missing twenty-four hours. But they said they would look for George, since he's a minor, and it's cold. There's a risk of freezing." She pursed her lips. "I asked them to send Kurt home, if they saw him. Hope he's okay."

As the guests prepared to leave—toddling toward the door in their herringbones and scarves, mumbling encouragement—Finley took my mother aside: "I think you'll notice," he said quietly, "that George has hurt his hands."

Mom led me upstairs to the bathroom and found a crinkly old aluminum bottle of calendula. She perched on the edge of the bath. Her movements were slow, marked by constant rests while she overcame some invisible stab of pain or adjusted the padding still taped to her jaw. She stroked my meat-red palms with the transparent, oily lotion.

"Why did you leave, George?" she asked.

I was too drained to speak. "Dunno."

"How did you hurt your hands?"

I said nothing.

"I want you to listen to me."

I did. Her ministrations ceased. She sighed. I could tell that moving her face pained her. She did not want to cry because it hurt too much.

"When your father died, I knew I had a mission." She sighed. "And that was to raise you as happy as I can make you." She sighed again, deeper this time. Her eyes were full of tears. "If you think you're better off with me than at the home," she said, "then I trust you. You're my smart boy," she smiled, as the tears spilled over, down her cheeks. "I'll keep you with me. We don't have to be apart again."

"I'm sorry I ran away," I slurred. The fatigue overwhelmed me.

She shook her head, slowly, holding the forgotten calendula in her palm. "I can't stand this," she wept.

"Mom," I said.

"I just can't. I can't, I can't." She cried. I sat slumped, fighting to keep my eyes open. Finally she wiped her face with her good hand. "We'll all run away," she sniffed, forcing a smile. "All together."

I awoke with sickly pale light on my face. I had fallen asleep with the drapes open. My head throbbed. Then I realized the pounding might be something else: someone was rapping on the front door.

I scrambled out of bed and down the staircase, with the comforter still wrapped around my shoulders and the floors freezing my feet. A head of light-brown hair was visible, man height, through the porch windows. I ran across the front hall and jerked open the door.

"Kurt!"

A policeman stood on the porch, heavyset, young, but somber. My face fell.

"Your mother here?" He did not smile.

"She's sleeping."

"Better wake her."

"She needs her rest," I said. "Can you come back later?"

"Come back?" he said, incredulous. "No. Tell her we found her friend."

"You found Kurt? Where is he?"

His mouth tightened. "Better get your mother," he repeated.

* * *

I shook my mother awake.

"Policeman's here," I whispered.

"Did they find him?"

"Yeah."

"They did?"

"That's what he said."

My mother rose stiffly, dressed, and limped down the stairs. She stopped short when she saw only the policeman in the hall. "Where is he?" she said, her voice now full of mistrust. "I thought Kurt was with you."

"Ma'am," said the policeman, shaking his head, "I don't know how in the hell he got up there. But I'm going to ask you to come take a look before we cut him down, see if you have any idea. You better leave the boy here," he added.

My mother's eyes widened. She gripped my hand. "I need you now," she whispered.

I helped her—slowly, painstakingly—down the drive and over the short wall of snow created by the snowplows, to the road. A police car was parked on the gravel shoulder, along the guardrail. Its lights twirled, its door stood ajar. We heard staticky voices on the CB. Day had scarcely broken into a cold, white morning. We shivered.

The policeman led us across the road.

My mother hesitated, confused. "Where are we going?" she demanded, irritably.

"This is the reason we didn't find him last night," explained the policeman. "We were looking for him, well . . . on the ground. We didn't think . . . we wouldn't've looked . . ." He stood gazing out over the water.

My mother and I followed and stood dumbly at the rail.

"I don't get it," said my mother.

In response, the policeman pointed. We followed his finger.

The sky remained heavy—later that day, it would resume snowing—and the bare trees' gray fingers seemed to reach into the clouds. I squinted along with my mother, trying to determine what in the world he could mean by leading us to the river and pointing at the sky.

I found him difficult to see, at first. The sky and the landscape intermingled in a patchwork of winter shapes—the bare boughs, the conifers on the opposite bank rising away to a rocky slope. Kurt's body dangled as if it were any other bundled frozen mass—a squirrel's nest, a broken branch. He had been hanged from the rope swing.

The rope was pulled taut. The frayed end had been coiled tightly twice around his neck. It wrapped around yet a third time, almost lazily, like a flung-over scarf. His head twisted at an acute angle. His stiff form—linear, arrowlike—pointed downward: an arrested plunge, a stillness that expresses violence.

Kurt's face bloated from the upward pressure of the rope. His cheeks, nose, forehead, were waxy gray. One lidded eye lay closed. The other eye had popped open—a freakish, accusatory witness. Kurt's heavy arms swung; his legs dragged in the river up to his knees, wetting his jeans to the crotch. The current pulled at him.

I felt something buzzing in my ears. A white noise, a terrible keening, which seemed to block out both sound and time.

Movement drew my gaze away. My mother had fallen to the pavement in a faint. The policeman rushed over and fell to his knees in the gravel, struggling to raise her up. I saw his lips moving. He was calling for me to help. I licked my dry lips. I could not stir.

April, This Year

I started whining, not like a child, pleading and negotiating, but like a dog does, a high-pitched, nonverbal beseeching, for release from acute discomfort. My eyes filled with tears, and my environs swam: just an ordinary examining room, crummy, beat-up, with a strong whiff of disinfectant that did not quite cover the odors of next-door garbage and urine. *Not enough like the one back in Charlottesville, not enough like the one they almost put me in*—because it should have been exactly like it. They needed to take me back to that exact spot where I had failed, where I had turned my mother and me into shadows; frozen the world; made us fakes, people who instead of April tulips or May graduation days or June weddings open their eyes and see a single day, a day full of cold and death.

"This isn't the answer," you said, shaking your head.

I had called you here, out of bed, in the middle of the night. *Meet me at Bellevue,* I had said, hysterically, dramatically. You paused in a way that translated to a very New York: *Are you kidding?* But I snapped my cell phone shut. You called back but I did not answer, and because I was a suicide risk, you had to come, drag yourself out of bed, and meet me in the waiting room at the Emergency Room entrance—the one with the plastic sheeting due to the endless refurbishments and construction on that block—and argue with me, beginning quietly, but due to my shouting and gesticulations and teeth-grinding and sweeping gestures that threatened even my catatonic fellow madmen slouching in the waiting room—junkies tipping over, filthy men davening and muttering—the burly male nurse had to ask us to quiet down. You flashed him your ID card for NYU Hospital where you're an attending physician, and you asked him, *at your patient's request,* to please find voluntary papers, and he showed us into this side examining room.

I rocked my body against the examining table, in a need to feel something solid, to knock myself against something, punish myself.

"It's not over," I said, tears streaming. I could not even see your face, but felt sure its expression blended patience and disapproval and nerves. "It didn't finish the job."

Your voice dropped apprehensively. "What are you referring to?"

I shook my head, refusing to answer. Instead I made sweeping gestures over my arms, my chest, as if scraping off some invisible, clinging muck. "I've still got it on me," I said, "I can feel it."

"Feel what?"

"You know what I'm talking about."

"Tell me," you challenged.

"The curse," I wailed, my tears beginning again. "The hatred. The *thing* that made me commit murder."

"You didn't commit murder, George."

"I did. I remember."

"You remember seeing the body. The man died while he was out looking for you—you feel responsible. You were traumatized. But you didn't actually kill him," you said. "The police never suspected you for a reason."

"What reason?"

"*A little boy cannot kill a grown man,* George—not the way you described it. Not by carrying him up a tree and hanging him," you said, exasperated. "It's a physical impossibility."

"*You're missing the fucking point!*" I screamed, jabbing my finger in the air. "The police didn't know what we know—okay? They didn't know about the demon."

"George, you've got to stop talking that way," you said. "Keep it up, you *will* be committed."

The door popped open. Drawn by my shouting, a doctor in a white smock—a stooped woman with stringy brown hair, hooded Slavic eyes, and clogs—barged into the room. "What's the problem?" she demanded.

"Nothing." You drew your hand over your eyes. "It's okay. Thanks."

She withdrew, casting a glance of wary annoyance at me.

"This isn't Betty Ford," you said, irritated yourself. "This is Belle-vue. A public hospital. You'll be in here with the homeless guys and the criminals."

"It's where I belong."

"No, it's not," you snapped. "The criteria, even for voluntary com-mitment, is being suicidal or homicidal. Far as I can tell, you're neither."

"I killed someone. That's homicidal."

"You *believe* you killed someone," you corrected.

"And my son?" I said.

You frowned. "What about him?"

"You said it yourself. I've been protecting him," I said. "I knew what the demons could make me do. I couldn't hold him because I was protecting him, cutting off the curse—from my father to me, from me to him. Now I'll finish it. Keep myself where I can't go near him, or anyone else."

In an instant, your face turned to stone. You strode quickly across the room and stood so close I could smell your breath—sour from your few hours' sleep.

"You showed up in my office four months ago so clean and sweet you could have been applying for a loan," you hissed. "Now you want to commit yourself to an institution because you think *demons* are after your family? We're moving in the wrong direction here, George. I'm sup-posed to be pushing you closer to the truth. Not into deeper delusions. Tell me," you demanded, eyes flashing, "are you serious about this?"

I merely closed my eyes. Folded my arms. Continued rocking. I wished you would go away. Wished I could melt. I squeezed my eyes, and felt the tears drip over my cheeks.

Demons are after your family.

Suddenly I stopped rocking.

I'm supposed to be pushing you closer to the truth.

I opened my eyes. I cocked my head, listening. You did not notice the change that came over me. Instead, you turned your back and began pacing.

"Okay," you said. "Go ahead. Voluntarily commit yourself. Pay your outstanding dues to society. While extreme, it's possible this will make you feel better—clearly, you believe it will. Half an hour ago I would have sworn at gunpoint that there is nothing wrong with you. Now . . ."

I saw the examining room with complete clarity. You were wearing tan slacks, badly wrinkled, I guessed the ones you wore to the office that day and had hastily redonned to meet your problem patient at the emergency room at 3:00 A.M.

You were right. The answer did not lie in here, in psychiatric incarceration. It was laughable—I had nearly imprisoned myself when precisely what I needed to do was slip away.

"Yes," I declared.

"Yes, what?" you grumbled.

"Yes, I'm serious," I said, suddenly lucid. "And you're wrong."

"Wrong?"

"I'm not deluded."

You looked up, surprised.

"Good-bye, doctor," I said, and bolted from the room.

"George!" you shouted.

I pushed my way through the narrow corridor. I ran so fast that I caught the attention of the male nurse. He maneuvered in front of me—great footwork, like a defensive back—gripped my arms, his biceps bulging, shouting, *Whoa, whoa, where are you going,* until I shouted in his face, *I haven't been committed, I didn't sign anything yet, I don't have a bracelet,* and you emerged, asking, *Where are you going, George? Maybe you were right, we can keep you here, just to get a proper examination,* and the nurse demanded what the heck was going on, was this patient staying or going, all at once, everyone with competing voices, drumming the whole room into an uproar, distracting Nurse Bicep so that with a single wrench and a lunge I reached the plastic door marked EXIT HERE and started sprinting around the corner, past the construction zone and the ambulances and the shuttle bus stop. Gone.

After a few blocks I pass through a black-painted iron gate, into a park. There are blossoms on the trees. Midnight blossoms. They hang heavy and fleshy in the rude orange light of the streetlamps. I have left my jacket in the ER, but the cold, even for the coldest hour of a spring night, seems severe. I shiver.

The circular stained-glass window of an Episcopal church looks out onto the park, its panes dark and blank—dead eyes. *Most merciful God,* I recite to myself, *we confess that we have sinned against thee in thought, word, and deed.* Then, to my surprise, I hear a response. I spin around. The park is deserted. Even the homeless are sleeping elsewhere tonight. I search the bushes with my eyes, expecting to see some horny couple emerging from the ivy, red-faced and stinking of alcohol, a wad of cash changing hands . . . but the shadowy corners remain still. I open my mouth to speak aloud, to call out. Then I realize what I have heard. Just a whisper. The labial smacking of a murmur in my ear, so close as to be on my shoulder, tingling the hairs on my neck; inside my head.

"I know you're there," I say aloud. "I'm not afraid of you anymore."

I'm a man now, after all, I say to myself. *I'm the one who stands up to you.*

Am I?

My mother and I never spoke of it again. Nothing between that first collapse in the shower, and the policeman's visit, existed for us. We never mentioned Kurt—and when we met or heard of others with that name, the barest blink did not pass between us. My mother packed the story away, the way she packed our belongings—in garment bags and labeled boxes—into the Toyota for the long drive north the day after I killed Kurt. She left her job, left our house in the hands of a realtor, left all the friends we knew without a phone number or address.

I walk, head bent, following a tight O, the circular path in the center of the park. I pass benches, the same benches, around and around. If I cannot enter the asylum, then at least I can find a place to pace, to clear my mind.

I'm not afraid, I say to myself. *The man is the one who stands up on the fortifications, braves the bullets, lays the strategy, and takes the consequences. The man is the one who fights.*

You can't.

I spin again. I know it is a voice. But suddenly it is not so much a matter of a voice, but which voice. They argue and hiss around me—somewhere at knee level, it seems—like a sea of tickling grass, each teasing, each vying for attention, nipping puppies wanting to be chased. I strain to hear them. Then stop myself. *No.* I press my hands against my ears and I groan.

On an overcast afternoon soon after we left Preston, a minister parked his canary yellow Honda in the gravel drive of my maternal grandmother's house in Killingworth, Connecticut. He wore casual clothes. We had the impression he did not wish to be seen in clerical collar making this particular house call. Over the objections of my Presbyterian grandmother—former member of the Women's Temperance Union, and for whom, I'm sure, this seemed scandalously Catholic—the minister, tall and gaunt in his flannel shirt and pleated blue jeans, gave me a "special blessing." No stole, no crucifix, no mentions of the serpent. Only stony February sunlight on three drawn Anglo-Saxon faces in a nervous circle. Fifteen minutes of mumbling from a Good News version New Testament. A cool damp hand on my forehead. Some stern staring into my face afterward—maybe to see if it "took." Then, after grave and respectful thank-yous from my mother, a parting line at the door: It's in God's hands now. *And no good-bye. I suffered no more visitations from my Friend, from Other George. The minister—a proper minister*

*of God—had been able to do what my father's friends, in their enthusiasm
and maybe their folly, could not do. Or perhaps it was just that the demon
had no more use for me.*

For me, I repeat to myself. Then it strikes me. *But what about him?*

I begin to run. Down the long block, past the glass office building,
past the off-Broadway theater and the W Hotel and the Disc-O-Rama
and into Union Square Park, where rats bumble across the pavement
like little furry footballs. I sprint through the park's dim and leafy center,
and just as I do, the streetlamps extinguish, click off—their light detec-
tors have sensed the sunrise. I rush around the corner past the medical
clinic and into our building, our lobby with the vinyl sofas and the dentist's office, and I wave to the slow-witted doorman, who nods—clearly
not aware that I haven't lived here in months—and I punch the elevator
button, but it's slow, so I round the corner to the stairs, force my tired legs
to climb two at a time, until I stand, heaving, in front of our door. I hear
noises inside. They are awake. Rising early with a hungry baby.

My heart pounds in my ears, and with every downstroke, the voices
rise, rumbling and scratching, so brutally loud they are like a pick
jabbed between my eyes. The throb of a headache begins. Trembling, I
take out my key. I open the door. Maggie never changed the locks.

The apartment is lit brightly. Music murmurs from the stereo.
I stand in the doorway and steady myself. The thrum in my head is
relentless. But I hear something else. A swooshing noise, and an irregular rattle.

I close the door softly behind me. The swooshing noise is the
shower—through the open bathroom door, I hear Maggie singing to
herself. The rattle is my son. He is standing in a baby saucer outside the
bathroom door—where Maggie has placed him to keep an eye on
him—spinning a plastic tub full of beads.

A few minutes later, the shower stops. "Paul, you okay?" Maggie calls
for the baby. "How you doing there?"

There is a silence.

"Paul?"

Maggie steps from the shower, toweling herself off.

"Paul, Paulie-cracker, where did you go?"

She opens the bathroom door wide and finds the saucer gone. Footsteps as she checks the bedroom. Then walks into the living room.

"OH GOD!" she screams, grabs her chest, draws up. "Oh God, you gave me a heart attack. How did you get in here?"

I am standing over the baby—still in the saucer that I have dragged to the far end of the room. He is now six months old, fat and round-headed, a whisper of hair across his pate, sucking on a bottle.

"Visitation," I whisper. "It's Sunday."

I reach down and grab him by the armpits. I lift him into the air, wrenching his fat, sectioned legs free from the saucer-seat. I hold him above me. *George—what are you doing?* exclaims Maggie. She runs toward me wrapped in her white towel, leaving wet footprints on the carpet. I swivel away from her, to be alone with him, to have him to myself. I smell his scent that mingles fresh laundry with a hint of pee. I stare into his eyes: they are a brownish black, a blackish green, as dark and alive as ocean swells. Maggie pulls at my shirt. *Give him to me,* she is shouting, *don't touch him.* I fend her off with an extended arm. She does not hear the voice, a single voice, now distinct and vivid, calling me.

I raise my eyes to see the figure in the window: the urchin with its straw-yellow hair. It has pressed its chewed fingertips against the glass. Its gaze is unblinking. Its eyes are dull. Its mouth hangs open, wet with the desire to consume us. Dawn casts rays of sunlight into the room, but in its presence, even the morning sun is moribund, shot through with decay.

I wrap the baby in my arms. I swear to him that I will never leave him, that I will stay, that I will protect him. *That's how we will break the curse,* I whisper. Then the figure in the window opens the void of its mouth and screams.

ACKNOWLEDGMENTS

Several sources were critical references in writing this story: *Witchcraft in England: 1558–1618,* edited by Barbara Rosen (University of Massachussetts Press, 1969), from which the Jean Bodin anecdote in chapter 11 is quoted and/or paraphrased; *The Roman Ritual,* translated by Philip T. Weller (1969), upon which I relied for the prayers of exorcism; a collection of essays entitled *Satan* (Sheed & Ward, 1952); *Mysticism,* by Evelyn Underhill (Random House, 1911); *Deliverance from Evil Spirits: A Practical Manual,* by Francis MacNutt (Chosen Books, 1995); a sermon by The Most Reverend and Right Honorable David Hope, Archbishop of York and Primate of England, on Ash Wednesday, 2004, at St. Thomas Church in New York City; and interviews with M. Scott Peck about demon possession, quoted in multiple sources in the press.

My first debt of thanks must go to my friend Dr. Christie Limpert, for tirelessly providing insight on multiple topics related to clinical psychology. All related mistakes and liberalities with fact are mine, not hers. It's my extraordinary good luck to have a friend so well-versed in her field who also happens to have the knack for story structure. A thousand thanks, Christie.

Deep gratitude also to three friends whose writing talents far exceed my own but who were generous enough to read (sometimes multiple) drafts and offer valuable assistance over several years. Special thanks to Heather Byer, Jim Piazza, and Holley Bishop.

Thanks to my wonderful agent, Diane Bartoli, for being an insightful and determined champion; to my editor, Sally Kim, for her laser eye and energetic support; and to the entire team at Shaye Areheart Books, especially Karin Schulze, for being thoughtful and attentive beyond all possible expectations.

I wish to extend heartfelt thanks to my dear friend Patricia Burke, for her unflagging support; and to my in-laws, Claire and Joe Massie, for the countless occasions of babysitting and hospitality that allowed this book to be written.

Thanks also for contributions of many kinds to friends and associates Marjorie Braman, Susannah Hardaway, John Kolchin, Sylvie Rabineau, Elisabeth Schmitz, Todd Siegal, and David Turnbull.

Finally, I want to thank my family—Martha and John Evans, and Rachel Evans Lloyd—for their confidence, love, and forebearance throughout the writing of this book, and through everything.

This book is for the loves of my life: my wife, Maria, and my son, Nicholas.

ABOUT THE AUTHOR

JUSTIN EVANS is a strategy and business development executive in New York City, where he lives with his wife and son. This is his first novel.

A B O U T   T H E   T Y P E

This book was set in Granjon, an oldstyle typeface designed by George William Jones in 1928 for the Mergenthaler Linotype Company. It was modeled after sixteenth-century letterforms of Claude Garamond and was named for Garamond's contemporary, Robert Granjon, who was known for his italic types.

Composition by Stratford Publishing Services
Brattleboro, Vermont

Printing and binding by Berryville Graphics
Berryville, Virginia